I0631318

D. Appelton and Company

Righted at Last

D. Appelton and Company

Righted at Last

ISBN/EAN: 9783337041519

Printed in Europe, USA, Canada, Australia, Japan

Cover: Foto ©Andreas Hilbeck / pixelio.de

More available books at **www.hansebooks.com**

"While I stood before her bit of mirror in the kitchen, twisting a refractory curl, she came suddenly behind me."

Righted at Last, p. 9.

A child of our grandmother Eve, a female;
Or, for thy more sweet understanding, a woman.
LOVE'S LABOR'S LOST.

WITH ILLUSTRATIONS.

NEW YORK:
D. APPLETON AND COMPANY,
549 & 551 BROADWAY.
1872.

NEW YORK:
D. APPLETON AND COMPANY,
549 & 551 BROADWAY.
1872.

CONTENTS.

RIGHTED AT LAST.

CHAPTER I.

SALLY HUNT AND OLLIE LEE.

I was a waif cast up by the Dead Sea of poverty upon the town of Bradshaw, Connecticut. From my earliest memory I was "town poor," and lived with Granny Hunt in the Pond District, a portion of the town not remarkable for the respectability or sobriety of its inhabitants.

I do not know how the select-men could have put a little child to live with such a woman as Sally Hunt; they certainly would never have subjected one of their own children to the ordeal, but they were acting for the public interest, and I suppose the public conscience absolved them, all the more readily, because she offered to keep me for a shilling per week less than any one else. Moreover, she was known to be neat, economical, and industrious, a "regular driver;" she would early initiate me into these saving habits, and what more could a town pauper need or expect? Why should I blame them?

Are there not many there now who deem these the cardinal virtues, and make them cover a multitude of sins? Then, I was an orphan, without a relative or friend in the world to care what did become of me, as the old woman often said.

Indeed, I remember no time when I was not made to feel that I had no business to be in the world, and I early became a sort of Ishmaelite, and gave back scorn for scorn, and hate for hate. I know now that I could have given love for love, for I made friends of all things without-doors; even the great turtles in the pond, I fancied, knew my voice, and when Ollie came—little Oliver Lee—I gave him my whole heart.

He was a pale, sickly boy, of ten, with great, sunken eyes, that looked like wells, and clubbed feet, turning inward, the scrofulous legacy which two formerly wealthy families had, through a long series of intermarriages, left to the town; and the town sent him to Granny Hunt, and paid her "nine shillings per week" for keeping him; at least, so she told our neighbor, Mrs. Smith; but I knew God sent him to be a good angel to me, for the taint touched only his physical system—a better, truer, more patient, loving soul, I have never seen. When blows and coarse abuse fell upon him, he did not swell with suppressed rage, or fire up with lightning-like anger and scorn, like me; he only shrunk a little, and pressed his pale lips together more closely. And in the summer evenings, when we were sent to our beds in the old kitchen-chamber, his bed occupying one end of the long, low, "lean-to" row, and mine the other, we would sit beneath the high, narrow window, still as mice, while he told me, in low whispers, why he bore this, and made me kneel by his side and say "Our Father" with him.

On the wall, opposite my bed, which was nearest the window, hung an old, coarse, wood engraving, intended to represent the Last Judgment. There were the flames—long, leaping, twisting tongues of fire, amid which writhed a multitude of devils, armed with pitchforks and spears—upon which they transfixed the unhappy, ghastly sinners, as they fell down into the horrible pit—while above the smoke and flames, seated upon the clouds, benignant-looking, more by force of contrast with the hideous group below, than by any skill of the artist, was the "Son of Man," surrounded by troops of the righteous, with crowns upon their heads and harps in their hands. Before Ollie came, I had been wont to study this picture occasionally. Although I had received no religious training, I was by no means ignorant of the name and character of Satan, and the contrast between these faces and that of the man in the clouds pleased me. I found a resemblance between the face of one of these fiends and that of Granny Hunt, and I gave it her name in my thoughts. Some days after Ollie came, Mrs. Hunt sent me to a neighbor's for some buttermilk, saying, in her usual sarcastic tone, as she gave me the pitcher:

"Be sure and fall down and break it, now."

I did. Coming through our old, rickety gate, my dress caught upon something, and I pitched headlong, breaking the pitcher, tearing my dress badly, and bruising my arm. The first and second offence brought a shower of blows about my head and ears, the last only elicited the remark that 'twas a pity 'twasn't my neck."

I did not cry, but stole up to our garret, where Ollie had preceded me, and gave way to such a burst of passion as fairly frightened the poor boy. He tried to soothe me; and, when all his arguments failed, he had recourse to that old picture. He explained its meaning as well as he was able; spoke of the dread day of doom in tones full of hushed, trembling awe; and his poor, puny frame shrunk and shivered as he told of that terrible lake of fire and brimstone, and the torments of the wicked, where I must surely go, if I gave way to my anger thus.

"Then she needn't strike me!" I exclaimed. "I can't forgive her—I don't know how to, and I don't want to!"

"Then you can never go to live with Him," and his preternaturally bright eyes glanced from my stormy face to the serene one of Christ.

"Will Granny Hunt live with Him?" I suddenly asked.

"I am afraid not, unless she stops using such bad words," he said, sadly.

"But you will, Ollie?"

"I hope so—if He will take me."

"Then I'll try to be good, if you'll ask Him to let me come, too—I'll try real hard, Ollie."

He sat down on the side of the bed, and, putting his arm around me, told me how people must die before they could go to Him; how some died young—younger even than I was. Then he told me about his mother—how good she was to him—how many things she had taught him; how she used to make him kneel by her bedside, and say "Our Father," until she grew too faint and weak to speak to him; and then—she died.

"She is in heaven now," he said, "and I promised her I would try to come to her."

"Is my mother there, I wonder, Ollie?"

"I hope so."

"Then I'll go, too!"

I was, indeed, a poor, ignorant child. I had no idea, even after Ollie's teachings, what my words meant; but, as I have said, God sent him to me as an angel, and ever after, violent and passionate as I was at times, I had a dim, undefined hope of attaining to some life better and purer than the one I was living. But that picture henceforth haunted me, and there came a time when its hidcous horrors were my nightly torment, and filled me with indescribable terror and disgust.

I did not attend school; the select-men said I was to have three months' schooling in the year, but Granny Hunt did not think much of schools, especially for town poor, and I seldom attended more than three days in three weeks. In the fall and winter I had to wind quills for her loom, for she wove for the neighbors occasionally, and in the summer I worked in the garden, picked berries, which she sold at the boarding-houses at "the Beach," about two miles south of us, scrubbed floor, and washed dishes, daily duties which were never omitted. I cannot say that I cared much for this deprivation. I was sensitive and proud, strange as it may seem, and resented keenly the slights to which, as "town poor," I was sometimes subjected. I greatly preferred wandering over the hills and through the pastures after berries; and, when I had filled my baskets, to sit perched upon the highest of the perpendicular cliffs that overhung the west side of the "Pond," and watch the white sails that flecked the blue waters of Long-Island Sound, heaving in sight and disappearing so silently and mysteriously; or to stretch myself on the cliff, and look down upon the dark, still waters of the pond, where every fleecy cloud and tiny shrub was mirrored so distinctly.

Yet I was not entirely without instruction. Among Ollie's treasures, which he kept in a miniature tin box, which had once been "japanned," was a small Bible, which had been his mother's (I have it now), the "Natural History of Whales," a tiny book called "The Twin Lambs," a simple allegory, and two or three certificates of good behavior and scholarship from his teacher, when he was so happy as to go to school. On Sundays he used to read to me from these books, and nothing I have ever read since has impressed me as did the story of the Twin Lambs. I liked to hear about the whales—"as big as houses," Ollie said—a statement which I should certainly have doubted, had I heard it from any one else. I liked the Bible stories, too, especially those which told about Vashti, and Esther, and Ruth; and did I not seem to know the very brook-side whence David took the stone which was to sink into the forehead of Goliath—the wood where Samson encountered the lion—and the identical field which Elisha ploughed with his twelve yoke of oxen? Indeed, I appreciated his skill as a teamster far better than I did the wonderful miracles which he afterward wrought. But those little lambs—my heart went with them in all their wanderings, especially with the truant which would stray from the fold; and when Ollie came to where, worn out with hunger, fatigue, and thirst, it lies down, far away from the happy fold, and the good shepherd, whose unwearied love had followed it through all its wanderings, finds it and gathers it to his bosom, I never could keep back my tears. Was it because that simple story dimly foreshadowed my own life?

I do not know but even now it is hard for me to forgive Sally Hunt for snatching that book from my hands and flinging it into the fire.

But, poor old soul, she knew not what she did. She had been born in a home, if such it could be called, where vice and crime tainted the very source of life, and made the mother's milk a fountain of bitterness and disease, instead of healthy, happy life. Energetic, ignorant, and violent, at eighteen she married a man whose oldest child was some years her senior, partly to spite her parents, and partly with the hope of bettering her condition, and thus missed the beautiful evangel of love, which so often makes up to a woman for the lack of other teachers. Her husband was old, infirm, avaricious, and ill-tempered; there could be no happiness in such a marriage—not even after their two boys were born.

Indeed, they only seemed to increase the discord, for, although she ruled them herself with a rod of iron, until they were large enough to defy her, she invariably took their part against their father, who revenged himself by giving every thing that he possibly could, even before he died, to his children by his former marriage.

Her oldest boy soon followed his father to the grave, the victim of premature vice, and the youngest ran away when a mere lad, and, at the time I lived with her, was married and residing in New York. The law allowed her the use of a third of the old house in which we lived, and the bit of land around it; the adjoining fields were owned by her stepsons, and there was a constant warfare carried on between them and us. I say us, for, little as I loved her, I liked them less, and with reason, for they always called me "town-poor brat," and asked me about my father, the "town-pump." They killed our geese, broke up our hens' nests, stole our eggs, put our cow in the "pound;" and we burnt their rails, and turned their cattle into their corn or grain fields whenever we found them in ours.

If there was any one person whom I hated worse than I did my mistress's step-sons, it was her son—Tom Hunt. He occasionally made us a brief visit from New York, which usually ended in a quarrel with his mother. I was afraid of him, and he knew it, I suppose, for he seemed to take a fiendish sort of pleasure in tormenting me—pulling my hair, pinching me, treading on my bare toes, snapping me on the head with his great fingers, and calling me all sorts of names. He was terribly profane, but his frightful oaths never troubled me much until Ollie told me how wicked they were. Their quarrels were usually about money, I believe, and Ollie and I used to get out of hearing of his oaths and curses, if we could, for at such times they did not seem to mind us; and many

a time I have stolen a glance at the old picture, as we sat in our garret, to see if the great devil was really there, and not down-stairs in the person of Tom Hunt. with whom I had come to identify him. Tom was always flashily dressed, and once he brought with him his wife and little girl, who astonished me by the splendor of their costumes. I suspect I had a natural love for the rich and gorgeous, or what my ignorance took for such, for the impression their finery made upon me was very deep. I doubted if any of the kings and queens that Ollie read about were finer—even Queen Esther herself, when in "regal state" she went into the presence-chamber "to save the Jews from dismal fate."

I soon made friends with this girl, and, during the Sunday which she passed there, to my shame be it said, I almost forgot Ollie. It was midsummer, and I took my new friend down to the pond to show her my fish and turtles, and waded knee-deep into the water to gather the beautiful water-lilies for her; but she called the turtles "ugly things," and flung my lilies back into the pond, because the "nasty things wet her dress." Then she looked at my old dress and asked what I wore such "an old patched thing" for, and why I did not curl my hair like hers—"'twas all the fashion."

Ollie was looking down from the narrow garret-window when I came back to the house, and I immediately went to him with these queries. He did not say much about the dress, but he took his pocket-comb and began to smooth out my tangled locks, and wind them around his fingers. They were rather longer than usual, and, when he took from the japanned trunk a little box, and showed me myself in the two-inch mirror set in the lid, I was filled with wonder and delight at the change. Pride in my personal appearance was aroused, and I smoothed my curls daily. At first Mrs. Hunt said nothing, and I fancied she did not notice the change:

but one day, while I stood before her bit of mirror in the kitchen, twisting a refractory curl, she came suddenly behind me, and, gathering my hair in her hand, took her shears from the window-sill, cut all the locks close to my head, and flung them into the fire.

"There," she cried, giving me a box and a shove, "go to your work, and remember that I don't keep young uns for a dollar a week to prink afore the looking-glass!"

I took the sheet upon which I had been at work and jerked my needle through it with a hearty wish that I could stick it through her in the same way. Ollie was at work outside the door, and, when he came in, his poor, pale face looked very sad, and I thought it was for the loss of my curls. So it was, in part, but more for the hatred he read in my face, for, when he asked me about it that night, and I burst into a storm of rage, and wished the old woman dead and buried, his face grew sadder still.

"O Lina! Lina!" he said, "I am afraid you will never go there!"

"Go where?"

"To live with Him, as you promised."

"I don't care if I don't!" I cried, passionately. "I don't believe He wants to have me, or he would not a let her cut off my curls!—What does God make such folks for, if He is good as you say, Ollie?" I added, suddenly struck by a new thought.

"He don't make 'em so," he replied, thoughtfully. "You know the walnut-sprout that I bent down for you to swing on, last summer, down by the pond. It has not come up straight again, and it never will, I guess. I s'pose something bent her just so, when she was a little girl, mebbye, and made her cross and crooked, and I s'pose she'll allers stay so unless He makes her better."

"Why don't He then, if He can?"

"I don't know; I never thought about it before. I guess it's cause nobody's ever asked Him."

"Then let's us ask Him, Ollie."

We did. Then and there we knelt down, and I well remember how earnestly I seconded Ollie's petition that God would make Sally Hunt a better woman, and how disappointed I was to find her, in the morning, more cross and captious than ever. Like many a soul of larger growth, my faith faltered. My heart was still sore about my curls, and there was little comfort in hearing Ollie say that God liked me just as well without them. I didn't like myself half so well.

One day, in the autumn, when Ollie and I were shelling out the dry beans in the shed, the bell of one of the churches began to toll. The day was very still, and, across the mile and a half between us and the church, we could hear every stroke distinctly. Ollie had counted up to sixty when I heard the voice of our neighbor, Polly Smith, talking with my mistress. Presently, Mrs. Hunt called me to get a pail of water, and, as I entered the kitchen, Mrs. Smith glanced at me rather curiously as she said:

"You'll take her to the funeral, I s'pose?"

"What for? She don't know him from Adam! Besides she hain't got a rag o' mournin'."

"An' 'taint likely the town'll buy her any. Between him an' her we've a pretty bill of expense a'ready. But then, I'd take her. Folks'll think strange if ye don't. Can't you borrow suthing?"

"Who'd want ter lend to town poor!" asked granny, dryly.

"Sure enough. But Steve Leet's girl down to the cove's got a black dress that 'ud jest about fit her," said Mrs. Smith, with another glance at me, for—to my shame, I confess I had not stirred from my tracks—"an' Polly Maria ain't over an' above particular about such things."

The woman's glance drew Mrs. Hunt's attention to me, and, with a cuff that sent me half-way across the floor, she said:

"Go to your work, an' don't stand there to swaller every word that's said!"

"Who's dead?" I asked, curiosity getting the better of prudence.

"Why, your gran'ther, child. Don't you know it?"

"Gran'ther!" I echoed, unmindful of Mrs. Hunt's angry gesture. "I did not know as I had one!"

"Well, you know it now!" exclaimed my mistress, "if that's any comfort! Old Nathan Day was your gran'ther, an' he's to be buried to-morrow. It would not be so easy tellin' who's your father. Now be off with you!"

I took the pail and made my way to the pond. It certainly was a comfort to me. For the first time in my life I felt as if I belonged to somebody—was somebody. I had had a grandfather! That he was even then lying dead made no difference; I scarcely thought of it. But I wondered what he was like. I had seen old gray-haired Mr. Gates, with his little grandson on the horse before him. Was my grandfather like him? Why did he never come to see me? Did he know I was here at Granny Hunt's? Why did not I live with him as Alfred Gates did with his grandfather?

Mrs. Hunt's voice calling me broke in upon my queries. As I again entered the kitchen I heard her say, in reply to Mrs. Smith:

"Yes, long before that. He was out of his wits when he sold out an' went West. They were pretty well run down, though, an' could not stomach bein' poor among folks they'd known all their born days. We heard tell as he'd set up some sort o' factory out there, an' got cheated, as of course he would. But the truth is, they hadn't no faculty, an' that girl must play the lady— Lina Day, how many times must I tell you not to drizzle water from that are gourd all over the floor!" I was drinking very slowly, filling my ears rather than my mouth. "There's another on 'em," she added, as I went into the shed, "the proudest, obstinatest,

shiftlessest critter that ever drawed breath—a regular chip o' the old block!"

"I don't see as she favors her mother the least bit—if, indeed, Harriet Day was her mother. She was a pleasant-spoken girl, I remember, and as pretty as a pink."

"Han'some is as han'some does!" muttered Mrs. Hunt. "We all know how she turned out!"

"I wish we knew for sartin. To be sure, the old man come back here crazy as a loon, with this girl, a baby in his arms, an' everybody s'posed it was Harriet's, but the old man never would say so, nor tell where it was born. Sister Janet's husband was one of the select-men then, and he tried his best, I'm sure. —Well, here I set, as if I'd nothin' to do. I'll come this way to-morrow, for I believe in paying some respect to the dead, even if he was town poor."

He had been town poor, then! Well, what did that matter? I had a grandfather, as I told Ollie, with a feeling of proud satisfaction.

That afternoon I was sent down to the cove, about two miles below us, to ask for the loan of little Adeline Lee's black dress to wear to my grandfather's funeral, and I can remember the feeling of importance with which I made known my errand to Steve Leet's grim-visaged sister. I had a grandfather!

I was somewhat cowed by the great black eyes, set in a circle of yellowish purple, which the woman fastened upon me, as she said in a low, solemn tone:

"So your gran'ther has gone at last, child. I hope you'll heed the warning."

I said, "Yes, m'am," but with no very distinct idea of what I was promising; and, before the thin lips opened again, a short, rather stout man, with a face tanned and burned to the complexion of sole-leather, entered, carrying upon his shoulder a little girl of about my own age.

"Two hungry uns, Polly," he began, but, seeing me, he interrupted himself with—"Why, here's a new un! A play-feller for you, Birdie. Jump down an' shake hands with her. Easy there!"

He swung her from his shoulder as lightly as if she had indeed been a bird, and she came shyly toward me, while the woman said:

"It's the child that lives with Sally Hunt. She wants to borrow Ad'line's frock to wear to her gran'ther's funeral."

"So he's gone at last, an' the poor thing lives with Sally. I guess it's kinder rough there at times. Sally used to be squally. But you'll let her take the dress, Birdie, an' she shall stay an' have some dinner, too."

We were still eying each other, as strange children and animals will before making acquaintance, when he added: "What are you playing shy for, like a couple of young porpoises? Can't you show her your traps?"

Little Adeline laughed—a little, quick, silvery laugh, like the sudden overflow of a tiny jet of water—and brought from an inner room a broken-nosed doll, a wooden box full of exceedingly beautiful shells, and some picture-books. With these we adjourned to the bench near the open door, while Polly Maria put some clams over the fire to boil for dinner, and Uncle Steve, as little Adeline called him, went into a kind of shed, and, rolling up his red-flannel shirt-sleeves, took off his tarpaulin hat, which left a red mark across his forehead, like the ring of a planet, and began washing himself, dashing the water over his head and face, blowing and sneezing, until I thought of Ollie's whales, then rubbing them with the coarse crash towel until his face was as red as the lobster-shell cradle I held in my hand, and his hair seemed glued to his scalp.

Then he came and sat down upon the bench, and, lifting Adeline upon one knee and me upon the other, he began to tell us about the pictures in the books. One of them was "The Natural History of Beasts," and was full of pictures of lions, tigers, sloths, and monkeys; "queer

critters," Uncle Steve said, "some on 'em he'd seen in the longitudes under the line."

Then Polly Maria called, "Dinner!" and we gathered around the table. The pine table, white as this sheet of paper, was set with four blue-edged plates, nice brown bread and yellow butter, and in the midst a dish of yellow earthen, full of smoking clams, from behind which beamed the kindly face of the old fisherman, only just visible, for the rush-bottomed chairs in which he and his sister sat were so low as to give them a dwarfish look, especially to me, who sat in Adeline's high chair, while she occupied a temporary elevation which Uncle Steve had "rigged up" for the occasion.

"Now, work sharp, or I shall eat all the clams afore you know it," he said, as he filled our plates.

But he did not. He was much more intent on spreading great slices of bread and butter for us, than feeding himself. I think it did him good to see me eat, for he leaned back in his chair and said:

"I guess we'll have to keep this little gal. Then I'd have a pair o' birds—a blue bird and a black bird—for see how black her eyes be!—What say ye, Birdie? Will you go halves with her?"

"Yes!"

"Give her half of all—half of Uncle Steve?" he added.

She jumped down, and went and leaned against him without speaking. He smoothed her silky locks tenderly with his great brown hand and said, smiling:

"Well, well, I s'pose 'twould come kinder hard arter being the baby so long. But we'll find a place for her whenever she'll come, won't we?"

Rough, coarse, and homely in speech and look, but with such a kind, loving heart—such a true, tender heart—such a noble, reverent heart! Among all the blessings which God has vouchsafed to give me, there is none which fills me with a deeper sense of gratitude than the gift, to my desolate childhood, of the friendship of this humble fisherman!

CHAPTER II.

MY MOTHER'S RING.

It was a pauper funeral. An open pit at the end of a long row of sunken graves, overrun with dewberry-vines and yarrow, with broken, moss-grown stones, some of the red sandstone of the region, and ornamented with those dropsical-looking heads with aborted wings attached, supposed to represent cherubs. Others of marble, for the Days had once been a family of some repute in the annals of Bradshaw. A pine coffin stood on the verge of the open grave; the minister, two of the select-men, a few white-haired old men, who had played with the deceased in his youth, a half dozen women, and some school-boys, who had left their play upon the common to see what was going on, composed the assemblage.

The men stood with uncovered heads, the more aged with their hats held behind the ear, to help catch the words of the minister as he lifted his voice in prayer. How strange and remote his voice sounded in the open air! Everything was strange—myself not the least so, in that black dress. Then the voice ceased, the undertaker began to unscrew the lid of the coffin, and the women began to converse in low tones, looking curiously at me.

"Not a single look like Harriet Day, as I can see!"

"Well, now, where are your eyes? That mouth is clear Day!" etc., etc.

At length the people swerved aside a little, and Mrs. Hunt led me forward to look upon the face of the dead—that was familiar. Somewhere—away—far away, and oh, how the thought seemed to recede, as I tried to grasp it!—I had seen that same white, thin face, with that fringe of soft white hair bending over me. While I continued to gaze there came memories—vague and dim memories, more like dreams than any thing else—of a place that was not Sally Hunt's—of boats and great sheets of water, that were neither the Cedar Pond nor the Sound—of dusty roads and wayside houses, where women gave me cakes and cups of milk, that were held to my lips by trembling old hands, laced by great blue veins, just like those folded upon the dead man's breast. I do not know what ghosts of memories that dead face might have recalled, if I had not suddenly felt Mrs. Hunt's grip upon my arm and heard her voice whispering:

"Are you going to keep 'em waitin' all day?"

I followed her and Mrs. Smith across the fields, still haunted by that face, and, as soon as we were alone, poured out these memories to Ollie. But there was nothing in his experience that could help me, only he sometimes dreamed of beautiful faces, and sailing away over the water; and so we set them down as dreams, and life went on as before.

I did not go down to the Cove with little Adeline Leete's dress—Mrs. Sally sent it by old Sam Grant; but, not long after, I heard the old fisherman's name mentioned in a way that made a deep impression upon my mind.

Mrs. Sally had been weaving a piece of toweling for the wife of one of the select-men; and the lady, when she came for it, felt it her duty, I suppose, to inquire after Ollie and myself. We were called into the room, hastily glanced over, told that we "must be good children, and not learn bad words or bad habits," and then she went on to speak of some changes relative to the management of the town paupers, and mentioned the sale of certain things that had belonged to some that had recently died.

"There were a few things that belonged to old Nathan Day," she continued, "which he had contrived to hide.

You have no idea, husband says, how cunning some of these people are. In a common steel tobacco-box he had hidden away a heavy gold ring, marked with the letters 'P. C.' and 'H. D.' on the inside. It just fitted my Sarah Ann, and I got it at a bargain!"

"Was there nothing else in the box?" queried Mrs. Sally.

"No, for I looked myself—nothing but some old cotton and a bit of dirty paper. Steve Leete, of the Cove, bid off the box, and even had the impudence to bid for the ring. To think of the like of him wanting rings!"

"He's got a niece, you know," said Mrs. Hunt, dryly.

"I've heard so, but he'd better save his money to buy her bread. If he were to die, we should have her on the town. I like to see folks know their proper places. But I must be going."

"An' she was Lois Bunnelle—poorer 'n pizen, an' went out to work afore she married Abram Barnes!" growled Granny Hunt, as the woman crossed the threshold. "Got it at a bargain! I guess she did. She'd skin a 'skeeter any time. Well, if I was as forehanded as she is, I'd never let my girls wear town-poor rings! An' that un, by good rights, belongs to some un else!"

"Lina," whispered Ollie, as we bent over our carpet-rags, "that ring was your mother's. Wouldn't you like to have it?"

"Yes."

He did not speak of it again for many months.

CHAPTER III.

THE HEALER COMES!

I AM back there again—in the old house—sitting in the kitchen, the narrow windows of which overlook the pond. It is winter; the surface of the water is hardened to thick black ice, mottled over in spots with that of lighter hue. The snow lies deep and hard in the roads—the drifts piled high over fences and posts in many a curve of rare beauty. All without is white and cold, and within one sits by my side with a face like the snow, and eyes deep and dark as the ice-bound lake, sewing with thin, trembling fingers the strips of carpet-rags which he has hardly strength to hold.

Need I say it is Oliver—poor, patient, uncomplaining Oliver? Again I help him up stairs and down, for he needs help now. Mrs. Hunt cannot have a bed down-stairs, for who is to pay for the extra fire? Not the town. She says it's "nothing but a cold—he'll be well enough when the warm weather comes—that he's full of notions, like his mother before him, and poor folks can't afford to be notional."

We do not read any more now, for he is too short of breath, even if it were not so cold in our garret, neither do we tell stories, but he kisses my cheek, and says, faintly:

"You are so good to me, Lina. What should I do without you?" And, though the tears fill my eyes every time he says this, I am very strong, for he calls me good.

I am ten years old, but if I were fifty I could not waken more regularly, when I hear that hoarse rattling in his throat, to give him drink—drink too often frozen—or to caulk with rags the worm-eaten clapboards that let the snow come sifting through upon his bed. Then, in the mornings—these long, cold, gray, winter mornings—I wake to find his eyes fixed upon the face of Christ in the old picture—always gazing on His face with such a pleading, expectant look. Then I think of the stories of the miracles which he has read to me, and I wish, oh, so earnestly, that He would come and lay His hands upon him, and heal him!

"He will, Lina. He will make me whole, by-and-by," he says, when I tell him my thoughts.

But I am impatient. I think when Dr. Moore is called in, and uses such long, hard words, and leaves such queer-smelling medicines, that possibly the time has come; but Ollie grows worse instead of better, and I lose all faith.

Oh, these weary days and weary nights! Ollie, growing weaker and weaker (he cannot get down-stairs now), and I growing quieter and quieter; and Mrs. Hunt darting about the house as usual, and talking of "the spring, and folks that have the spleen."

Then He comes!

It is night—night in the old, lean-to garret-room. The winter moon shines white and silent in the wintry sky; the small uncurtained window is frosted all over with rare devices, beautiful as dreams; the ice on the pond cracks and splinters beneath the action of the frost —and all is still again. I rise up in my little bed—is it Ollie that calls?

"Lina!"

In a second, I am by his side.

"Oh, I'm so cold—so dreadful cold!" he murmurs.

I strip my own bed of its covering to put over him, and, crawling upon his bed, take his hands in mine. They are like ice—so cold and damp.

"Are you any warmer now, Ollie?"

There is no answer, and I think he sleeps; but, presently, he whispers, and I bend my head to listen:

"'Suffer little children to come unto me, and forbid them not.'"

The words are broken and faint, but I know the verse. He has read it to me from his Bible and the story of the "Twin Lambs," and I whisper:

"Do you feel better, Ollie?"

"Yes—lie down Lina; put your face close to mine; I want to tell you something."

I creep under the coverlid, and lay my cheek close to his, with my arms about his neck. Still he does not tell me—does not speak.

"Ollie!"

"You'll try to be good, Lina—not to say bad words, or think bad thoughts— you'll try?"

"I'll never say a bad word again, or get mad, Ollie, if you'll get well, Ollie," I say, crying; for there is something in his voice that awes me. I wish I could see his face, but it is so dark here; and I cast an imploring glance toward the wall, where I know the benignant face hangs, and think:

"Oh, if He would only come now!"

Now he is still—maybe asleep. No— hark!—he whispers:

"Don't cry, Lina! What was it I wanted to say?—Oh, the little trunk and the books are to be yours; and there's two ten-cent pieces in the box—mother gave me—mebbye they'll help to buy back that ring for you—your mother's ring."

"Yes. You feel better, Ollie?"

"Easier. Kiss me, Lina."

I kiss his cold cheek, and he lies still, only now and then making a low moan; that and the splitting of the ice are all the sounds I hear; presently I cease to hear even these, for I fall asleep and dream—dream that Ollie and I have the boat we have so often longed for, and are sailing on the pond, which grows narrower and narrower, until it shrinks to a swift, rapid river, shut in between high walls of rock, upon which grow cold-looking lichens and long green ferns. Onward still, while the stream grows narrower and deeper, the sky darker and gloomier, and the lichens and ferns give place to snow and ice—nothing but snow and ice! Chilled to the heart I awake; the ice is in my arms—that cold, icy body. The gray morning light is struggling through the window, and I start up to catch a sight of his face. I know that look, I had seen it on the face of my grandfather; and, with a loud shriek, I spring to the floor.—The Healer had come and found me sleeping! Ollie was dead!

I believe the suddenness of the event

and my fright touched even Granny Hunt's heart. After the first shock was over, I was very quiet, and she left me to sit all day long in the kitchen corner, without once calling me to take part in the house-cleaning going on in anticipation of the funeral; while the neighbors who assisted her went back and forth, from kitchen to parlor, stopping to ask me the same questions again and again, until, worried out, I refused to speak.

Then I was lectured for my evil temper, and bade to think of poor Oliver, and what would become of me if I were to die.

God knows I did' think of him, and how, in my grief and loneliness, I longed to be with him, wherever that might be. But when, standing by his side after they had laid him out, my dumb grief broke into convulsive sobs at the sight of that still immovable face, and I uttered this wish, they were filled with horror—shocked that one so young could be "so wicked."

Weak enough and wicked enough I was, but not in that one feeling. I did not believe it then, and I do not now. If I am wrong, let Him who stood by that grave at Bethany, and wept for His young friend, judge.

Then came the funeral. I wore no mourning this time. No one would "think it strange" for the little town pauper to follow her dearest friend to the grave in a party-colored calico dress. Indeed, I never thought about it, but sat in the low chair in the corner of the room, where Mrs. Sally had placed me as soon as the neighbors began to come in, with my eyes fixed upon the coffin that hid him from my sight, crying out in my heart, "O Ollie! Ollie!"

CHAPTER IV.

PERSECUTION.

I DID try to be good after Ollie's death. I did *long* to be good; but, alas! it was the parable of the sower over again! There was the good seed, sown by his feeble hand—there the ground, not incapable of bearing good fruit, and there were the tares also—and in that cold, ungenial atmosphere, under the constant harrowing of Sally Hunt's unhappy temper, is it strange that the tares choked the good seed, and the ground remained unfruitful?

I did not forget Oliver. Night after night I went to sleep with his little Bible and the "Whale Book" beneath my pillow (Mrs. Sally had burnt the "Twin Lambs"), but it was easier to do this than to keep my temper, and I gradually grew discouraged, and lost all hope of being good—almost all desire.

Sundays were our holidays. When Ollie was gone there was no more reading for me, no more telling stories, no one to teach me to spell out words, and these days were very long and lonely. The words did not sound right when I spelled them alone, and I could not look at our old pictures forever. Mrs. Sally usually spent the day in cleaning up the house, looking over her drawers and bundles of pieces, bags of stockings, etc., "putting things to rights generally," as she expressed it. She never went to church, but it occurred to me that I might; so, with a childish attempt at diplomacy, which betrayed its nature at the outset, I asked her one day if Mrs. Smith did not "go to meeting."

"Yes, I s'pose so."

"Why don't you go?"

"Because I hain't got no seat. They've took to selling the slips, and I ain't a goin' to set with niggers and every thing. I guess I'd be as able to buy a seat as Nance Smith, if I had my rights!"

She was netting seine for the fisheries

at the Cove, and her needle flew like lightning.

"I should like to go some time," I said, after a pause.

"You would, would you?"—slackening her hand. "Who put that notion into your head?"

Like all people of her stamp, she was exceedingly jealous and suspicious.

"Nobody, ma'am. Ollie used to tell me about going when he was a little boy, and he wanted me to go. Mayn't I?"

"Yes, I guess you'd better, an' have up prayers. If you're gettin' so mighty pious, you'd better mind an' wind that are twine a little evener. A pretty figger you'd cut a gwine ter meetin'!—not a shoe to your foot, nor a decent rag to your back! They'd turn you out o' the house."

I did not believe it. Ollie said God did not mind about clothes; why should the people at church care?

To be sure, I had no decent shoes; the town provided such luxuries only for winter, and mine were sadly worn by May, but I had a blue-and-white calico dress—the one I had worn to Ollie's funeral—and a sunburnt straw bonnet, with the bit of limp black crape across it, which Mrs. Smith had put on when my grandfather was buried. I took Mrs. Hunt's words in earnest, and determined to go. But, somehow, I did not like to say any thing more to her about it; so, after taking a bath in the pond one pleasant Sunday morning, I went to my garret, and spent nearly an hour in curling my short locks and dressing myself before the bit of looking-glass in the lid of the box I had inherited among Ollie's treasures.

Luckily for me, Tom Hunt had arrived the evening before, and, as usual, there was some trouble between him and his mother, or rather some trouble in which he needed her aid. I heard talk of selling the cow, and, finally, they went down the lane toward the pasture. Then I hurried on my bonnet, and took—ah, what woman, who remembers her childhood, will not understand the temptation!—an old green veil of Mrs. Sally's, which was spread over some blankets in my room, and hurried out of the house. Then I made one more addition to my toilet. Mrs. Barnes's daughter, when she came to our house about the weaving, had flowers on her bonnet—why should not I? Especially as there were several beautiful lilac-blossoms on the stunted bush by the gate. I gathered one, pinned it upon my bonnet, and struck across the fields at a rapid pace.

The bell for the afternoon service ceased ringing before I reached the church, and, seeing no one about the door, I was afraid to go in, so went and sat down by Ollie's grave, for the graveyard, as is customary in some of our country villages and towns, was close by the church. At length, I saw a man going toward the church, and I hurried forward that I might go in with him. He did not see me, and I followed him in, and up the middle aisle. My bare feet made no noise, but the man's boots creaked as none but the Sunday boots of some respectable gentlemen can, and, although the minister was at prayer, most of the heads, especially of the younger portion of the congregation, were turned to see who entered, and, seeing me, continued to gaze in astonishment. Some smiled and whispered, and one or two little girls giggled out when the man, turning to fasten his slip-door, became aware of my presence, and stood looking at me in blank surprise. I felt my cheeks glowing from anger and mortification, and was turning to run away, when the slip opposite was opened by a young lad, and the lady within reached forward and drew me in, and seated me by her side.

She did not look at me again until the prayer was ended, then she quietly removed the obnoxious bonnet with its veil and flowers, and smoothe' my hair with her ungloved hand. I thought it looked like the apple-blossoms, it was so soft and white, when she opened a hymn-book and held it out for me to take. I did not know what the book was for, but I held it as she did hers, until the minister ceased to read, and the organist began a soft prelude on the organ, when I dropped it in my astonishment. I had never heard any instrumental music before, and I stretched back my neck as far as possible, to see whence the strains proceeded that filled me with wonder and delight. Suddenly I thought of Ollie and the golden harps of the angels he used to read about, and, before I knew it, the tears began to come, and one or two had fallen upon the lady's book, which I had picked up mechanically and held in my hand. I glanced at her in a great fright, but she did not notice them, only put out her hand, closed the book, and fixed her eyes upon the minister. My eyes followed her eyes. I had seen the minister at Ollie's funeral, and, though I understood little that he said, I liked his face and voice, and sat very still through the remainder of the service. When it was over, the lady put on my bonnet, but the lilac-blossom and veil were missing. She waited until most of the congregation had gone out, then took the veil, and, throwing it over my shoulders, led me by the hand down the aisle.

"What made you cry?" she asked in a low, pleasant voice, as we entered the porch.

"It was thinkin' of Ollie, ma'am."

"Ollie! Who is he?"

"He's dead, ma'am, and that's his grave yonder," I replied, pointing to the portion of the graveyard where he lay.

"Aunty," said the lad by her side, turning his bright, handsome face toward her, "don't you remember that I told you of seeing a lame boy and a little girl down by the pond, when we were here last summer? This is the girl."

"And the boy is dead?" said the lady.

"Yes, ma'am."

"Where do you live?"

2

"With Sally Hunt at the pond."

"She isn't your mother?"

"No; I hain't got no mother."

"And your father—where is he?"

I hesitated, and she repeated the question, and asked if he was dead.

"I don't know, ma'am. I never see him. Mrs. Sally allers says I'm a child of Satan."

Her grave look checked the lad's rising smile, and she said, as kindly as before:

"You can tell me your name, at least."

"Zerlina Day, ma'am, and," I added, proud that there was any thing I could tell her, "my grandfather is buried out there, too."

She was silent a moment; then, seeing some of the people looking back at us curiously, she led me toward the street, saying:

"Do you know the place call Fernside Cottage?"

"Mr. Eames's, ma'am—over the hill, below Bill Williams's place?"

"Yes. We are staying there at present. Will you ask the person you live with to let you come there some day? I shall be glad to see you."

I readily promised, and stood watching them until they turned the corner by the store; then, with one glance at Ollie's grave, I hurried toward the pond.

But I did not return as light-hearted as I had come. That veil troubled me. I knew I had no right to take it. I fancied the lady knew this when she looked at it so gravely. I feared to meet Mrs. Sally's eye, and before I reached home I took it from my shoulders and held it behind me while I watched an opportunity to get into the house unobserved. Presently, I saw Mrs. Sally come out and pass around the corner of the shed, and I ran through the gate, turned the corner of the house and—met her face to face. She had a long, lithe apple-tree sprout in her hand, which she laid over my shoulders vigorously.

I had long since learned the uselessness of dodging, and, intent on concealing the veil, I stood and took the lashes in silence.

"There, madam!" she cried, as she paused for breath, "next time you take a notion to run away, you can have as much more of the same sort!"

What was it moved me to hold out the veil and confess my fault? Was it the kind lady's words, or poor, crippled Ollie's spirit pleading with me to choose the right? I don't know, but I held it forth, and said, as steadily as I could for the pain:

"You said I might go, ma'am, only I hadn't oughter took the veil!"

"Took the veil, you good-for-nothing little hussy! What business had you to even tech one o' my things?" she cried, as she jerked the veil out of my hand. "Where've you been to?"

"To meetin'!"

"Ter meetin'! Ter meetin'! In that rig!"

"You said I might go, ma'am!"

"It's a lie! I never said such a word!"

"You did, ma'am. You said—" But she dropped the switch, caught me by the shoulders, and shook me until I had no breath left for words.

"There!" she cried, as she pushed me reeling toward the house, "tell me I lie, will ye! I guess you won't want ter go to meetin' agin in a hurry. Into the house with you!"

"Hillo, old lady! You seem to be havin' a time of it! What's the row?" and Tom Hunt's coarse face looked out of the door.

"She's been ter meetin'. Ask her!" sneered the old woman.

"And this is a part of the blessin'—the layin' on of hands, I s'pose, mother. Well, you haven't forgot your old knack, it seems. Some is whipped for goin' and some for not goin', and it's all the same in the long-run. But, Madam Parson, supposin' you give us a piece of the ser-

mon?" and he caught me by a lock of hair, and drew me into the house.

"No kickin', now. Your pious folks never kick."

I did kick, and strike too. The good spirit was gone. I could bear blows from the mother, but neither the touch nor the ridicule of the son; and, jerking away from him, I flung myself on the floor and screamed wildly.

Is it any wonder that I did not make known the kind lady's request? Any wonder that I did not keep my promise to Ollie, but thought bad thoughts and said bad words, until I almost deserved the name which Tom Hunt gave me— "little devil!" Indeed, I should have quite deserved it, if it had not been for that one angel which God had set to watch over me. He would not quite leave me to myself.

Tom Hunt was much at home this summer, and, very soon after the scene I have described, it became necessary for Mrs. Sally to go to New York. What to do with me was the question. She would not leave me alone in the house, and as for having any one come there to stay with me, that was out of the question— she said she'd stay at home first. She was always in a quarrel with the neighbors, and happened to be "out" with both Mrs. Smith and Mrs. Grant at this time. I ventured, finally, to suggest going to the Cove. She caught at the idea. Polly Maria had asked her to let me come and see Adeline, and she'd send down by Sam Grant, that very day, and ask if they could have me for a few days.

"Come and welcome," was the answer, and I spent six days there—the happy precursors of many more, before the summer was over—days that fringe with light that most miserable period of my life. How they come back to me now, and the scenes that they enclose! There is the little, low, brown house, stuck under the steep bank, like a swallow's nest beneath the eaves, originally a fisherman's shanty, but enlarged and repaired by Uncle Steve until it forms a nice kitchen and two bedrooms, exclusive of the shed; the wide-curving beach stretching away for a mile or so, and ending in high, rocky points—the wet, brown sand strewn with smooth variegated pebbles, and "silver shells," and large rocks cropping out here and there; an occasional fish-house, with its great reel for drying the seine, its lazy, listless, jolly occupants lounging upon the rocks, waiting for signs of the coming prey—the broad expanse of water, bounded by the dim, distant outline of Long Island—the restless, foam-capped waves that came rolling in upon the beach, sending their spray mockingly in our faces, as we sit on the bench beside the door, each chanting its part in the solemn, mystic anthem, which goes up ceaselessly from the heart of old ocean—weird, low notes, caught up by the tall, dark pines on the bank above the house, and wafted far inland to the ears of dreaming poet and maiden—the fresh, glad breeze, symbol of the Spirit of God, "that moveth on the face of the waters," with health and healing in its touch—and, best of all, the simple, homely, loving hearts and faces that met me there.

Tears! well, let them come! It is much that the child of the almshouse has memories which can call forth such as these.

Uncle Steve had been a sailor in his younger days, and I think he must have garnered in his heart a large share of the sunshine and warmth of those "furrin" parts under the line," about which he used to tell little Ad'line and me, for his fund seemed inexhaustible. It could thaw even the hard visage of Mrs. Sally, and penetrate the husk of black melancholy in which his sister had ensconced herself, for I soon found it was but a husk (the result of a combination of high Calvinism and bile), and I used often to wonder why Uncle Steve never sent her on a "v'yage across the line." But underneath the husk was a fund of real though undemonstrative kindness which neither the hard discipline of life nor her hopeless temperament could petrify; and, although she looked upon us as "conceived in iniquity and born in sin," she was, practically, as tender of us as if we had been angels.

They were such a contrast—the inmates of that cabin—my childish imagination was never tired of watching them. One day, when Polly Maria was silently stitching away on a red-flannel shirt for Uncle Steve (he always wore red flannel, and I used to think the color had something to do with his high complexion, for I could hardly tell where the one ended and the other began), I asked him what made her always so sober.

He paused a moment from his work—a lobster-car which he was weaving from smooth lithe ash-splints—and, glancing at her a moment through the open doorway, said:

"Disap'inted!"

"Disappointed!" I repeated, and, after maturely considering the meaning of the word, I said:

"You wasn't ever disappointed, were you, Uncle Steve?"

"Bless the child, no!" he returned, laughing. "I never took to sech ways. Howsomever, I s'pose it comes more nateral to womankind than it does to us. —Give me another splinter, Blackbird."

"How more natural?" I asked, handing the long splint.

"Well, I dunno exactly — but I've known lots on 'em to be so, though they pretty ginerally picked up arter a while. Then, you see, Polly Maria has had trouble."

"Trouble?"

"Yes, when she was a young gal she broke off with Jim Dean, or Jim with her, I never rightly know'd which, for I was in the Aurory at the time, but it don't matter which; Jim, he went and married Jane Toroner, an' Polly, arter peakin' around a while, up an' married

Bill Stevens all ter once, as you may say. I'd no perticular grudge toward Bill as I know'd on, an' I don't want ter say hard things about him; but he didn't turn out well—took to drink, and 'bused her—a woman! An' now, you see, she has trouble with me and Bluebird."

"With you! O Uncle Steve!"

"Yes. You see I hain't been much used to wimmen-folks's ways—I've got a notion o' flingin' things about an' litterin' up the room, an' it worrits her, I know it does; an' then, when I take Bluebird off to the reef with me, an' it's a bit rough, that worrits her. To be sure, these here winds ain't the trades, an' a body can't allers tell when they'll chop right about, as I tell her."

"What's become of her husband?"

"He's dead. Arter he died she took to meetin's an' doctrines, an' I hoped she'd light up a bit, but I don't see it yet, poor woman!"

Oh, what a kindly, affectionate glance was that which he cast toward the dark, silent woman!

I watched his stiff, clumsy fingers as they wove, with geometrical precision, the octagon-shaped apertures in the car, until he had made two or three rounds, when I resumed the conversation.

"Whose girl is Ad'line?"

"Brother Joe's."

"Where's he?"

"Dead—knocked overboard in a hurricane off St. Kitts."

"Were you with him?"

"No; I was on a whalin'-v'yage ter the Nor'west coast. When we got inter port, his wife was dead, too, and Birdie yonder" (his eye glanced to where little Ad'line sat on the bank above, beneath the pines, tossing the dry cones down at us) "was a leetle bit of a thing not bigger'n a lobster and a'most as red as one biled. So I got a woman to keep her, for Joe's wife's mother had enough of her own ter look after, an' went on a vy'age up the Straits. When I got back she could run alone. Polly's husband was dead, an' I

thought I'd give up the sea for a spell an' make a berth for 'em on shore. I used to lobster an' fish about here when I was a shaver no bigger'n you, an' I know'd I'd make both ends meet somehow, an' so I have."

He set the car up, stepped back, shut up one eye, and took a critical survey of his work.

"She's a trifle lop-sided, Blackbird, but we'll bring her up with the next round, won't we?"

"Yes. And you've never been to sea since, Uncle Steve?"

"No; I'm allers talkin' about it, but don't get away. Birdie'd be so lonesome, for she (nodding toward his sister), though mighty good in the main—wuth a dozen o' me—can't be to her jist what I've been—larnin' her to swim—playin' porpoises, an' whales, an' bears, an' kangaroos. It ain't nateral she should, you know."

I said, "Of course not," though, upon reflection, I did not see why, for, sitting there, at her work, so upright and unbending, she bore far more resemblance to a kangaroo, as delineated in Ad'line's book, than I could possibly conceive of Uncle Steve's attaining with his best effort, and I knew he never stopped short of that.

This conversation opened an inexhaustible topic between Uncle Steve and me—that of whales. I told him about Ollie's book; and he would take little Ad'line and me upon his knees, and tell us stories about them, far more wonderful than any contained in the book, and go on to talk about the *natyves* of the Northwest coast, and bring out his favorite book, the "Narrative of John R. Jewett," who was cast away in the region of Nootka Sound (he had but one other besides his Bible and Almanac, viz., an "Account of Remarkable Shipwrecks"), and refresh his memory with regard to their peculiar habits.

I seem to see him now, reading the title-page, slowly pointing with his finger along the lines, and the expression of honest confidence and satisfaction in his face and voice when he came to the couplet which served for motto to the book:

"Dire scenes of horror on a savage shore,
Of which, a witness sad, a part I bore."

"That's truth, every word on't, for I've been there myself, an' know all about it; an', what's more, I've seen the man himself, an' bought this ere book of him. If you are goin' ter buy books, Birdies, it's a good plan to buy them as you know to be true."

Then, perhaps, to our great delight, he would finish by giving us, in a voice as hoarse as the winds of that region, a song purporting to be an authentic account of the dreadful massacre perpetrated by those savages—

"On board the North America, at anchor as she lay,
In Queen Charlotte's harbor, Nor'west America."

I have heard some famous voices since, but I doubt if I ever enjoyed any singing as I did that!

I do not know why I should single out this particular day from all those happy ones, but in all the after-years the memory of this stood out with vivid distinctness—Uncle Steve and myself in front of the open shed-door; little Ad'line on the bank above, her fair hair lifted by the sea-breeze, laughing so gleefully when one of her light missiles fell close to our feet; was it because I was to see her lie there, one day, so white and still—so very still—when no breeze stirred her hair, and there was no sound of laughter —not even of woods—only a low, hushed sobbing to mingle with the solemn requiem of the pines! But I must not anticipate.

In spite of Polly Maria's fears, we were often off with Uncle Steve to the reef to look after his lobster-pots or to throw our lines for the rock-fish that frequented those waters. We had our hooks and lines carefully prepared for us, and no mother threaded needles for her little

daughters with more unwearied patience than Uncle Steve showed in baiting our hooks and disentangling our lines from among the rocks and sea-weeds. We had but one order—we must not talk; talking "scart the fish." When we grew restless under this rule, he would bid us run to the other end of the island and "slacken our tongues a bit," or leave us rocking in the boat, while he went a little distance and fished from the rocks.

On one of these occasions I bound his heart to me forever, even if my friendlessness had not done it before. He was only a few rods distant, on the opposite side of the rocky point, where our boat was moored, when little Ad'line, in reaching after a bit of floating sea-weed, lost her balance and fell into the sea. I do not think she would have drowned, the boat was so near she must have caught it when she came up, but I, who could swim like a duck (thanks to my experiments in the pond), was over after her in an instant, and had one arm about her, and one hand on the edge of the boat, when Uncle Steve came in sight on the rocks above. He dropped his line, and the great fish dangling at the end slipped back into the water, taking the tackle after him, while he sprang to my aid. He drew us into the boat, and, taking us in his arms, carried us up the rocks without a word. Then he held us close to his breast, and choked, and choked, as if something were in his throat, and he turned away his head, but not before I saw the tears standing in his eyes.

I was never "town poor" there. I was "Blackbird," and treated just as kindly as little Ad'line herself; only, if Uncle Steve petted her a little more, it was because, as he once said, in a half-apologetic tone:

"She'd allers been such a little mite of a thing an' needed broodin' so much ," and, though by that very remark he unconsciously showed that he felt the essential difference in our characters, he never permitted that to influence him further, and if we had been birds, indeed, he could not have treated us more tenderly or been more thoughtful of our comfort.

———

CHAPTER V.

A CHANGE FOR THE BETTER.

But, behind these glints of sunshine, lies the dark, dreary background of my life at Sally Hunt's; made drearier than ever this summer, by the fact that, in some way, she had become involved in Tom's affairs, and found herself compelled to raise, upon short notice, what was for her quite a large sum of money. Moreover, the minister, Mr. Brae, probably reminded of my existence by my appearance at church that Sunday, had been making inquiries about me, particularly as to why I was not sent to school; and, between her trouble about the money, and indignation at the minister's "impudence," her temper became unbearable. I learned of this interference incidentally, by "twits and flings," for she never told me any thing that concerned myself directly, and I knew, by the way she drove me at my work, that she meant to get as much out of me as possible, fearing that something might come from these inquiries. To me, any change would have been most welcome.

It was coming, but from quite a different source than that which she feared.

On her return from New York, she had brought a lot of (what seemed to me) very nice clothing, though some of the articles were exceedingly dirty and "hogged out," as she expressed it, which had been given her by Tom's wife. Among these things was a bit of thread lace so delicate and fine, that I was never tired of looking at it, though I did not dare to touch it. She intended it for a cap, and put it out upon the grass with some other things to bleach. Some time in August, she had occasion to look for the lace, and could not find it. She searched the

house thoroughly, but without success, and then remembering, I suppose, my special admiration for it, charged me with stealing it. Of course I denied the charge, and—but why stain this fair page with a detail of what followed? Heaven knows I have no pleasure in recalling scenes like this, but I must take account of all the circumstances and influences that have moulded me into what I am.

You can readily guess what it was—rage and violence, strength and injustice on one side—wild passion, scorn and defiance on the other, and I do not know how the conflict would have ended, for I would have died before I would have admitted the truth of the charge, and she believed it her "bounden duty to whip the lie out of me," if it had not been for the appearance of old Sam Grant.

He was employed about some small job for her, and, hearing the fray, came to see what it was about.

I think he pitied me and tried to intercede in my behalf—but she never listened to other people or deferred punishment on account of their presence. But, when he finally comprehended the cause of the trouble, his face brightened at once.

"Lord bless me, Miss Sally, I'll bet I'll find that are stuff in a minute! If my eyes sarved me, I seed it yesterday built into that are robin's nest in the old apple-tree yonder. I remember lookin' at it, but didn't think 'twas of any 'count."

He returned in a few seconds, with the bird's nest in his hand, and, woven in among the sticks and straws, was the piece of lace for which my body and soul were still smarting, but so mildewed from exposure as to be good for nothing.

I was innocent, and old Sam gave me a look of triumph. Mrs. Hunt did not acknowledge her error or apologize; she merely began a tirade about the wickedness of town-poor children, and myself in particular, which I did not stay to hear. With a burning feeling of anger, hatred, and degradation in my heart, I fled from the house to the pond, and, throwing myself upon the ground, gave way to a passionate flood of tears. I do not know how long I had lain there, but I was still sobbing in the spasmodic way common to children when grief has nearly exhausted itself, when some one addressed me, and, raising my head, I saw a lady and gentleman standing near me.

I sat up and stared. The lady asked questions in a high, *falsetto* tone, and the gentleman eyed me fixedly.

"Give the child time to recover herself, Cousin Agnes. We have taken her by surprise," he said; and there was something in his voice, and the way he spoke, that helped to quiet me far more then the lady's words.

Presently he took me by the shoulder, and, raising me up, said:

"Now, tell the lady what you are crying for." I did tell her, and he listened quietly, occasionally glancing at the lady, to check, as I thought, her frequent exclamations of pity.

"You are sure you have told the truth?" he said, sternly, as I finished my tale.

"To be sure she has, Cousin Ralph. Don't be so suspicious!" cried the lady.

"Let her answer for herself, if you please, Agnes!"

"Yes, sir. You may ask Sam Grant. I never touched the lace; 'twas the old robin!" I said, indignantly, for I read distrust and suspicion in his keen glance.

"I shall not take that trouble," he replied, with a smile. "I believe you. What is your name?"

"Zerlina Day, sir."

"But what makes you live with that odious woman?" broke in the lady. "Why don't your friends take you away?"

"Hain't got no friends, ma'am. I'm town poor."

Whether my words destroyed any little romance the lady had been weaving about me, I cannot say, but she suddenly removed her hand from my shoulder,

and even the end of her scarf, which touched my dress. This movement did not escape the quick eye of her companion, and it brought a smile to his lips, that did not make his face half so pleasant as the one he had given me a moment before.

"A capital illustration of the subject of our discussion, dear cousin," he began —"a proof of that high state of moral and religious development with which you have been striving to impress me during our walk; quite providential, I should say, for this poor little wretch's daily life is a gauge which shows just how much that development or culture, or whatever you please to call it, amounts to. The people of this town, I presume, are a fair sample of humanity, in this nineteenth century; moral, well educated, intelligent, and pious, as the world goes. Let any millionnaire offer them a sum of money, for a course of lectures, or for founding a library, a school, or for any benevolent purpose, how gladly they would receive it; how unanimous would be the vote of thanks, and how scrupulously they would carry out the conditions imposed by the donor! But here is a child, an heir of immortality, as your faith and mine teaches, endowed with powers that make it little lower than the angels; passions and affections that will —nay, *must* even here, on earth—make its future a heaven or hell, bequeathed to them by their professed Master, in the memorable words, 'The poor always ye have with you!' and what do they do with it? Accept—no, endure it as a burden—put it out to live with some Sally Hunt at the lowest starvation price, and then go to church and thank God they are not like other men, left to bow down to "stocks of wood or stone!" Talk to me of my rationalism, Agnes! It is better to believe in any thing, if it be a reality, like this piece of granite, then to be a professed humbug!"

"You always have such a queer way of putting things, Ralph, that there is no use in arguing with you. Your long residence abroad has made you so unpractical!" said the lady, impatiently. "But this poor child—what can we do for her?"

Again that peculiar smile lighted up his dark face, as he said:

"If the Baltic were not going to sail on Saturday, I'd try to be a little practical for once, and relieve your mind by looking after the child myself."

"You! You are joking, Ralph."

"No, I am not. Why shouldn't I?"

"I don't know; only it seems so queer to think of your troubling yourself with a child."

"There are a great many queer things in this world, cousin, and it is very true that I have had little to do with children. But, however highly I may think of the Eastern custom that transfers superfluous female infants to the arms of Father Ganges, in comparison with some of the features of our much-boasted pauper-system, I should not quite venture to put it in practice in this case. If I had the time, I presume, I could find some decent woman who, for love and money, would treat her kindly, at least as kindly as I do my dogs, which seems not to have been her fate heretofore," he said, gravely.

"Indeed, I always said you had a good, kind heart at bottom, Ralph."

"It's a family trait, I'm sure, for I was just thinking the same thing of you, Agnes, and, therefore, was about to propose that you should take her yourself. You will then have something to occupy you—something to love, the lack of which you were lamenting not long since—an object in life—the great need of your sex. And, look here, cousin "—he caught my head in his hands, and turned it toward the lady—"there is something here that will pay better than *crochet* or embroidery. Wilful, fiery, I should say, but capable of being wrought into a noble character, and finely tempered. Will you try it, cousin?"

"I wonder I did not think of it my-

self, Ralph. It will be, indeed, a delightful task to mould that plastic mind after one's highest ideal; to watch it as it expands beneath the hand to perfect symmetry and grace, like the statue under the chisel of the artist, and to feel that it is the work of one's own hand!" cried the lady, enthusiastically.

"An occupation worthy of the angels, or—woman," he returned, gravely; "but you must remember that the artist finds no perfect block. The material will prove more or less flawed, and you must not expect too much. You will doubtless take with her a great increase of care, responsibility, and disappointment. But we all have to creep before we can walk, unless it be some such favored mortal as yourself, cousin "—and his lip curled with a mischievous expression—" and I have faith in your ultimate success. What I recall of my own childhood leads me to think that those who have the care of children often, unconsciously, nullify their most earnest efforts by indirect influence. What are you laughing at, Agnes?"

"How can I help it? To hear you talk, one would suppose you a grave *pater-familias*, and not a confirmed old bachelor. Excuse the adjective, cousin—it slipped out unawares. But I know so little about children."

"Trust to your womanly instincts, Agnes, and you cannot fail—that is, if you decide to accept this gift from God."

"O Ralph, I wish you would leave off that irreverent way of speaking."

Another comical expression glimpsed over his face as the lady turned to me and asked:

"Would you like to go and live with me, child?"

"Yes, ma'am."

"And will you promise to be very good, and—"

"Enough, Agnes! Don't begin by making the child promise impossibilities. —Zerlina!" I started at the deep, firm tone—"this lady will give you a pleasant home; she will be kind to you, and will teach you to be a good and useful woman. What can you do in return?"

"I can try to be as good as I can, sir."

"And love me?" added the lady.

"Yes, ma'am."

"Very well.—Are you satisfied, Agnes?"

"Yes; but how are we to manage? I can never face that odious Hunt woman."

"It is not necessary. I will arrange the business with the proper authorities this afternoon." Then, turning to me, he added: "You had best go home now, and mind and keep your own counsel. Do you understand?"—seeing my puzzled look.

"No, sir. I don't know just what 'counsel' means."

"Hold your tongue, then! I suppose you understand that?" he replied, smiling.

"Yes, sir. That's what Granny Hunt allers tells me."

"Well, obey, then, until you see me."

He drew the lady's arm through his, and they took the path through the woods in the direction of the beach. I watched them until they were hidden by the trees. Was it a dream? Would I really live in some other place? What would Ollie think? I looked up to the blue sky, flecked with white, fleecy clouds, as if I expected to see his face looking down upon me, with the old, pleasant smile brighter than ever at my good fortune. He had told me that heaven "was away up beyond the clouds;" and often, sitting on the hot, still hills, amid the whortleberry-bushes, I had paused from my labor, and, looking up to the yet stiller sky, had thought how easy it would be for him to look down on me there.

Then I thought of my new friends—of the lady. Her face was pretty, the features small, delicate, and regular, but it had a kind of *wilted* look, like my water-lilies when I held them too long in my hand, or laid them in the sun for any length of time. Her eyes were blue, and her light-brown hair, arranged in long, loose ringlets, was mingled with a profusion of blue ribbon that ornamented the inside of her straw bonnet. She was younger than and not so pale as the lady I had met at church; her dress was more fashionable, but, somehow, I did not like her so well. I rather preferred the gentleman, at least when he smiled. I thought, from his dark, sunburnt face, his firm tones, and decided manner, he must be one of those "bold, brave captains" that Uncle Steve sung about. This thought suddenly brought to my mind the probability of my being separated from my friends at the Cove; and I was sorry I did not ask if I might not sometimes go to see them; and, last of all, I remembered Sally Hunt, and oh, how I did long to tell her! Had the gentleman desired to try my power of self-control, he could not have selected a better test.

She was in rather better humor than usual when I entered the house. She took no notice of my long absence, neither did she make any reference to the affair of the morning. The road upon which we lived was little travelled, and no one passed that day but John Wilford with a flock of sheep. And I went to my garret that night with a sadder heart than ever, for, until that day, I had really never hoped.

I was on my knees next morning, scrubbing the kitchen-floor, when I heard the sound of wheels rapidly approaching, and, dropping my brush, I sprang up and ran to the window. The carriage had passed the corner of the house, but I knew it had stopped, and my heart seemed to stop beating also.

A thump on my head, from the yard-stick with which Granny Hunt was measuring cloth, set it in motion again.

"What are you starin' at, you fool! 'Tain't nobody arter you, I guess!"

"I guess 'tis!" I cried, triumphantly, for, spite of her reminder, I had maintained my position and had caught sight

of Squire G—— and my new friend, as
they came round the corner of the house,
for no one ever thought of entering by
the front door.

"No so good news as that!" she
muttered, as she rose and began to
gather up the scattered threads that had
fallen from her cloth, for she too had
seen them.

They soon undeceived her. She was
too wilful to manifest any surprise when
Mr. G—— went on to say that a lady,
distinguished for her benevolence and
many excellent qualities, Miss Agnes Lathrop, wished to adopt the child, Zerlina
Day. The town authorities, satisfied
that it was for the good of the child, had
consented, on condition that she should
not again become a charge to this place.
The necessary papers had been signed,
and he had come to give the child into
the hands of Ralph Annesley, Esq., etc.

Mr. G—— seemed in high spirits; he
called me to him, patted me on the head,
hoped I would "be a good girl, and not
form bad habits."

All the while Mr. Annesley sat listening, with that queer smile curving his
lips.

It takes but little time to pack the
wardrobe of a pauper. And, with one
lingering glance at the old picture on the
wall and the corner where Ollie's bed
used to stand, I followed my old mistress
down, with my bundle in my hand.

"The lady'll find all her things clean,
an' the young un knows how to keep
'em so, if she's a mind ter," said Mrs.
Hunt.

"Is the child honest?" said Mr. Annesley, turning suddenly to her, and addressing her for the first time.

"It's plaguey little you know about
young uns if you don't know that the
best on 'em'll bear watchin'," she replied sharply.

"Why, Mrs. Hunt!" began Squire
G——; but Mr. Annesley motioned him
to be still, and, fixing his keen gray eyes
upon Mrs. Hunt, said

"Did this child ever steal from you?"

"I never gin her a chance. I've
dealt with the likes of 'em too long for
that, I hope!"

"Indeed, Mr. Annesley, I can assure
you we have never had any complaints
of that nature about this child," interrupted Mr. G——, nervously. "I think
she bids fair to make a useful member of
society; she can hardly fail of doing so,
under the training of your accomplished
relative. There are, it strikes me," he
went on tapping my forehead with his
fat finger, "capabilities here—comparison large, you see, causality fair—and
capabilities, as I tell my wife, must make
themselves felt, sooner or later, sir."

Oh, what an excellent thing is faith!
Especially in a town magistrate. It was
this conviction, I suppose, that reconciled
Squire G—— and his respectable con-
frères to leaving me to take my first lessons under the tuition of Granny Hunt!

"Certainly, sir—in one way or the
other," said Mr. Annesley, dryly, as he
took my hand to lead me out. We were
followed by the town magnate; and,
from the carriage, in which Mr. Annesley placed me, I caught the last glimpse
of Granny Hunt's froze-and-thawed visage, peeping at us from behind the paper
shades in her spare room.

We drove to the village, and stopped
at a house near the church; where, with
a request to be "as quick as possible," to
the woman who met us at the door, Mr.
Annesley left me. The woman took me
into a back room, where another woman,
with her foot on a bonnet-block and her
mouth full of pins, sat sewing; but I nowhere saw the pretty, faded face of my
lady friend. I soon understood that I
had been left there for new dresses. The
woman tried on several of pretty prints
and muslin, with frequent injunctions not
to drop my shoulders in *that* way, or
draw in my breath, while they both plied
me with questions as to who the person
was with whom I was going to live, and
where I was going, with a kind of run-

ning commentary upon the condition of town paupers generally, while the pins, though they thickened her speech somewhat, seemed to be not the slightest impediment.

I knew absolutely nothing about my new friends or my destination, and, therefore, could give them no satisfactory information, and was glad when Mr. Annesley returned and put an end to their questions. He spoke a few seconds with the woman, paid her some money, and, quite unmindful of her voluble thanks and hopes that "the lady would be satisfied—the fit was quite wonderful, seeing it was all guess-work"—he stalked out of the room and deposited me and the large package which the woman handed him in the carriage, without so much as giving one look at my pretty new dress.

We took the road to the beach, a small hamlet overlooked by a large hotel and several boarding-houses, much frequented by lovers of sea-food and seabreezes. Mr. Annesley did not speak, but, with slackened reins, let the horse plod on at its own gait, while I, proud of my new clothes—prouder still of the astonishing fact that I was actually riding in a real carriage—looked down upon the people on foot or in open wagons whom we passed, with an exceedingly self-satisfied feeling, until, in smoothing out the folds of my dress-skirt, I let Ollie's little japanned trunk, which, as the most valuable of my possessions, I carried in my hand, slip to the floor of the vehicle, and a sidewise lurch sent it to the ground.

"Oh, stop—please, do stop!" I cried, attempting to follow it.

He caught hold of my dress, and asked what I had dropped.

"Ollie's little trunk, sir. Please let me get out!" which I did as soon as he checked the horse.

"And what precious valuables is that tin box supposed to contain?" he asked, as he helped me back to my seat by his side.

I had a fancy that he was laughing at me, and answered timidly, "Books and—and things, sir."

"Books and things"—a woman's answer. I felt quite sure he was laughing at me now, for that queer smile gathered round his mouth as he muttered:

"A special subject for Agnes's literary mania—so much the better. What books, child?"

"Ollie's Bible, that his mother gave him, and the 'Whale Book,' sir. It's got a picture of the very one that swallowed Jonah," I said, eagerly.

"Authentic, no doubt. But who is Ollie?"

I told him about him, and was still talking when we drove up to the "Mansion House." He lifted me out and led me across the piazza to a parlor, where there was quite a party of ladies and gentlemen, among whom I quickly recognized Miss Agnes. She ran forward to meet us, very much as little Adeline Leete might have done, and, taking my hand, presented me to the company as her *protégée*, saying something very pretty about "a waif cast up by the sea," which I did not then comprehend. Then she related my story, or I supposed she was talking about me, for she repeated my name and Mrs. Hunt's, but I was puzzled to recognize myself through the romantic covering in which her imagination clothed me. Of course every one praised her "benevolence," etc.—all but Mr. Annesley, who stood with his back to the company, looking out of the window, and when he turned round he looked decidedly cross.

In a few hours we were on our way to New Haven, and, tired as my eyes were, from looking at every object to be seen through the car-window, and halfblinded with dust, I could not help gazing with delight at that beautiful city. I had never seen any place larger than Bradshaw before, and the elegant houses, the elm-arched streets, the high bluffs rising like sentinels on either side, the long semicircle of undulating green hills in the background, made me think of the paradise of which Ollie used to tell me, and this child's fancy clings to me still. God's blessing on every leaf of those noble elms that shade alike the weary and the light-hearted!

Here, Mr. Annesley left us to take the boat for New York, whence he was to sail for the East. He did not tell me when he left that I must be a good girl and love my protectress; perhaps he thought the ladies at the beach had impressed that duty upon my mind sufficiently; he only shook my hand and said "Good-by, my girl," in a pleasant voice, and, turning to Miss Agnes, added something about having as much patience with me as she would have with a Choctaw or a Chinese.

Next morning, before we left, Miss Agnes took me to Miss Ford's, on Chapel Street, to select a new hat. Shall I ever forget that pretty, English straw, with its wreath of rose-buds, and the many times she had occasion to caution me "not to crush them," in my eagerness to see every thing from the stage-coach windows, on our way to her home in Chesterwood?

CHAPTER VI.

MY NEW MISTRESS.

THERE are many of the progeny of Reuben yet living, and my new friend was a true daughter of this line. Kind, unselfish, generous, and impulsive, she had little firmness, and no self-reliance. Moreover, she was surrounded by a large circle of intimate friends, who claimed the right to criticise her for burdening herself with the care of a child, who "belonged to nobody," and to advise her as to the best method to be pursued in bringing her up, and, *par conséquence*, when I left her, at the end of four years, she had never quite decided how or for

what station in life I was to be educated.

Yet she prided herself greatly on her method, which consisted in carefully writing out, in her delicate "Italian hand," a set of rules for the employment of my time (she having decided to teach me herself), and the regulation of my conduct for every hour in the day, and hanging them up over the mantel-piece in her small sitting-room, which henceforth was called the "study."

It did not take long for me, child as I was, to discern that, whenever these rules interfered with her business or pleasure, they were set aside, and I very naturally followed her example. It need hardly be said I was a poor scholar for my age. I found no difficulty in learning any thing that was taught orally, and easily understood the principles involved when familiarly explained (at least I did in after-years, and suppose I might then), but I detested saying things off by rote, without changing or missing a word of the text, and this was Miss Agnes's idea of a perfect lesson. Very sore were my trials with English grammar and arithmetic under this system, and very sore my heart too, for I almost always failed, and was sent away in disgrace with the tearful reproach, which cut me far deeper than had Mrs. Sally's blows, that I did not love her, or I would not try her patience thus.

I *did* love her, but I should have loved her better, more spontaneously, if my obligations to do so had not been so continually kept before me by herself and others, while no one ever seemed to think of my need of love. I have no desire to make a special plea for myself —I know what I was then; and, many a time since, I have gone down on my knees and prayed that the errors and sins of that period of my life might be forgiven. But there was one thing of which neither Miss Agnes nor her friends took sufficient account—the half-savage life I had hitherto led, and my utter ignorance of the common forms and usages of society. Especially was this true of the first months of my residence with her, when I was expected to "behave like a lady" when presented to her numerous friends and acquaintances; not to "wriggle or twist" my body, or cross my limbs, "like a vulgar, ill-bred child," and to be very careful not to tumble my mistress's collar or hair when I kissed her upon entering or leaving the room, which was one of the established rules.

Of course, I failed—but I think my eagerness to please her was as often the cause of my failure as my awkwardness, and poor Miss Agnes felt my *gaucherie* as keenly as if her own reputation was at stake. And indeed it was, for each of her friends claimed the right to criticise her action in adopting me, and there is no tribunal like that to be found among one's friends and relatives in a country town or village.

Chesterwood was in a sort of transition state at this time. Formerly, a wealthy agricultural town, its wide green common was set round with large, heavily-timbered, roomy old mansions, with gardens and "home lots" behind them—the homes of wealthy farmers, who drove out, as their fathers had before them, daily, to their farms amid the hills.

They were strongly conservative, and as aristocratic, in their way, as any Guelph that ever filled a throne, making it a point of conscience to patronize the same lawyer, doctor, minister, and storekeeper, year after year, without a thought of change. But they lived in the nineteenth century, and the introduction of the steam-engine changed the whole aspect of the town, and gave a new tone to the life of thought there. There had sprung up within a few years a class of men, chiefly mechanics, upon whom the members of the old *régime* had been wont to look with a friendly, patronizing air, with views broader and deeper than their purses, to be sure, but

active-brained, enthusiastic, busy-handed, whose keen eyes detected at once the available power of the beautiful streams that laced the fine old township with their silver threads; who bought privileges, cut channels, built dams, dug flumes, put up machinery, set hundreds of hands to work, and lo! at the west end of the old town there sprang up the pretty village of Bubbleton, so named in honor of the senior partner of the firm of Bubble & Hum, to whose enterprise the village owed its existence—or, in the words of Orville A. Grindwell, Esq., the talented young lawyer who had taken up his residence there, it had "sprung, Minerva-like, from his brain."

Squire Gaines, who belonged to the old town and visited at Miss Agnes's, said that the crop had exhausted the soil, with how much truth I cannot say. But I know that the old *régime* looked down upon the place as a sort of Jonah's gourd, and prophesied for it a like fate, and, for a time, their prophecies seemed likely to prove true, for the first attempts failed, a fate nowise uncommon in the history of manufactures, but, like the giant Antæus, every time they touched the ground they gathered new strength, until they became firmly established, and the manufacturing interest was in the ascendant. There were new stores, schools, lawyers, doctors allopathic, homœopathic, botanic, dentists, etc., etc., and a new church with a spire far overtopping the old one, and a new minister. The majority of the townspeople soon felt their interests to be identified with the new movement, but a few, the most aristocratic of the old *régime*, wrapped about them that mantle of family pride, to the preservation of which the air of certain localities in New England seems peculiarly favorable, and kept on "the even tenor of their way" with unabated dignity.

In most of these families, there were one or more unmarried daughters, not, as I can well believe, for lack of opportunity, for several of them must have been very pretty in their youth, but chiefly because, their circle being limited, the offers did not come from the approved grade. Professional men and merchants were considered the only desirable parties, and, as these had been somewhat scarce in Chesterwood in their early days, and those who had come into town in the train of the manufactures were either provided with wives or preferred youth to rank, they were still left hanging upon the ancestral tree, though occasionally one dropped off into the arms of some wealthy old bachelor or widowed divine.

To this set belonged Miss Agnes, she being the only child of their old physician, from whom she had inherited a competence, and whose dying wish she respected by still living in the house which he had built at the time of his marriage, and which was one of the pleasantest of those fronting upon the common. Miss Agnes had been very pretty and quite gay in her girlhood (of course all this I learned in after-years), had been educated at a celebrated female school in Hartford, and spent several successive winters in New York, with her maternal relatives. If reports were true, she was several times engaged to be married, but they ended, where they began, in mere gossip, for it was not until she was near thirty that she announced her engagement to a New-York merchant, and the gentleman visited Chesterwood as her betrothed husband. Her father's illness and death caused the marriage to be deferred at first, then it was put off on one pretence and another, the gentleman's visits became less frequent, his letters more cool, until, finally, he wrote requesting her to cancel the engagement, giving, as a reason, the state of his affairs, and a serious doubt of his ability to make her happy. The letter reached her about the same date as the announcement of his marriage to a lady who possessed a few more thousands than the old doctor had been able to leave his daughter.

Like Polly Maria, she had been "dis-p'inted," and I am inclined to think there is some truth in Uncle Steve's remark, that it "comes kinder nat'ral to women," for, although her most intimate friends said she had never recovered from the shock, I think they must have been mistaken, from the fact that she was always ready to refer to it, in her usual manner, on all occasions. Indeed, it was the pet sorrow that gave a pleasant sentimentalism to her whole life. I hardly know what she would have done without it; it was the bond between her and the young people of her acquaintance, and this alliance, coupled with a kind of half recognition of the "new folks," subjected her to a good deal of criticism and scrutiny from her own set. Her adoption of me, as I said before, was a fruitful theme for discussion. Had she assumed the responsibilities and duties of a missionary, for which she was in no wise adapted, they would have lauded her self-sacrifice and devotion, and been proud of the slightest line written by her hand, but this "whim" of adopting a town pauper was "quite another thing," and it met with more condemnation than congratulation.

"Agnes dear," Miss More would say, after discussing the last number of *Graham* or *Godey*, and that "love of a poem" by Willis or Morris, "you are wearing yourself out with that child. Remember that you have other duties— you were not at the society yesterday— duties to yourself and your friends. You must not confine yourself in this way; you can never bear it!"

"But I do not feel it, Fanny. It is so pleasant for me to have something wholly my own—some one to love me better than any one else in the whole world. I have been so much alone since papa's death—and I need affection so much!"

Then, perhaps, there would follow something about the "dear gazelle" from Moore, and Miss Fanny, who was sentimentally given also, would admit that "dear Agnes had had her trials," and they would go on quoting poetry or talking over some piece written in their albums by some distinguished politician or preacher, when a student; one reminiscence calling up another, until they grew quite young again. Of all Miss Agnes's circle, I liked Fanny Moore, with her poetry and sentimentalism, the best.

She would be followed by the dignified Miss Griffin, whose ancestor originally owned one-third of the whole township, and whose mother's grand-uncle had once been secretary of state. To be sure, most of the land had long since passed into other hands, but it must have been very strong land, indeed, for even the memory of its ownership gave a loftiness and stiffness to the Griffins, which were to be accounted for in no other way. Like the condemned heroine in Ben Jonson's play, Sarah Griffin was "Duchess of Malfy still!" She never would recognize my existence, in spite of Miss Agnes's manœuvring, otherwise than by a brief—

"Ah! that child. I think I heard Fanny Moore say you had taken one."

Miss Beach was the wit of the set, who liked, above all things, to hear people say, "Now, Anna, don't be satirical!" and she shook her black curls defiantly at me every time she came, and ordered me off to play, vowing she was not going to be cheated out of her usual quiet chats with Miss Agnes, for all the brats in Christendom. "Turn your cosy sitting-room into a nursery if you choose, dear, or your house into a foundling hospital—make a second John Rogers's wife of yourself, but don't expect me to tolerate them. I came here to see my old friend, and I am going to see her! The idea of your adopting a child!—and one in no way connected with you—whom you know nothing about—and you so exclusive! It is preposterous! I wonder you don't apply for the position of matron of the orphan asylum in H.—— Shall I write you a letter of recommendation, dear?" and the black curls would toss with mirth

at Miss Agnes's annoyed look and deprecatory tone as she pleaded:

"But you cannot understand how lonely my life was, Anna. You have a plenty of brothers and sisters to love and care for you."

"Love! Fiddlesticks! You might as well say to quarrel with me too. Give me your position and independence, and you may take the love. Don't let us be silly in our old age, Agnes."

But the most dreaded of these ladies, the *bête noire* of those days, was Miss Harriet Hart, and I think Miss Agnes shared my feeling. She was such a superior person; every one said so, though in what the superiority consisted, save in a hard, inflexible will and unfaltering self-assertion, I never could make out. Under the pretence of a regard for truth, she made no scruple of saying the most disagreeable things, or meddling with the most intimate personal affairs. Her features and figure, though large, were good, and she was always most carefully dressed, but there was something hard and metallic about her—you felt it as soon as she entered the room. I had a fancy that this property extended to her clothes, for her silks and muslins had a rustle and stiffness peculiar to themselves. She had an adroit manner of drawing people out, and then coming down upon them with her own views—generally some oracular utterance of an old truism that, for the time being, would quite disconcert a more self-reliant person than Miss Agnes.

She had been absent from town when we arrived, and I had seen most of Miss Agnes's friends before she made her appearance. I was seated at my table, striving to master my lessons, when she called, and the rustle of her silk caused me to look up. Miss Agnes signed for me to go on with my studies, and conversed some time with her visitor, before she said:

"Zerlina, dear, come and shake hands with Miss Hart.—A little waif,

Harriet, which I picked up on the sea-shore, a few weeks since."

"Ay, I've heard about it." She gave me two fingers and a sharp glance, before she added, "You can go on with your lessons, child."

"She may as well take a recess, now, for I have a great deal to ask you about, Harriet.—Zerlina, you may get your hat and go out."

"Permit me to observe, Agnes, that I think your course decidedly wrong, if the child has not properly learned her lessons yet. Children should be made to pursue their studies under any circumstances, and thus form habits of concentration and self-control. Don't you think so?"

"I presume you are right, but I confess I never thought of it before," replied Miss Agnes, timidly.

"And you have actually adopted this child without carefully weighing all the responsibilities, Agnes!"

What a weight of condemnation there was in her voice and manner! Miss Agnes blushed as if caught in the commission of some crime, but said, with charming frankness:

"I am afraid I have, Harriet. The truth is, I did not think much about it. I met the child when she was suffering from the violence of the person who had charge of her; my cousin, Ralph Annesley, who was with me, suggested the idea of my adopting her, and I did."

"That was just like you—impulsive as a child—but, unfortunately, something else is needed when we come to training her for her proper sphere in life. Have you decided upon any plan?"

"Oh, yes; I shall train her to be my child—companion, friend—and, at the same time, a useful member of society, I hope. But I shall be glad of any suggestions."

"Then let me suggest that you train her for the humble condition of life in which she was born," returned the lady, dryly.

"Oh, no, Harriet, I cannot do that!" cried Miss Agnes, eagerly. "I must do better by her than that, or where is the good of my taking her?"

"A very pertinent question, and one which should have occurred to you before, my dear," said Miss Hart, with a grim smile. "I presume you are teaching her yourself—what is your method?"

Miss Agnes pointed proudly to our neat schedule of exercises.

"Reading, writing, spelling, defining, grammar, geography, arithmetic!—um!—um!—the first three are essential—drop the others and send her to the kitchen to take lessons of Hannah Smith. In this way she may really become of some use to you and others. To attempt any thing more with her is a complete absurdity, and will prove an utter failure, take my word for it."

Consciously or unconsciously, Miss Hart did a good deal toward a seeming fulfilment of her prophecy. She had a habit of coming in to hear me recite; or about the hour of recitation, and often when I knew, by Miss Agnes's look, that she was satisfied with me, Miss Hart would take the book from her hand and, in five minutes' time, so completely confuse me that I could answer nothing correctly; then return the book to my mistress without a word, but with such a look! Why, Miss Agnes could no more have stood up and defied that look than she could have made a world.

Besides, she knew that I had a much better knowledge of my lessons than my answers to her friend indicated, and was both grieved and angry. I could not make her understand how that lady's presence, even the rustle of her dress, seemed to act upon me like a spell, freezing all my faculties. I did not understand it myself. It did not help the matter to say simply that I did not like Miss Hart, for then my failure was attributed to sheer obstinacy, and I was generally sent to the kitchen in disgrace, as the only fitting place for me, until the kind heart of my mistress recalled me to her side.

But, in causing me to be sent to the kitchen, Miss Hart did me a kindness of which neither of us was aware at the time. Hannah Smith was a genuine New-England woman—sensible, clear-headed, and kind-hearted. She had been in the family many years. At first she had been kind to me from a sense of duty, but gradually she came to like me for myself, or, rather, for the habits of neatness and order which had been instilled into me by Granny Hunt. Hannah often trusted me to do things about the house, taught me the routine of duties in a well-ordered household, and made me her aid in assisting the sick and the poor; for Miss Agnes, though a liberal giver, shrunk from close contact with pain and suffering.

In two studies, and precisely those with which Miss Hart said I had nothing to do, I made rapid progress—music and drawing—and, in spite of that lady's contempt, Miss Agnes was very proud of my performances. They were crude enough, for my teacher (one of those peripatetic young ladies who make the round of country towns) might have practised weeks on Giotto's "O" to advantage, herself. Miss Agnes's praise might have made me vain if I had not so keenly felt my stupidity and backwardness in the more solid branches, which I was not likely to forget under Miss Hart's criticisms.

The second summer after I came to Chesterwood, I went to a day-school. Miss Agnes, I presume, was quite satisfied with her experiment in teaching, for a slight indisposition in the spring served as an excuse for the change. My dislike of schools soon wore off under my new circumstances, and Miss Agnes was so pleased with my progress that she took me with her to the sea-side, as a reward, during the summer vacation, instead of leaving me at home with Hannah.

We went to the beach, where we spent four weeks, or Miss Agnes did, for most of my days were passed at the Cove with Uncle Steve and little Adeline. Miss Agnes had some hesitation as to the propriety of my renewing my acquaintance with "people of that sort;" but, hearing a gentleman speak in the highest terms of Uncle Steve's heroism in saving the lives of two unlucky boys, during a sudden squall, her curiosity was excited, and she not only permitted me to go, but took me over herself, when Uncle Steve quite won her heart by his resemblance to one of the characters in Scott's "Pirate."

Uncle Steve, who had his own opinion of pirates, did not feel at all complimented by the comparison, I could see; but Miss Agnes was quite charmed with little Adeline, and he could forgive any thing to those who were kind to her. I need not say how unchanged I found the simple hearts there, nor how glad they were to see me. I was "a whole head taller than Bluebird," Uncle Steve said, when he placed us "back to back" and sighted the difference with his right eye shut close and set round by a sea of wrinkles; but not too tall to sit on his knee and listen to his stories with the same interest as of old. I shall never forget his astonishment and delight when I made for him a sketch of the cottage, with the curving beach, and the "Dart" coming in from the Reef. He even saw a resemblance to himself in the upright, black mark, crowned with a tarpaulin, with two horizontal curves for arms, which occupied the stern of the boat. He got a carpenter to frame it, and, when he had "slung" it at the proper angle over the mantel, and stepped back to admire it with a true nautical squint, Michael Angelo could never have received a look of more loving reverence and admiration than he bestowed upon me.

Little Adeline had grown too, grown prettier—more like my old favorites, the pond lilies—but her pet name seemed just as fitting as ever, for no one who saw her childish grace of manner, or looked into her eyes, could ever think of her growing old or mature. Polly Maria was the only one in whom I noted any change. She seemed to be more gloomy and discouraged, in view of her own shortcomings, than ever before, but I was beginning to form my own estimate of people and things, and, when I saw her laboring so unweariedly, day after day, not only for our comfort, but for the parties of country people who were always wanting some favor, lending them her kettles and dishes to help out their picnics and finding them dirty, if not cracked or broken, when returned, without a word of complaint, I found it difficult to believe her the "sinful worm of the dust" which she affirmed herself to be. I was beginning to understand that people are generally better than their creeds; that the moods resulting from a morbid, diseased digestion, and an earnest, thoughtful, religious experience, are quite different things.

I had not been there many days, however, before I began to suspect her anxiety was in some way connected with the visits of a certain Mr. Nat Frisbie, who frequently called to look after the seine she was netting for him, he being a large owner in one of the most valuable fisheries; and they held, sometimes, quite long conversations together, which, however, did not seem to brighten her up in the least—why, I could not tell, for he was a brisk, cheery little man, with a clear, treble voice like a fife.

At last, I asked Uncle Steve what it meant.

He continued to look gravely, for a minute or so, at the point of the horizon on which his eye was fixed when I spoke, before he replied:

"I s'pose it's cause he's a widderwer."

"A widower?"

"Yes. He's been hangin' round, off and on, all summer. Widderwers are pretty good at hangin' on, I've minded, but,

somehow, Polly don't seem to bite—not right sharp," he added, meditatively.

"Do you mean that he wants to marry Polly Maria?"

"A'cordin' to my observation, that's it, though she never's opened her head to me about it, but I know'd she'd feel oneasy in her mind about Birdie and me, if she had a mind ter go, so I tried to talk to her a bit, and lay out a clear course for us all, an' she said as how 'twas a world o' changes, and 'twas best to be prepared for whatever as was to come ter pass—which I take to be as nigh true as any thing out o' the Bible. Them as has had troubles like her ought ter know," said the old man, humbly.

"But you wouldn't let her go! you couldn't spare her?" I said, in surprise.

"Well, yes; 'cause, as I said afore, that's Bible truth, an' there's no sheering off from that. Nat's a good feller—he's well to do, and he's got three little uns, who need lookin' arter. You see, Blackbird, it don't come quite so handy for most men-folks to look arter little uns, as it did for me to look arter Birdie. Nat thinks she'd be a good hand ter look arter 'em, an' so she would. An' I shouldn't wonder if among so many on 'em they brightened her up a little, for she never'd be alone as she is here, when Birdie and I am off in the Dart. 'Twouldn't be so lonesome for her."

Rough, unpolished old sea-shell, but with a strain of the eternal melody in his heart—unselfish to the last! But I did not see it then, and this matrimonial project seemed to me a kind of proof of Polly Maria's sinfulness, and I bluntly expressed my thought.

Uncle Steve opened his mouth, something after the manner of a fish, and laughed silently; then letting his eye drop on me, he said:

"Not sinful, but nateral, Blackbird. You don't understand it now, but you will bime-by. Some on 'em play shy awhile, but I've minded they 'most ollers give in at last."

"But how will Birdie and you manage?"

"Well, it seemed kind of a hard kink to me when I first thought on't, 'cause you see I ain't very sharp, an' I hadn't observed as Birdie was a growin' up inter a tall gall till she minded me on't t'other day. Polly had gone up ter Harriet Stone's ter evenin' meetin', and I kinder sounded Birdie about the matter."

"What did she say?" I asked, seeing that he paused.

"Say? She made it all straight, in course! Nothing ever puzzles her! You see I bore down hard on Nat's little gals as hadn't no mother, 'cause I thought 'twas a good p'int, an' when I axed her would she let Aunt Polly go to look arter 'em, and be content with old Uncle Steve and what he could do for her, why, Lord bless ye, I had her a cryin' an' a laughin' all ter once: cryin' for the poor little gals as hadn't got no Uncle Steve, she said; and laughin' to think o' the weddin', an' 'cause she'd have some little gals ter go ter see. I never'd thought about that afore, Blackbird," he added, thoughtfully, raising his tarpaulin, and drawing the back of his red hand across his still redder forehead, as if all this unusual amount of thought pained him. "I'd never thought about her bein' lonesome, though she won't 'low she is. But it's nater for her to want ter see somebody besides Polly an' me, an' she can't go agin nater—though, if anybody can, she can. I've thought a deal about it sin', Blackbird, an', if 'twarn't makin' too much 'count of old Steve Leete, I should say the Lord had jist took a turn at the wheel Himself ter lay out a clear course for me—leavin' a kink here an' there ter make me keep a sharp look-out, an' all for Birdie's sake, in course. An' sin' you've come, I've thought on another p'int. She ought ter have some larnin'—not that she don't read glib enough now, an' knows all the capes from the Horn up to Sandy Hook, but she don't know much about the land as

you seed when you was talking to her about Chicago t'other day; an' she can't write nor make picters, 'cause she hain't been ter school much, it's sech a long ways to go; an' Polly nor I ain't much given to sech things. If Polly marries Nat, Birdie can stay up there some, an' go ter school with his chil'ren. You see, the kink is clear; it all pays out with a clear run, Blackbird!"

"Yes; but what will you do all alone, Uncle Steve?" He looked straight over my head at the distant horizon, so that I could not see his eyes, as he said:

"Blackbird, you used ter like my clam-chowders: I guess I'll go an' make one for dinner!"

Even the thought of my favorite dish could not hide from me the figure of the lonely old man, and I persisted in repeating:

"But you will be all alone, when she is up there."

"I can get used to it, Blackbird, I s'pose," he said, slowly; and I much doubt whether the spars and lines of the schooner off Faulkner's Island (upon which his eyes were fixed) did not grow indistinct, for a moment, from other causes than distance and the salt-sea spray.

I learned from Uncle Steve that Sally Hunt had become entangled in a lawsuit with her step-sons, which had been decided against her, and the damages and costs would be very heavy for one of her means. Miss Agnes had forbidden me to renew my acquaintance with her, and the prohibition was a severe trial to me. Not that even Miss Agnes's teachings had led me to feel any thing like love or forgiveness toward my old mistress, but I longed to have her see my pretty dresses, my new hat, and sun-shade—to show her that "town-poor Lina" was somebody. I thought there would be no harm in just walking past there; the temptation to do so was very great: and one day, when Uncle Steve was off to the Reef, and Polly Maria and little Adeline gone up to Rogers's store, where I had declined to accompany them, I dressed myself in my prettiest dress and set off for the pond. It did not occur to me that the very dress which I was so proud of would prevent my old mistress from recognizing me, even if my growth did not. But, as I drew near the old place, there came memories of Ollie, gentle memories that drove away the proud, vain feelings with which I had set out, and left only tears. The sting of Granny Hunt's blows, so keenly remembered when I started, were forgotten, and, yielding to a sudden impulse, I sprang over the fence, and, instead of walking proudly past the house, sought my old retreat on the edge of the pond. Looking into the water there, I saw all that poor boy's life pass before me; even the patient face seemed to mirror itself there, and I continued to gaze until I could see it no longer for the fast-falling tears.

As I turned to go, I came in contact with a bent sapling; it was the one Ollie had bent for me years before, and by which he had illustrated to me the reason of Granny Hunt's existence: "God does not make 'em, He lets 'em be. Something made her cross and crooked, I s'pose."

Again I seemed to hear his earnest voice repeating these words; and, my heart melting within me, I went down on my knees and uttered again that prayer for our old mistress's redemption which our childish faith had put up years before.

God deals wonderfully with the heart of childhood; let us reverence, not scorn His teachings.

CHAPTER VII.

THE REV. MARCUS TYLER.

"I would also give notice that the Rev. Marcus Tyler will preach from this pulpit this afternoon, on the subject of foreign missions, when he will give some account of, the great field for missionary enterprise among the tribes of Central Africa," etc.

How well do I remember the above announcement as it fell from the lips of Father Mason in Chesterwood Church one wintry Sunday morning, and the look of eager curiosity which I lifted to the somewhat stout, bland-looking gentleman leaning back in the pulpit!

Not that there was any thing strange in the presence of an agent, for Chesterwood received frequent calls from them; but this man would speak of Africa, that wondrous land, "under the line," of which Uncle Steve had told little Adeline and me, where they raised lions and elephants, and hump-backed camels, pictures of which he used to make for us in the wet beach-sand before his door, and where the coast was bordered with a beach of bright gold-dust. Had I not spent hour after hour, when Miss Agnes thought me conning my lesson in the geography before me, open at the picture of the sphinx, in traversing the Great Desert, feeling its hot breath upon my cheeks, its burning sands scorching my feet, boundless, vast, and silent as the great, luminous sky over my head?

Therefore, I listened eagerly to the preacher's words that afternoon; but oh, what a different Africa was his from the one Uncle Steve and my imagination had pictured! My rich, warm, luminous image was blotted out in the universal darkness, moral and physical, in which the speaker shrouded the "swart mother of nations." With measured, sepulchral tones, he dwelt upon the terrible retribution that would come upon those churches which from sloth or selfishness withhold the means of conversion from those perishing millions, until I shuddered from terror, and expected to see Miss Agnes and every one else tear off their jewelry and rich clothing, and, wrapping about them the mantle of sackcloth of which the preacher spoke, lay them upon the altar, as an offering to the cause. Miss Agnes did no such thing. She wiped away the tears which the preacher's flowery peroration had drawn forth, and, joining Fanny Moore when the service was over, discussed the sermon as they walked home; the minister's style, looks, manner, and small, white hands; quoted some passages from Dumas's "Sinai," a copy of which, presented by Mr. Annesley, lay upon the centre-table; and Miss Fanny rejoined with some stanzas from Mrs. Hemans's "Traveller at the Source of the Nile;" and that was all.

No; for that week the reverend gentleman attended Miss Agnes home from the "sewing circle," and followed up the acquaintance by frequent calls, whenever he happened to be in our vicinity; remained to dinner or tea, did ample justice to the good things set before him; while he enlarged, in that subdued, suave voice of his, upon the beauty of self-sacrifice and devotion, and how remarkably these qualities had been illustrated by woman in all ages.

Miss Agnes early introduced me to his notice, related my story, and Mr. Annesley's connection with it.

"Ah, Mr. Ralph Annesley! I had the honor of meeting that gentleman at a friend's house, during the anniversaries in New York, some years since. A gentleman of a good deal of general culture and observation, but tinctured with the pernicious evil of our times—the pride of human reason. But Providence sometimes chooses to work with strange instruments. I can scarcely conceive how a person bound in the sweet tie of relationship with yourself, and enjoying the inestimable advantage of your society, can hold such views."

Miss Agnes blushed, and said that her cousin "had lived mostly abroad for many years; that his errors of opinion were indeed a source of grief to her, but that he was one of the kindest-hearted people in the world."

"Ah, the heart, my dear Miss Lathrop, if we could always judge people by the heart! But we know that the unregenerate heart is deceitful and desperately wicked. A man may be charitable, virtuous, honest; but, without religion, I need not tell you that these are the poor, filthy rags which self-righteous morality wraps about its deluded victims," returned Mr. Tyler with a mournful sway of the head, which gave an undulating motion to his double chin behind the barrier of his white cravat. "Now, in reference to this child," he went on, with a wave of his soft, white hand toward me— "the motives which actuated you were as different from his as light from darkness: his could be but a blind impulse of our poor, fallen humanity; yours the truly Christian yearning to save her — to snatch her, as it were, as 'a brand from the burning.' You must not confound them, in your charming humility, dear friend."

The soft hand fell slowly, as if by accident, upon the small digits of Miss Agnes, which rested upon the table by which they were sitting; and the "brand," as Mr. Tyler often afterward designated me, was sent to the kitchen, not to be consumed by the fire—before which Hannah Smith was cooking a nice veal cutlet for the reverend gentleman's supper, he having "found his duties very arduous during the past week, and having but a delicate appetite at best," Miss Agnes said, with a timid, blushing air, when she had come to the kitchen to order it—no, not to be burned, but to ensconce myself in a corner out of Hannah's way, and recall Mr. Annesley's dark face, his clear, keen eyes, his full, distinct tones, and wonder what made them say he was so wicked. He certainly was not a bit like Granny Hunt, or Polly Maria, or myself, the three types of wickedness with which I was most familiar. There was no question about my state, for I felt, then, that I would much rather live with Mr. Ralph than Mr. Tyler, though the latter often reminded me of the life from which I had been snatched, and my obligations to Miss Agnes, in that tone which he deemed most impressive to a "brand," and I could recall no such proof of interest from Mr. Ralph.

Somehow, Mr. Tyler's advent seemed to disturb the current of our quiet life. Hannah Smith no longer laid out her work for weeks to come, but went about the house with a look of patient endurance upon her face, varied by glances of commiseration at Miss Agnes, who was constantly falling into reveries, seemingly very pleasant, from which she would start at the first word, with a blush and a pretty, childish air of confusion, and beg pardon, over and over again, for her inattention. Sometimes, when we were alone, she read to me from "Memoirs of Mrs. Van Lenness" and other devoted women, and would often pause and exclaim:

"Ah, what a precious privilege! To be permitted to devote one's life to the nations sitting in darkness!"

Dear Miss Agnes, how her eye kindled, and her pretty, delicate face gathered strength and firmness, as she spoke! How her slender figure grew strong and erect with the strength of a noble purpose! The frail, fading flower had taken a draught from the perennial fountain of life, and the subtle element brought not only freshness and beauty, but also strength and earnestness of purpose, and that overflowing love which would have all the world the happier for its happiness—a woman's experience, often, too often, brief as the life of a rose, but its fragrance and beauty still linger to bless the weary after-life, hints of the immortal and eternal beauty.

I needed not Miss Agnes's enthusiastic words and look to enlist my most ardent sympathy in behalf of missions. Ever since that Sunday, I had dreamed of being a missionary, some day, when I had become sufficiently good. No other way of life seemed of such pressing necessity and importance as this. Many a child can look back to a similar experience, and possibly recall, with a sigh or a smile, the doubts and struggles which the discrepancy between the words and practice of those around him raised in his mind. There is no realism like that of childhood.

Part of this painful experience was spared me by Miss Agnes and a few of her friends. They became deeply impressed with the duty of retrenchment in dress, but they did not put on sackcloth. They only exchanged their dainty bonnets and French flowers for those of rich, white satin; their striped and plaided silks and grenadines, for those of solid colors or elegant satins, and India muslins guiltless of spot. To be sure, they cost twice as much as the former— three times as much as the gaudy outfit of the factory-girl for whose benefit they had, in part, made this sacrifice— but they *meant* well. Of this I am certain; and who shall say that the satins of Miss Agnes, and the flimsy finery of the operative, do not count equal, in the eyes of the angels, with the sackcloth of St. Theresa or the hair-shirt of St. Ignatius?

Of course, the reader has already inferred that Miss Agnes was about to marry the Rev. Marcus Tyler, and go out to Africa as a missionary, as soon as arrangements could be made to that effect. The affair was duly discussed in Chesterwood; and, while some thought it a very suitable match, there were many dissenters, even among her own particular circle, who were supposed to have her interest most at heart, and the most active of these was Miss Harriet Hart. She did not joke her friend, like Miss Beach, or sympathize in her happiness, like tearful-eyed Fanny Moore; she was too "superior for that," but she overwhelmed her with her responsibilities; humbled her to the dust, by pointing out to her (all in her great love for the truth) her weaknesses, dexterously hunting out her little foibles; and ended with the sincere hope that she had not mistaken a mere human passion for that Christian fortitude and devotion which could alone support her in the position to which she aspired—a position which *she* (how her silk rustled as she spoke!), with all her strength of character, "had always shrunk from assuming."

Poor Miss Agnes! would that, on thy pretty head, self-esteem had risen like a mountain! But, after all, it would not have made thee a more lovable woman than the humble, trusting faith that answered, amid tears:

"I can suffer, Harriet dear. This deep and abiding love, which I feel for—for Marcus, will make me strong to do that!"

"I am afraid you mistake, Agnes. You are not of the stuff of which martyrs are made!"

Another mistake of Miss Hart's. Many a martyr is made of just such stuff as Miss Agnes Lathrop, but they do not go to Smithfield or Boston Common; neither do they cry, with Madame Roland, "O Liberty, how many crimes are committed in thy name!" Some of them may be even ignorant of that famous martyr's name; but they are slowly roasted, in private, before a domestic fire, kindled by unthinking egotism, and fed by morbid irritability; suffocated by the close atmosphere of a home whose narrow creed forbids them to follow the leading of their own taste, or even share in the social life and labor of the day; or they suffer the slow torture of a life of endless exactions and reproofs, dropping, at regular intervals, like the water upon the heads of the victims of the Inquisition, until madness or idiocy comes to their relief.

Yet these are the women whom men admire and love—women who "are content to go through life, gracefully leaning on the arm of man," as a reverend gentleman recently said in a public lecture—a sentiment worthy of the Rev. Marcus Tyler. And they are worthy of this love, even as Miss Agnes, with all her weakness, was more lovable than the hard, metallic Miss Hart; only let all good souls pray that they may find that arm strong and steady—a support even from their own weaknesses, as it should be—and that they may have the wisdom to see that this love (God be thanked for it!) can not only make them strong to endure, but has the power, beyond aught else, to make them noble, and place them on a level with the best and noblest man that ever lived—and that man was *not* the Rev. Marcus Tyler!

CHAPTER VIII.

MY STEP-FATHER.

"COME here, Lina!"

Miss Agnes is sitting in "the study," with her writing-desk open before her, upon which lies a letter with a few rose-leaves scattered over it. Her long, flaxen curls are put back carelessly behind her ears, and she wears a morning-dress of delicate pink lawn, with a *chemisette* of plain muslin and a tiny apron of black silk, and looks very bright and happy when I enter from the porch, where I had been studying my Sunday-school lesson, and lay the book before her.

"Oh, it's not about the lesson, dear, that I wish to speak now; I wish to tell you that I have received a letter which—Lina, wouldn't you like some one to share your plays and studies—a little brother to guard and protect you?"

"What from?" I ask, unconsciously looking round to see from what quarter danger is to be apprehended.

"Why, from the dangers and trials, the temptations and sufferings, which fall upon woman. 'Her lot is on you, silent tears to weep!' my child."

"I guess I can do it pretty well myself, ma'am, but just as you say."

"Quite right, dear. I do think it best. I am going to give you a papa in Mr. Tyler, and a brother in his little boy, Augustus. I suppose you may have heard Hannah speak of my engagement?"

"Hannah never said so, but Miss Beach did one day, and she said Augustus Tyler would 'put my nose out of joint!'"

"What a thoughtless creature! You must not mind Sara's jokes. But I am about to change my condition sooner than I had anticipated. Mr. Tyler will consent to no longer delay, and what I wish to say to you is this: my marriage will make no difference with you—you will still be my daughter, and I want you to remember what I say, because there are people who may try to make you think differently; they have even made the attempt already, it seems—but it has ever been my lot to be misunderstood. I'll show them their mistake, if I live," she goes on talking rather to herself than to me, while her cheek kindles with love and pride. "I will make them confess that Marcus's justice is as unimpeachable as his love, and that forestalls my slightest wish."

It was true—if you took his word for it, no man had a keener sense of justice —it was a fertile subject with him; he would dilate most eloquently upon its moral, political, and theological aspects; but, when he came to a personal application of its principles to the daily events of life, Justice, it would seem, never laid aside her scales to dirty her fingers with such common affairs as these.

They were married, the ceremony being performed by Father Mason, in Miss Agnes's parlor, in the presence of a few of her parents' old friends, and the ladies of her own circle. None of Mr. Tyler's family were present.

The evening before this ceremony, Miss Agnes came to my room after I was in bed, and talked to me about their plans. When they returned from their wedding tour, which was to be a visit to Mr. Tyler's dear mother, and became a little settled, Augustus would come to live with us, and go to school with me. He was an excellent scholar, and would help me so much. Then, if Mr. Tyler, as they hoped and expected, should be sent out to "Walla Basheen," or any other foreign station, Augustus and I would be left at school, for, of course, they would be obliged to renounce the parental relation until we were old enough to share their labors and trials.

She spoke rapidly, as if she was conscious that her time already belonged to another, but, before she left the room, drew from her pocket a small gold locket, and, touching a spring, showed me a set of clear-cut features which there was no mistaking.

"Do you know it, Lina?" she asked, letting the lamp-light fall full on the face.

"It is Mr. Annesley—only it looks like a boy."

"Yes; he was quite young when it was taken. We were much together in our childhood. I thought you would like to keep it, because he was so kind to you, and I suppose it will not be quite proper for me to be keeping it now—at least, Mr. Tyler might not think so—but—there —he calls, he misses me in a moment!" Be a good girl!" and, with a kiss on my forehead, she left the room.

"Umph!" said Hannah, when I showed her the locket, the day after the wedding, and repeated Miss Agnes's words, "so it's begun already. I wonder where was the harm o' her keeping it? Well, there's one thing—if Mr. Ralph had been at home, she never'd a got married—at least, just as she has!"

"Why not, Hannah?"

"'Cause she wouldn't a durst to. I've nothing to say again Mr. Tyler—

"Now, tell me who that lady is?"

he's a good man, I s'pose, and a minister o' the gospel, but she wouldn't a done it."

"You mean she would have been afraid?" I asked, in some surprise.

"No," she answered, pettishly, "not that she'd be afear'd of his being cross or unkind—but he would have told her it wasn't suitable, and he would have made her see it too!"

"If you were going to be married, Hannah, and Mr. Ralph was to tell you it was not suitable, would you give it up?" I asked, after gravely considering the subject awhile.

"Don't talk such nonsense, child! Them that's always known what's suitable always will, I hope!" she replied, loftily.

"Miss Agnes—"

"Is that the proper way of addressing my wife, child?"

It was the morning after the arrival of the newly-married pair; and, with childish eagerness, I had entered the sitting-room with some request to Miss Agnes, when Mr. Tyler, for whose comfort the large stuffed easy-chair of the doctor had been brought forth, suddenly laid down the *New-York Observer*, and, crossing the skirt of his handsome new dressing-gown over his knees, interrupted me with the above query, followed by a gleam of astonishment from above the bows of his gold spectacles.

Thus checked, I began again, more slowly, "Miss Agnes—"

The glance of astonishment turned to one of rebuke, and, tapping with his fat finger on the paper to command attention, he exclaimed:

"Do you hear, child? Is that the proper way to address my wife? Now, try again!"

I glanced from him to Miss Agnes, who was dusting some ornaments upon the shelf. She looked a little troubled, and was about to speak, but, with a lofty motion, he warned her to keep silent.

Left to myself, and really not knowing my offence, I repeated the name in a tone scarce above a whisper.

He pushed his glasses down as far as they would slide upon his fat nose, and, drawing in his chin until it was quite hidden within the folds of his cravat, gave me a look which was intended to express not only reproof, but astonishment and commiseration, while he mournfully waved his head, saying:

"I fear we have here a great deal of obstinacy or ignorance—perhaps both."

Miss Agnes stepped forward and began:

"My dear—" But he checked her with a counter "my dear" and a deferential wave of the hand, as he added:

"Don't let this little incident worry you, my dear. We"—Mr. Tyler had at one time been connected with a newspaper, and the editorial plural still adhered to him—"we perfectly understand children. There are few of their tricks and subterfuges with which we are not familiar, it having pleased divine Providence to place us over them in the capacity of instructor as well as parent.—Now, Zerlina, come here!"

He folded his hands, the backs of which looked like pin-cushions, over his knee, and, looking me in the eye fixedly a moment as I stood by his side, said sternly:

"Now, tell me who that lady is?"

I had been frightened at first, now I was irritated, and returned his look in silence, until he added:

"Well, we are waiting. We know how to manage obstinacy."

"It is Miss Agnes Lathrop, sir, and she is married to you."

"Very well," lying back in his chair complacently; "we thought we should succeed in getting a suitable or at least an approximate answer. Now, remember, girl: this lady is my wife, and henceforth you are to address her as Mrs. Tyler. We know nothing about 'Miss Agnes' any more. She has merged her name with her being into mine—*Mrs. Tyler.* Do you think you can remember?"

"I will try, sir."

"I think, my love," my mistress began, coming forward and timidly laying her hand on his shoulder, "I am afraid I am to blame—that is," she added, seeing him turn slowly in his chair, "I wish to say that it was by my wish that the child called me Miss Agnes, so you must put part of the reproof upon me. The change is so recent, you know; but I am sure henceforth Lina will remember."

. He gave her a look of unctuous fondness. "Ay, of course, you are sure! Your artless nature is so easily convinced —and I trust you are right. We have certainly no desire to mar the serenity of this auspicious marriage morn, as we may say, with any thing of a disagreeable nature, but duty is duty, my love. Therefore, we will give the child a lesson to read, and dismiss her."

He opened the Bible at the chapter which gives an account of the fate of the ill-mannered children who mocked at the prophet's baldness, and said:

"Go to your room and commit that portion of divine truth to memory as a warning of the fate of those who are disrespectful to their superiors."

When I came down to dinner, I found a new arrangement. Hitherto, Hannah, who had been more like a mother to Miss Agnes than a servant, had been accustomed to take her meals with us, unless when company was present and she was needed to wait at table. Now, her place of course was vacant, and my plate, instead of being laid next to that of Miss Agnes, was put quite at the lower end of the table, out of the neighborhood of the others. But it was not beyond the reach of her kind hand. Seeing that her husband had helped me to nothing but bread and vegetables, she reminded him of his oversight by passing it back for some of the nice boiled fowl before him. He had helped himself bountifully to the chicken and the various vegetables and sauces, and was just raising his well-filled fork to his mouth when she preferred her request. He laid down his fork and sat for a full second gazing at her with an expression of mingled grief and pity, which finally (the dinner was cooling) found vent in words.

"Is it possible, my love, that you have made the pernicious mistake of permitting this girl to eat meats!"

Miss Agnes looked confused, flushed a little, but recovered herself and answered gently:

"I may have been mistaken. I am quite ignorant of dietetics; besides, papa used to say that growing children needed animal food."

Again he bestowed upon her another benignly commiserative look, which was followed by a pitying smile.

"A very common notion among the professional men of his time, but fallacious, my dear, completely exploded by the modern science of dietetics. Vegetables and farinaceous substances are the only suitable food for children or—even adults. But habit is strong with us of older growth," he reached for the drawn butter as he spoke, "we may—nay, we *must*—always regret, my love, that our parents were not wise enough to rear us on this simple, rational system. But this subject will only add another to the delightful paths of knowledge, along which we hope to lead you with a gentle hand. Augustus has been trained under this system, and, when he joins us, we hope to make some progress with this girl. His example will be of great value to her."

Having delivered himself thus, his eye fell upon my plate, which Miss Agnes, in listening to him, had left standing where she had placed it; and, after denuding a leg of almost all the flesh, he passed it to me, adding:

"In the mean time, I have no objection to the child's picking a bone. It is never best to make changes too suddenly. Besides, bones are nutritious; the French compound some of their most appetizing dishes from them. A little more of the cranberry-sauce, my dear.—Now, this is an article," he continued, glancing benevolently down upon the crimson fruit in the pretty glass dish which he balanced in his hand, "of which children are very fond, yet nothing is more injurious, it being productive, in the tender stomach, of flatulencies and acidities, and a long train of evils."

He was evidently quite at ease as to the state of his own stomach, for he half emptied it, and, replacing it, continued:

"This is a very interesting topic in a psychological view, proving, as I think it does, conclusively, the perversion, not only of the moral, but physical nature, by the fall of man. What were those lines from Milton which you were repeating, to this effect, yesterday, Mrs. Tyler?"

"'Earth felt the wound, and Nature from her seat,
Sighing through all her works, gave signs of woe
That all was lost!'"

quoted Miss Agnes.

"That all was lost!" echoed the gentleman. "It is always a pleasure to find Milton coinciding with one."

I was making my escape from the room, when he recalled me with—

"Stop! Can you tell me the name and proper mode of addressing this lady?"

"Mrs. Tyler, sir."

"Right. Our lesson was not lost, it seems. Can you repeat that Scripture story?"

I did so, to his satisfaction, and he added: "Don't you think those wicked children were justly punished?"

"I don't know, sir. I would not have let the bears eat me. I would have run away!"

"Child! I am astonished at you! Run away from the penalty due to sin! You could no more have escaped than you could have changed your depraved nature! You might have been one of the very first to fall into the power of those ferocious animals!"

I did not venture to reply, and the gentleman, after a few more remarks, such as he deemed applicable to my condition as a "brand," and a few more to my mistress on the necessity of a personal application of Scriptural truths, dismissed me.

For a person of such an adipose, spongy look, or, as Miss Agnes expressed it, one "so thoughtful and considerate of the rights and happiness of others," Mr. Tyler developed a remarkable degree of executive force. He began with the kitchen table. "The sin of waste and the pampering of the appetite," was a topic upon which he enlarged eloquently; and, either because his spongy body had a tendency to absorb all sorts of good things, or his great benevolence prompted him to make a martyr of himself for Hannah's and my sake, few of the nice things sent to the dining-room ever reached our plates.

Love is a great strengthener of patience, but even the almost maternal love which Hannah Smith felt for Miss Agnes would never have induced her to put up with these innovations, not to say insults, or even so much as the "nose of a hen-hussy" in her department, if she had not looked upon her mistress as one doomed to be eaten by the cannibals of "Walla Basheen." She really believed that her "time would be short" (why should not she, hearing the subject discussed so often?), and was determined that she would bear any thing rather than trouble her. Too conscientious to express her growing dislike of Mr. Tyler, and too simple to think she could betray it otherwise, she went round at her work sighing:

"Ah, well, folks must live and learn. 'New masters, new times,'" etc.

But she was mistaken in her apprehension of Miss Agnes's nearness to martyrdom, or rather she mistook the location and manner, thereby doing the natives of "Walla Basheen" a great wrong; for, after Mr. Tyler had taken possession of our pleasant old home, he manifested another sponge-like trait, by attaching himself so tenaciously to it, that he seemed to lay aside all thought of moving. Doubtless, he thought it his duty to forsake all things, and " cleave unto his wife—" and her possessions, especially when there were numbers of brethren, unencumbered by domestic ties, who could take his place.

There is no " sesame " like the possession of property to open one's eyes to the beauty of stability, and the sacred nature of responsibilities !

Not that Mr. Tyler gave utterance to any such thoughts ; but he suddenly became aware of the delicacy of Miss Agnes's constitution ; and, though he still talked of the " nations that sit in darkness," and the probability of their " burning out their feeble lights " among them at no very distant day, it was in a very indefinite manner, very much as Uncle Steve used to talk about going " on a long v'yage " once more.

As to Miss Agnes, she was as well as usual, but I think she really felt disappointed in seeing the realization of her cherished hope postponed, and not a little annoyed at the frequent inquiries of her friends as to how soon she " expected to sail."

CHAPTER IX.

MASTER AUGUSTUS.

NOT many weeks after Miss Agnes's marriage, Mr. Tyler's mother came on, bringing with her Master Augustus, the " model child," whose example was to prove such a blessing to me.

I had gone to the dress-maker's for Miss Agnes when they arrived, and it was about sunset when I reached home. Miss Agnes was standing by the front window of the chamber which she had occupied from childhood when I came up the walk, looking rather sad, I fancied, as she pointed out the church-spire, half hidden by the trees, to an elderly female in a cap beside her. I thought she felt sorry to give up the room which her own mother had arranged for her, and the bed over which that mother had often bent in silent prayer, for the room below, in which she had seen both father and mother breathe their last. I knew that this change was to be made, for, in anticipation of the arrival of " our venerable mother," the subject had come up between the newly-wedded pair some days before. Miss Agnes had expressed her pleasure at being able to offer her a room on the ground-floor, but Mr. Tyler cast upon her such a look of surprise and grief that she hesitated, and finally added that of course she should be guided by his wishes in this, as well as every thing else.

That look had a kind of magical effect upon my mistress. I have often seen her, while conversing with something of her old enthusiasm, grow suddenly confused at meeting it, catch at the most plausible word, and, perhaps, give her sentence a widely-different meaning from that which she had intended.

Are women " deceitful and false, unreasonable and unreasoning," gentlemen? Then beware what lessons you teach them in the sweet privacy of domestic life ! Remember that this " deceit and double-mindedness " in women and children is usually the result of fear or injustice—of rights denied or perverted—and neither lectures, nor sermons, nor quotations from prophets or apostles will avail to remedy the evil—nothing can, until perfect justice shall permeate every heart with a sense of the divine significance and sacredness of individual rights, and thus become synonymous with that perfect love which casteth out fear.

Mr. Tyler would occupy the room below, that was certain. No one who knew him, but his wife, would have questioned it, any more than they would have questioned its proximity to the warm, cosy sitting-room, or the fact that Miss Agnes's old room was up one flight of stairs, with a cold landing above and below. Of course, he did not give these facts as reasons—he merely said it was "proper for the head of the family to occupy the lower room;" and, as his sense of propriety always seemed to be synonymous with his convictions of right, he could not be expected to violate his conscience for the convenience of his mother; therefore, when Miss Agnes suggested that her age and feeble health seemed to make a room below desirable, he very magnanimously assured her that his "mother's presence in the house was never to interfere with their domestic arrangements—*never*—she might rely upon that!" And Miss Agnes really thought he had conferred a favor on her, so full of impressive condescension was his manner.

It is so easy to be magnanimous—at other people's expense!

Mother Tyler made no objection. Indeed, there was hardly energy enough in her whole body to make an objection to any thing, but there was a great deal of a certain kind of passive endurance that would have led her to climb a dozen flights of stairs, had her son so ordered it, when once her *inertia* was fairly overcome. Her leading traits seemed to be devotion to her son—and the headache, she being one of those people of whom it is no misnomer to say that they "enjoy poor health."

But I forget that figure of my girlhood standing at the gate. Miss Agnes saw me, and came down. I delivered my package, and went to the kitchen with the intention of reaching my room by the back-stairs, but I paused at the upper landing, for some child, evidently in my own room, which adjoined that of Miss Agnes's, was saying, sulkily:

"I tell you I won't, and so—there!"

"There—there—don't go to being naughty—there's a dear!" replied a drawling, coaxing voice. "I'm sure it's a great deal prettier than your old room at home."

"I don't care if 'tis! I won't have it! I won't sleep there—all alone—in the dark!" And the sulkiness now changed to a whimper.

"Well, well, you needn't cry! The dark won't hurt you. There's nothing in the dark to hurt good boys. You needn't be afraid!"

"Who said I was afraid? But I won't sleep there, that's flat! I'll have this room close to yours."

"But it's the little girl's room, and your new mother mightn't like it."

"What'll she care? The house is pa's, ain't it? You said 'twas, and I'd have lots of nice things!"

"Well, well! only wait till things get settled a bit—there's a good boy. Oh, my poor head!"

"I won't wait—and—so—there—and you may as well go down and tell 'em! What's the use in having a new mother and a new house, if I've got to go off, alone, into that little room? I won't stay here—I'll run away, and so!"

The boy began to sob, and Miss Agnes came running up directly to see what was the matter.

"Is that all?" I heard her say, in reply to Mrs. Tyler. "Of course, it's quite natural he should have some such feeling in a strange place. We ought to have thought of it before.—Don't cry, darling. Lina, I dare say, will willingly exchange rooms with you. I will speak to her about it—oh, here she comes!" for, hearing my name, I came hastily forward.

"Lina, dear," she went on, "this is our dear mother, Mrs. Tyler, and this (patting the cheek of a boy of about my age) is our dear Augustus, of whom I have so often spoken to you."

I courtesied to the old lady, and turned to the boy. He did not offer his hand, but stood looking at me, from under his half-shut eyelids, with pouting lips, until Miss Agnes, laying her hand on his head caressingly, said:

"Won't you shake hands with Lina,

dear?" He just touched my hand, and let his arm drop heavily to his side again. It was very evident that this model child could *sulk*. Perhaps Miss Agnes thought so, for she said, pleasantly :

"Augustus is very tired, Lina; besides, he is feeling very badly, because the room prepared for him is on the other side of the house, quite away from his grandmother, near whom he has been accustomed to sleep. He is quite a stranger, and we must consider his feelings; his father, to be sure, thought he would prefer that room, but you won't mind changing with him, Lina, or doing any thing to make him happy?"

"I will do any thing to please you, ma'am," I said, decidedly, for neither Master Augustus's manner nor looks inclined me to make many sacrifices in his favor.

"You mean you will be glad to do it to please him, as well as me, I know, Lina. You must remember to express yourself more politely, dear. You are naturally a little blunt."

"But that would not be the truth, and you always tell me to speak the truth, ma'am!"

"To be sure—but there are different modes of—but we won't discuss this, now. We must consult my husband about this change of rooms."

We descended to the sitting-room, where Mr. Tyler was dozing in his easy-chair, with a copy of the *New-York Observer* laid over his head, to shield its bald apex from any current of air. He was in the habit of solacing himself daily with these "little naps," and, as he usually placed that paper over his head, I childishly inferred that there was some soporific quality connected with that sheet. If I erred, I humbly beg pardon.

He roused himself on our entrance, and manifested a trait, not uncommon even among people who have attained to his state of perfectibility—a slight irritation at being disturbed—which showed itself in a disposition to snub Master

Augustus's wishes at once; but, on a clearer understanding of the case, he assented to the change, not, as he solemnly assured us, from any desire to indulge his own child—he sincerely hoped he should be kept from such weakness—but because in the future there would, doubtless, arise little differences between us children; concessions must be made, and this was an excellent opportunity to enforce the great duty of self-denial, in the practice of which, he feared, owing to the peculiar guilelessness and gentleness of the person who had had the care of me (with a look of tender pity at Miss Agnes), I was sadly ignorant. He hoped Augustus, too, would profit by this example; we should overlook no example which would tend to our profit.—"Augustus, my son," he added, "what was it you learned, when I was last with you, to this effect?"

"Precepts are the chart with which we start on the voyage of life, example the beacon which teaches us to avoid the sunken rocks upon which others have foundered," promptly repeated the boy.

"Very well, very well, indeed.—It has been a part of my system with my children, dear, to insist upon their learning, daily, some moral or divine precept. The mind should be like a granary, well stored with moral and religious truth."

With what an air of wisdom and benevolence he glanced around the group, and with what a look of loving pride my mistress regarded him! "So wise and good, and to think he should have chosen me!" it seemed to say.

Such was my introduction to my "little brother," as Miss Agnes had been fond of calling him before her marriage, though the fraternal title was soon dropped. I took the chamber which had been prepared for him, but I am afraid this example of self-denial was lost on us both, for it had to be repeated many times in the ensuing months, and always at my expense. There did arise little and great differences between us; and, although Mr. Tyler always affected a strict impartiality on weighing the testimony on both sides, yet, in view of my questionable parentage, my pauperism, and the condition of the people with whom my early years were passed, it might be safely predicated that I would be more likely to be guilty than his own son, and therefore the case was invariably prejudged. I felt the injustice of these decisions, and resented them, frequently, in a way that, unfortunately, went far to sustain Mr. Tyler's assertion that my mistress had been "wholly blind to my true character and disposition."

One of the most sorrowful things in human experience is the power of one unjust act to call out evil in others, to multiply and perpetuate itself through all time. Under the training of Mr. Tyler, and the example of his son, I became a sad illustration of the truth of this; yet, let me do him justice. He did not see it; he was the victim of certain formularies of life and thought; thoroughly self-deceived, and incapable of judging others.

If I had not told lies before I knew Ollie, it was from no particular sense of their wickedness. Mrs. Hunt was not in the habit of asking questions; her blows fell too suddenly for any attempt at palliation, and it suited my nature to show my scorn of her violence by my indifference. But once, to save Ollie from punishment, I told her a downright lie; I am not sure but I should do it again under like circumstances. I assumed the guilt, and took the whipping, but his grief hurt me far worse than her blows, and he would not be comforted until I had promised I would try never to be guilty of a falsehood again.

But Augustus Tyler "made no bones of lying," as Hannah Smith expressed it, the consequences of which, owing to the sins of my fathers, and his own consummate adroitness in the business, were visited upon me. As I look back to that time, and recall his face and figure, I am as much puzzled to understand how he contrived to deceive his parents as I was then. He was a fat, dull, heavy-looking boy, with scarcely so much muscular power in his whole body as a lad of his age should have in his ten fingers, the result, probably, of the *stuffing* process by which his weak, doting grandmother tried to make up for the vegetarian diet imposed by his father. As a consequence, he was always "munching," and the habit of tucking the half-masticated food away in his cheek, or of swallowing it hurriedly, at the approach of any one, or when addressed, often brought tears to his eyes, and gave him a very pitiable as well as grotesque look; and this look, added to the imperturbable coolness and obstinacy with which he persisted in sticking to any falsehood he chose to tell, must have been the secret of his success. He looked stupidly innocent, yet those cold gray eyes could leer with malicious triumph when he chose.

Mr. Tyler had spoken truly when he likened his head to a granary. He had a good verbal memory, and in all our Sunday and weekly catechisings he was ready with chapter and verse, but, for all practical influence upon his character, his acquisitions might as well have been stored away in the granary of the Pharaohs.

As his father seemed to mature no plan for our training, save in what related to our diet, we were sent to school, but I failed to profit by his example, of course, much to Miss Agnes's disappointment. Indeed, I grew worse; for, although not forbidden the sitting-room, I was no longer called to Miss Agnes's side to read to her, or questioned about my lessons, all such questioning having devolved upon Mr. Tyler, and I had a kind of feeling that she wished to keep me out of the way as much as possible, though her manner to me was as kind as ever when she did notice me. Perhaps, it was the kindest thing she could do for me, but I did not think so then; I felt slighted, and withdrew myself more and more from her presence. Even the kitchen was no longer the same place. Between Mrs. Tyler and his dietetics, and old Mrs. Tyler's foraging expeditions after tidbits for Augustus, Hannah Smith was almost beside herself, so I went abroad for amusement. I had, by this time, a plenty of acquaintances among my schoolmates; and many an hour, when Mrs. Tyler thought me in my room busy with my lessons, I was sitting in Helen Hall's pleasant chamber, devouring the contents of an old copy of the "Arabian Nights," which belonged to her oldest sister.

Oh, for those hours of wonder and delight!—of utter self-forgetfulness and confiding faith, when I sat at the feet of Scherazaide, and listened to her tales of all that happened—

"In the golden prime
Of good Haroun-Al-Raschid!"

I dared not take the book home, for I knew Mr. Tyler would not permit me to read it. He was sternly opposed to what he termed "light and profane" reading, and classed every thing under this head, except works of the heaviest, driest kind. Very soon after his marriage, he had examined the contents of the doctor's bookcase, and purged it of various works, among which were some odd volumes of old English plays, Scott's "Antiquary," and "The Heart of Mid-Lothian," an old copy of "The Scottish Chiefs," and filled the vacant places with bound volumes of "Religious Miscellany," "Disquisitions on the Will," etc.

The condemned volumes had excited my interest from certain peeps I had taken of their contents, and Miss Agnes had promised that, when I was a little older, I should read them aloud to her. When I saw them consigned to the garret, therefore, with a strict injunction to Augustus and myself not to touch them, I felt not only disappointed but wronged; and the feeling was not at all lessened when Miss Agnes showed me a bookcase in the sitting-room, and told me that the books it contained were expressly for the use of Augustus and myself.

"Mr. Tyler is very particular to have you read good and useful books, dear, and he has selected these himself."

It was the small compact "Religious Library" issued by the Tract Society, and contained many a name dear to the cause of truth and Christianity, Baxter, Doddridge, Mason, and Edwards, strong meat for strong men, but little to interest a girl of thirteen. My heart still clung to the exiles in the garret, and, looking up to Miss Agnes, I asked:

"Your father was a very good man, wasn't he?"

"Certainly, one of the best. Why do you ask?"

"Because I was thinking of those books you told me he used to like to read so much—those Mr. Tyler had carried to the garret because they are so wicked. Did he know they were such bad books?"

"No, indeed, he did not think so. Many good people think differently about such reading," she said, thoughtfully. "I remember hearing papa say that one of our most distinguished divines, who was a classmate of his, was particularly fond of 'The Heart of Mid-Lothian,' but Mr. Tyler disapproves of all fiction, and thinks such an admission by a professed Christian likely to lead to much evil. If I had seen the subject as I do now, I would never have promised that you should read those books. But Mr. Tyler's conscientiousness is remarkable—equalled only by his humility and goodness."

The closing sentence was a happy soliloquy, rather than a sentence addressed to me.

I need not say how dry I found the contents of those uniformly bound volumes in the small bookcase, or how little I profited by reading them every Sunday after church, taking alternate paragraphs with Augustus, while Miss Agnes listened reverently with an occasional half-suppressed yawn, and Mr. Tyler reclined in his easy-chair, with closed eyes, "inwardly digesting the words of truth," as he said, but the process seemed to me more like digesting his hearty dinner, especially when taken in connection with his long, regular breathing, which frequently culminated in a loud snore. I could not understand or appreciate what I read in this way; yet there were two books which proved exceptions to this charge—"The Life of Dr. Payson," and "The Pilgrim's Progress." The first interested me, but in a very different manner from the last. I could find nothing of myself in Dr. Payson, he was too good. His goodness, too, was so constant and unvarying, that it seemed to me a little unreal—as well as a little tiresome, on this earth—but it chimed admirably with my notions of angels in white robes, with golden harps.

But, man or child, the heart clings to that which has a touch of earth about it, like itself, and I turned with delight from the saintly Payson to the sinning, stumbling, doubting, fighting Christian. With him I was at home; I struggled by his side through the "Slough of Despond," mourned with him for his lost roll, fought the terrible giant, descended into the Valley of Humiliation, and swelled his song of faith and trust:

> "He that is down need fear no fall,
> He that is low no pride;
> He that is humble ever shall
> Have God to be his guide."

The flames which consumed poor Faithful scorched my cheek, and, letting go the Pilgrim's hand on the banks of the Dark River, I leaned eagerly forward with eager eyes and clasped hands, for, amid the white-robed band on the farther side, I always recognized one face—that of little Ollie Lee.

Meantime, I had my own pilgrimage to perform; neither Christian nor Ollie could do that for me, and it lay through Miss Agnes's garret straight into the pit of falsehood.—I could not forget those forbidden books, the names of which I had caught when I had opened them. Jeannie Deans, Effie, Douce Davie, Monkbarns, and Edie Ochiltree, haunted me, Miss Agnes's old promise that I should read them, rose between me and the interdict; and, one day, I stole to the attic and read the first chapters of "The Heart of Mid-Lothian." I was in for it then! I took care of my own room always, and, day after day, when I had hurried through my sweeping and dusting, I stole to the garret and read awhile. Presently I grew more bold, and brought one of the volumes to my room. One evening, when I sat with my book on the window-sill, to catch the last rays of daylight, I was startled by a noise, and, turning suddenly, caught a glimpse of Master Augustus retreating from my door and heard him "scuffing" along through the passages, for he always walked with a kind of dragging step. I immediately slipped the book beneath my pillow and went down-stairs to meet my punishment, for I thought he would betray me at once. To my surprise, nothing was said about it that night, and the delay proved my rock of stumbling. I began to tamper with my conscience: "He did not know what the book was—you can put it back, and they will never know any thing about it," etc.

Who does not know the process? Mean enough, sorrowful enough, in all conscience; I have no need to describe it, else the Liturgy is a libel. We are all miserable sinners, or we make ourselves miserable liars, every time we repeat its solemn responses.

I did not replace the book. I was sent on an errand before going to school, and had no opportunity to do so; but I was hardly over the threshold that evening, when Augustus came to tell me with a grin that his father wanted me in the study—a room now wholly monopolized by him.

4

Mr. Tyler was sitting by the table, and Miss Agnes stood looking out the window, with her back to the door, when I entered. She did not stir even when Mr. Tyler addressed me sternly:

"Zerlina Day, what book were you reading last evening?"

"Say 'Barnes's Notes,'" whispered the Tempter. I obeyed.

"My dear, will you ask Augustus to come here? We may need him before we get through."

Augustus was probably listening, for my mistress barely crossed the threshold, before she returned with him.

"My son, take your place by this table.—Now, Zerlina Day, I put the question once more. What book were you reading last evening?"

"'Barnes's Notes,'" again whispered the voice. "You know you looked over some portions of your Sunday-school lesson last night;" and again I obeyed.

"O—h! o—o—h! o—o—oh! what a lie!" cried Augustus, bringing his hands to his mouth in a sort of funnel-shape as if to prevent his astonishment and horror from blowing him up. His father dropped his arms nervelessly across his lap, as if wholly overcome by the spectacle of such wickedness, and my mistress sighed heavily. That sigh was like a needle to my conscience, and I turned to fling myself at her feet and confess guilt, when Mr. Tyler laid his hand on my shoulder. I had always been susceptible to the touch, and when his soft, damp, clammy hand fell on my bare shoulder, I instinctively recoiled. His face flushed with anger as he exclaimed:

"Don't show temper like that to me! Why did you twitch away?"

"Because I don't want you to touch me, sir."

"She rejects the hand that would save her. You must be convinced now, my dear," turning to Miss Agnes.

She removed her handkerchief from her face, for she was weeping, and made a step forward, but he motioned her back by an authoritative gesture.

To my surprise she did not heed him, but came forward, saying eagerly:

"Perhaps Lina can explain—"

He bestowed upon her one of his compassionate glances.

"We do not want explanations in this case, my dear, but a direct categorical answer; and we have, just what I feared —a downright falsehood.—Now, Zerlina Day, what book is this?"

He drew the volume I had been reading from beneath a paper and held it before me.

"'The Heart of Mid-Lothian.'"

"How came it in your room?"

"I took it there from the garret."

"To read?"

"Yes, sir."

"Had you not been strictly forbidden to read it?"

"Yes, sir."

"How dare you touch it, then?"

"Miss Ag— Mrs. Tyler promised that I should read them before you came here, sir."

He seized me by the ear and drew me toward him; but in a moment Miss Agnes was by my side, saying:

"I did indeed; she speaks the truth!"

He let go my ear and looked at her. Immediately she began to color and shrink in self-abasement, and went on in a frightened manner:

"It was wrong, but I did not think so then. Pray don't punish her for my fault."

He didn't turn aside his eyes or alter a muscle of his face for a full second, then said, with a deep sigh:

"It is very easy to see how you fell into such an error. The fathers have eaten sour grapes, and the children's teeth are set on edge. I do not punish her for *that*, but because of her being guilty of downright falsehood. If you had faithfully used the rod, you might possibly have cured her of this dreadful habit. I readily cured Augustus.—My son, you go—"

He had seized me by the ear again, but I hardly felt it, so intent was I on watching my mistress, for the blood rushed to her neck and cheek in a torrent as he spoke, but the next instant she was white as death.

"You will not beat her?" she cried. "Surely, Mr. Tyler, you cannot mean it? Remember, she is a girl—almost a woman!" and she burst into passionate, convulsive weeping.

I can see the face even now, white with suppressed anger, with which he regarded her for a second before he removed her hand from his arm, and said in his hardest, most inflexible tone:

"You are nervous, Mrs. Tyler. You had better retire until you can command yourself—at least, before these children."

I could not see her face, but I fancy he read something in it that either touched or warned him, for he immediately added in his softest tone of reproach:

"I had hoped that my experience as a parent and instructor would have given you confidence in my judgment, my dear, even if your own observation has not, but it seems I am mistaken."

He had not miscalculated the effect of his tone. She hid her face upon his shoulder sobbing, and begged to be forgiven, just as if she had been guilty of some heinous crime.

It was accorded, magnanimously and condescendingly; and, to prove her confidence, she proposed to retire and leave him to deal with me as he thought best, but this did not suit his present mood; he seated her, and entered into a disquisition of the punishments best adapted to different dispositions with a critical acumen that showed him to be master of the subject.

"With Augustus, who is exceedingly susceptible to physical suffering," he went on—"a peculiarity which he inherits from me, I have ever found corporal punishment very effective. Our strength lies in the mind, my love; any amount of mental labor or anguish we can bear; but this child is of a different stamp. You have quite mistaken her disposition and character. Her heart is full of pride, ambition, self-will, and vain, inordinate affections. This will must be broken—this pride humbled, these affections tempered; and they can only be reached through the heart.—Zerlina Day, do you confess that you have been guilty of falsehood and disobedience?"

"Yes, sir."

"Are you ready to ask our pardon?"

"I will ask Mrs. Tyler's, sir.—Indeed, indeed, ma'am, I am very sorry for my wickedness!"

"Very well. Now, ask pardon of us —Augustus and myself."

I hesitated—at length, I said, "I am sorry I told you a lie, sir."

"And Augustus?" he asked.

"No; he tells lies every day. Yesterday, he stole the cake, and told Mrs. Tyler the cat—"

"Zerlina Day!" thundered Mr. Tyler, "we want no accusations from an avowed liar like yourself. It will not lessen your guilt to accuse others.—Augustus, open that Bible at Acts v., and read aloud the punishment that overtakes liars, even in this world!"

Mr. Tyler sat with folded hands, and reverently closed eyelids, though I felt that he was watching me all the while. Miss Agnes sat with her face bowed upon her hands, but, from the convulsive motion of the cords in her white neck, I knew she was weeping while Master Augustus read in clear, emphatic tones the story of Ananias and Sapphira.

"Thus God punishes liars!" said Mr. Tyler, when the boy ceased to read, "and such may soon be your fate. Will you confess your sin before my son now, and ask forgiveness?"

I do not know how it was, but, instead of being softened by that terrible story, my heart grew harder and harder all the while the boy was reading. I felt that I did not care if I did die, and I answered doggedly—

"No."

"Then, until you can subdue your wicked, rebellious spirit, you must not be permitted to hold any intercourse with this family or your school-mates. Your teacher and they must be warned of your character.—My dear, will you hand me the key to the small room in the attic?"

They would tell the whole school! I saw myself scorned, avoided, pointed at; and, unmindful of Mr. Tyler's order to follow him up-stairs, I sprang past him, and, clinging to Miss Agnes's dress, implored her to have mercy on me.

"I will never; never tell a lie again!" I cried. "Please don't hate me, and make everybody else hate me, too!"

She put her arms around me, but they were removed by her husband, who unclasped my hands from her gown, and, without a word more, dragged me up-stairs and thrust me into a small, dimly-lighted room or large closet rather, to which the unsold medical paraphernalia of the doctor had been removed after his death, locked the door, and left me.

For a long time I sat with my head bowed on my hands, weeping bitterly, not from sorrow because I had refused to ask Augustus's pardon—I felt that I had not sinned against him—but from a feeling of miserable wretchedness that I had never felt before, born from the consciousness of my guilt, and the conviction that every one must loathe me as I loathed myself. I thought of Ollie. He, too, must hate me. If I should be struck dead like Ananias and Sapphira, I should go away to everlasting punishment, and never see his face again. I shuddered at the thought. A feeling of faintness overcame me, partly caused by exhaustion, and partly by the closeness of the room and the suffocating odor of the drugs upon the shelves, and I fell from my crouching position to the floor. I have no idea how long I lay there, or whether I woke or slept, but the horrors of that time I shall never forget. The old picture of the Last Judgment was before me, but so large that it filled all space—the whole world was one mass of darting, leaping, hissing flames, and the hideous devils were multiplied to legions. Above, on the luminous clouds, was the "Son of Man," and on His right, close to him, stood Ollie. I knew him at once, though the deformity which had marked him on earth was gone, but, oh, despair! the faces of both were turned away from me! The ears of both were deaf to my imploring cries, as I clung to Miss Agnes's skirts (for she, too, was there in the lower rank of the blessed, and strove to shake off the grinning devils that clutched at my feet). There were Ananias and Sapphira in the midst of the flames, drawing me toward them with such a look of unutterable horror, woe, and anguish, in their still human eyes! And Sally Hunt beckoned me with her hard, skinny hand, and said mockingly, pointing to the flames—

"Went ter meetin', did ye? Come an' see your father, child!"

And then there came a voice, hard, stern, and unpitying, rising far above the shrieks, and yells, and curses, echoing like thunder amid the hills, and it said— oh, how the cold, damp sweat started from every pore in my body, and my soul shrunk and trembled within me!—"All liars shall have their part in the lake which burneth with fire and brimstone!"

It did not seem to come from above, for, although the faces of the Divine One and His young disciple were still averted, I felt that there would have been a strain of compassion and sorrow in His tones; but, while I still shivered and shrunk, sweeter than all music, hushing for one moment the shrieks and the torments of the bottomless pit, came a second voice, saying:

"Inasmuch as ye have done it unto one of the least of these my brethren, ye have done it unto me!" At these words, Miss Agnes was drawn up, as it were; but I, poor wretch, went falling—falling — falling—struggling—gasping!—oh, the unutterable agony of that feeling! clutching at the thin hot air as if that could stay me—sinking—sinking—until, in unspeakable terror, I sprang up.

What was this? Were those hideous things real? There were no flames there! The corner of the room where I sat was dark as pitch, but the strong moonlight, through the small skylight, fell upon the shelves which lined the opposite side of the room, transpiercing the glass jars there, and revealing their contents, hideous, contorted reptiles, bloated, swollen toads and frogs, with white bellies which gleamed with a kind of phosphorescent light, lizards and human monstrosities—thumbs and fingers and toes—trophies of the old doctor's skill as a surgeon and naturalist.

I had never seen these things, though I had more than once heard Hannah Smith speak of them, and my previous dream or vision had so paralyzed reason and memory that I sat staring blankly at them until my frenzied imagination had endued them with life and they began to crawl. I had always had a horror of spiders—and, now, the room was full of these cold, slimy, crawling abominations. I tried to shriek aloud, but it seemed to me as if my paralyzed organs refused to utter a word. But I was mistaken; Hannah Smith heard me, and, when she burst open my prison-door, I lay upon the floor, to all appearance, dead. It was that good woman's first intimation of my punishment, and, even in heaven, I think it will be hard for her to speak of it with patience.

CHAPTER X

IN HANNAH'S ROOM.

WHEN I returned to consciousness, the first thing I recognized in the dimly-lighted room was a large bag of gay chintz hanging against the white wall, at the foot of the bed. I knew that bag—it was Hannah Smith's! I tried to turn myself, in order to make out where I was, but I was limp as water, and forced to lie still, and contemplate that object, assured, by its presence there, that I was not beyond the reach of that good woman's hand. The room was perfectly still, and with a delicious feeling of safety from some evil—what I could not tell, for I was yet too weak to recall the past—my heavy eyelids were again closing, when I became conscious of the smell of camphor. This was one of the odors, or one of the combination of odors, that had impregnated the air of my prison, and I closed my eyes with disgust, though old Mrs. Tyler's voice, asking if I was awake, sufficiently accounted for the smell. She seated herself by my bed, I knew; but, much as I wished to ask how I came to be in Hannah's room, I could not overcome my dislike of the woman so far as to ask her. Presently steps approached from the kitchen, and some one said in a whisper:

"You here, ma'am? Pray don't disturb her."

Before the old lady could gather breath for the long sigh with which she usually prefaced a remark, I said:

"I'm not asleep, Hannah. How did I come here?"

"My goodness, child! Ain't I glad to hear you speak once more?"

She came to the bedside with her hands white with flour, and her kind face red with heat, for she was baking, her lip and forehead beaded with great drops of perspiration, but it was as welcome to me as that of an angel—indeed, more welcome, for I was longing for companionship of flesh and blood.

She looked at me intently a moment, before she said, "You are sure you know me, Lina?"

"To be sure! Why shouldn't I? And why don't you tell me why I'm here, in your bed."

"'Cause 'twas handier for me to take care of you here."

"Have I been sick?—I don't remember."

"Yes," interrupted Mrs. Tyler—"you've been sick ever since you told that lie; don't you remember?"

Hannah turned and faced the old lady so suddenly as to make her start.

"There's some things that had better not be remembered, Mrs. Tyler, and if you had just as lief as not come in here—why, it will be quite as agreeable, for I ain't used to seein' all sorts of folks in my bedroom," she said, dryly.

"Dear me! You don't say so! I only just dropped in to see how the girl was. They'll be glad to know she's got her senses again," said the old lady as she left the room.

"Come here, Hannah," I said, for the old lady's words had quickened my feeble memory, and brought back the events of that day and night with fearful distinctness—"tell me about Miss Agnes—will she never forgive me? never speak to me again!"

I shuddered and trembled, and there was a troubled look in the good woman's face, while she smoothed back my hair and arranged my pillows.

"There, don't worry, child. I have no doubt Miss Agnes would come to you if she could. But she's been sick herself, an' its new times here. I have not seen her for a week! Mr. Tyler's sister has come, an' she carries things with a high hand. I little thought I'd ever live to be told in this house that my opinion was not wanted—an' about the dear child, too, that I've nussed since she was a baby!"

There was grief and indignation in Hannah's voice, but I did not heed it. Miss Agnes was sick, and I had doubtless made her so. I might be a murderer as well as a liar—that was why Ollie's face had been turned away from me, and I felt deserted by God and man. I asked no more questions—why should I? but covered myself with the bedclothes and gave way to my grief and despair.

Oh the long weary days that followed! The doctor said I needed nourishment only—but it was for the soul rather than the body, and, among all Hannah's broths and syrups, there was none that could do that! That lie haunted me. Why shouldn't I be weak, when night after night I started from my sleep with my flesh creeping with fear, and wet with perspiration, at the repetition of the fearful scenes of that night of horror? All that I had ever read of retribution or punishment seemed to come back to me in those nights of mental anguish and physical weakness. Sometimes I was with the strayed lamb, and the Good Shepherd would not look at me, when He drew the lamb to His bosom; and sometimes it was no longer a lamb He bore, but Ollie. Sometimes I was with Christian, passing through the valley and shadow of death—striving to overtake him — while the horrible, undefined shapes that peopled the abyss on either hand clutched at my garments and filled my ears with mocking gibes and jeers.

Hannah tried to cheer me up, but it was quite evident that her own heart was heavy; besides, she was ignorant of my sufferings, for I shrunk from acknowledging them to any one.

Sometimes I heard a strange voice in the kitchen, giving brief but decided orders, which I took to belong to Mrs. Reed, Mr. Tyler's sister; but I never heard that of Mr. Tyler or Augustus, and this seemed so unusual, that I asked Hannah about it.

"Augustus and Sara—for Mrs. Reed brought her girl with her—were sent away, the day after she came. Dr. Guthrie said the house must be kept perfectly still on account of Miss Agnes, an' Fanny Moore took 'em home with her. As to Mr. Tyler—there's no use in his comin'—*she's* enough! "

"She?"

"Mrs. Reed, child. She had not been in the house a day, before she'd got the keys, even of Miss Agnes's drawers, an' she'd be glad to have nobody breathe, without asking her leave. But there's one that'll never knuckle to her. She'd have the house to herself quick metre, if 'twarn't for Miss Agnes, poor child."

She had hardly ceased to speak, when Mr. Tyler and his sister entered the kitchen. Hannah hurried out, but their business was not with her, for they came on to my room. I have said I did not like to have Mr. Tyler touch me, and now it seemed as if I could feel his presence the moment he entered the kitchen, and I involuntarily closed my eyes, that I might not be obliged to see or speak with him. I had no wish to deceive—no farther thought about the matter, save the one stated, but, when he spoke my name, although I did not unclose my eyes, I could not prevent a slight shudder from moving my frame.

Mrs. Reed observed it, and said:

"The girl is as wide awake as you are, brother. She is only shamming sleep."

This charge, so wholly unexpected, caused me to open my eyes at once, and the dark, strong-featured woman before me, with a triumphant, "There—I told you so!" added, before Mr. Tyler could speak:

"Look here, miss. I've got something to say to you. You have got one to deal with, now, that understands all such tricks. You can't cheat or cajole me as you have Mrs. Tyler, nor kill me, neither, as you have come near killing her. I am made of different material. I am neither weak nor nervous, and, if you are ugly and obstinate, I can be obstinate too!"

I heeded but one portion of her words, that which referred to Miss Agnes, and, cut to the heart by the taunt, I burst into tears, and begged to be permitted to see her.

Mr. Tyler interrupted me with—

"I trust your grief is sincere, Zerlina; but, after such shocking conduct as you have exhibited, you cannot expect to be received into Mrs. Tyler's presence or favor at present. Your ingratitude and wickedness have blasted her cherished hopes, and brought her to the borders of the grave; and, were she weak enough to wish it, I cannot permit you to see her. You were warned of the fate of liars in the example of Ananias, and for a time a like fate seemed likely to overtake you, for I can but view your illness as the legitimate consequence of your sin. You have been mercifully spared this time, and I trust you will heed this warning, and remember that, although we still bear with you, the day of reckoning will surely come."

Oh, could he have known how I had suffered—how, in sorrow, and anguish, and ignorance, and darkness, I had already reckoned with my soul, would he have spoken thus? I cannot believe it. Hard, and narrow, and selfish, as he was, he was still human, and must have had some pity.

I could only sob, and he had hardly ceased to speak, when Hannah appeared in the doorway, saying, indignantly:

"Mr. Tyler, if you want to get that girl out of the world, you had better go on in that way a little longer. I hope I know my place; if I don't, it won't be for want of tellin' in these days; but I've lived in this house fifteen years, and I'll speak my mind now if I'm hanged for't. This child's sickness is none of God's sending, but your own! I don't excuse her fault—she told a lie, and she ought to have been punished for't—but it was a cruel, heathenish piece of business to shut her up with all them nasty snakes and bugs. No wonder she went into a flt.—Mercifully spared! If she hadn't 'a been, I'd like to know whose reckoning'd 'a been hardest, your'n or her'n!'"

I opened my eyes, and hushed my sobs in fear and astonishment. Mr. Tyler seemed speechless from anger, while Mrs. Reed only surveyed the defiant Hannah with a cool, supercilious stare—then, turning to her brother, she asked:

"Really, brother, I would like to know what position this"—again her hard, gray eyes were turned upon Hannah—"person has held in this house? I understood she was a servant."

"It's little matter what you call me," returned Hannah, making a step forward, and confronting Mrs. Reed—"so long as those whom it concerned were satisfied. As I said before, I've lived here fifteen years, an', if I'd been a queen, I couldn't have been treated with more kindness and respect. The doctor wanted me to stay with his child, and I have; but I'll never stand by and see a friendless child driven out of her wits, without saying what I think on't, if I have to budge the next minute!"

"And you shall!" exclaimed Mr. Tyler, for the first time finding his voice. "You may depend upon that!"

"Very well, when my mistress, Mrs. Tyler, says the word, I'm ready to go!" and Hannah walked back to her baking.

Mrs. Reed looked after her with compressed lips, but, mindful of my presence, she did not give vent to her anger, otherwise than by taking the phials of medicine upon the table, and, after testing them by taste and smell, flinging them out of the window.

"There," she said, "no wonder you don't gain strength. Drugged and dosed with such stuff. A few homœopathic granules is all you want.—Brother, you will send some down.—And, remember this, girl, you must be up and out of this room before the week is over. You can do so if you choose. The will is all that is needed, and you have a plenty of that, if you choose to exert it!"

They left the room, and the next moment I heard her giving orders to Hannah, in that same hard, inflexible voice, as coolly as if the scene just related had never occurred.

But Hannah's words had aroused again a sense of wrong and injustice that had been crushed into silence beneath the weight of conscious guilt and self-reproach. But it did not rise with the passionate vehemence with which I used to meet Granny Hunt's injustice—it only added a new ingredient to my wretchedness.

I brooded over what Mr. Tyler had said about Miss Agnes, until I became hopeless and wellnigh reckless. Mrs. Reed's orders as to my getting up were behind me, and I knew I must obey them. I was trying to dress myself, one day, and had partly succeeded, when Hannah entered the room.

"What are you trying to do, child? You ain't fit to get up!"

"I must get up. Mrs. Reed said so."

"Well, what if she did? She can't put strength into a body's bones, nor breath into their bodies, I guess, though I've no doubt she thinks she can. Accordin' to her, nobody ever need be sick, and she's driving that poor girl, Agnes, just as she is you! Nothing but *will* wantin' to give her strength to get up, an' she frettin' so about her baby, poor thing!"

"Her baby, Hannah!"

"Yes; I never told you about it, because I thought 'twould worry you; besides, when 'twas born, you didn't sense any thing. It didn't live but a few hours, an' she can't help mournin' about it, though it's better, perhaps, as it is, for it's a world o' trouble to be born into."

"Is that why they sent for Mrs. Reed?"

"Yes, I s'pose so—nobody said a word to me about it, though."

"Is she going to stay, you think?"

"Stay? Of course she will! Isn't this a nice, pleasant home, and don't the

Bible say, where the carcass is the eagles are gathered together? An' what's more, she'll make Miss Agnes feel that she's doin' her a great favor by staying."

"And will you stay, too, Hannah?" I asked, after a pause, during which I had been reflecting upon these changes.

"As long as I can bear it for her sake and yours, child!" and the eyes she turned on me were full of tears.

I don't know how it came about, for the good woman was by no means demonstrative, least of all in evidences of tenderness, but I found her arms around me, and my cheek pressed close to her breast, while she said slowly:

"You have no relations, they say—or none that you know of, and if ever you do go away from here—that is, if they make it so hard that you can't stay, even for Miss Agnes's sake, I'll do what I can for you, for the sake of old times. But, you must stay if you can, for I know she's set to have you."

"Then she don't hate me? She will let me see her again, some time!" I cried, sobbing.

"Hate you? No!—When did Agnes Lathrop ever hate any thing, 'specially a friendless child!"

"But I made her sick! I killed her baby—Mr. Tyler said I made her sick!" I cried.

"But truth is truth, an' will stand!" said Hannah, solemnly. "'Twas a dreadful thing for you to tell a lie, child, wicked and mean, but it was not that which made her sick—it was the sight of your white face and starin' eyes, when I brought you from that room. She does not know how very sick you've been, I would not tell her, but she asks after you every time I see her. You were crazy as a loon at first. It was a mean, cruel thing to put you in that room, an' I believe in her heart she thinks so, though she dursn't say it."

There was comfort for me in her words, though I could not but feel that it was my conduct that had given her the first shock; and, forgetful of Mrs. Reed's orders, I lay there dreaming of that little dead baby.

The next moment Mrs. Reed entered my room, and, after feeling my pulse, ordered me to get up. She had brought some linen in her arms, and, turning to Hannah who came in to remove my breakfast-dishes, said:

"You will see that this girl gets up to-day, Miss Smith. She will need no medicine or waiting on any longer. Exercise is all she wants. In a day or two, she will be able to turn these sheets which I have brought down. They ought to have been seen to before."

Hannah's face crimsoned deeply. "Those sheets were Miss Agnes's mother's, ma'am. She sets greatly by 'em because her mother spun 'em herself. Perhaps, you'd better not meddle with 'em until she gets about, an' can see to 'em herself."

Mrs. Reed drew herself up, and said with the utmost deliberation:

"When I need your opinion, Miss Smith, I can ask. Having accepted the charge of this house, at the request of my brother and his wife, I shall in all things act as I think best. Any further remarks or suggestions from you will be quite unnecessary.—Zerlina, you will turn those sheets. You can do a little every day."

I shivered as if an iceberg passed me when she left the room. Hannah looked after her with compressed lips for a moment; then, with a long sigh and a glance at the fine linen on the table, went about her work in silence.

I tried to obey. The sheets were heavy and my fingers weak, and I made slow progress. One day, while I sat thinking of Miss Agnes, a hand light as a snow-flake was laid upon my bowed head, and her own voice said:

"That work is too heavy for you, Lina dear. Why do you try to sew?"

She had come so softly that I had not heard her footfall, and, as she stood there

in her white wrapper and bright scarlet
shawl, with her cheeks so thin and white,
and her brown hair put away behind her
ears, I stared at her without speaking, as
if she had been a ghost.

"I have frightened you, Lina," she
continued, sinking into the chair from
which I had taken my work—"but I
didn't find Hannah in the kitchen."

She was not angry with me, then!
She could not have spoken more tenderly to her own dead baby, and I flung myself beside her, crying:

"O Miss Agnes, you don't hate me,
then! I know I was wicked, but you
will speak to me again!"

She did not speak just then, but
bowed her head upon mine, and I felt
her tears upon my forehead. I needed
no words; I felt I was forgiven.

"Miss Agnes—dear child—you here!
Crying, too! Dear me—we shall have
you down sick again!"

"Let me alone, Hannah. I believe
it will do me good to cry—only I'm
ashamed to be so weak," she said, looking up, and holding out her hand to that
faithful friend. "They are all gone out,"
she went on, "and I longed so to come
down to the kitchen once more, and see
you and this sick girl. What's the matter with her, Hannah? She is white as
a daisy; and what do you make her
work for?"

"Mrs. Reed said she must," was the
brief reply, as Hannah took the work,
and laid it out of sight.

"Mrs. Reed, probably, does not consider how weak she is," she replied. "I
have given her so much trouble of late,
that she has had no time to think of any
one else. But Lina must have been very
sick indeed."

"She's been a good deal down, and
don't gain strength as I wish she did. I
think some good syrup, or bitters, such
as your father used to give you, would be
good for her, but Mrs. Reed thinks them
little sugar mites 'll cure any thing.
Mebbe they will, but I should like to

know what your father would 'a said
about 'em."

"Sister Reed is a very ardent believer
in homœopathy, as well as my husband;
it is, at least, a harmless practice, as papa
would say, I think. I think it agrees
with me, but something else may be
needed for Lina."

Hannah was called out by a neighbor,
and Miss Agnes, drawing me to her,
looked at me intently for some moments,
before she said:

"What made you think I would hate
you—never speak to you, Lina?"

"Because I told that lie, and made
you sick—and—and—"

"And what?" she asked, seeing me
hesitate.

"Because they said you wouldn't want
to see me, ma'am," I replied, slowly, for
I had a kind of instinct that my words
might wound her.

"They were mistaken," she replied,
using the plural pronoun in the same indefinite way that I had; "they are so
strong and good themselves that they
hardly know how to make due allow-
ance for others. But I am weak, and
full of errors—I feel it daily, more and
more deeply—and it is not for one like
me to condemn another, especially a
child whom I am bound to love and protect. Did they think you made me
sick?"

I nodded.

"Their great love for me has made
them over-anxious. It was not altogether that. I was deeply grieved, of course,
but many things conspired to make me
anxious; besides, I had not felt well for
some time."

Then she went on to speak to me of
her baby, and how much she had hoped
I would have loved it, if it had lived. "I
thought its coming might help us to understand you better, Lina, for I, at least,
am very ignorant, and I have sometimes
thought that people who have never had
any girls of their own can hardly understand them; and Mr. Tyler has had only

boys, you know." Then she talked to me about my sin—of her promise that I should read the books, and took great blame on herself for thus leading me into temptation, as it were, until it seemed as if the innocence and gentleness of that little babe which she mourned had entered into her own soul, so kind and gentle and wise were her words. She spoke of Augustus and Sara, saying Mrs. Reed would take charge of us all for some time to come, for Mr. Tyler could not consent to have her burdened with any care in her present state of health, and she hoped I would try to be a good girl, and live pleasantly with Sara and Augustus, and not make any unnecessary trouble. As the eldest, she expected me to set the example. With a kiss on my cheek she left the room, telling me not to follow, for Hannah would help her up-stairs.

When her pale face disappeared, I made a vow in my heart; I felt the energies of my nature reviving, and I knew, by God's help, I could keep it, and I did try.

CHAPTER XI.

TROUBLE AND RELIEF.

THERE would be little use and no pleasure in recalling my life for the next six months, if it were not that it developed in me a fixedness of purpose, and a silent energy of will, for which I had great reason to be thankful in after-years. I do not know what Miss Agnes said or thought about it, but from the time of Mrs. Reed's arrival it seemed to be decided that my place was in the kitchen. I felt quite content as long as Hannah remained, but that good woman had uttered words during that interview by my bedside that could not be forgotten, and the experience of each day made it more and more apparent that she must leave.

A letter from her brother, in which he spoke of the serious illness of his wife,

served as a plausible reason for a necessity which she felt as strongly as did Mrs. Reed. It was a sad day for me when she left, and a sad one for my mistress also. Hannah had an interview with her before she left, and, when she bade me good-by, she said:

"Keep up a good heart, Lina. I spoke to her about you, for all *he* and *she* were there. I told her it was no place for you in the kitchen, with furrin' servant-girls, after treatin' you as her own child so long, and she said she'd do what was right. I hope she will—I know she will if they will let her. And you must do your best for her sake; for, Heaven forgive me if I wrong them, but I do believe some folks don't care how bad you do, the worse the better. You must spite them in this, child, and mebbe it 'll be all for the best, though it's hard seein' or sayin' it, with so many things stickin' in one's crop. But if you can't stay—if worse come to worse—come to me. Remember, Eli Smith, W——, child!" and, with a grasp that made my fingers tingle, she departed.

Now, the old home was indeed gone, and I was almost as solitary and friendless as when Miss Agnes brought me there three years before. Hannah's place was supplied by a series of Irish girls, for, Mrs. Reed being one of those mistresses who always act on the assumption that all servants are dishonest, seldom kept one more than four or five weeks, and I had no time to make friends of them, if I desired. I suppose Sara Reed was no worse than other children, but, seeing her mother treat me with dislike and neglect, she improved upon her example, and attempted to order me about at her pleasure. Of course I refused to obey, and there followed high words, of which she gave her own version to her mother, who solemnly assured Miss Agnes that I was "the worst-tempered child she ever saw." Augustus and Sara, though they quarrelled constantly, were ready to become close allies against me; and, knowing there was no redress, I bore their gibes and tricks with a stoicism I was very far from feeling. I instinctively shrunk from Augustus; he knew it, and delighted in ferreting me out from every nook where I thought to hide myself, during my moments of leisure, which, after old Hannah left, "were few and far between." Only in my own room was I safe from his impertinence; but not from the insatiable curiosity and greed of Sara Reed. She made no scruple about entering my room when she chose; peering about among my things, and begging for such as happened to suit her fancy. One of the things she specially coveted was Ollie's little trunk. It would just hold her dissecting maps—wouldn't I give it to her? When I refused, she offered several of her things in exchange; but, finding me firm, she flew into a passion, and taunted me with being "town poor, without a decent rag to my back when her aunty took me!"

The hot blood rushed to my cheeks— the angry words to my lips—but I remembered my interview with Miss Agnes, and, choking back my anger, kept on with my work in silence.

Seeing this, she said, with a sneer:

"You needn't sulk, miss; though nobody cares whether you speak or not. I guess it will be as mamma says about the trunk."

I made no reply, but, as soon as she was gone, I burst into tears. I felt so homeless, so friendless, and unprotected. Why had I no parents and friends like Sara and Augustus? Who were my parents—where did they live or die? Sara's words had recalled Bradshaw— Sally Hunt, Uncle Steve, and little Adeline. I wondered if I could not find my way back there—if Uncle Steve would not let me live with them if I should. I thought he would, but the experience of the past two years had unsettled my confidence in many things. Why did they all hate me? Why did Miss Agnes so seldom see me, and speak so hurriedly

when we did meet, as if she was afraid some one would see her?

Oh, how wearily, and in what a chaos of darkness and childish ignorance, I brooded over these questions! Later, when I was old enough to read the world, I could have answered some of them, at least those that referred to my position in that house. I was in the way. I was a present expense, and, in the future, I might, as the adopted child of Mrs. Tyler, come in for a share of her property. Besides, I had nothing in common with them, and they could not love what they did not comprehend.

But my work waited in the kitchen, and on my way there I met Miss Agnes in the hall. I was unwilling to have her see the traces of my tears, and was passing her hastily when she laid her hand on my arm, and, placing the other under my chin, asked:

"What makes you so pale, Lina?— And you have been crying, too! What for?"

I made some hasty answer, for Mrs. Reed entered as she spoke, and she released me, but, from a few words I caught as I went out, I suspected Miss Agnes was speaking to her of me. I was right, for half an hour later, when Mrs. Reed entered the kitchen, she said in her sternest, most inflexible tones:

"Zerlina Day, if you choose to sniffle and cry all the while, I trust, henceforth, you will keep out of Mrs. Tyler's presence. She is still weak, and it seems as if you took pleasure in distressing her. I wonder how any one could be so ungrateful. Don't let me have occasion to speak again. I never cry."

I don't think she did, and it was the last time she had the pleasure of reprimanding me for a like evidence of weakness, for a circumstance occurred a few days later that made my expulsion from the house a necessity.

I have said that Mr. Tyler was something of a gourmand, and that Miss Agnes had delighted in preparing little delicacies for him, particularly upon occasions when his business or pleasure prevented him from eating with the family. Mrs. Reed, who affected to consult his comfort above all things, had continued the practice, and since her arrival there had been hardly a day in which, upon plea of his fastidious appetite, we had not prepared some extra dish for him, and I used to wonder how he could enjoy them, with the greedy eyes of Augustus, who inherited all his father's appetite, fixed upon him, for we children were still nominally confined to a vegetarian diet.

One day, toward the last of February, some business had kept Mr. Tyler away long after the family dinner-hour, and a nice "porter-house" steak with fitting accompaniments was prepared for him, which I was ordered to carry to the dining-room. I did so, and, seeing that one of the blinds was loose, raised the window, fastened it, and left the room. I did not observe any one in the room, but, a few moments after, Augustus came out and stole softly up-stairs. I had gone into the hall for something and saw him, and saw also that his mouth, as usual, was stuffed with something. The next moment I heard Mr. Tyler and his sister enter from the study, and his voice saying angrily:

"How is this? Some one has been meddling with my dinner. Look at that toast!"

I did not hear Mrs. Reed's reply; it was not necessary, for immediately she opened the door and ordered me to come in.

Mr. Tyler was very angry, I knew by his flushed face and quick, spasmodic breathing.

"Come here!" he cried, as soon as he could gather breath. "I want to know how long I and my household are to suffer from your wickedness! Look at this," pointing to the half-emptied dish —"how dare you steal the food prepared for my necessities?"

"I did not, sir."

"Beware! Don't think to deceive me. You were ordered to place it here, and no one else has entered the room!"

Before I could reply, Mrs. Reed, who had listened to his words with scornful impatience, broke out:

"What earthly use is there in talking to her in this way, brother! You can't believe a word she says. You know she did it, and it is not the first thing that has been missing lately. Last week I had some change. If I were you, I would send her back where she came from."

Somehow, the woman's looks and words stirred the passion of anger and aversion so long fermenting within me to an explosion. Miss Agnes was not present with her timid, pleading eyes to restrain me, so I burst forth:

"I suppose you would, ma'am, but that will be as Mrs. Tyler says, though. If it were not for her, I would not care how quick I go!"

"Just hear the impudent, ungrateful hussy!" she exclaimed, with a malicious smile.

"I am not ungrateful; I would work my fingers to the bone for Miss Agnes, and I have as much right to be here as you have!"

"You little saucy wretch! How dare you speak so to me?"

I was trembling from anger and excitement. All the slights, wrongs, misconstructions, and coldness I had endured for months past came rushing to my lips to find expression; and Mr. Tyler must have read something of this in my face, for he looked at me in perfect astonishment while I retorted:

"Because it's the truth! I wish Mrs. Tyler would send you away, and bring back Hannah. She don't seem one bit as she used to before you came. It's you who have made her sick!"

"The girl is beside herself!" exclaimed Mr. Tyler.

"She's just as she always is, as you would know if you saw her every day as I do. She is the worst-tempered, slyest, most deceitful child I ever saw!" returned Mrs. Reed.

"I am not sly—I don't open drawers and peek into other folks' things like Sara, and I'm not deceitful, for I don't pretend to like folks and then talk about them when they are gone away, as you do. I never pretended to like you, and I could not if I tried; but, if you want to know who eat that toast, ask Augustus. I saw him come out of this room with his mouth crammed full of something, and there are the leaves of his Latin grammar under the table; and if you want to know who took your change "— I went on with a strange feeling of exaltation at Mr. Tyler's look of consternation and Mrs. Reed's lowering brow and set teeth—"ask him where he got the money he spent for oranges, the day you went to the sewing-circle, and how many he gave Sara not to tell!"

"I will ask them both!" she said growing pale beneath her thick skin. "But you need not think to get off by accusing them; for if—"

"Call them now!" interrupted Mr. Tyler, sternly; "and Zerlina Day," he added, turning to me, "if it proves, as I presume it will, that you have again been guilty of falsehood, as well as dishonesty, we shall be forced to send you away, as my sister suggests. I cannot consent to have my son and niece ruined by your pernicious example; your language and manner are utterly disgraceful, more those of a fury than a young girl!"

Half an hour later, when the ferment of passion had subsided, I knew they were. If it was the truth which I had uttered, it was not for me, a child, to speak it in that manner, but I did not feel it then, and made no reply.

Augustus and Sara came; the former stoutly denied all knowledge of the food or of being in the room, saying he had been up-stairs studying his Latin.

"What is your lesson for to-day?" asked Mr. Tyler.

"Nouns of the fourth declension, section 126," and he was going on with some further assertion, when his father thrust the stray leaf from his old grammar containing that very section under his eyes, saying in a voice that shook with anger—

"Enough! Tell me, then, how came this leaf here upon the floor?"

The boy trembled in every limb, and, at last, burst into tears.

"Now, sir, own the truth—did you meddle with my dinner?"

He blubbered forth a confession, and begged for mercy.

I should have pitied Mr. Tyler's grief and surprise at finding a flaw in his model boy, if I had been in any mood to pity. Besides, I had no time, for Mrs. Reed said, with a glance of mingled dread and aversion toward me:

"Brother, there's no use in keeping this girl here any longer. She has brought trouble enough, for in Augustus you see the fruit of her evil example. If you choose to put up with such language and conduct, you can, but, if she stays, I quit the house!"

Mr. Tyler made a gesture for me to go. Not a word of apology for their false and degrading accusations—no admission of their mistake—only—"Go!"

I left them with a hard, angry feeling burning in my heart, but, when the fierce flame cooled, I felt, as I have said, that I had done wrong. No provocation could excuse my intemperate, disrespectful manner, and, instead of enjoying the vindication of my innocence, I was very wretched indeed. Many and many a time had I longed to have Augustus and Sara discovered at some of their tricks— I had anticipated a fierce satisfaction—a triumph; but, now, I could think of nothing but my own violence.

I went to my room; no one called me, as usual, to take my share in the work, and I sat there and thought of my broken vow to Miss Agnes, while the tears rolled slowly down my cheeks. I thought of the future. Would they send me away? I had a dreary kind of satisfaction in thinking they would. Again the thought of Uncle Steve and little Adeline recurred to me, a light amid my dark world. I was quite sure they would shelter me. It was my first day of liberty, but, like all liberty gained by violence and wrong, a curse clung to it, and poisoned all its sweetness.

The next day I went down to the kitchen, and performed my usual share of the labor, but Mrs. Reed, when she came, did not notice or speak to me. Had I been a block or stone, she could not have been, or affected to have been, more unconscious of my presence, and my half-formed resolve to ask pardon for my violence was petrified by her indifference.

During the morning I saw Mr. Tyler and Miss Agnes drive away, and I watched the carriage with a heavy heart, for I felt that she would be told of my violence, but not of the provocation, and that she was lost to me forever. Augustus and Sara, though they came, it seemed to me, much oftener than usual to the kitchen, followed Mrs. Reed's example—they even failed to make grimaces, and I felt that I was banned beyond redemption.

Two more days passed, full of suspense, loneliness, and misgivings of the future, when, on the third morning, I was summoned to the study.

I thought I was prepared for any thing, but certainly not for the kind look which Miss Agnes gave me when I entered. Mr. Tyler spoke to me pompously—condescendingly of course, but not so very sternly. He had, as it seemed, decided to permit his wife to introduce the subject under consideration, for she said, with a pleased expression, and much of her old, kind manner:

"Lina, we have something to tell you. How would you like to go away to school?"

"Very much indeed, ma'am."

"Well, Mr. Tyler—" she looked at him, and he waved his hand, as if to say "proceed"—"moved by his desire to benefit you, and gratify me, has been looking out for a suitable school for you. We think we have found one at Oaklawn, a seminary for young ladies, near M——, the principal of which kindly consents to receive you into her family."

"On certain conditions," Mr. Tyler continued. "You will be expected to perform certain portions of household labor during your leisure hours, as an equivalent for your board. The tuition fees we shall discharge as long as you give satisfaction to Mrs. Ellis. This arrangement we think rather beneficial to you than otherwise, as you will, in the future, have to depend, in a great degree, upon your own exertions for support. Mrs. Tyler thinks you have capacities for teaching—I am willing you should try."

"I had hoped that my cousin Ralph would have returned before this, for I would have liked to consult him—" began Miss Agnes, but Mr. Tyler raised his eyebrows, and she grew confused, as usual.

"Mr. Ralph Annesley's opinion in regard to training an immortal soul could be of but very little value, my dear. Were it a dog, it might be otherwise."

Miss Agnes sighed. Perhaps she thought of what he had said down by the pond in Bradshaw. I did.

I thanked them earnestly, so earnestly that Miss Agnes said, rather sadly: "Then, you are very glad to go, Lina?"

"To be sure—she ought to be!" returned her husband. "Few girls, of her condition, have such advantages offered them.—You will be prepared to take the stage Monday morning, at five o'clock."

"So soon, dear? I am afraid we shall hardly be able to get her ready on such short notice. She will need some new clothing!"

"Very little will be necessary. A few plain, substantial garments will be all that will be needed in that rural retreat."

So it was decided. The "brand" was to be sent away, but did Miss Agnes know why? I never could answer this question, but I think she did not—I think she saw in this plan only another evidence of her husband's great kindness and benevolence.

The three succeeding days were very busy ones to me. My trunk was packed very late on Saturday evening, and on Sunday night Mr. Tyler ordered me to take leave of Mrs. Tyler, as he did not wish her to be disturbed at so early an hour as that in which the stage would stop for me.

I was struck dumb at this proposal, or rather command, and so I think was Miss Agnes, for she said something about it being no trouble for her to rise at that hour, but Mr. Tyler silenced her by a look; so, kissing me tenderly, she whispered her "Good-by," adding that I must make her "happy by being a good girl."

But, before I fell asleep that night, she came to my bedside, and, stooping over me, let tears and kisses fall on my cheeks. I lifted my arms (there was no fear of crushing her collar then), and clasped them around her neck without a word.

"Lina," she said, "I want to say to you that if any thing should ever happen to me, that I could not look after you, and help you, I want you to apply to Cousin Ralph—he will help you—that is, if you should ever require help. I have not heard from him these two years, but I have written to Miss Annesley to know when she expects him home, and she says, 'Always, until he arrives.'"

"Miss Annesley! Has Mr. Ralph a sister?"

"No; Miss Anne Annesley is a cousin of his father and my mother—old enough to be his mother. He is very fond of her, and since his mother's death she has had the care of his house."

"Does he keep house?" I asked, for I was very curious to learn something more of this person, of whom I had so often thought.

"Yes; he has his house kept in just the same way it was in his mother's lifetime, though he is seldom there but a few days at a time, even when in this country. I have written down the address on this card, which I wish you to keep, in case you should ever need it. It is No. 90 Bleecker Street."

She was silent a moment; then, gathering my hands in hers, she said:

"I am afraid I have not done for you all I ought—all Cousin Ralph hoped. I think if we could live over again the time—I mean the time before my marriage—I could do better. I have thought a great deal about those days, since my little baby was born; it, somehow, seems as if it had made me better acquainted with young children—or else it has made a child of me."

I felt her tears dropping upon my hands; every drop seemed to weigh down my heart with a sense of my own failures and ingratitude. I tried to tell her something of this, but not the half of what I felt, and so we parted.

Five o'clock was not, since the advent of Mrs. Reed, an unusually early hour at our house. She was an early riser, and indulged no one in morning dreams, but her brother and his wife. However, Mr. Tyler, probably to please Miss Agnes, was up this morning to see me off, and put me into the coach himself, saying he really hoped I would improve my time and give satisfaction to Mrs. Ellis and the teachers—that nothing could give him more pleasure than to hear that I had been able to overcome evil with good.

He spoke kindly, and I think now, sincerely; and I am grateful that I have been permitted to live until I have learned to see how sincerely and honestly a person may pursue a mistaken course—to separate the sin from the sinner, and forgive him, as I have long since forgiven the Rev. Marcus Tyler.

I need not describe my journey, the excitement of the morning, or the weariness of the latter portion of the route; for the state of the roads was horrible at that season of the year, and the coach so crowded that it was not until quite dark that I was set down in front of Oaklawn. The driver set my trunk, through the gate-way, into the yard, mounted his seat and drove on, leaving me standing at a large, square, three-story building, in the drizzling rain of a March evening.

At such an hour, and in such an atmosphere, every thing looked dreary enough. The long walk leading to the front door was bordered with the blackened and mildewed stalks of the last year's flowers, and the bare, pendant branches of the elms, swaying in the chilly east wind, had a most melancholy appearance. I trembled as much from a feeling of loneliness and dread, as from cold, while I stood waiting, for I had expected that some one would meet me at the gate. No one came, and I finally mustered sufficient courage to walk to the door and ring—nervously, and consequently loudly, for I started to hear how the sound reverberated through the house. It answered my purpose, for immediately a servant opened the door; I uttered the name of Mrs. Ellis, and was ushered into a small room where there was a fire, which was specially grateful to my chilled body. The servant saw me seated, and went to announce my arrival to Mrs. Ellis. Presently she entered, a tall, erect, dignified lady of middle age, who walked directly up to me and said;

"The new pupil from Chesterwood, I presume?"

Her voice was firm, clear, almost sharp, but not unpleasant, and I answered in the affirmative.

"You are earlier than I expected. Mr. Tyler said the 20th—to-day is the 19th—yes, the 19th, he said," she added, consulting her tablets. "But you are weary and hungry." She rang the bell and the same servant entered.

"Remove Miss—Miss—"

"I am Zerlina Lathrop," I said, giving the name by which it had been Miss Agnes's wish that I should be known in Chesterwood, though Mr. Tyler seldom honored me with it.

"Remove Miss Lathrop's wet wraps," she said. "It is past our hour for tea," she added, turning to me, "but you will follow Mary to the dining-room, where she will provide you with refreshments; then she will show you to your room —No. 10, Mary, next to Miss Nichols. I will have your baggage sent up. The rising-bell will ring at six,—the breakfast-bell at half-past six. You will be expected to be punctual."

With a slight gesture she dismissed me, and, an hour later, I had forgotten Chesterwood and Oaklawn, in a dreamless slumber.

CHAPTER XII.

OAKLAWN SCHOOL.

"Who is there? Open the door, and you will have more light!"

I had risen in the morning, without waiting for the bell, and was groping about in my dimly-lighted room, which was rather a large closet which had at some time been partitioned off from the adjoining room, when I heard the above words. Not supposing them addressed to me, I kept moving about until the same gentle voice said again.

"Who is it? Why don't you open the door?"

"It's me," I said, timidly opening the door, for I was not quite sure that I was the person addressed.

"Well, come forward and let me see me," said the voice.

I entered, and advanced to the bed-side, where some one lay supported by pillows. A small night-lamp burned upon the table near the bed, which the

5

occupant extinguished with her thin hand, saying:

"Please raise that shade, and let in the light. I think it must be near sunrise."

I did so, and in the gray dawn of that morning I looked into the eyes of one whose memory, even now, is like the presence of an angel, whose brief existence here has made all holy and beautiful things possible to womanhood. It was the face of a girl of twenty-two or three years, though she seemed older, for there was that expression of maturity and serene self-poise about it which children and young people are apt to associate only with years; still it was only an expression, for the face was fair—clear almost to transparency—toned down by large eyes of deep, clear gray, which, in the dim dawn, I mistook for black. She had cast aside her cap, and her abundant, fine hair, of that neutral brown so grateful to the eye of an artist, was carelessly folded round such a head and brow as make

"The old Greek marble with the goddess glow!"

Her cheeks were thin and sunken, but her eyes were like stars. She looked steadily into my face for a few seconds, but I neither turned away nor looked down, for I felt that her look did me good. Presently she smiled, and, sad and lonely as I had felt a moment before, I could not help returning her smile.

"I trust we shall be good friends," she said, "for I suppose you know you are to be under my care."

"No, ma'am; but I shall be glad of it."

"Why?" she asked, still smiling.

"Because—because—I can't exactly tell why," I said, stammering and coloring, "but I *feel* that I shall."

"Well, I suppose that is about as good a reason as the wisest of us can give. What is your name? I have forgotten, if my mother mentioned it."

I told her, and she repeated it, musingly—"Zerlina does not sound much like a New-England name, but I like it. I am Michal Ellis, and you are to be

hands and feet to me for the present, while I am to help you with my head and heart, too, I hope."

"May I begin now? Shall I help you to dress?" I asked.

"No, not yet, for two long hours, and then my toilet will be quickly made. But you may open that blind, dear. I like to see the level sunbeams strike the tops of the trees yonder; and then you may go back to your room and put it in order. You will have ample time before the breakfast-bell rings. After breakfast my mother will tell you what she expects you to do."

Following the sound of the bell, I went down. In the hall, several girls passed me, smoothing their hair with uncertain fingers, and yawning, as if not yet quite awake. I followed on to the dining-room, near the door of which I paused timidly. Two or three teachers, for such I judged them to be from their age and air of authority, had already taken their places at the long table. I had scarcely time to note this when the bell ceased to ring, and Mrs. Ellis stood by my side.

"Ah, good-morning, miss," she said. "Young ladies, this is Miss Zerlina Lathrop.—Miss Gay, she will take her place next to you.—Miss Thatcher, will you see that she is properly helped?"

Miss Lathrop! I had cared little for that name before, but now it was very pleasant to hear it. It seemed, as I have no doubt it was, a proof that Miss Agnes's love and care followed me still. But I had no time for reverie. The thin, nervous-looking lady, addressed as Miss Thatcher, saw me seated between two flaxen-haired misses, who seemed, as yet, half asleep. Then there came a light tap on the table, and every hand was folded, while Mrs. Ellis said "grace before meat" in a few brief, earnest words. The food, of which, be it noted, there was an abundance, was eaten in silence, and the pupils filed out after the teachers. I was the last, and Mrs. Ellis, who had remained standing near the head of the table, beckoned me to remain.

"You are an orphan—with no relatives, I have been told," she said, as she drew near the stove, whither I gladly followed her, for the room was chilly with the raw March air.

"Yes, ma'am."

"And they say, also, that you are bad-tempered and intractable."

She paused for an answer, and, with a sinking heart, I replied:

"They say so, ma'am."

She stood for a second or so looking down—for she was very tall—into my eyes, and there was something in this clear, direct look, that gave me courage; and when she added—

"But what do you say?" I replied instantly:

"I would much rather you would try me, ma'am."

The answer seemed to please her, for she said:

"I will. I think it is a mistake. I do not believe in intractable girls—we don't have them here. Our pupils are expected to be polite, orderly, and obedient; and such you must prove yourself. You know you are taken on peculiar terms?"

"Yes, ma'am."

"You will be required to wait upon my daughter Michal, for the present, and, at her special request, you will study under her supervision, and recite to her. She will examine you, and decide what branches you had best pursue at present. Wednesday and Friday afternoons are devoted to short lectures by the teachers, and a general review. On these occasions, you will be expected to take your place in the school-room. You will also attend prayers there every morning; then return to my daughter's room, where I understand you have already been, and obey her orders as you would mine."

In just so many words, my place in the family at Oaklawn was decided, and, for the next six months, I do not think

"our principal," as she was always called, addressed as many consecutive sentences to me. But I had no reason to complain —she was not a woman of many words. Quiet, firm, direct, and strictly just, I felt that I was cared for equally with the rest, and the "peculiar terms" that consigned me to the service of Michal Ellis brought advantages which no gold could have purchased. It is not necessary for me to describe this school; it was, in some respects, superior to many of its class, for the conscientiousness of the principal led her to fulfil, as far as possible, the terms of her circulars. Of course, there were grumblings, for most school-girls in their teens seem to think it their business to grumble, and the teachers looked jaded and nervous, as if it would do them good to sleep a whole year. There were three resident lady-teachers: Mademoiselle Berthier, who taught French and music, a lady of fine presence and graceful manners; Misses Stevens and Thatcher—the former always busy, but good-natured—ready to put the fairest construction upon every thing; the latter nervously exact and precise, always in a worry, and always hurried. Our drawing-teacher walked out from M—— daily; and the teacher of the more advanced classes in Latin and mathematics was an old friend of the principal, who resided at a short distance from Oaklawn, at a very pretty place called "The Pines." The garrulous school-girl, who gave me these particulars the day after my arrival, said that the latter was an odd sort of person, who lived all alone, with the exception of an old housekeeper, who never went anywhere, nor saw any one, though sometimes a lady came there, and stayed awhile; some folks said she was the old gentleman's sister, and that there was something queer about her.

"Queer! How so?"

"Oh—queer—you know;" she returned, with true school-girl indefiniteness. "That's what all the girls say.

Some think she's kind o' crazy because he would not let her marry a foreign gentleman, who used to visit there. Mary Sherman saw him once, and she says he was quite like a corsair, with such magnificent eyes."

"Did you ever see the lady?"

"No; I'm only here since last spring, and, when she's here, he keeps her mostly shut up, they say, though they do, sometimes, walk for hours, in their own grounds. They say the old gentleman don't like it much when she goes off; at any rate, he's queerer than ever then, and sometimes even forgets to note whether they answer correctly or not."

"Goes off? I thought you said he kept her shut up."

"So he does; but she contrives to get away from him. I wonder she don't stay away. I would."

"Is he a good teacher?"

"Yes, I s'pose so. He knows lots, they say. But he's as full of points as a chestnut-burr. We think he breakfasts on them occasionally. But there goes Thatcher—I can tell you, you won't like her—she's a regular fidget, always finding fault, and you'll be in her classes, I think."

"I sha'n't, for I am to recite to Miss Michal Ellis," I said; then, seeing her look of surprise, I added, "I am poor, and shall wait on Miss Michal to pay for my board."

"Well, you are a queer one too!" she said, after a moment's silence. "I'm poor, too, at least my guardian says so, but should never thought of owning it here. I don't believe there's another girl in school that would have owned up in that way. But I would not much care if I could have Miss Michal for a teacher. She's splendid, I tell you. Seemed as if her looks helped me. I wish she'd get well and take her classes again, for that Thatcher—she's worse than the old professor!"

"What professor?"

"Why, Cavendish—that we have been talking about all this time! Aren't you a little bit stupid?" And, with this compliment to my mental perception, the laughing girl ran away.

I felt the peculiar influence of which Sophie May had spoken, every time Miss Michal's clear eyes met mine. It was magnetic, I suppose, and she did "help me even by her looks," as every noble, truthful human face does. Alas! that they should be so disguised by the dusty turmoil of life! All my troubles, passions, vexations, and wrongs, as I held them, grew to look poor and insignificant in her presence.

"How minutely and vividly you remember these things, and how keenly you must have felt them!" she said, thoughtfully, one evening, looking, as it seemed, right into my heart with her serene eyes.

A week's acquaintance had worn off the timidity and reserve I had felt in the presence of strangers, and she had led me to speak of my early life with Sally Hunt, and my subsequent residence with Miss Agnes, and I had dwelt on the petty tyranny of Augustus Tyler and Sarah, and that night of horror in the attic chamber, until my face flushed, and my voice trembled with excitement.

"And why shouldn't I, Miss Michal? I have nothing else to remember!" I replied, passionately.

"Are you not mistaken, dear? Even by your showing, you have received much love and kindness. Why not dwell upon this with equal intensity? Surely it would be pleasanter."

I blushed, and my glance fell slowly beneath hers in self-abasement. Then she took one of my thin brown hands in hers, and went on:

"Your lot has been hard and sorrowful, Lina; but, it does not make it a bit brighter or pleasanter to dwell upon its wrongs. No one—not even the wisest or most favored—can escape sin and suffering, wrong and sorrow. But these we know are transitory—passing away in the light of God's truth, while good is eternal, blessing us even in its memories, and it is so much wiser to recall this."

"But there is so little good," I said, despondingly.

"So I thought once, but it was because I would not see it. I put my personal wrongs and grievances between myself and that, and how could I expect to see it? I fancy you have done the same. Think—have you really nothing pleasant to recall?"

I thought of Ollie, Uncle Steve, Miss Agnes, and felt ashamed.

She smiled as she said:

"You need not look so distressed, dear; we are all alike in this—far readier to see the trail and slime of the serpent than the footprints of the angel."

"But how can I forget these things? How can I stop thinking of them?"

"When you climbed that steep cliff that overhangs the pond, and sat looking down at those beautiful pictures of cloud and tree and sky, mirrored in the clear, still waters which you described a few moments since, did you think of the roughness of the ascent—the stones and briers that had impeded your way?"

"No, I forgot all about them—only, when I tore my dress, I cared, for then Mrs. Sally whipped me."

"But that did not keep you from going again?"

"No, it was so beautiful!"

"Then, when we know that, before us, it may be but a few hours' journey, there lies another world, where, instead of these shifting shows, we shall stand in the presence of the real and eternal, where all that has been dark or sad or painful to us will not enter—all that has been mysterious will be made clear—all our aspirations realized, and even evil itself be seen to praise Him—why should we think upon the stones, the brambles, and briers, that beset the way?—why darken the little light which falls upon our path?—There, it will be all light!"

She was looking at a point in the western sky where beautiful Hesper was visible above the tree-tops, and, when she again turned her eyes upon me, I felt the resemblance between her face and that star. The light of that world of which she had spoken beamed from them both. I never look at that star now, without seeming to hear her sweet low voice, saying: "Good is eternal—blessing us even in its memories; remember that, dear!"

It was so strange that she never once seemed to think of my birth—that I was "conceived in iniquity and born in sin," a circumstance which Mr. Tyler deemed it so necessary that I should bear in mind; or that she did not remind me of how grateful I should be for her attention. She even did not seem to think me any ways different from herself—a minister's daughter—save in my lack of years and experience; and, what was quite as strange, I seemed, when with her, to forget all these things myself, and to feel that I really might become as noble and good as herself. Perhaps, she felt that self-respect is as much the birthright of the pauper as the king.

CHAPTER XIII.

PROFESSOR CAVENDISH.

"I will not sit down! You have convinced me of the truth of the doctrine of total depravity, Michal! Haven't I told you to let your books alone—that there is death in them? And you mind me no more than you do the hootings of an owl! You might well teach perseverance to the saints. No—I won't sit down. I don't affect the company of suicides!"

But he did sit down, even while he spoke—that gray-haired, gray-eyed, long-limbed, round-shouldered man, who stood shaking his long, bony finger at Miss Michal and her books, when I entered her room and stole quietly to my usual seat, within reach of her chair.

Miss Michal smiled pleasantly, as she laid her hand upon the shrivelled one that continued to point ominously at her books, and said something in a language I did not understand.

"He who can look on death fears no shadows!" repeated the gentleman, and there was a bright twinkle on his deep-set eyes, that belied his querulous tone as he went on:

"Umph! So much for training a house bantam like an eagle. I much doubt if your wise father ever gave a thought to your sex, Michal, and I, like a fool, have followed in his steps. But I'll not have manslaughter or womanslaughter on my conscience. Does not the wise man say, 'He that increaseth knowledge increaseth sorrow?'"

"Certainly, but you always say that truth, to be of any value, must be tested. Now, I must, like all who have gone before me, prove the truth of the wise man's words myself. Besides," she added, more gravely, "we are sure that death will meet us somewhere, and there is so much to learn, and so little time."

The twinkle in the gentleman's eye softened into an expression of fondness and admiration, yet it did not affect his voice or words, for both were harsh and impatient as he took a book from the table, and, running his eye over a paper that lay within, exclaimed:

"What's this? Circles and attractive forces; precession and recession of the equinoxes; zodiacal light—ay, the zodiacal light of March 20th was a most beautiful phenomenon, Michal. The pyramidical form, from base to apex, was perfectly distinct. I wish you could have seen it."

His face was glowing with enthusiasm, and Miss Michal smiled a little mischievously as she answered:

"I did. I watched it for more than an hour."

"You did! You, Michal Ellis, with that cough!"

"Yes, you had so often described it to me, and I wanted to see it so much."

"I! I wish my tongue had been blistered before I ever mentioned the thing before you! But when did a woman ever use any reason! An hour in this raw, March air, just to look at a light space in the heavens—a mere will-o'-the-wisp. I was a fool to have watched it myself."

Miss Michal took no notice of this burst of irritation, but said, quietly:

"Little as I know of astronomy, I believe I can comprehend the enthusiasm with which men devote their lives to its study. You remember telling us, in the class, one day, how Rittenhouse fainted from excess of emotion at witnessing the last transit of Venus. I think it the most natural thing in the world. It must be sublime to grasp with one's own strong, untiring will at the comprehension of the mighty plans of God; and, if this comprehension grows wiser, more and more perfect, to become at one with Him — to grasp at God's secrets and catch them! The thought almost takes away one's breath! Ah, if we were not such cowards—so weak and faithless! It sometimes seems as if the child might grasp the sunbeams, the man remove mountains, if he really comprehended the power of a strong, persistent *will!*"

Now the look of loving admiration softened and brightened, for an instant, every line of that worn face—but he resolutely put it out. I could see the effort to do so, by the working of the muscles of his scraggy throat, and he said, in a voice that seemed to me more sad than tears:

"Ay, the old story of the moth and the candle; but suppose it were true, would the child or man be the happier for what they had achieved? Would they not always see before them, just beyond their reach, other treasures far more beautiful and more difficult to obtain?"

"Yes, but what if it does seem the task for ages, perhaps of eternity, to reach that point where one may stand face to face with the great Centre of Light and Truth, and read His secrets! Surely, if one strives, he can approximate toward this, even here, and it is far better to make the effort, than to sit down and mourn because the task is so hard, the way so difficult and far, or grumble because we cannot compass every thing by one effort."

Again I was reminded of Hesperus—the same clear, starry light was in her eyes, and I felt vexed that the iron-gray head and the iron-muscled face should turn away from her just then, to mutter, as it seemed, only these words:

"Dreams—dreams!"

"No, I will not believe it. I cannot put my convictions into words, for it is with the *heart*, not the intellect, that 'man believeth unto righteousness.' My faith in God and the soul is assured—then why should I distrust the deepest, purest hopes and aspirations of the heart? They may grow dim, they may seemingly fail, but I know that nothing suffers change unknown to God—nothing is really lost, and, somewhere in His universe, I shall find for them a full and complete realization, and I am content to wait."

"It will not be here—not here, child," murmured the guest.

"Perhaps not—but *elsewhere*, then, dear master, and I am not the less content."

I have never seen a look so full of loving admiration, pity, and regret, as that with which the master, as she called him, regarded her, and his voice was full of tenderness as he said:

"Ah, Michal, you should have been a boy; you should have had the strong vitality and steady nerves of our sex—our unfailing egotism—our varied resources and independence of the affections."

"Are men, indeed, so independent of affection?" asked Miss Michal, thoughtfully.

"Not always. But, between the world, the flesh, and the devil, they either learn to put up with empty husks, or do without it!"

"Well, why cannot I learn to do without it, too?"

"Because you are a woman, with a woman's heart and a man's head, and your judgment will make sad work with the cravings of your heart. But what have you here? Where did you pick up that little brown gypsy?"

His eye had accidentally lighted on me, and Miss Michal could not help smiling at his comical look of surprise, while she said hastily, as if fearful that his look or manner might wound me:

"It is my new pupil. I forgot that she came while you were away, and, therefore, you had not seen her. For various reasons, my mother has placed her under my care, and we get on nicely. —Come here, Zerlina, and speak with Professor Cavendish," she added, turning to me. "You need not mind his words, for he is just as good as he can be."

"It's no such thing, Zingarella! I am—"

"I said Zerlina, sir," interrupted Miss Michal.

"And I say *Zingarella!* Don't you think I know that look? I have seen it in every country in Europe. There are the true gypsy eyes and skin. I don't know where you found her, but her progenitors are, no doubt, swapping mules and telling fortunes, this moment, somewhere in Spain."

I laughed as I met his half-serious, half-comic look. Instantly he seized my arm, and, drawing me forward, said eagerly:

"Laugh again with just that look, child!"

He might as well have told me to fly. I was not one to laugh by order, and instead I made an effort to elude his grasp, which was none of the gentlest. He felt it, and, shoving me from him, said:

"Contrary, as I might have known she would be!"

Miss Michal laughed. "Lina is not used to your autocratic ways, dear master. But what was there peculiar about her laugh?"

"Nothing," he answered hastily; "I only fancied a passing resemblance to one I once knew. 'Twas nothing; the girl is eerie-looking enough to give rise to any fancies." Seeing she still looked curious, he added, in a tone of testy impatience: "What should I care for the giggling of a girl? Where is the German lesson for to-day?"

He took a book from Miss Michal's hand. His whole manner changed, as he read in a voice deep-toned as the trumpets that called Egmont to the scaffold, those heroic words with which the condemned prince greets them:

"*Horch! horch! Wie oft rief mich dieser Schall zum freyen Schritt nach dem Felde des Streits und des Siegs! Wie munter traten die Gefährten auf der gefährlichen römlichen Bahn! Auch ich schreite einem ehrenvollen Tode aus diesem Kerker entgegen; ich sterbe für die Freyheit, für die ich lebte und focht, und der ich mich jetzt leidend opfre.*"

He closed the volume, saying:

"Thus a true man meets death, Michal."

She answered only with a glance, but I saw it, and thought of Miriam and Esther, my old Bible heroines; and then, for an hour or more, they went on reading those strange-sounding words, while I sat and watched them.

Finally, the professor flung down the book, and, with a grave command to Miss Michal to "let reading alone, and mind her netting," left the room, apparently without remembering my presence.

This was my first introduction to Rothsay Cavendish, and here for the next six months our intercourse ended, save what was required by my weekly attendance on his lectures; but not the acquaintance, at least on my part, for I felt drawn to study him just as I would any of the strange animals Uncle Steve used to tell me about years before. Whenever he spoke to me, he used a tone of positive authority, which I could neither resent nor disobey. Besides, he had called me "eerie-looking," and I was at an age when girls are somewhat sensitive about such things. It was true, I knew. I needed only to look in my glass for confirmation; but, then, it was none of his affair. If any one in the class was reproved, his eye always seemed to rest on me; and a failure on my part to answer any question which he chose to ask, in the course of his lectures on English history, would irritate him more than if Sophie May or any of the other girls had blundered a dozen times. I was convinced that he disliked me, and I drew myself within my shell of reserve, which was growing quite hard by this time, and was as stolid and indifferent as a turtle whenever he came to read with Miss Michal.

She knew nothing of my feeling, for in this matter I kept my own counsel; but she was evidently annoyed that he took no more interest in *her* pupil, and always tried to place my achievements in the most favorable light. I had a truer eye and a more facile use of the pencil or crayon than herself, and, urged on by her praises and the approbation of our drawing-teacher, I had finished some quite commendable sketches, for a school-girl, of which I heard her speaking to the professor one day. I was in my own room, and could not avoid hearing all that was said.

"Clever!" he repeated. "Well, it might be thought so, perhaps, if that shot-tower — light-house, is it? well, light-house, then — was not quite the eighth of an inch out of the perpendicular; and that gray space of sand—water do you call it?—well, then, that thing in the distance is a ship I suppose. Really, Michal, your pupil's efforts are beyond criticism!"

It was my pet piece—a water-scene— to which all my memories of the Cove had lent an interest; and it had been praised by Herr Heller and Mademoiselle Berthier, who was herself an accomplished artist, and I drew my breath hard while I mentally vowed that it was the last time he should have occasion to criticise my drawing. I did not hear Miss Michal's reply, but the rejoinder was very audible.

"Remarkable? Yes, as a child's first attempts to walk. Zingarella is not a genius, Michal. She has the ordinary abilities of girls of her age — nothing more, I assure you."

The next day I surprised my teacher by requesting to go back to the rudimentary lessons in drawing; and for several weeks I worked at lines and circles, angles and curves, with a zeal that delighted him. It was good practice, and, thanks to the professor's criticisms, I have now a true and steady hand.

Our principal, after coming upon me very suddenly during my dusting and sweeping hours for the first few weeks, was apparently satisfied with my manner of performing my work, and left me to myself, though I never felt quite sure that her eye was not on me, except when in Miss Michal's room. She usually came there in the morning to inquire after her health, then went below to her duties; and so well did she know how to oil with smooth words or to cut with keen, decided ones any difficulty that occurred between the members of her large family, that there were few more peaceful households to be found. She deferred to no one but Mr. Cavendish; his slightest suggestions were listened to with respect, and generally adopted. Some of the girls insisted that she designed to make him "our principal" by marriage, but there were few that really believed so.

As the weather grew warm, and the days lengthened, Miss Michal was able to go down-stairs, and, with my assistance, to the lower end of the garden, where there was an old-fashioned grape-arbor. Here, when my lessons were over, I was permitted to read to her, and our reading was as varied as our moods. Science, biography, history, poetry, each had its turn, and opened to me a new world, to which her rich and varied culture gave an additional charm. One day she sent me to the school-room for a manuscript, which she thought I would find in a desk formerly used by herself. She gave me the key, and I ran to execute her commission. It was after school-hours, and the room was vacant, as I had expected. I unlocked the desk, and was laying aside the papers in search of the manuscript, when I observed among them a pencil-sketch, and with an irrepressible exclamation of surprise I ran with it to the window. It was a sketch of the Cedar Pond; a mere outline, faulty enough in some respects as compared with the one in my memory, but sufficiently accurate for me to identify each locality. There were Granny Hunt's house and barn, with the loose boards hanging by the end on the east side; the old barn-yard gate, with a stick set against it to keep it fast. I had handled that stick hundreds of times. There were the pond, the trees, the bluffs—rocky shelves and rough seams as familiar as life. The small figure by the pasture-bars—might it not have been Ollie waiting for me? And unconsciously the tears began to mingle with the smiles with which I had recognized each object.

"It's wonderful! The faces so like and yet so unlike!"

I had seen no one, heard no step, but there was no mistaking the voice; and I turned to meet the eager, questioning yet perplexed look of Mr. Cavendish—a look that seemed ready to wrench from the heart its most hidden secrets. For a second I cowered before it; then, raising my eyes, I looked right into his face.

"There—that movement!" he muttered, without withdrawing his eyes (I had raised my hand and swept back my falling hair), "it's as like as life. Who are you, girl?"

His tall form was bent forward in eager expectation, his tone hoarse from suppressed feeling; but I did not understand it then, and, impatient at being detained, I replied, a little maliciously:

"La Zingarella, sir."

He lifted his long finger and said impatiently:

"I am not trifling, child! Who are you?"

"Zerlina Lathrop."

A black shade of disappointment darkened his face, and he answered hastily, contemptuously, as I thought:

"Yes, I know, adopted daughter of Mrs. Lathrop Tyler, pupil at Oaklawn, etc."

"Add pupil by the charity of Mrs. Ellis, and pauper by birth, and the history will be complete," I said, quickly, irritated by his tone.

He looked surprised a moment, then stretched out his hand, saying in the gentle, tender tone I had never heard him use before, save when speaking to Miss Michal:

"I did not mean to wound you, child. I am sorry your lot has been so sad. Let us be friends."

I touched his hand, and hastened away. When I joined Miss Michal, with the manuscript, she was coming up the garden-walk with Mr. Cavendish. She took the paper, saying we would read it some other time. He did not notice me at all—I doubt if he saw me, so absorbed did he seem in some sad train of thought; but, lingering in the porch for Miss Michal, I heard him say, as he turned to leave her:

"No, child, there is no hope. Dr. B—— thinks her days are numbered."

"God help them! It is terrible!" she murmured, as she watched him going with long strides toward the woods.

CHAPTER XIV.

MOTHER AND DAUGHTER.

"Your brother's coming, Miss Michal?"

"Yes, my mother's son, James Sancroft, and our brother Edward, born after her marriage with my father."

I resumed my work. I was putting the trimming upon a travelling-dress for Mrs. Ellis, and remained silent for some moments. I had heard the girls speak of Mrs. Ellis's sons, but this was the first time that Miss Michal had spoken of them to me, and the announcement that they would spend part of the summer vacation at home took me by surprise.

"It will be very pleasant for you, Miss Michal," I said at length.

"Yes, indeed. Poor fellows, they have not been home in a year!"

"Why don't they come home every vacation?"

"Our mother does not think it best, as long as she is at the head of such a school. It is very hard for her, for she dotes on her boys."

"She!"—Miss Michal looked up at me, and I felt constrained to add—"I did not think any thing hard for her."

"You misjudge her. Her manner is undemonstrative—but she is a woman of very strong affections. If their channel is narrow, it is deep—all the deeper because they are never permitted to overflow, but are met on all sides by her idea of duty, backed by an inflexible will. One must live with our mother to know her. She is no dreamer like me, but, if she is exacting with others, she is no less so with herself."

She had let the dress which she was folding fall upon her lap, and seemed lost in thought. I fancied my heedless remark had stirred some memories not altogether pleasant, but still I clung to the subject, and said:

"You are not at all alike, I think."

"No; I have naturally no practical

" His tall form was bent forward in eager expectation. "

Righted at Last, p. 74.

talent, and little executive force. My mother has a great deal, and it was a long, long time before we could understand each other—a time when I could see nothing but the briers and thorns in the way, Lina."

"Are your brothers like you?"

"No; James, who is only brother by courtesy, has much of his mother's energy and business talent. He is a fine scholar, took the 'Valedictory' two years ago, at Amherst, when he graduated. He is now studying law. Our mother has high hopes of him. Edward is still a boy, preparing to enter college—not much older than you, frank, truthful, merry, and kind-hearted. You will like him very much."

The school had closed for the long summer vacation, the day before. All the morning, the halls and stairways had echoed with the bustle caused by the departure of the pupils; and it was in the stillness that had succeeded, that Miss Michal had spoken thus of her brothers. We were sitting in her room, very busy in giving the last touch to some dresses, for, the next morning, she and her mother were to leave for Springfield. It was Mrs. Ellis's native place, and she felt quite sure that her old physician there would be able to restore Miss Michal's health. The brothers were to meet them there, and return with them to Oaklawn.

The programme of my holidays had been announced by Mrs. Ellis, the evening before.

"Zerlina," she had said, "Mr. and Mrs. Tyler wish you to spend your vacation here, if I can find any thing for you to do that will remunerate me for the trouble. It is not convenient for them to receive you, but they express great pleasure at hearing such a favorable report of your progress and conduct. Here is the key to the linen-closet; you will find a large basketful which needs mending. I notice that you are a neat sewer, and I want you to look it all over, and put it in perfect order. The cook will remain in the house, as will also Miss Rathburn, and I shall expect you to look after her until I return."

I answered with a brief "Very well, ma'am," for her whole air and manner shamed me from showing the repugnance I felt to one part of my duty. I would rather have mended or made up all the linen ever spun by Penelope and her maidens, or taken Irish Margaret's place in the kitchen, than been compelled to spend twenty-four hours with Ann Rathburn, to say nothing of three weeks. She was the half-witted daughter of a very wealthy New-York family, who kept her at school in the country to "keep her out of sight," paying lavishly, it was said, for the extra care and attention she required. She was obstinate, self-willed, and ungovernable by all save Mrs. Ellis; and, indeed, it required all her authority to make her keep herself personally decent. My "town-poor breeding" held her and her habits in infinite disgust, and something of this feeling was visible in my face, I suppose, the following morning, when, after watching Mrs. Ellis and Michal enter the carriage and drive away, I turned and met her grinning, leering face; for, during the next ten days, she made my life a torment. I had studied very hard for the past four months; I had also worked hard, at hours when other growing girls were at play or asleep; and now, when the strain was relaxed, and my overtasked brain and irritable nerves cried out for rest—mere physical rest—to be obliged to look after that girl—to care for her slatternly, ill-kept person—to see her stolid eye and hanging lip—to watch her at her meals, and see that she did not overeat—to baffle her sly malice, or contend against her mulish obstinacy—nearly drove me mad, and every day's experience increased my horror and disgust.

Margaret was little help to me, for all her leisure was given to gossipping cousins, who took advantage of the mistress's absence to visit her, or in trudging into the city to attend some ceremony or *fête* of the Church, and I was left alone for hours with this girl. I think I was growing idiotic or insane myself, for my head throbbed and ached as if all the blood in my meagre body was centred there; and, one afternoon, I grew so dizzy that I could no longer see to sew. I laid my head down upon the pile of linen on the table before me, and fell into a kind of stupor, I suppose, for, after a while, I was aroused by a torrent of Irish objurgations, among which I only distinguished the name of Miss Rathburn.

"What of her? Where is she, Margaret?" I said, rousing myself with difficulty, for every bone in my body was full of pain.

"Where is she! An', shure, ain't she in the pantry—an' hasn't she gone an' made a baste o' herself, and eat all me illigant leg o' mutton, and the beautiful pears the misthress saved for the sweetmates, an' shure won't she be in purgathory the morn, an' the divil don't help her, for the saints never'll dirthy their fingers wi' the likes o' her!"

I followed Margaret to the pantry, and there the miserable girl sat upon the floor, still munching the pears. She looked up at me, more like some wild animal than any thing human, while Margaret pointed to the roast joint, which was all haggled up, saying:

"It's a divil a bit you or I'll be touchin' the lave o' that, miss!"

I told Ann to get up and come with me. At first, she only swelled up, and looked at me like an angry toad; but, finally, by dint of coaxing, I got her to her room, and turned the key on her, as Mrs. Ellis had told me to do every night. True, the sun was not yet down, but I was glad to get rid of her, and glad when Margaret left me—after assuring me, over and over, that she only left the pantry-key in the door for just a minit, while she went to the door to speak to Bridget Flanaghan, an' the creyther slipped in unbeknownst—for my head seemed bursting.

I flung myself on the lounge, and, after tossing about for a while, fell into a kind of drowse, in which the face of that girl still haunted me. At length, a strange noise startled me, and, with every nerve throbbing, I sprang up. It came again—a low, gurgling sound, as of one choking, and from Miss Rathburn's room. I hastened as fast as I could to the door, and entered. I had no light, but the mellow August moonbeams flooded the chamber, and fell full upon the convulsed features and writhing limbs of that unfortunate girl. She was in a fit. I had heard that in her childhood she had been subject to them, and I ran to call Margaret—then returned to her bedside. The white foam was about her lips—flecked with blood—for she had bitten her tongue badly, and her face was livid; but disgust was swallowed up in pity and terror, and I hung over her, entreating her to speak. Encouraged by a slight cessation in her struggles, I bent lower, and tried to raise her head, which lay all awry, when she suddenly flung up her arms, seized me around the neck, and drew my head down into the bed with the force of a vice, while she fastened her strong, yellow teeth in my arm. I screamed—a faint, smothered scream—for my position was suffocating, and that might have been my last cry, had not Margaret reached the room, and set up such a howl as only Milesian lungs can utter. I was just conscious of a crash below—of a quick step along the hall—and Margaret's emphatic "God save ye, sir!" when, with a strong but futile effort to release myself, I fainted.

I was in my own room, and on my own bed, when I again became conscious. The door of Miss Michal's room was open, and a lamp on the table there revealed the features of two men standing by my bed. The one with his fingers on my wrist was Dr. Herrick, and the other Prof. Cavendish.

"Fever?" asked the latter, as the doctor removed his fingers.

"I am afraid so, but we will see what can be done," was the reply, as he walked into Miss Michal's room, and took a pencil to write a recipe.

A spluttering, unearthly noise at the other end of the hall, reminded me of the horror there, and I shuddered from head to foot. Mr. Cavendish's face, so full of pity and almost motherly tenderness, changed at the sound, his eyebrows sharpened, and he said to Dr. Herrick, who entered, prescription in hand:

"Doctor, that idiotic fiend will kill her if she remains here."

Again the fingers were applied to my wrist.

"I am afraid you are right, but, unless removed very early in the morning, I will not answer for it. Where are her friends?"

"Too far off to be of any use. But she can be moved now, without any ill effect. Carried a half mile or so?"

"Yes; and it will be better than to leave her here. Her nervous system seems completely unstrung, and she needs careful nursing, and great quiet."

A scream from Margaret, and a supplication in the name of the saints, rang through the hall, and the doctor hurried away.

"Zingarella, poor child, will you go home with me? My housekeeper will look after you, and you cannot stay here. That cannibal will eat you up. Will you go, child?"

I put my hand in his, and made an effort to rise. I should have gone to the world's end in answer to a look and a tone like that.

He smiled, went out of the room a few minutes, then came back and began wrapping the bed-coverings about me, when I noticed, for the first time, my arm. Below the short sleeve of my dress, where Ann Rathburn had fastened her teeth, it was bandaged with fine white linen. I saw it with dismay, and asked, instantly:

"Where did you find this bandage?"

"What, now! Where? Why, on the table, yonder. We tore up some trash or other!" It was the old, testy, impatient voice again.

"Oh, dear! It was one of Mrs. Ellis's best pillow-slips. What will she say?"

"Mrs. Ellis be ——!" he muttered something between his teeth, and I sank back again, too deathly faint to care what became of me, so that I was beyond hearing the voice or seeing the face of Ann Rathburn.

CHAPTER XV.

THE PROFESSOR'S FAMILY.

"ALL man's days, he eateth in darkness, and he hath much sorrow and wrath in his sickness!"

I was an exception to these words of the Preacher, or they did not exactly apply to town poor in the nineteenth century. It was very pleasant for me to be watched over, cared for, and consulted about, pleasant to listen to the hushed tones and careful footfalls, pleasant to feel that I *was* somebody in the universe, cared for with love and tenderness, even though it was only by an elderly woman, and a man in middle life, who, with no companion but his great dog, sat day after day in a room adjoining the one I occupied, surrounded by books, maps, manuscripts, telescopes, and quadrants, with every muscle of his iron face corrugated and seamed by intense thought, as he pored over them, but ready, at my lightest movement, to step to my bedside, and discharge the duties of nurse with womanly tenderness and skill; all the pleasanter because God had mercifully rendered me unconscious during the hours of my greatest peril, as I learned from Mrs. Ross.

"Mr. Rothsay, that is, the professor,"

she said, correcting herself, "drove up here one evening, and brought you into the house in his arms, just as I have known him to carry a poor, motherless lamb when he was a lad, and laid you down there. It was all we could do to keep the breath of life in you for more than a week, and all the time he watched you, and would let no one give the medicine but himself. It is just his way always. But, by God's blessing, we conquered the fever, and you'll soon be about again, I reckon."

Not a word of her own unwearied care, only a face expressive of the utmost thankfulness for my recovery! I might have been a child of the house all my days, and she could not have spoken more kindly or gratefully, and I took her hand and covered it with kisses. She withdrew it hastily, but not unkindly, saying:

"I am only the housekeeper, miss."

"But none the less Rothsay Cavendish's friend, and Zingarella's friend, Alice," said the professor, looking in at the door. "A poor time she would have had of it with gruels and broths if this hand had had their stirring.—Come, let us look at that arm, child."

He unbound my arm where the marks of Ann Rathburn's teeth still showed red and swollen, and dressed it carefully. The bandage then in use was not Mrs. Ellis's torn pillow-slip, but we both thought of it, for, with a comical grimace, he said:

"Alice Ross has taken very good care of it, Zingarella. She's a careful woman, specially of old linen. I told her that Mrs. Ellis set great store by that piece, and she'll be careful of it, I assure you."

"She was indeed very choice of those covers, and you oughtn't to have torn them, sir."

"No; I suppose we ought to have left your arm undressed while I made a journey to the tombs of the Pharaohs, and stripped the mummies for a piece of waste linen. Indeed, I suppose I ought not to have burst through the back window that night, but have left that vampire to eat you up. But I don't confess daily that I have done those things I ought not to have done, for nothing, child."

I could not help smiling at his words, and instantly he became very grave and thoughtful. He turned slowly back to his room, and for three or four days he scarcely addressed to me as many words; yet, more than once, when I looked at the still figure seated by the table, I knew that his glance had been fixed upon me with a look that seemed to search my heart.

I was soon able to sit up and have on my clothes, then I began to walk about my room, which was in one of the angles of the cottage, and to look with delight upon the beautiful views from the windows. The country wore a very different look now from that which met my eye that March evening when I stood at the gate of Oaklawn in the rain. The location of the house was very beautiful, and, though the grounds contained but few acres, they had been laid out by one who had been content to follow Nature rather than attempt to rival her. On the north and east of the house circled that beautiful growth of wood which I had so often admired from Miss Michal's window. Here and there an opening had been made, through which one caught the silvery gleam of the waters of the Connecticut, and glimpses of the line of rugged hills beyond. To the south were fair meadows, orchards, and cornfields, with clusters of farm-buildings, overshadowed by green trees. On the west, the garden sloped down to a chattering mountain-brook, that leaped upon you unawares from beneath a fine growth of pines, and went hurrying onward to lose itself in the beautiful river. Beyond this stretched a broad expanse of undulating country, bounded by the hazy outlines of the Hartford-County hills. Beautiful as it was then, with the rosy flush of summer deepening into the golden haze of autumn upon the hills, I came to love it none the less in its bare and wintry ruggedness; for, when wearied of the tiresome routine of school duties, I frequently turned my steps toward the grove of pines, and sat, folded in my cloak, listening to their weird murmurs, in the hush of the wintry sunset, until the farm-house lights came out one after another, and the pale gleam of the wintry moon tipped the skeleton trees with silver.

But thoughts of my neglected duties at Oaklawn began to haunt me; and one day, when Mr. Cavendish entered my room, I spoke of my return.

"Not to-day, nor to-morrow, nor next week, Zingarella. You are not strong enough yet. You are a pale, puny, good-for-nothing thing. You can't go to Oaklawn yet. But, if you are weary of this room, you may ramble over all this wing of the house, which all consists of but two rooms besides this; the one adjoining contains some things at which you may like to look; the room beyond, books—such as a young girl may like to read. It's not an extensive promenade, you see," he added, as he threw open the door, "but it is better than a tramp to Oaklawn."

I stood on the threshold for a moment in surprise; the room was long, running the whole length of the building, east and west, and lighted by a deep bay-window in the west end, and skylights of soft, ground glass above. A heavy curtain of rich, crimson silk was looped away from the window, one part flung carelessly over the back of a large stuffed chair, as if it were done with a hasty hand. A low rocking-chair, covered with the same rich material, stood near, with a hassock to match. Near the great window was an elegant piano, with the lid thrown back, and the westering sunbeams fell full upon the white keys, and made it easy to read the name and notes of the Scotch melody open against the music-rack. The floor was covered with a carpet more beautiful than any that I had ever seen, and the delicately-tinted walls hung with pictures, with pieces of armor, weapons of offence and defence, interspersed. It was so different from anything I had anticipated—so different from my own room, which was amply though plainly furnished—that I looked round for the professor, hoping for some word of explanation, but he had disappeared. I stole lightly forward to the piano, for I was not sure that an extra jar would not cause the whole scene to vanish. The dust lay undisturbed upon the keys, and upon the right, close by a vase of withered flowers (spring flowers, I knew by the leaves), lay a lady's glove, as if the wearer, after arranging her flowers, had flung it down to play out the melody they had stirred in her heart. That glove I thought must have belonged to the lady of whom Sophie May had told me when I first came to Oaklawn—his sister, I knew now, from some words of Miss Michal's; but where was she, and what made her absence so terrible, as her words that night had implied? Busy with these queries, I passed on to the other end of the room, where a curtain of the same hue and texture as that over the bay-window depended from a wide arch; lifted it, and stood within a smaller room, with a corresponding window, fitted up as a library. Giving a hasty glance at the books through the glass doors, I returned to the other room to examine the pictures. They were chiefly landscapes —views of English and American scenery, and, whatever I might think of them now, they seemed masterpieces of art then. I no longer wondered that the professor had spoken so slightingly of my drawing. At length, I paused before a group of portraits, three of which were of the usual proportions, the fourth what is usually termed cabinet size. The two at the right were evidently father and son; neither was handsome, as far as regularity of feature and beauty of outline

were concerned, but the deep-set gray
eyes and square brows were instinct with
conscious power, while the strong jaw,
and close, firm lips, indicated courage to
perform, and strength to endure. That
they represented the professor and his
father I did not doubt. On the next
canvas were two children, a boy and girl,
with arms interlacing, fair-haired, blue-
eyed, with faces that seemed to light up
the dark background with sunshine. Both
were very beautiful, and, at first sight, as
unlike the former as possible, yet a closer
inspection detected the same look of latent power which gave to them such
marked individuality, with this difference in the elder ones, it was power sub-
ordinated to reason and high principle ;
in the face of the handsome, self-willed
boy it was simply a laughing defiance,
" I will do as I please, if the heavens
fall ! "

The other frame encircled a face of a
different type from either of the above—
that of a boy, hardly beyond the first
stages of childhood, small, dark-eyed,
dark-haired, daring, resolute, and impetuous. Something there was familiar about
this. I climbed upon a chair to get a
better view—I was not long at a loss—it
was very like the miniature of Mr. Annesley, which Miss Agnes had given me on
her marriage.

" That face seems to interest you
greatly, Zingarella," said the professor,
who had entered the room unheard and
unobserved by me. " Naturally enough,
for he has something of a gypsy look, as
well as yourself, but let me assure you
he is ugly enough by this time."

" Are his ancestors even now swapping mules in Spain ? " I asked, gravely.

" No ; though he may be, for aught I
know," he answered, smiling. " Ralph
Saville's ancestors were rooted, for many
centuries, in the north of England ; but
some chance drew his father to this
country, where he died. But what of
the other faces, girl ? Speak out."

I told him my thought of the father

and son. " Right ! " he said, slowly ;
" they did try to do their duty honestly
and without murmuring, even if not always wisely—man proposes, but God dis-
poses—let us therefore take heart.—But
what of these, child ? One would think
that face," pointing to the fair-haired boy,
" as worthy of your high consideration as
that little fire-eater — it was twice as
handsome, at least."

" Yes, sir ; but—he thinks more of
having his own way than any thing
else."

" And what if he did ? " he growled,
his eyebrows running up into angles and
working restlessly. " Who was to blame
for it, but those that petted and indulged
him, until he never knew the meaning
of self-denial ? Poor Philip !—I wonder
how I could ever think you like him ? "

So this was the friend I was supposed
to resemble. I took another look at the
handsome face, and wondered too—not
if I was like the picture, but if my companion was not a little insane—then
turned to the one he called Ralph Saville,
and asked :

" Were they brothers, these two boys
and that girl ? "

The momentary excitement had subsided, and he answered pleasantly :

" No ; there was only a distant cousin-
ship between their families. We all had
Saville blood in our veins."

" Those children are your brother
and sister," I said.

" How do you know ? "

" Because they have something of the
same expression," I returned, glancing
again at the portrait of himself ; " only
they are—"

" Are what ? "

" A great deal handsomer, sir."

" Wonderful, Zingarella ! So, with
beauty and ugliness right before you, you
are able to tell the difference. Your
artistic perception is worthy of Michael
Angelo."

He spoke in that dry, ironical manner which he sometimes used, but I had

a feeling that he was not angry, and I said, bluntly:

"I suppose you are laughing at me, sir; but that face," pointing to the youth, "is not ugly, neither is that of the gentleman. They are good, strong, honest faces, and I like them."

"Well, how do you like one of them now? I suppose you will say age has improved it?" he returned, with one of his odd grimaces.

"No, sir. But I like you now very much, if you would not make such ugly shapes."

He laughed almost a merry laugh as he said:

"Truth from a gypsy. You are as outspoken as you are odd, Zingarella."

He was turning away, when, anxious to know more, I said, with a glance at the brother and sister—"Are they still living?"

He looked me intently in the face for a moment, and, somehow, my own eyes filled with tears as he said:

"One is dead, and the other—dying in an insane retreat."

The hard-lined face quivered with suppressed emotion, and, turning suddenly he left me alone. A few moments later, I saw him pacing slowly back and forth beneath the pines.

"Mrs. Ross," I said, that evening, when that good woman came, as usual, to see if I was comfortable before she slept—"is there no hope of Miss Cavendish's recovery?"

She looked at me a second, in great surprise, before she said:

"Is it Miss Helen you mean, miss?"

"Yes—Mr. Cavendish told me about her himself."

"Indeed!"

"Yes; we were looking at the portraits, and I asked him about them—he has thought me like his brother, it seems."

"You are not a bit like his brother, miss, and so I told him; but you sometimes have a look like Miss Flora Saville, or like her portrait that used to hang in the old hall at home."

"Where was that, Mrs. Ross?"

"Far enough from here, miss," she said, with a sigh. "The Cavendish family are English, and they lived at a place called the Holm, and a beautiful place it was, too."

"Was Mr. Cavendish born there?"

"No; he was born in the West Indies, when his father went on his marriage, but he and his mother spent some years at the Holm, during his childhood."

"And where were the others born?"

"In Jamaica, too—first Miss Helen, then Master Philip."

"How did they come here?"

"Some business changes—I never knew what rightly, made their father move to New York, where he died just after Mr. Rothsay entered college."

"Did their mother die too? I saw no portrait of her," I said, recalling that circumstance.

"No; she soon married a gay young officer; not much older than Mr. Rothsay, whom she had known in Jamaica. Mr. Rothsay made Captain Eastlake a present of her portrait."

"And the children, Mrs. Ross?"

"They stayed with Mr. Rothsay. He sent for me to come over to this country —I had been raised in the family, miss, my old master was dead, my husband too. I had no ties to keep me, for Mr. Edwards's family were mostly abroad, so I came."

"Here—to this house?"

"Dear heart, no! We had a beautiful place just out of the city. Philip, poor boy, fretted hard for his mother at first; he had been her idol, but he finally got accustomed to the change. Dear, dear, how merry they used to be!"

"Did he die then? Mr. Cavendish said he was dead."

"No; but I've sometimes thought 'twould have been better if he had. He grew up brave, bright, high-spirited, and handsome — generous, affectionate, but

6

self-willed and passionate. He would not hear to any one, not even his brother, who would have laid down his life for him—and—so—well-a-day—there was trouble, and he went away—to India, we heard, for he never came to say 'good-by' to us, nor sent us so much as a line; and, a while after, we heard he was killed in a skirmish with the natives there, for it seemed he entered the army."

"Did this make Miss Helen crazy?"

"No; though she began to be poorly about that time, and Mr. Rothsay took her to Europe, where they were absent some years, travelling about. After we had news of Master Philip's death, her mind began to wander. Mr. Rothsay had all the doctors far and near, and it was a long time before he would consent to send her away, though the doctors all advised it. Finally, she grew so wild that he decided to put her at the Retreat in H—— where the chief physician is his friend and classmate. He bought this place, and we came here to live, to be near her. Sometimes, she seems as well as ever, and she will stay with us weeks, and they will read, and walk, and sing, and it will seem quite like old times, if he could only forget the terrible curse that is likely to come back at any moment, and compel him to take her back to the Retreat. He watches and waits upon her, as if she were a little child, and when I think of the place and honor he has given up to be near her—O miss, there's never another like him in the whole world!"

The faithful woman's eyes were full of tears, and perhaps it was because she saw mine were, also, that she lingered, candle in hand, while I asked:

"He teaches at Oaklawn, I suppose, to while away the time, then?"

"Yes, Mrs. Ellis's husband was a distant relative of his family, and he is glad to help her educate her children. He is very fond of Master Edward and Miss Michal— But, there—I hear his step. If he has a fault in the world, it is being so irregular about eating and sleeping. I doubt if he eats a morsel to-night, but I'll see. Strange he should have told you about the children, child!"

In a day or two, I was out of doors wandering about the garden among Alice Ross's old-fashioned flowers, or leaning over the low wall, listening to the babble of the brook, and the low murmur of the pines. They reminded me of a project I had decided to execute during vacation—that of writing to Uncle Steve and little Adeline. In term-time, all our letters passed under the eye of our principal, and I had a feeling that I could not write to them like myself if Mrs. Ellis's critical eye was to scan the letter. The next day, while I was waiting to ask for some paper, the professor entered with an open letter in his hand, and gave me a note addressed in Miss Michal's writing, saying:

"There's something for you, child."

I ran it over eagerly—then, more slowly, for the contents took me by surprise. At length I looked up, and met his amused glance.

"Well," he said, "have you nothing to say?"

"I am very grateful to Mrs. Ellis, indeed—"

"Grateful to Mrs. Ellis!" he interrupted impatiently. "Nobody doubts that, but let me tell you, she never would have made you the offer if she did not expect to benefit herself as well as you! She is an excellent manager—circumstances have compelled her to be so, but she never deals in humbug; therefore, she will not expect any specific mark of gratitude from you. Have you no feeling about the matter personally, child? That is what I mean?"

"Yes, I am very glad to be independent of Mr. Tyler—to be in a position to take care of myself. You can't think how I have longed to do this, sir!" and, overcome by a crowd of memories, I burst into tears.

He stared at me a moment, in surprise; at length he said:

"Look here, Zingarella, was not this Mr. Tyler kind to you?"

"I don't think he ever liked me, sir; besides, he had a child of his own, and it was natural that he should think more of him than of me."

I was in no mood to enter into the details of my life with Mr. Tyler, for Miss Michal's words had made me somewhat unsettled about it myself, and I was glad my vague reply satisfied him, for he said:

"Very true; but I had been thinking how proud they would be of your success—for it is a success, child, notwithstanding what I said of Mrs. Ellis—for, not even to serve herself, would she place any one in a position of trust whom she did not thoroughly approve and respect."

"They will be glad, at least Mrs. Tyler will, and so will two other friends, to whom, with your permission, I wish to write to-day."

In a few words, I told him of Uncle Steve and little Adeline, and his consent was readily given.

Reader, I was to be a teacher at "Oaklawn Seminary." Promoted to that honor in consideration of my "scholarship, diligence, discretion, and practical talent," which, it pleased our principal to say, were "beyond my years."

True, my department would only include the juveniles who were coming in at the commencement of the term. It had but a trifling salary beyond my board, for the first term, but it was no less the realization of a long-cherished dream. It was probably well for my credit for discretion and practical talent that Mrs. Ellis did not see the letter I wrote to little Adeline Leete that day.

Two days later, I went back to Oaklawn, in compliance with the request of Mrs. Ellis, to prepare for her arrival. I was very sorry to leave the Pines, its odd master, and Alice Ross; and the latter really regretted my departure, I knew—but the master—it was just as if a stout shag-bark hickory had given shelter to some poor, stray, weary-winged bird for awhile, and, when the storm was over, had said: "Go, you have no further need of me; I never needed you!" At least, so I read the close, grim face that was opposite me at the breakfast-table the morning I left, and the quick voice that said: "I am going to H—— to-day, so, good-by, child;" and I was ready to cry, as I thanked him for his kindness, and said I would like to come sometimes to the Pines, to walk in the grove, if he pleased.

"Come to the Pines, yes, you'll be welcome; but to walk in the grove, nonsense! What does such a girl as you want of such a place? Go out in the sunshine, and among the roses, and let the pines alone. They are not good for you!"

"I think they are, sir. I never had any roses, but when I was a little girl I knew the pines well, and they seem like old friends. I like their murmur and their strong aromatic smell. It makes me strong."

"You are an odd child, Zingarella—but come when you please—talk to the pines, or to Alice, as you list, but come *alone*. Remember, I will have none of the other girls here."

Thus we parted. I had grasped Miss Michal's hand, felt her kiss upon my cheek, replied to Mrs. Ellis's kind but brief inquiry after my health, and been presented to the young gentleman as Miss Zerlina Lathrop, the junior teacher, and, with a passing glance at them, was following Mrs. Ellis to the hall to receive some orders about the baggage, when I overheard one of them saying:

"*That* your *protégée*, Michal! She ought to possess the seven cardinal virtues, for she's homely enough. Here I have been conjuring up visions of a fairy-like little mortal, and you introduce me to a brownie, who gives one glance from her eerie-looking eyes, and then vanishes!"

"Hush, Edward! I never told you Lina was pretty, so you may thank your own vain imagination for your mistake. But I like her face—it is good, bright, and very expressive. I know James will agree with me."

"It indicates a good deal of character, I should say," returned a voice I supposed to be James Sancroft's, "but of what quality I must be excused from deciding, as I gave it only a passing glance. Pretty it certainly is not."

His voice had all the clearness of his mother's, but was much more carefully modulated.

Edward Ellis laughed merrily. "There spoke Judge Sancroft, that is to be, Michal. You have no idea how cautious and sententious James is getting to be—all his words are sifted and weighed before he speaks. He is already accounted a 'rising man' in Amherst; his nod will be equal to Lord Burleigh's one of these days."

"Edward is rather hard upon us law-students, sometimes, sister. We are obliged to be very industrious, and, besides, every one does not possess the fortunate privilege of saying just what comes into one's head with impunity."

"Fortunate! Is it not rather dangerous, James?"

"No, Michal dear," returned Edward, "not if one feels friendly with all the world. But that girl's name haunts me. Zerlina—I have heard it somewhere, I'm certain."

"Probably, in Mozart's opera," suggested James.

"No; I remember now; it was a scene from the 'Beggars' Opera,' rather! It must have been the name of that funny-looking girl that Aunty Lester and I encountered in Bradshaw Church, when we were visiting at Fernside. Her name was Zerlina or Zillah, or something of the kind!"

So here was a *dénoûment*. Edward Ellis was the boy who had opened the slip door for me in Bradshaw Church, and the gentle lady was his aunt. She must have made that sketch of the Pond, and Granny Hunt's house, which Miss Michal had told me was drawn by a relative many years ago. I did not tell her why the picture interested me, then, for she was occupied, so I had no fear of being identified with that child, unless I chose to avow the truth.

Should I do it? Should I drop the shawls and satchels I had been slowly gathering, and go into the parlor and announce myself the heroine of that scene?

I did not; no person, especially at my age, likes to appear ridiculous in the eyes of others, and I instantly decided to keep my own counsel. By this time, I had learned the value of Mr. Annesley's advice.

Edward Ellis's opinion of my face occurred to me rather unpleasantly that night, but after all we were, perhaps, far better friends for my lack of beauty. Nature had been no niggard in forming him. Less intellectual than Michal or James Sancroft, he seemed to revel in the perfection of physical life. Handsome, affectionate, frank, buoyant, and self-confident, his sanguine temperament craved a confidante, and he chose me, probably, because I was the best listener in the family, and some one to *talk to* is generally a desideratum with boys of eighteen.

There might have been danger to me in this had I not been so often, unintentionally, been made to feel that my lack of beauty was supposed to indicate a corresponding lack of sensibility. Yet, so wholly unpremeditated were these chance sayings, that I never thought of being vexed or wounded, though I sometimes wondered if the owner of this or that pretty face which he described to me so enthusiastically (he had a half-dozen every vacation) really did care more for him than my plain self.

Mrs. Ellis herself, who shared in her

son's admiration of beauty, held, I suspect, to this theory in regard to plain women; for she never seemed to feel any anxiety about our intimacy, though if Sophie May's fair face, or Annie Fairman's roguish eyes, looked in upon us while he was there, she was always on the alert. Beyond the usual commonplaces, my acquaintance with James Sancroft did not extend. He had no need of me as yet, and never wasted time on people whom he did not need.

CHAPTER XVI.

THREE YEARS LATER.

I am conscious that I have dwelt too minutely on the events of my childhood. I will now pass over three years, premising that I am still at Oaklawn Seminary. I have left the place but once in that period, and then I went by request to Chesterwood, to attend the funeral of Augustus Tyler. He was a member of the Freshman class at Yale, but his was not the kind of character to withstand the temptations of college-life, and several complaints had reached his parent's ears, when he was drowned by the sudden upsetting of a boat—drowned on Sunday, with the sound of a score of church-bells mingling with the rush of water in his ears as he sank. The brief note that recalled me to my old home was signed by his father, and, during the ride, I wondered much how he would take the blow, and what special lesson he would read me in view of this terrible event. But when I returned the distant bow of Mrs. Reed and Sara, who, in their heavy robes of deep mourning, looked more impenetrable and unmalleable than ever, and, with Miss Agnes's tears upon my cheek, followed her into the well-remembered study, and saw that face, so shorn of its arrogant self-conceit and self-righteousness, so shrunken with horror, and wan with grief—

when I noticed his shrunken limbs and his effort to greet me in the old condescending, patronizing manner, which, after a few syllables, broke into smothered sobs—I felt he was learning a lesson himself which would leave him little time for others. In taking from him his idol, Death had stripped him also of his wrappings of creed and conventionality, and left for the time the nerves of the man bare. I stayed there two days, during which there was no allusion to my past, but much pleasure expressed by Miss Agnes at my success; and, when I took my leave of Mr. Tyler, and he said, with a kind of bewildered air: "I am glad you came, Zerlina. I thought it would be a comfort to Mrs. Tyler to see you, for your course at Oaklawn has been very commendable indeed, and I want to say that I may have erred in my method with you in the past. I fear I did with *him*"—I felt that henceforth, so far as I was concerned, there was peace between us.

Miss Agnes whispers as she parts from me with many tears: "He is so conscientious, so self-exacting, and it's so hard for men to bear trouble!" while I think that her sweet face is more than ever like my pond-lilies, so fair and pale, and ride back to Oaklawn half pitying and half envying her simplicity.

A few months later, I received a letter from her, saying that, as God in His wisdom had left them without any very near ties to bind them to home on earth, they were about to dedicate themselves anew to His service, and, in pursuance of their long-cherished plan, would sail in the spring as missionaries to the East. "We go at the eleventh hour, my dear," she went on, "and at times I tremble at my own weakness and inefficiency; but I remember the parable of the laborers in the vineyard, and I feel also that my little dead baby will help me to find my way to those poor heathen mothers' hearts, and, for the rest, I seem to hear His blessed voice saying, '*Lo, I am with you alway, even unto the end of the world!'* That you may hear it and trust it always, my dear child, will be my earnest prayer."

God forgive me that the thought should ever have crossed my mind that *she* was too weak for this sacred office! —that I should forget for one moment who it was that "sat over against the sepulchre" and watched out that night of terror and despair—that it was a woman, a repentant Magdalen, whom He selected to bear to the chosen disciples the blessed tidings, "*He is not here; He is risen!*"—tidings that have sounded down the ages above the din of sin and strife, bringing life and immortality to light. If a life of patient endeavor, of humility, and humble, hopeful trust, have power to win those heathen mothers to the better way, Miss Agnes will not have gone in vain. She has already joined that noble army of martyrs who have laid down their lives for the truth's sake, but not without hope of success, for already "the day is breaking in the East of which the prophets told," and those lonely scattered graves gleam like beacons in the morning light.

Mr. Tyler was less single-minded and unselfish, for it is only when the soul is lifted out of and above self that we are able to "see no man save Jesus only;" less humble and devoted, yet "whatsoever is right he shall receive," therefore, God be with him.

I received another letter about this time, which contained news of great interest to me. It was from little Adeline Leete, and told of changes at the Cove, which had brought certain families of Methodists to reside there; of an earnest-minded, excellent man, who had been stationed near there to look after them, and gather into the fold such stray sheep as are usually found about sea-shore hamlets; of a camp-meeting in the woods, where many had been converted, and among them little Adeline herself. Her letter announcing this was the *Jubilate Deo* of a young,

fervid soul, through which trembled the low minor chord of humility and self-distrust. I could feel the young heart palpitating with alternate hope and fear as I ran over the lines, and my own throbbed in unison. I was not like her. Nature, aided by circumstances, had made me less impressible and sympathetic, cooler and more cautious; but I rejoiced greatly in her joy, and many times the thought of that letter—some word or sentence—pierced the darkness and mistrust which shrouded me, and sent me to my duties with a patient if not a contented heart.

Does it seem strange that I am not content, reader? Remember, I am back at Oaklawn; teachers and pupils have changed, but I am still "teacher of the higher English branches," and considered by our principal, and sometimes by myself (God help me!), a part of the mechanism of the institution, and am referred to as a sort of walking compendium of the rules and regulations of the place. I have a salary which, if not large, suffices for my necessities — a "home," which means a room shared with another teacher, and am therefore considered respectable and independent. Our principal says so; she frequently says to our minister, Dr. Smith, and others, that "Miss Lathrop is quite indispensable—Oaklawn would not be itself without her—she is so useful;" and, sinner as I know her to be, it sometimes irritates me to hear it; and I often watch the birds and squirrels when out with my division on our long walks, and wonder if indeed the whole end and aim of life is to be *useful*—wonder, if compelled to go on thus year after year, dispensing the treasures of the heart and brain to the many, with no return from any source beneath the sun, how long one's individuality and amiability will last. Not always, I fear; for at times I am conscious of such a hollowness and craving within me that I know well if there is that "which scattereth yet increaseth," it is not always the heart of a solitary woman whose right to be on earth is made to depend on her capacity for being merely *useful*. The human heart is a hungry thing, and it sometimes seems to me no wonder that there are so many that are fain to feed on husks.

Sometimes I send my thoughts beyond Oaklawn, with the resolution to follow them. But where? I call to mind my ignorance of life, my staid "school-ma'am manners," for I am conscious that I have them, the reports teachers give of other schools, and try to stifle my unrest.

Was it wrong that I had not learned, in whatsoever state I was in, therewith to be content? It was not until his eyes were smitten with blindness by excess of light, and he lay prostrate at the feet of the Highest, that the great Apostle to the Gentiles could say this, and I—was a girl of nineteen.

While Miss Michal remained at home, this feeling slept; but consumption had set its seal upon her, and she, at last, far too late, as my fears told me, had gone to try the influence of a tropical climate. It was only after much consultation as to "ways and means," that she was persuaded to do this, for there was no superfluity of money among them; the expense of educating the boys, for the sake of which both she and their mother devoted themselves to a life of toil, necessitated the most rigid economy. But this difficulty was met in some way, and she sailed with the family of a friend, with far less of hope, and even less of fear, than was felt by those she left behind.

Another face was missing, also; one which I had come to regard much as one does some friendly rock, within whose shadow the frail wild-flowers and helpless animals creep for protection—that of Professor Cavendish. At the commencement of the fall term, Mrs. Ellis had announced that he would no longer take his place among us—that a gentleman from the university in M—— would fill his position. This change filled me with surprise and disappointment, none the less because, as I told myself, I had

no just cause to complain. I was not in the confidence of either our principal or the professor, but this knowledge did not reconcile me to the change, or dispose me to join in James Sancroft's praises of the new lecturer, who was his friend. Mr. Sancroft had now opened a law-office in M——, and boarded with his mother, and seemed to have a general oversight of the whole household. Whether he still remained undecided as to my character, I do not know; but lately he had given me a much greater share of his attention than was either pleasant or desirable; not the spontaneous and graceful attention common from his sex to mine—for that I should have been grateful; nothing that denoted a warmer interest—that I should have deprecated; but a kind of polite *espionnage* which was easier felt than described, coupled with a kind of diplomatic smoothness that would seek to lure me on to lay myself open, and let those cold, keen blue eyes read me through and through. I had not much to conceal, but I was not to be scrutinized, least of all by him, so I shut my "school-ma'am" reserve about me as an oyster does its shell.

"Ah, Miss Lathrop, I came near forgetting that there came a package for you by express to-night," said Mrs. Ellis, one evening, when I lingered longer than usual in the parlor, to discuss something connected with my classes. "Pardon my neglect," she added, as she laid the package on the table; "but it is so unusual for you to order things by express."

There was a little, just a little curiosity in the tone, if not in the face; and, more from a spirit of contrariety than any thing else, I kept back any expression of my own surprise, and took the package as coolly as if I were accustomed to receive one every day.

She turned away, and, being quite alone, I began to untie the cord, for the address was in a hand I did not recognize. It contained, as I had thought, books —Ruskin's "Modern Painters," and Mrs.

Browning's, Whittier's, Bryant's, and Longfellow's poems. I suspected whose hand had opened for me this new fountain by my lonely wayside, and felt that I was still within the shadow of that presence I so much missed.

"That selection must be a fine one," said a low voice near me. I started, for Mr. Sancroft had entered so softly (all his movements were stealthy and feline) that I had not heard him, nor did I dream that he stood opposite me at the table.

"Mr. Cavendish's taste is unquestionable," he added, as if he had not observed my movement.

"I do not see that Mr. Cavendish's taste is called in question," I said, shortly. "This address is certainly not his writing."

I pushed the paper across the table, and glancing at it he said, slowly: "No, but I inferred it was from him, because it would be so like him."

"You can make such inferences as you please, sir; I believe it is a part of your profession," I said, provoked at his impertinence, as I took up my books to leave the room.

"Miss Lathrop is disposed to be severe, I see, but"—he took from the table a slip of paper, which must have fallen from the package when I opened it, and passing it to me said, with an air of mock humility, "possibly I may retrieve my character when she reads this."

It bore only the words "For Zingarella," but there was no mistaking those letters, more like Hebrew in their regular, square outlines, than any thing else, and I said hastily:

"You are right, sir. It is the writing of Mr. Cavendish."

"Miss Lathrop will seldom find my penetration at fault in reading handwriting or—character," he returned, with a peculiar smile.

The words were nothing, the tone, as usual, soft and low, but the expression was that of one who had, or thought he had, read my character, and summed up

its most latent possibilities; and, with an indignant and but half-suppressed— "Who cares for your penetration?" I passed him and left the room.

I had not seen Alice Ross for some weeks, and the next day, about an hour before sunset, I set out to walk to the Pines. It was a bleak November day, heavy racks of dark, leaden-hued clouds swept at intervals across the heavens, filling the air with fine particles of snow. But my rapid walk kept me warm, and I fully enjoyed these alternations of sunlight and shadow, and the reedy piping of the wind as it swept across the dry stubble and withered herbage. Sometimes it drove the great, dark clouds eastward, and in the hush which followed I could hear the muffled roar of the Connecticut, swollen now by the late autumn rains, and the fainter soughings of the brooks that circled upland and meadow. It was almost sunset when I reached the house, where I found the good woman suffering severely from an attack of rheumatism. She seemed delighted to see me, and I soon learned that Mr. Cavendish's absence was caused by the rapid decline of his sister. As her physical strength failed, the dark shadows seemed to be lifted at intervals from her brain, and he stayed by her constantly, watching these fitful rifts which he well knew betokened the coming of the friendly angel, Death.

While she spoke, we heard the ringing of a horse's feet upon the frozen ground. It paused before the door, and, almost before we could speak, the bell was rung by an impatient hand.

"Dear, dear, some bad news, I fear," said the faithful woman, striving to rise and reach for a light, for we had been sitting in the pleasant twilight of a wood-fire.

"Let me go to the door, Mrs. Ross, I do not need a light," I said, and, hurrying along the hall, I reached the door just as the person without gave another impatient pull at the bell. I unlocked the door, and the person, whose face was so muffled by his fur collar and cap that I could not distinguish a feature, flung the bridle of his horse over one of the clipped cedars, which supported a wistaria, and entered the house, asking for Professor Cavendish as he closed the door.

"He is not at home, sir."

"I suppose Alice Ross is," was the reply, as he strode along the hall to the pleasant room which, after her English fashion, she called "the housekeeper's room." I had left the door slightly ajar, and a bright gleam of light from that direction assured me that she had succeeded in getting a light. The gentleman entered without ceremony, saying:

"Ah, Alice, old friend, I knew I should find a warm corner here."

She was peering at him through her glasses, with her candle raised high in her hand, when I passed in and slipped into a chair in the corner.

"Am I, then, so changed, Alice? I should have known you anywhere!"

His voice was no longer muffled by his fur, which he flung aside as he spoke, and I looked eagerly from my shadowed corner, while the old lady dropped her light upon the table, and cried, eagerly:

"Master Ralph! Surely it is Master Ralph Saville himself!"

"It's what's left of him, anyway, Alice. But where is Rothsay?"

Alice began to speak of Miss Helen; the guest listened attentively. "Poor Rothsay!" he said, as the old woman paused; "so I've been within a mile of him to-day, and did not know it!"

He was standing now with his back to the fire, slowly unfastening his loose overcoat with his left hand, and the light fell full on his face. It was thin, dark, and imperious; would have been sarcastic, had it not been softened by memories stirred by Alice's words. There were lines about the firm mouth, but whether of sorrow, passion, or remorse, I could not tell; but, as I continued to gaze, I began to identify it with the one I had seen at the Pond, with the miniature in my possession, and I was satisfied that Ralph Saville and Ralph Annesley were the same person.

Presently he started from his musing posture, and a twinge of pain contracted his features as he attempted to draw off his coat. Alice's eye, which had been perusing his face with tender interest, observed it at once.

"What is it, Master Ralph? Are you hurt?"

"A trifle, Alice. We had a smashup this morning on the cars, and my arm got jammed somewhat; I didn't notice it then, but the pace of that beast they saddled for me at M—— has not helped it. Where's Mark? Is he living?"

"Yes; I will ring for him."

In a moment the old negro man entered, and his wrinkled face shone with joy at the sight of the guest and his hearty greeting.

"Now, Mark, bear a hand, and help me off with this coat. There," he continued, when the heavy overcoat was removed, "now, you must look after that horse; you haven't forgotten how, I suppose, though it's a long time since you used to saddle Kelpie for me."

"Ah, der's no horses nowadays, Mass Ralph, like what der was in de old times, an' no boys nudder," said the old negro, with a grim shake of his head, as he went out to obey orders.

"Now, Alice, if you will—" began the guest, "but you are lame," he interrupted, seeing her limp forward.

"Can I be of any assistance?" I said, coming out of the shadow.

"Oh, it's so fortunate! Miss Lina will help you, sir," said Alice. "She's so handy."

Without another word, I helped him remove his coat; and he rolled up his shirt-sleeve, and began to press his fingers on his arm, which was badly bruised and discolored above the elbow.

"O Mr. Ralph, your arm is broken!"

cried Alice. "Do let me send Mark for the doctor."

"No, Alice; it is only bruised badly. Have you any of your liniment? You see I haven't forgotten its wonderful virtues, or the time I sprained my shoulder in trying to make old Samson leap the gate, and your liniment cured it. The famous balsam of Don Quixote was nothing to it, I know."

The old dame brought out her liniment, and proceeded to apply it. But her hand was unsteady from excitement, and, after a few moments, the gentleman said pleasantly:

"Now, Alice, you sit down, right there, where I can see you, and let this young woman finish the job. You are too lame to be kept standing."

He evidently took me for a servant, and I had no fear that he would identify the thin, dark person, with demure face and close-braided hair, with the half-wild child he had found sobbing on the bank of the Pond, so many years ago, even if he was, as I believed, Mr. Annesley; so I again came forward and applied the emollient, while he went on chatting with Alice.

"Hungry? yes," he said, in reply to Alice, as I finished binding up his arm. "That beast's pace is conducive to an appetite. Just bring a tray in here, and I'll make myself comfortable."

I remember thinking him not far from it, then, lying back in a deep-cushioned chair, with his feet on the fender, looking into the fire, while, with his left hand, he thrust back the tumbled black hair from his forehead. The firelight softened the hard lines of his face, and gave him more the look of my Mr. Annesley than ever, and I was passing into the kitchen to assist Alice, and settle this question, when old Nep came rushing in, almost knocking me over, and with one bound was at the gentleman's side, with his black muzzle on his knee. I glanced back, saw the haughty head raised quickly from the cushion, the left arm thrown caressingly around the dog's neck, heard the joyful words of recognition, and I walked into the kitchen where Alice was preparing some refreshments, and, instead of questioning her, said, quietly:

"Mr. Ralph Saville Annesley has taken you quite by surprise, Mrs. Ross."

"Yes, it's his way! But—you aren't going, miss? I was just thinking I didn't tell who you were. I was so flurried at seeing him. I hope you will excuse me."

"Certainly. Old Nep seems delighted," I added, for the dog's joyful whimpers, mingled with the caressing tones of the gentleman, were now distinctly audible.

"Yes; Ralph Saville was always fond of dogs, and he sent Nep to Mr. Rothsay three or four years ago. I wonder the creature knew him!"

I did not.

"It's almost like seeing Master Philip," she said, arranging the slices of bread with mathematical precision; "for, after Mr. Ralph's father died, he was much with us, and he took greatly to Master Philip, though he was some years younger. What madcaps they were! Dear heart, it seems but only yesterday since I had them all about me!"

She hastily brushed away a tear, and, lifting the tray, she added:

"I wish you would go in now, and let me tell him who it is that has bound up his arm so nicely."

"I will carry that tray in for you gladly; but I would much rather you would not mention me to him at all, or only as a teacher from Oaklawn, if he asks, which is not likely."

I was quite sure he would not, and now that I was certain it was Mr. Annesley, I felt a strong aversion to thrusting myself upon his notice. He had probably never thought of me since he left me with his cousin in New Haven, and why should I compel him to do so now?

"I am glad I have seen his face again," I thought, as I walked rapidly across the fields to Oaklawn, "for, if it is haughty and proud, it is the pride of conscious superiority and self-reliance, not of insolence or arrogance—a face with manhood behind it, and that is something worth looking upon, even if there are some traces of the old archenemy there also."

CHAPTER XVII.

UNEXPECTED REVELATIONS.

This meeting with Mr. Annesley caused a break in my monotonous life. I liked to recall his face, so unlike the boyish portrait in the gallery at the Pines, far less handsome than the one in my locket, more haughty, stern, and wilful, with something of the granite look that marked Mr. Cavendish's features cropping out about the jaw and mouth. I liked also to speculate upon his character. It was the one mysterious picture hanging among my gallery of commonplace, still-life portraits, and of course created a sort of charmed atmosphere. I determined to ask Mr. Cavendish about him, and tell him of our meeting, years ago, by the Pond. But that gentleman was absent until after Miss Helen's death, which occurred in February, and when I met him again, and saw the sad, suffering look in his eyes, I could not bear to trouble him with words.

The school was unusually full this term, and my duties proportionally severe; therefore, I availed myself more than ever of the interval, between tea and prayers, for exercise, and my feet instinctively turned toward the Pines, although I did not often venture into the house, fearful of seeming to intrude on their sorrow.

On several of these occasions, I either met or was joined by James Sancroft; once or twice under circumstances that led me to think he watched my steps, and yet the idea was too absurd to be entertained; so the next time I met him

I paused, determined to treat him courteously. I was standing by the gate leading into Mr. Cavendish's grounds admiring the delicate and intricate network of interlacing boughs against a background of clear sky, when he came up, and, after admiring the effect, began to speak of the fine taste indicated by the arrangement of the professor's grounds, the grouping of the trees, etc.,

He spoke well, and I listened with pleasure.

"Edward thinks," he went on, "that, if yonder group of beeches and hickory was removed, the view toward M—— would be finer; but I do not agree with him, and I hope, when he comes in possession, his respect for Mr. Cavendish will prevent him from making the change, even if his own taste does not."

"Edward!"—Surprise got the better of discretion, I knew, as soon as the word was uttered, and I saw his peculiar smile. It vanished, however, in a moment, and he added, carelessly, switching the silvery-gray umbels of the everlasting, by the fence, with his cane.

"Yes; and I ought to have united Michal's name with his. I did not know, however, that I was betraying family secrets when I spoke, for you have been so long a member of our mother's family —quite in her confidence, and on such a friendly footing at the Pines, I thought you could hardly be ignorant of this fact."

What soft, insinuating tones! what apparent frankness!—and yet, he did not believe six of those daintily-uttered words. Strict justice, unvarying politeness, formal and monotonous—necessarily, perhaps—I had received from Mrs. Ellis, but *confidence* never, as no one knew better than James Sancroft. But, if he wished to assume it, I wished to know for what end; I, therefore, led him on by asking:

"What fact?"

"That Michal and Edward are to be Mr. Cavendish's heirs."

"And yourself?"

"I have none of the Cavendish blood

in my veins, and with no one is the old adage more true, that 'blood is thicker than water,' than with the professor. I have no reason to complain, however, for he has already done much for us all. It is only since his sister's death that the business has been definitely arranged, and the papers signed."

" Was it by his liberality Miss Michal went to Europe ? "

" Yes ; and he wishes her to remain until her health is completely established."

" I hope she will, and that she will live long to enjoy her good fortune."

" I am glad to hear you speak so warmly. Indeed, I thought the arrangement would meet your approval."

I hardly knew whether the words conveyed a sneer or a compliment; it was too dark to read his face, so I answered briefly, as I made a movement to walk on :

" My approval or disapproval can be of little consequence. But I rejoice in any thing which will add to Miss Michal's comfort and happiness."

He bowed, and proceeded toward the Pines, while I retraced my steps, musing on the motives which could have led him to communicate this matter to me.

Two weeks later we had a half-holiday, and I walked into M—— to make some necessary purchases. This was soon done, and with my package in my hand, I went to the post-office to inquire after letters, at Mrs. Ellis's request.

" None for Mrs. Ellis, but one addressed to Oaklawn, for Miss Z—mena D. ——"

" Zerlina D. Lathrop," I said.

" Yes, that must be it," said the clerk, handing me a great, awkwardly-folded letter, bearing my name, evidently written by a hand unused to the pen.

I did not know the hand, and the postmark was illegible. I thrust it into my pocket, and went round by the Pines to see Alice Ross. Mr. Cavendish was on the lawn, giving Mark some directions about clearing off the old year's withered herbage, and he called me to him to see the hyacinths and crocuses that were just pushing through the ground, and, with some words more in his own vein than any I had heard of late, bade me " run into the house and see Alice Ross, who would be glad enough to hear the sound of a woman's tongue."

Alice was not in her room, and I sat down by the fire to read my letter. It was from Polly Maria; something unusual, I knew, must have occurred to call forth such an effort from her, and I ran my eye over the cramped, ill-spelled lines with a foreboding heart. It was not death, it was marriage : little Adeline was married to a Mr. Heath, of New York. She referred to a letter which little Adeline had written me a few weeks ago, "telling all about it," which I had failed to receive, and, between the prolixity which uneducated people seem to think essential to letter-writing, and scriptural quotations, observations about " carnal affections " and " days of probation," it was difficult to get any definite idea of the man she had married. She "did not know much about the young man," she wrote; he seemed a well-disposed person enough, quite serious-like, and she hoped he wouldn't prove a castaway, for Birdie's sake ; but men, at best, were but broken reeds; we could be sure of nothing in this vale of tears, etc.

Of Uncle Steve she wrote this: " Brother was quite downhearted about the marriage, at first, but he picked up a bit after Birdie went away with her husband, and now had made her write to give you his love, and say as how he had concluded to go on a v'yage up the straits once more, cause he'd like to be able to do a little something for Bluebird when she went to housekeeping, and the Magnolia, Captain Hood, was about ready to sail."

I laid down the letter, for the thought of the lone, loving old sailor, in his solitary house, striving to hide his sore heart by planning and working for his darling's happiness, though another had taken from him her heart, brought the tears to my eyes, and, for the moment, I felt almost angry with little Adeline for leaving him.

"Bad news, Zingarella?" said the professor, when he entered, and began poking the fire, as usual.

"No; I suppose it oughtn't to be, for this letter tells me of the marriage of a friend."

"And this, I suppose, is the certificate? It's yellow and old enough to be the quitclaim Laban gave to Jacob," he remarked, picking from the floor a bit of paper, stained and worn, and handing it to me.

"Then it must belong to you, sir, I think. It would be too precious a document for the children of the bondwoman to inherit. What is it?"

He carelessly unfolded it, and, with a sharp exclamation of surprise, made a long stride to the window. I watched him a moment, then started up, for his gaunt frame shook with some strong emotion, and his face turned white as a woman's.

"Where in Heaven's name did you get this paper? Speak, girl!"

"I don't know any thing about it. Indeed, I don't. Perhaps the letter will explain," I said, startled by his vehemence.

I ran it over; it was the paper that Mrs. Barnes had spoken of as being in the old tobacco-box which Uncle Steve had bid off at the sale of my grandfather's effects. The honest old soul had persuaded Polly Maria to write and send it to me. I hastened to explain, and the gray old face, looking down into mine with such trembling eagerness, began to light up as with some untold hope or joy.

"Day! Day! Was your mother's name Harriet Day?" His fingers griped my arm convulsively.

"I have heard Mrs. Hunt and others say so, sir."

"And your father?—they call you Lathrop—was that his name?"

"No; I went by my grandfather's name until Miss Lathrop took me. I never knew my father's name."

"It was Cavendish, child! my own brother, Philip Cavendish! O God, I thank Thee!"

The long arms were folded about me, the grim face was bowed upon my head, while his tears fell fast upon my cheek.

Suddenly he lifted his head, and, putting me from him a little space, though one arm still encircled me, he scanned my wondering face with a look of womanly tenderness, while he muttered:

"I felt it—I felt it from the very first, child, but I thrust the thought out. I strangled it as a phantasm of a diseased brain—the spawn of incipient insanity. God forgive me!"

I stood like one in a dream. I felt the clasp of his arm, I heard his words. I knew it was Rothsay Cavendish who spoke—the odd, harsh, stern professor—his face that bent over me quivering with emotion, and yet I dared not stir, lest it should vanish away. But my eye fell on that time-stained paper, which he still held fast. That was something tangible, and I asked:

"That paper—does it speak of my father?"

"It is the certificate of his marriage with one Harriet Day!"

He spread it before me on the table, and I read the brief lines which certified that, "on the 18th of October, 184-, at the Catholic Mission, in the State of Michigan, Philip Cavendish and Harriet Day were legally married by Father François Dupré." Andre Leudru and James Gibson's names were signed as witnesses. But I could scarcely realize its importance to me. Those pale, faded words—were they what I had needed to give me a right to be in the world? Would they give me name and family, home and friends? Would they fill my hungry heart?

But, when I looked up and met Mr. Cavendish's face, I doubted no more; for the first time in my life, I wept from excess of joy, while my father's brother drew me closer to him, and passed his hand caressingly over my hair, as he muttered:

"Poor, homeless child! What a weary time you must have had of it, drudging away down there, and I hardening my heart like Pharaoh all the while!"

Alice Ross entered, but he did not stir, only answered her look of astonishment by bidding her "Come and welcome Philip's child!"

She was bewildered and incredulous at first, but he soon convinced her, and she grew almost wild in her joy, not only because God had remembered them just then, when their hearts were so sad and sore, but it was Miss Lina who had already made herself a home in their hearts with her Saville look!

Sitting between them, I listened while Mr. Cavendish told how my father, while still a mere boy—hardly twenty—had accompanied a friend of the family to the West as his assistant in surveying certain lands for government; that after a while they received letters from that friend, telling of an intimacy which he had formed with a young girl of that region, speaking of the connection as disgraceful and disreputable, and urging Mr. Cavendish to recall him home. The gentleman's interest in Philip was beyond dispute, and the elder brother wrote, urging the younger to return home. He refused, but, after some weeks, his superior, Mr. Morris, induced him to go down to Louisiana on some business, and contrived to detain him there several months. Finally, he returned to Michigan without leave, but the surveying-party had already left that region. Some weeks later he suddenly made his appearance at home, in a state bordering on insanity, and demanded of his brother his wife, whom he insisted Mr. Morris and Rothsay had carried off and concealed somewhere, in order to keep him from her. It was a terrible scene, I knew by the look of Mr. Cavendish's face and Alice Ross's low sobs, and it ended by the young brother's leaving the house in anger, never to return. He went back to Michigan in search of her whom he called his wife, followed by his brother and Saville Annesley, who had hitherto been his dearest friend; but he utterly refused to see them or hold any communication with them. They kept trace of him until he returned to New York, and took passage for India, where he entered the British service, as they afterward learned, and fell in a bloody but obscure contest with the natives.

They could find no proof of his marriage, and Mr. Morris always doubted it. They ascertained, however, that the girl in question was the only child of an elderly man, who, a short time before the advent of the surveying-party, had located in the region of Grand Traverse Bay, and whence he had suddenly disappeared, taking his daughter with him. The girl was said to have been very delicate and beautiful, and the attentions of the handsome young surveyor had been a matter of gossip among the settlers, and there were hints that she was obliged to flee to conceal her shame. Others, more charitable, held the father to be partially insane, and likely to make sudden changes.

"That mission of the French fathers is some twenty miles from the point where the surveying-party made headquarters," said Mr. Cavendish, after a pause. "Some of the persons who witnessed that marriage may be still alive, and, God willing, I shall see them soon. Now, my child, let us know where you have stayed your little weary feet, before you came to Oaklawn. Not inside the gates of paradise, I'll wager."

I told him briefly of my early life, leaving out much that I knew would pain him. He questioned me closely about the ring which had been found in the box with the certificate, and bestowed several muttered anathemas upon the town magnate's wife, who had got it at a bargain.

"It was, doubtless, your mother's wedding-ring, and we must have it, child," he said, noting down Mrs. Barnes's address. "To-morrow morning I shall start for Bradshaw—but go on."

I obeyed, and spoke of the meeting with Miss Agnes and Mr. Annesley.

"Ralph Annesley! Ralph Saville Annesley!" he exclaimed. "Are you quite sure of the name, child?"

"I think it was the same person I saw here some weeks since, whom Mrs. Ross called Ralph Saville; but his cousin, Miss Lathrop, always called him Ralph Annesley."

"You think! Didn't you speak to him? Make yourself known, child!"

"No, sir; he has doubtless forgotten all about me long ago, and I did not like to obtrude myself upon his notice."

"Obtrude! A real school-ma'am's whim. What if he had forgotten? Do you suppose that any man whose nature has become coated over with the hard larvæ of sin, to say nothing of the shards of broken hopes and good intentions, will not bless the hand that breaks through it, and holds up before him some evidence that he was once, as Moses hath it, *a living soul?* There is no surer way of casting out devils, child, and a woman can do it as well as an angel. Besides, Ralph Saville would have been glad to see a dog that retained a kind memory of him!"

"Indeed, he was very glad to see Nep, sir."

"To be sure he was, and Nep had no fear of seeming intrusive, but acted out his dog nature honestly. But you needn't look so grave. Nep has never been under the protection of the select-men of Bradshaw, and that makes a world of difference."

I then spoke of my life at Chester-

wood. He listened intently, knitting his eyebrows, and interrupting me at times by a kind of running commentary.

"Lathrop! I remember to have heard the name—a good woman—likely, I should judge, to exchange her sentimentalism for those real trials 'whereby men live, and in all of which is the life of the spirit,' as King Hezekiah found out ages ago. Rev. Marcus Tyler—ay, I know the species; a walking formula, bridging the way to heaven with his own narrow creed, a mighty man at 'fighting extinct Satans,' but blind as a bat to the real devils of modern civilization. It's a long time since his infernal majesty confined his operations to the Thebaid. Lied, did you! That was a sin against your own soul, and, if the fear of punishment was but the fear of sin, I should say he served you right. Never lie, child. I despise a liar as I do the devil."

"So do I; therefore, I must go back to Oaklawn. It is already past the hour when I ought to have been at home."

"Go to Oaklawn? I'll not hear of it!—Just look at her, Alice Ross! She comes in here, and gladdens our hearts with a joy we never hoped to feel this side of heaven, and then gets up and talks quietly of going!—Would you really leave us, child?"

For answer, I silently placed my hand in his. He smiled, and drew me to him, saying:

"Old folks hold their blessings with a close grasp. Alice and I can't afford to lose you."

It was very pleasant to hear these words, and, for a moment, I rested my hand against his breast, and enjoyed the happiness they brought; but I did not forget that I was still with the "English teacher at Oaklawn," that there were duties to be performed before I slept, and, gently as I could, I explained this.

"You are right, child. I would not have you false to your duties, but I will go down myself—or send Mark with a note."

"I would rather you would not. It would take long to explain; besides, if you leave for Bradshaw to-morrow, I would much rather that things remain as they are until you return. It will save a great deal of gossip and explanation."

"Possibly you are right, but I shall not be gone a moment longer than is necessary, I assure you; and then we will have done with lessons and recitations. So, I *was* right—you are a regular tramper, a true Zingari, after all!" he added, with a grin, as I put on my bonnet and shawl.

"Yes; and I am about to prove it by begging."

"Beg away, then, and see what you'll get."

"Please say nothing of this change in my affairs to the people at Bradshaw. Uncle Steve Leete is the only one whom I would wish to be told, and he has probably sailed long before this."

"Do you suppose I am a garrulous old woman, to go gossiping about my affairs from house to house?—No offence, Alice; I wish that old man was at home. I could not die easy without grasping his hand. That's a poor beginning! Beg again."

"Well, then, I beg permission to come to the Pines, while you are absent, just as often as my duties will permit. I want to help Mark trim the roses."

"Worse and worse! That's not begging. Isn't it your own home—roses and all? You'll have to try again!"

"Let me look at your hand, then."

"There! But I'll have no palmistry, girl. It's forbidden by Scripture, and Alice and I call ourselves Christians."

I took the thin, large-veined hand in mine, and raising it to my lips, kissed it again and again; then, dropping it, and, leaving a kiss on old Alice's cheek, I made for the door.

"Zerlina!"

I paused, while he came forward, and,

laying his hand on my head, stood for a moment as if in silent prayer. All that was audible was, "God bless and protect you, my child!"

A kiss sealed the benediction, and I left the house.

What a walk was that over the oft-trodden path to Oaklawn! I was no longer alone—a waif and a stranger in the world! The thought filled my heart with joy unspeakable, and clothed the gray, damp fields with beauty.

"You are late, to-night, Miss Lathrop —a full half hour," said Mrs. Ellis, when I entered the parlor, after attempting by a dash of cold water to remove all traces of recent excitement.

"I beg pardon. I was unavoidably detained."

"'*Unexpectedly*' would be the better word, Miss Lathrop. I do not like my ladies to find things unavoidable. Few things are, save death."

I had occasion to recall these words vividly before the close of the coming twenty-four hours; then, I only bowed and took up my work, while one of the teachers read aloud from some work on education, which task, always wearisome enough, now seemed to me more so than ever; so much did I long to get away by myself, to think over this new era in my life. At length, yawning teachers and pupils were dismissed. I lingered a moment to give Mrs. Ellis some trifles I had purchased for her, half expecting some more serious rebuke for my lack of punctuality, but she seemed willing to let it pass. Not so Mr. Sancroft; he looked up from his book, and said, in a low under-tone:

"You look excited. I trust your delay was caused by nothing unpleasant. You came round by the Pines, I think."

"Yes." I closed the door, but his words recalled our conversation that evening, by the gate leading into Mr. Cavendish's grounds. I hurried to my room. Fortunately, my room-mate, a person of soporific temperament, was already half asleep, and, putting out the light, that I might not be guilty of a double breach of the rules in one day, I wrapped my shawl about me, and sat down to think. In my joy at finding my kindred, and such kindred, I had entirely overlooked the change which this discovery would make in the prospects of Mrs. Ellis's family; but James Sancroft's words, or rather his look, reminded me of it, and I could not help feeling troubled at the thought of their disappointment. Many chance expressions of Edward's, and even some of Miss Michal's, recurred to me, and I was convinced that Edward, at least, expected to succeed to an inheritance, which he would not only enjoy, but grace. He and Michal, nay, even Mrs. Ellis, had always treated me not only with kindness, but as an equal; and should I now step between them and their long-cherished hopes? The thought seemed mean and selfish. What I craved was not money, but love, and I determined to persuade my uncle to consider us as equally his children, and, kneeling before "Our Father" in gratitude for which my words were but a poor expression, I sought my rest.

CHAPTER XVIII.

CHANGES AND CHANCES.

"WILL ye step into the mistress's room? Mr. James is after wishing ye, miss."

I met the chambermaid with this message, when I came to breakfast next morning, and went at once to Mrs. Ellis's room. James Sancroft was leaning over her bed, and, without raising his head, or moving, he signed for me to approach.

"What is the matter?" I asked—but I needed no reply when I looked upon her face, the vacant eyes, the contorted mouth, the flaccid, speechless lips. It was paralysis.

"When did it occur, sir?"

"I found her in this state, a few mo-

ments since, when, knowing it to be beyond her usual time of rising, I came to inquire the cause. I sent for you, because she is used to you, and you have more nerve and firmness than the others. I wish you to stay by her while I go for a physician, and allow no one to enter the room. I wish to alarm the house as little as possible. You can call Margaret, if you really need any one."

He spoke as quietly as if she were only sleeping, but I saw his lip tremble as he arranged the pillow, and the yearning look with which he turned away was more expressive than words.

It was two days before she spoke, and then with great difficulty, and in monosyllables. In the mean time, it was said in the house that "our principal was suffering from a severe attack of liver-complaint, with slight numbness in the limbs," etc. My duties were willingly assumed by the other teachers, and, aided by Mr. Sancroft, I passed day and night by Mrs. Ellis's couch, save when I went out for a breath of fresh air.

It was the fourth day after the attack, when, in quite her natural voice, she asked her son, who spent all his leisure moments in her room, to whom he was writing.

"To Michal, mother."

"You have not told her—" She did not finish the sentence, but a look of pain and distress clouded her face.

"No, mother," he replied, rightly interpreting that look. "I would not distress her or Edward, or write until I could tell them you were better."

"Don't tell them at all—at least, not Michal."

He looked at her with a penetrating glance for a moment, and seemed about to speak, when he was called out of the room.

"Let him be," she murmured; then, seeing her make an effort to turn herself, I came forward to assist her, and, looking up in my face, she asked:

"What was it my daughter Michal

7

said, in her letter to you, about being happy, Miss Lathrop?"

Michal had recently sent me an unsealed note enclosed in a letter to her mother, but I was not before aware that Mrs. Ellis had read it. She was in Florence when she wrote, and seemed to revel in its delicious atmosphere, its associations, artistical and historical, like some bird set free. I have the note now, and this is the passage: "Now, for the first time, I truly live, Lina, for my nature is no longer thwarted, my tastes cramped and contravened by tasks at once irksome and disagreeable. Yet these tasks were dignified by a noble aim; and some of the saddest hours of my life have been those in which I scorned and loathed myself for that weakness, physical and mental, which could not elevate them to the rank of joys."

I briefly repeated the substance of this to the mother, not daring to do otherwise, but I doubted if she comprehended me, for she seemed to be sinking into one of her fits of lethargy. But I was mistaken; presently she muttered, "Tastes contravened; irksome tasks; I never compelled her; 'twas necessity; she would have written verses, poor child! not knowing that none of us do what we *would*, but what we *must*, in this world.—James!"

He entered, just then, and went to her side. He had a paper in his hand. and she said, sharply, "I told you not to write."

"I have not written, mother; you will soon be able to write yourself."

"I shall never write again, James, never. I have finished my work. My sons are educated men. I have secured for them position, influence, and wealth —Rothsay Cavendish would never have chosen a boor for his heir. Michal said it was a noble end to work for, but she has gone among strangers to be happy. —Duty should be happiness, but, perhaps, all cannot see it."

Thus, for some days, I caught glimpses of the workings of that resolute soul —betokening doubts of the infallibility of her theory of life—sometimes, regret; then, as her strong constitution gained upon the disease, she sat up again, weak, but cool and reticent as ever.

More than a week had elapsed, and I had found no time to visit the Pines. I knew old Alice would excuse me, for James Sancroft had, as he told me, called there the day after his mother's attack, to inform them, and found that the professor had left, at an early hour, for New Haven. I felt very anxious and sad. I longed for my uncle's return, yet dreaded the effect the announcement of my kinship to him would have on Mrs. Ellis, in her present state, and half regretted that I did not let him avow it, that night, as he proposed.

I found, at length, a leisure hour. It was the 25th of April, but the day had been gray and chilly, with, now and then, a passing gust of wind and rain. As I went down the walk, something in its aspect reminded me of the first time I saw it, and I was leaning upon the gate thinking of the change "'twixt now and then," when James Sancroft came up the street rapidly. He seemed unusually excited, but, not caring to meet him, I was hurrying in the opposite direction, when he called out and asked if I was going to the Pines.

"Yes."

"Then please defer your visit for the present. I have sad news for Alice Ross —indeed, for us all."

I felt what was coming; an overshadowing presentiment of sorrow chilled my heart and palsied my tongue. I made a sign for him to speak.

"Mr. Cavendish is dead!"

I could not speak nor stir; I only shivered as if I felt the cold wind of desolation again beating upon my path.

When I could command myself, I looked up to find his keen eyes fixed upon me.

"I am glad to see you bear this sudden shock with such composure," he said. "I anticipated as much, and, for that reason, desire your assistance in breaking it to my mother."

I, with the knowledge of my loss—my earthly all knelling in my heart!—I comfort others! Why, what was he to her? What her loss to mine, that I should speak commonplaces of resignation, with the waters of bitterness flooding my soul?

The words pressed to my lips, but I thought of that pale, weak woman in her room alone, and, with a forced "I am ready, sir!" followed him to the house. But I took no part in the preliminary words with which he prefaced his news, and he seemed content.

After a few tears of genuine sorrow, the mother signified her wish to know when and where he died, questions which I had been vainly trying to school my lips to utter.

He had learned of his death through Mr. Spencer, Mr. Cavendish's friend and lawyer in New York. It seemed that, a week previous, Mr. Spencer had received a brief note from Mr. Cavendish, dated at New Haven, saying he should be in New York in a day or two, and might possibly wish that gentleman to accompany him to Michigan. He reached New York on the 22d, and called at Mr. Spencer's office. Not finding his friend, he appointed an hour for calling next day, and returned to his hotel. He did not keep his appointment, and, fearing he might be ill, Mr. Spencer called to see him. He found his room locked, and, upon forcing the door, discovered him dead in his bed — having apparently passed away without a struggle.

How coolly and deliberately he spoke, and how every low word seemed like a nail fastening down — encoffining the dearest hopes of my life!

There was a pause—a space for the mental "dust to dust, ashes to ashes"—before he added:

"He will be buried at Greenwood, by the side of his sister, and, being aware of his intentions toward our family, Mr. Spencer thinks it advisable that Edward and myself should attend the funeral, both if possible, as Mr. Ralph Annesley, his only blood-relation, is absent from the country. If you approve, I will telegraph to Edward to-night to start immediately. I will go down to-night. There may be some business matters to talk over, though the will is all right."

"It is best."

"In that case I must beg our friend Miss Lathrop to break the news to Alice Ross. It will be a heavy blow to the old dame, but none will know how to soften it better than Miss Lathrop, who has been such a friend to both—that is," turning to me, "if she will accept the sad office?"

I bowed—I felt, if I attempted to speak, the words would choke me. I thought of my uncle's look that night, when he blessed me on his threshold, of his kiss on my cheek, and that man talking so decorously of business and death —daring to speak of "softening" the blow to that faithful old friend and servant—of walking as chief mourner to his grave!

I was glad, however, of the privilege of meeting old Alice alone. If my words bowed that white old head with grief, I alone, of all on earth, had the best right to mingle my tears with hers. To her I represented the house which she, and her father before her, had so long served, and she clung to "Master Philip's child," with all the tenacity of her class.

"Thank God, I'll not be left to die alone in this strange land!" she said, between her sobs. "My master's child will close my eyes and lay me in the grave. You will come here to live soon, Miss Lina—come home!"

"Home!" How pleasant the word sounded! With that pale, sad face before me—those faded, blue eyes looking so fondly and trustfully into mine, I shrank from speaking what I knew would pain her so deeply. She saw me hesitate, and, mistaking the cause, said:

"I know, dear, it'll not be the same place, with his step no more on floor or stair—but, I think, it would please him. He fretted sore that he didn't keep you that night."

"Alice," I said, pressing her withered hand to my cheek, "I will do all for you that Philip Cavendishes daughter can do —but I am afraid I shall have to go far from here to find a home."

She sighed. "Well, well, child, it's natural for one so young to like a gayer life—but you always seemed so quiet-like. But it's all one to old Alice, city or country, so that her master's child is content."

It was evident that she did not conceive of the possibility that any person save "Master Philip's child" should succeed to Rothsay Cavendish's property, and I was forced to explain to her in so many words.

"No will!" she interrupted, when I spoke of the suddenness of his death; "the Cavendishes needed no wills; the property went from parent to child, brother to sister!"

"No will in my favor, Alice. I have reason to think that, very soon after Miss Helen's death, having no near relative, as he supposed, he made a will in favor of Mrs. Ellis's children, and the property will go to them."

"To them! They sit here, sleep beneath this roof, walk these rooms; and you, Philip Cavendish's child, driven out, a hireling? You, with Miss Flora Saville's own eyes!"

She had risen, and stood before me, trembling with excitement.

"Dear Alice, it's little good Miss Flora's eyes will do me in this case, I fear. They cannot break a will, or undo what is done."

"I don't believe it! I don't believe Rothsay Cavendish ever made such a will, and said nothing about Master Philip! He would say he was dead, but I know he always hoped that the story would prove untrue. I don't believe he ever quite gave him up. I have heard him and Ralph Saville talk it over many times, and I don't believe he would give away his property to strangers, without a word of him."

"Possibly not; but, Alice, my uncle died without acknowledging me, and it may be utterly impossible for me to prove my birth—my right to bear my father's name."

"Prove! Didn't I hear him say it? Don't I mind his very look and tone, when he called me to welcome Philip's child? Let me go to these folks, Miss Lina! I will tell them the truth, and the word of an honest woman should be believed."

Again I tried to explain to her that, even if there should be a clause in the will relating to my father, the law would require other proofs of my right than her assertion; but all I could gain from her was an impatient—

"What need of law, Miss Lina, among honest folks?"

What need, indeed! But my chief object was to keep her from going to Oaklawn to "right her child." Possibly, very probably, my father was not mentioned in that will; in that case, I had no wish to set the gossips of the place busy by asserting a claim I could not prove. If it were, I must have time to think well, before I took any decided step; and, finally, more through her habitual reverence for my right to her obedience, as her master's niece, than the force of argument, I won her promise to be silent.

I also ascertained that she had a niece residing in Westchester County, New York, to whom her thoughts had sometimes turned, when a chance expression of her master had suggested the possibility of her surviving "the family," and I was certain that Mr. Cavendish had signed no will that did not make ample provision for her.

By Mrs. Ellis's request, I took charge of the school during her son's absence, and was too much occupied to give more than a passing glance at the strange path which I mentally saw leading far away from there, and along which, something whispered me, I must walk before many days.

On the fourth evening of Mr. Sancroft's absence, when I went into Mrs. Ellis's room with my report, I found Edward with her. James would follow with Mr. Spencer, he said, in a few days.

He was speaking rapidly, and his handsome face was flushed with a pleasant excitement when I entered. I would have withdrawn, but Mrs. Ellis bade me enter, saying, with much of her old, decided manner:

"Wait, my son, until I have looked over Miss Lathrop's report."

He left his position by the grate, and, crossing to his mother's side, said, with that pleasant air of confident self-trust that sat so graciously upon him:

"No reports to-night, mother. It is doubtless all right if it is Miss Lathrop's work; so lay it on the table, or under it, I beg. Thank Heaven, we have done with reports and such drudgery! Besides, I want Miss Lathrop to congratulate me. Mother, you must give a holiday to-morrow, and Miss Lathrop shall make the announcement. I want every one to share my happiness."

"Then you will have to speak a little more rationally. You have puzzled Miss Lathrop already."

"Well, now for the effort." He tossed back his waving brown hair, and, assuming a grave look, said:

"By the will of Professor Cavendish, made some months before his decease, Michal and I inherit the bulk of his property, amounting, Mr. Spencer says, to fifty thousand or more. Now, as I have my doubts as to money's being the root of all evil, and cannot, of course, feel the weight of all the responsibilities with which mother here says wealth is burdened, I want you to congratulate me on my good fortune."

How proud, and handsome, and happy were the deep-blue eyes bent on me! I think they exercised a mesmeric power, for I felt compelled to speak, and began to stammer something, but broke down.

Mrs. Ellis looked at me wonderingly, as if one of her well-tried rules had suddenly proved faulty; but Edward sprang forward, and placed a chair for me (I had remained standing), saying:

"Pardon me; I ought to have remembered that Mr. Cavendish was your friend also, and you must miss him sadly, just as Michal would if she were here. I did not mean to speak lightly of his death. God knows I honored every hair of his head; but I was thinking, just as you came, of what a life of constant care and toil mother had had, and how fortunate it is that now, when she needs rest and change so much, I have such ample means to give it."

"Yes, sir." I spoke the words as mechanically as I had spoken them to Polly Maria so many years ago.

"Stay! I wished to speak to you of a pet project of mine, which I am sure will meet even James's approval—of mother's I am certain. It relates to you and Oaklawn. We owe you much for your unwearied care during her illness; James speaks of it in the highest terms. —But, how pale you are! How thin and care-worn you look! You are ill.— Mother, James has been putting too much upon Miss Lathrop. It's just his way— he is iron himself, and he uses every one else, or every one that will let him, just as if that person were a tool or machine, made for his special use."

"Edward!" said Mrs. Ellis, reprovingly, "we will, if you please, leave your brother until he is here to answer for himself.—Miss Lathrop, if, during my illness, I have borne too heavily upon you, and it may well be—forgive me. It is human to bear heavily where one trusts. Are you really ill?"

By this time I had called up my will to school my faltering tongue, and I answered, clearly:

"No, ma'am."

She put on her glasses and observed me closely. "You are anxious," she said, "ill at ease. That is not your usual look!"

"Possibly; but be assured it is not from overwork. A dependent woman has cause enough for anxiety always."

"Not unless she be weak or ambitious. But no woman who can command the means of honorable self-support, however humble, can really be termed dependent; and duty conscientiously performed should, to a well-governed mind, be a sufficient reward."

There spoke "our principal" as in the days of her prime—there was the same measured, didactic tone—there the Oaklawn measure of woman's needs; but, dear Heaven, how weak and ill-governed must have been my mind, for her words touched me no more than if she had said, "The whole is greater than a part," or any other axiom.

I could not reply, and Edward relieved me from that necessity.

"Mother," he said, "in view of all these changes, it is quite natural that Miss Lathrop should feel a little unsettled, but my plan will lay all these anxieties like a charm. Just listen: I wish her to succeed you as principal of Oaklawn. The school, you say, is prosperous and profitable; your connection with it must cease at the close of the present term, or before, if she consents. It will be a nice situation for her, and she can have the house and furniture at the same nominal rent we have been accustomed to pay Mr. Cavendish. Michal, I know, will be pleased; and it seems to me just the thing for us all. What do you say, mother?"

"It has my approval," she replied, thoughtfully. "I should be very sorry to see the school go down.—Miss Lathrop," she continued, turning to me,

"since you have been with me, you have proved yourself honest, efficient, faithful, and capable; you are fully competent to fill the position, and I willingly give place to you, as my son suggests. As you have been faithful to me, may your assistants prove faithful to you, and God prosper you in all!"

I was surprised—touched deeply by her solemn manner, and, taking the hand she extended to me, I bowed my face upon it a moment—a liberty I should have hardly dared to take under other circumstances—then, moving back to my former position, I said:

"I thank you both from my heart, more for the kindness your offer shows, and the trust it implies, than for any mere worldly advantage it might bring; but I must decline it. I must leave Oaklawn at the close of this term."

"Leave Oaklawn, when I have set my heart on having you for a neighbor! You are not serious, Miss Lathrop! you have not had time to secure a situation elsewhere?"

"Edward, my son, you are speaking hastily, if not officiously. If Miss Lathrop declines our offer, it is doubtless because she has something she deems more advantageous in view. Do our past relations warrant me in asking what your plans are?"

The tone was measured and constrained. I had wounded her; I had refused to adopt a plan which *she* had sanctioned—to accept a favor which she had offered — and, deeply troubled at the thought, I said, hastily:

"I have no definite plan—no situation in view. The idea is so recent—indeed, I have only thought of change."

"Then think of it no more, Miss Lathrop! It will be so pleasant to Michal, with whom you were always a favorite, to find you here when we return next spring. I say *we*, for I am determined to leave business affairs to James, and take mamma to Europe. You need not compress your lips, and take that independent air; there is no favor in the case, I assure you; we owe you this much and more!"

I shook my head. "It cannot be, Mr. Edward. I could not live here—life must have a new setting; besides, I must have leisure—time to think."

"And is there any thing in the air of Oaklawn to prevent that?" exclaimed he, laughing. "I wish there was, and we should be gayer. To look at you, one would think that this fortune with its responsibilities and temptations had fallen on your shoulders instead of mine. You are tired out—morbid from grief and fatigue. Take time to rest, and stay at Oaklawn—do!"

Before I could reply, Mrs. Ellis said, with a slight touch of impatience in her tone—a weakness seldom betrayed until since her illness:

"Edward, there is nothing remarkable in the mere love of change, a desire of novelty; and such is, as I understand her, Miss Lathrop's only reason for refusing what, in our judgment, seems a permanent good—a position of usefulness, honor, and profit, in which I have spent the best years of my life."

"You mistake!" I broke in, shrinking from the cool irony of her manner, and with difficulty restraining my tears. "It is not from mere love of novelty, or fickleness, that I refuse. It is because I must go. I cannot remain; my whole nature cries out against it."

"Miss Lathrop, a simple 'yes' or 'no' would be much more intelligible and to the point, especially as I do not claim any right to inquire into your reasons. It is to be hoped that they are valid, but melodramatics are unnecessary."

Her look and tone nerved me at once, and I said, calmly and decidedly:

"Then, with all gratitude to you both, I say *no !*"

She muttered the word "Weak," and I turned away.

Edward opened the door for me, saying:

"Well, here's disappointment number one; but remember, Miss Lina, the offer is open yet, and, whatever may be your decision, there will always be a cosy corner for you at the Pines, or anywhere else where I am master."

CHAPTER XIX.

THE DEPARTURE FROM OAKLAWN.

DURING the two succeeding days, I pondered over the course suggested by old Alice, without coming to a decision.

"You can live alone," said Reason, when, in the gathering twilight of the second day, I lingered over my desk in the deserted school-room. "You are accustomed to a life of isolation, labor, and self-denial; why should you start up here, like some ugly *Kobold*, to disappoint the hopes which this family have, with good reason, cherished for years? To be sure, you have the right, but rights are not always easy to vindicate or establish in this world. These people have been your friends; will your path be any the brighter because you have darkened theirs?—brought Michal back to a life of drudgery, and shut the sunlight of hope from Edward's future?—You will still have the memory of Rothsay Cavendish's loving words, of his kiss on your cheek, and his tears on your forehead, and that should be able to lift you above mere selfish ends."

Then uprose the heart. "Ay," it said, "and by that memory, that kiss, and those tears, it seems mean, cowardly, wanting in reverence to him, to forego your birthright, your father's name, even though the attempt to claim it should cover you with doubt and suspicion, and darken your life still more."

Thus, the heart had the last word, and I looked up to the wide, dumb sky, with a silent cry for help, forgetting that God sends no angels down to make for us the decisions of life, but that now, as of old, the question is to us—"Choose ye this day whom ye will serve!"

Presently, I became aware of the presence of some one in the room. A stealthy footstep crossed the floor and paused by one of the desks, and, although unaware of his return, I was certain that step was James Sancroft's. I was right, for in a few moments, with the same cat-like tread, he drew near one of the windows, to make out, as it seemed, by the fast-fading daylight, the contents of a paper which he held in his hand.

I could see him very plainly from my seat, and, hoping to escape his observation, I drew back as far as possible behind my desk, and sat as quiet as a mouse, while I scanned his handsome face, and wondered what could have brought him there. Suddenly he turned, approached me, and, leaning carelessly over my desk, said:

"Good-evening, Miss Lathrop. Are you inditing a sonnet to the moon, that you sit here so silent?"

"No, sir."

"Concise, as usual, I see," he replied, blandly. "Most young ladies like you would have given a little shriek or start of surprise at the sudden appearance of one supposed to be absent."

"I have been aware of your presence some time, Mr. Sancroft; besides, I am not nervous."

"No, nor affected, either. But people who are above these frailties do sometimes find a civil word wherewith to welcome home a friend."

Friend! I was curious to know what he was aiming at, and answered, somewhat bluntly:

"Possibly; but I have never been quite sure whether we are friends or—enemies."

"There is some comfort in talking with you, Miss Lina; you always speak to the point," he said, with a smile. "I have had that same feeling myself with regard to you, but we never doubt where we are wholly indifferent; therefore, I accept it as a sure proof that we were born to be friends."

"You found friendship on a doubt, then?"

"Yes; a much better foundation than impulse or the usual sentimental rubbish. You have refused to become Principal of Oaklawn, I hear?"

"Yes."

"You did well—another proof that we were meant to be friends."

"Perhaps—but—at a distance. A too close proximity might bear hard on such a foundation, you know."

"No—not at a distance; and I say 'well,' because, Miss Lathrop, I would draw you still nearer to me." He leaned over the desk and laid his hand on mine, as he added: "I rejoice at your refusal to accept this position, because I wish to win you for my wife."

"Your wife!" I exclaimed, eluding his hand, and springing to my feet. "Do you come here to mock me, sir?"

"Mock you? Is it so very strange that I, a man, should make such a proposal to you—a woman? Such things have been done before, I believe, without incurring the charge of mockery. Were it another, I might think her nervous."

I fancied I could detect something like triumph in his quiet, subdued tone, and, vexed at myself, I answered:

"Perhaps not, but such a relation should be based on something besides doubt. There is a wide difference between friendship and marriage, I believe, and, but a moment since, you doubted if we were even friends."

"The recent doubt was yours, not mine. I spoke of mine in the past tense. What you say of the difference between friendship and marriage, shows simply that you speak without due reflection. Recall the married people of your acquaintance, and see what the usual love-matches amount to. You have let the romance of your pupils becloud your own clear vision."

"You mistake, sir. I have not yet

learned to doubt, for one instant, the existence or truth of that love which has its root in the necessities and yearnings of the heart; or not to dread, as I would God's curse, the union that would seek to consummate itself without it. Your ideal is far too high or far too low for me to hope to realize it, seeing you do not even profess to love me."

"A very woman, after all, Miss Lina," he said, pleasantly. "It's not my *forte* to sigh and rhyme and play Romeo with 'white, up-turned eyes.' I leave that to Edward, as you know. The very reason why I have not professed to love you, is the highest compliment I can pay you—because I think or thought you preferred truth to flattery—and to say I love you, in the common, sentimental acceptation of the word, would be to speak falsely."

"May I ask with what motive you do approach me, sir?" I said, after a moment's silence, for his apparent frankness puzzled me. "I have neither beauty nor position of connections to attract a young man like you."

"No; personally, you are but passable, though your face, under different influences, would not be without a peculiar beauty of its own. But you have that which to me is more essential than beauty—intelligence, firmness, self-reliance, and self-control—remarkable for a woman; acute perception and keen insight, with indomitable perseverance in carrying out your plans; else, believe me, you would never have won your present footing with the Principal of Oaklawn. I have studied you somewhat, you see, and I say frankly that, to one like me, these qualities are of more value than wealth or beauty. I have my way to make in the world, and you yours. Become my wife, and trust me for wealth, position, and all they include."

"If I understand you aright, you want a wife for use, and you think I possess just the qualities most needed to hoist you up the hill of ambition, or scotch your wheels when weary?"

"You put it plainly, but I answer, yes; with this difference: we will rather breast the hill side by side."

"Mr. Sancroft, you are aware that I am a pauper by birth?"

"Yes; but why refer to that?"

"Because, I wish to assure you that God did not make me, as your words seem to imply, a pauper in soul, that I should sell myself for such husks as these! Let me pass, sir!"

He looked a little surprised as I confronted him, but made room for me, saying:

"Most men would take that as a refusal, I suppose, but I, too, am very persevering; and a woman who admits of no intermediate ground between friends and enemies should not make her decisions hastily."

All at once a light broke in upon me. I was no longer perplexed over this proposal, and, vexed at my previous stupidity, I exclaimed:

"You have seen Alice Ross, Mr. Sancroft? You know who I am!"

"I have seen Alice Ross. I left Mr. Spencer to come on alone, and walked round by the Pines. I do know who you pretend to be."

"You doubt it, then?"

"Members of my profession have a way of doubting things until they are proved. I need hardly tell a person of your discrimination that there is quite a difference between the assertions of an old, doting servant, and a young, ambitious, and, what some of my brethren of the bar, knowing her antecedents, would term, *needy* woman, and a well-established fact."

"Your own discrimination does you credit, sir," I courtesied gravely, glad that he could not see the hot blood flushing my cheek. "But the case is not yet in court. I asked you if you doubted it."

"Excuse me, as you observe, the case is not yet in court. When it is, I shall be there to give my opinion."

"You found the name of my father in the will?"

"The name of Philip Cavendish is in the will, but it is a mere matter of form. Mr. Spencer says he never married, and has been dead many years."

"Mr. Spencer is mistaken. He did marry, and I hold the certificate—" I paused, for the recollection that the only proof I had of my parents' marriage had been in Mr. Cavendish's possession when he died, and was probably lost to me forever, filled me with dismay.

"You were about to speak of a marriage-certificate, I infer; but the possession of such a certificate is no proof that the holder is the child, or legal heir, of the parties therein named. As the adviser of Michal and Edward, I shall subject all such evidence to the severest scrutiny."

"You speak plainly, sir, and I thank you. But the disinterestedness that would wed a woman with one hand, while with the other it branded her as a needy impostor, is quite beyond my appreciation. We will drop the subject, sir."

"As you please, but remember, henceforth, you and I recognize but two classes in the world, *friends* and *enemies*."

I left the room with that feeling of relief which we often feel when we unexpectedly stumble on the solution of some question that has perplexed us. I was no longer at a loss to understand James Sancroft's motives or character. He was ambitious of power and position, rather than of wealth; by marrying me, he might achieve both; by opposing and disgracing me, as I knew he would do remorselessly, he would attain nearly the same end, but with much more trouble and expense, for no one, who knew the family, would doubt that he would have the whole management of the business affairs.

"Friends and enemies!" The words rung in my ears above the heavy breathing of my room-mate that night, as I sat in judgment on myself. Had I done well in rejecting his offer? He was handsome and talented; he could establish my birth as no one else could; and Michal and Edward would not refuse to share the wealth proffered by a sister's hand. With him, were ease, affluence, respectability, honor—more: for, when I recalled the tone in which he had spoken of the certainty of his future success, I was conscious of a real sympathy and admiration, which justified his assertion of a likeness between us. Besides, there was a kind of charm in the tribute he had paid to my abilities. I was but a woman, young, and not overwise, and the voice of worldly wisdom whispered in my ears, as in those of my old hero, Christian: "Hear me; I am older than thou. Thou art like to meet with, in the way thou goest, wearisomeness, painfulness, hunger, perils, nakedness, swords, lions, dragons, darkness—in a word, death!"

But the very words, as I recognized them, defeated their aim. I knew the voice of the tempter, and I said: "Get thee behind me! I will not consent to a lie! I do not love this man. I do not respect him. I will not face God or man with a lie in my mouth! Neither will I conceal my birth or parentage! I will speak what I believe to be true, let the consequences be what they may."

I slept well that night. James Sancroft and I met, as usual, at the table, next morning, where I met, also, Mr. Spencer, a nice-looking gentleman, of about Mr. Cavendish's age. When we rose from the table, Mr. Sancroft said:

"Stay, Miss Lathrop.—Mr. Spencer, this is the person to whom your envelope is addressed."

"Ay, indeed!" returned the lawyer, who took from his pocket an envelope, and, looking at the address, and then at me, observed:

"This sealed envelope was found in Mr. Cavendish's pocket-book after his death. It bears the somewhat singular address—For '*La Zingarella, Oaklawn*.'

" ' None save these,' I said, as I laid the ring and certificate before him."

Righted at Last, p. 107.

Mr. Sancroft and his brother say that he was wont to designate you by that name. I am happy, therefore, to transfer it to you."

I took the paper and opened it on the spot. It enclosed a heavy ring of plain gold, and the marriage-certificate. I glanced at them, then looked at James Sancroft. He smiled a quiet, cool, self-possessed smile, while Edward, who had caught a glimpse of the ring, begged to know what it meant.

"Please interpret, Miss Lathrop," he said, gayly. "Some information is due Mr. Spencer. Who knows but it is an engagement-ring, enclosing all sorts of hopes and joys in its narrow circle?"

"Edward never sees but the bright side; but the Sybil," said James Sancroft, fixing his eyes on me with a significance I well understood, "is wiser. She can see that it may enclose also trouble, disappointment, and possibly disgrace."

"She will not shrink from speaking the truth, nevertheless, at the proper time," I said, quietly.

Mr. Spencer laughed, and Mrs. Ellis, who had appeared at the table in compliment to him, said, reprovingly: "Come, boys, you trifle while business waits."

I had heard the class in history, when a message came from Mrs. Ellis, requesting my presence in the parlor for a few minutes. I fancied the crisis had come, and, summoning all my courage, I walked into the room. Her first words undeceived me.

"Miss Lathrop," she said, "will you do me the favor to witness some business papers between Mr. Spencer and James? I prefer some one besides my own family."

I walked up to the table, about which they were grouped, glanced over the paper which Mr. Spencer placed before me, and, taking the pen offered by James Sancroft, wrote deliberately—"*Zerlina Cavendish*."

"Cavendish! you must be dreaming, miss!" Mr. Spencer's exclamation drew the attention of the others; James San-croft said nothing, but Edward laughed merrily, saying:

"What a blunder for you to make, Miss Lina!"

"It is no dream or blunder," began James Sancroft; "I have recently learned that Miss Lathrop *claims* this name as her own."

"Her own! Miss Lathrop! James, are you mad!" exclaimed his mother, while Edward stared in astonishment, and the lawyer quietly surveyed me from head to foot.

"By what right, miss?" inquired the latter, without waiting James Sancroft's reply. "As a relative of the late Rothsay Cavendish?"

"As his niece—the daughter of his brother Philip, sir."

There was an almost breathless silence in the room as he went on:

"What proofs have you of the truth of this assertion?"

"None save these; whose authenticity Mr. Cavendish acknowledged, and his own words," I said, as I laid the ring and certificate before him.

He read the certificate over aloud amid that silence; he examined the initials upon the ring, pronouncing them very slowly "P. C.—H. D.;" then laid them down, and looked around the silent, waiting faces until his eyes again rested upon me.

"You claim to be the child born of that marriage?"

"I do."

"The late Mr. Cavendish believed you to be so — acknowledged you as such?"

"He did."

"Before whom?"

"His housekeeper, Alice Ross, and myself."

"How long since the discovery of this relationship?"

"Since the 12th of April; the night before he left home on his last journey; and that journey was undertaken to obtain proofs of what I have stated."

"Then he doubted the claim?"

"Not in the least. But I told him of this ring, which I had reason to believe belonged to my mother, and he wished to obtain it."

"Why did he not make known this relationship—at least, to his and your friends here?"

"Because I begged him not to do so, until his return. He told me he should be absent but a few days, and I was so confused—I wanted time to collect my thoughts."

"So you knew this all the while, Lina!" cried Edward. "You knew it when I insisted on your congratulating me for taking away your inheritance? You let me urge upon you the privilege of gaining your bread by a life of toil under my patronage! O Lina! was it right to treat me thus?"

I would have replied, but Mrs. Ellis said quickly and decidedly: "Edward, you are interrupting business. I wish, for the sake of all concerned, to have this singular claim made clear, if possible. —Mr. Spencer, I beg you to assist us. What is your opinion?"

The gentleman again examined the certificate.

"It is, indeed, a singular affair," he began, slowly; "but I see no reason to question the validity of this certificate, especially as the date corresponds with the time when there were reasons for believing, as he himself asserted, that Philip Cavendish had married a young person of the same name, I think, as the one herein mentioned—Day. Of the credibility of this young person's claim, I cannot judge at present. If she can *prove* that she is the child born of that marriage, she will, of course, succeed to the property, to the exclusion of all others, for the terms of the will are: 'To Philip Cavendish or his heirs, provided they appear and prove their claim within the space of two years from the death of the testator.' This paper, of course, is but the first link in the chain of evidence

necessary to establish her claim, yet it may be done."

Here James Sancroft arose. "I wish to say," he remarked, "that, as one of the executors of the will, I shall subject every proof advanced to the strictest scrutiny of the law, it being well known that the late Mr. Cavendish was a somewhat eccentric person, and liable to be *deceived.*"

"Of course," replied the lawyer, blandly; but, stung by the insinuation, I said, with all the firmness I could command:

"Mr. Sancroft speaks of deception. Whether I am one likely to attempt such a part, I leave his mother and brother to decide. My life, for more than four years, has been passed in their family, and will answer for me, I think. For the rest, in speaking of my claim, you understand one thing, and I another: you think only of the property; I, of my right to bear my father's name, and be recognized as his child. You cannot understand this feeling, you, whose lives have been set round with sweet household affections. Had you been friendless and homeless from your birth, kept by your poverty and loneliness outside of the happy family circles which you might look in upon, but not enter; had you been made to feel that you were born for *use*, and nothing else, you might have grown ahungered like me! We do not cheat and juggle about things we hold sacred, sir. That certificate of my parents' marriage was accidentally discovered in the town where she was born, and where her father died, and sent me by a friend. Mr. Cavendish saw it by mere chance, and acknowledged and blessed me as his brother's child. Such I honestly believe myself to be, and, of all that he left, I claim nothing as mine, but that blessing, and the right to bear his name."

Before James Sancroft could speak, Edward was by my side. "I believe it, too!" he cried—"not only your right to the name, but the inheritance; and here, in the presence of these witnesses, I re-linquish my claim!"

"But your sister?" said Mr. Spencer.

"I speak for Michal as well as myself, sir!" he said, proudly.

"Your impulsive temper and generous spirit make you unjust to yourself as well as others," said James Sancroft, gently. "You cannot answer for Michal, and it would be well to have our mother's opinion before we discuss this matter further."

"I speak just what I believe, James," returned Edward, warmly, "and I know Michal will feel the same.—Pardon me, mother," he continued, turning his glow-ing face to her, "for forestalling you thus, but I know I spoke your sentiments as well as my own. We are not robbers, thank Heaven!"

We all turned to Mrs. Ellis, who had risen to her feet at Edward's sudden movement, and was still standing, but —dear Heaven, what a face! It was as if we could see the life slowly fading out of it, leaving behind that strange, awful ghastliness which I had seen on it once before. Yet, as if conscious of what was coming, the will still struggled for the mastery, for, when Edward sprang forward to support her, she put him fee-bly back, while her lips worked painfully in the effort to articulate something. One by one, we caught the words as they came in gasps:

"Not—a—cent!—Work—beg—but—let—her—prove—it."

She fell into Edward's arms, and James Sancroft, with a look at me that said, plainly, "This is your work!" as-sisted his brother in bearing her to her room.

Of course, all business was postponed for the present. James and Edward re-mained with their mother, and Mr. Spen-cer went to M——, where he had some business to attend to. Instead of return-ing to the school-room, I went to my own room, and sat wondering if old Sally Hunt had not been right when she said I had "no right to be in the world!" I had been sitting there some little time; when the chamber-maid brought me a slip of paper. It bore, in James Sancroft's writ-ing, these words: "The class in natural philosophy await their teacher."

Here was a duty. From my earliest memory, every one around me had im-pressed upon me my obligations to per-form my duty. Had I, then, no rights? I thought of Sally Hunt and Mrs. Ellis—so different, and yet both practically teaching the same thing—and I wondered if it was the "turpitude of the carnal heart," upon which Mr. Tyler used to lecture me, that had all these long years been uttering silent protests and yearn-ing for something else! I knew not, but Mr. Sancroft's note was plain; duty called, and I descended to the recitation-room.

That night I met Edward in the hall. I think he had been looking for me, for he came hastily forward, as soon as he saw me, saying:

"I thought you would be anxious about mother, Miss Lina. The doctor says the shock is less severe than the former one—the result of over-excitement, prob-ably. She is already conscious, and can speak intelligibly." He paused, then add-ed, earnestly: "Don't mind what James says, Lina. He is a lawyer, and sees things only after the manner of his pro-fession. Whether you can prove it or not, I believe, as I said before, that you are the heir, and so will Michal, I am sure, when she knows all the circum-stances."

The next morning Mr. Spencer called, and requested to see me a few minutes in the parlor.

His manner was kind and friendly; he referred to my singular position; said he had seen Alice Ross, and was con-vinced that, whatever might be the re-sult, I was guiltless of any intention to deceive; that both Mr. Cavendish and Mrs. Ross believed me Philip Cavendish's child, etc. He wished, if I did not object, to know the history of that certificate—how it came into my possession.

I told him briefly—also of Mr. Cavendish's intention of looking up the witnesses.

"That accounts for his projected journey West, and his anxiety to have me go with him. Pity he couldn't have lived to settle this business himself! The chances are, that one of the witnesses is living; the next step would be to find the place of your birth, and your mother's death; then to trace your grandfather's wanderings—um, um! It's a pity this young Sancroft is interested on the other side; he has the kind of talent needed for this—your grandfather crazy—it will cost time and money, and you have—"

"Neither!" I said, seeing him hesitate.

"Just so; therefore, let me give you an honest piece of advice: compromise with these people."

"I thank you, sir, but I have nothing to compromise."

"Do you still adhere to what you said yesterday morning?"

"Yes, sir. I ask nothing but the name."

"You are either a very proud or a very foolish woman. Here is property enough to make you all comfortable, but each party refuses to take it until it has been dragged through the law, and decimated by half a score of lawyers. Who shall say we lawyers stir up strife, after this?"

"You mistake; if such was their wish, and I might take my share as an acknowledged right, I would do so gladly. Mr. Edward and Miss Michal, I doubt not, would consent to this; but Mrs. Ellis, while she will not permit them to touch a dollar that is not clearly theirs, will require the most indubitable proof of my right; and—"

"Mr. Sancroft?" queried the lawyer.

"Will be even more exacting, and in the end contrive to bring them all to adopt his views—or all but one."

"The sister?"

"Yes."

"I wish she were here, then, for I believe there is some truth in your character-drawing. But will you give me leave to propose a compromise; not as coming from you," he said, seeing my gesture of dissent, "but as a suggestion of my own?"

"As you please, sir."

He did so, and, after some preliminary discussion, apparently succeeded. There was to be a compromise, the exact terms of which could not be arranged until Michal had been consulted. In the mean time, I was to bear my father's name, and go on with my duties as usual, for the present.

Mr. Spencer returned to New York, pleased with his diplomacy, and I remained to watch, day by day, the fulfilment of my prophecy—to feel the subtle insinuations and suspicions of James Sancroft infecting the atmosphere around me; to hear Mrs. Ellis's daily allusions to the want of the "necessary proof;" to know that Edward's faith in me, if not shaken, was sometimes troubled; to be required to unroll my past life to James Sancroft's scrutiny, and listen to his cool, cutting comments!—

> "Being observed
> When observation is not sympathy,
> I just being tortured;"

but being constantly watched, from lack of confidence, by those who call you friend, is rack and thumb-screws to boot. I could not endure it.

One evening, when I entered Mrs. Ellis's room, I found her looking over a letter with a troubled face. Her face was easily troubled nowadays, and always fearful of bad news from Miss Michal. I ventured to ask if she had heard from her.

"No," she replied, querulously. "I suppose you are impatient. It is natural, perhaps, for one so ambitious of wealth and independence."

I was weary—jaded by a hard day's work—in one of those moods where a kind word is of more value than "apples of gold," and it was some time before I could summon courage to reply:

"You entirely mistake the purport of my question, madam," I said, finally, "and the taunt conveyed in your words is unmerited. If I have sometimes longed for a freer life—if it has seemed hard that all my days must be spent in barely providing for the body, it has not been from overweening ambition or greed. The terms on which I have remained here prove that, and, if you refer to Mr. Cavendish's property, you will please remember that I claimed nothing but the right to bear my father's name."

"True; but, knowing the generous, impulsive disposition of Michal and Edward, you, probably, felt quite safe in making that display."

"Display!"

"The act of declining that to which one has no legal right can hardly be called any thing else, whatever pretensions it may assume."

I felt the force of her words, and for a brief space stood silent, humiliated before the image they presented, but, conscious of my integrity of purpose, I said:

"It certainly was not intended as such; moreover, the proof in my possession was sufficient to induce your lawyer and your sons to offer a compromise."

"Edward, you mean; neither my son James nor myself favored the proposal."

"Yet you preferred that they should work or beg, rather than accept the property that I renounced!"

"Yes; I scorn to have my children take that to which they have not a clear, undisputed right!"

"You think me mean, then!"

"I did not say so; the inference is yours, not mine. But I do think, when one in your circumstances makes such a claim, and, what is very singular, defers speaking of it until the only person, whose slightest word could have settled the matter beyond dispute, is dead, she should make some effort to prove it.

Money—is a sore temptation; there are few who can pass its ordeal scathless."

"It is, indeed, and a sore curse too, since it has the power to make poverty synonymous with baseness," I said, indignantly. "But it will not tempt me to bear a life made intolerable by degrading suspicion and insinuation. And here, Mrs. Ellis, our relations end. Michal and Edward will believe me; and possibly, when we meet again, I shall not lack the proof of which you speak."

She looked at me quietly a second, before she said:

"I think I have had occasion to remind you once before, Miss Lathrop—I beg pardon, Miss Cavendish—that these tragedy airs are unnecessary. The window is raised in the hall, I think. You will please close it as you pass."

Was this my dismissal?—or had she really not understood me?

I went to my room and tried to settle upon some plan for the future. Stay there I would not.

"What! Go and leave James Sancroft master of the field?" said Pride.

"Yes; better do that, than stay to endure scorn, suspicion, and contempt!—and I will go at once," I said, for I heard the voice of Edward in the hall—"go before he learns to despise me!"

I took no counsel of calm Reason, but immediately folded such clothes as I could put in my satchel, placed it by the side of Ollie's little trunk, and went to bed. Miss Roe soon came up, and, thinking me asleep, crept quietly down by my side, and was soon sound in slumber. Toward morning I arose, dressed, put the small sum remaining of my last quarter's salary into my pocket, and, taking my satchel and the little trunk, made my way down-stairs and out into the silent night.

I paused for a moment, and looked up at Miss Michal's window with a silent blessing; then, stood looking at the diverging roads, uncertain, as Hagar in

the wilderness, which to take. A breath
of wind moved the tree-tops; I fancied I
could distinguish the murmur of the
Pines, and I struck across the fields toward them. The house with its quaint
gables looked beautiful in the moonlight,
and, for a brief while, I fancied myself
its mistress. I paced its rooms, trained
its roses, planted its flower-beds, enjoyed
its sunsets, but always *alone*. Then, I
put Edward there, with some fair young
wife, whose loving hands only left his
arm, as they strolled through the walks,
to caress the dimpled little children that
frolicked around them, or paused from
their play at sunset, to listen, with
hushed voices and large, round eyes, to
the solemn murmur of the pines; I saw
refinement, graceful hospitality, domestic happiness, in the place of isolation;
and my decision was made. I did not
awaken dear old Alice, but, with a silent
benediction, I turned and went away.

CHAPTER XX.

IN A NOVEL SITUATION.

WHITHER? This was the question
that occupied my thought when I entered the solitary "ladies' room" at the
depot in M—— and looked out on the
diverging tracks. Anywhere beyond the
reach of Edward Ellis, who, I felt sure,
would leave no means untried to find me.
The parting words of Hannah Smith had
recurred to me more than once. Of her
they knew nothing. And late in the
afternoon of that day I stood in the
streets of the busy manufacturing town
of W——, making inquiries for her
brother's house.

A rosy-cheeked lad, who sat on a box,
whistling a popular negro melody, un-
puckered his lips long enough to reply,
and, tempted by the offer of a trifling re-
muneration, agreed to show me the way
to the house. He resumed his melody,
and we marched on for a mile or more,

when he halted, and to one of a row of
two-story buildings broke off with a decided *staccato* and a—"There, that's the
house!" took his fee, and, taking up his
strain again, went down the street, clink-
ing his money as an accompaniment. I
looked after him a moment with envi-
ous eyes, then mounted the steps, and
knocked. No one answered, but several
children left their play on the sidewalk,
and stared at me. I knocked again, but
my effort not seeming sufficiently energetic for Young America, one of them
ran up the steps, saying:

"Let me give it a thump—I'll raise
'em!"

He did, for he had barely time to run
back and hide his laughing face among
his companions, when the door was
opened; a young woman, of no very benignant aspect, thrust out her head, crying:

"You young rascals!—" but, seeing
me, she drew back with a hardly more
amiable—

"I don't want any thing. I never
trade with pedlers."

I looked down at Ollie's little trunk,
which I carried in my hand, and could
not help smiling, but, seeing her about to
close the door, I asked: "Does Miss Hannah Smith live here?"

"She stays here, when she's in this
place."

"Can I see her?"

"She ain't here. She went to live
with Sally's children in Ohio, last fall."

I suppose something of my disappointment was visible in my face, for
she added, in a softer tone: "Did you
want to see her?"

"Yes, very much, indeed. Can I
see her brother's wife?"

She bridled a little and said, with a
silly laugh: "I s'pose I answer to that
name. Will you walk in?"

Heaven knows I was faint and weary
enough to accept even a more grudging-
ly-given invitation than this, and I followed her into a room, where several

women were tacking a quilt. She gave me a chair, sat down at the frames, and, for a few minutes, they went on with their work in silence. Presently, they began to whisper and giggle; then, one remarked aloud, "That's a piece of Aunt Hannah's dress."

"Yes," said the bride, "she gin' it to me when I was nussin' his wife."

"She'd 'a kep' it till doomsday if she'd thought you'd ever been mistress here!" said another, laughing.

"Yes; an' here's a woman come ter see her. I s'posed everybody knew she was gone, an' why she went."

"Sure enough! Everybody does know, about here. Did I ever tell you what Betsey Blake said?"

A tirade of neighborhood gossip here set in, while I waited to gain some more definite information, if possible. The condition of the room and the tone of the conversation made it very evident to me why Hannah had left. At length, I asked if there was a quiet, respectable hotel near there, where I could obtain lodgings for the night.

"None nearer than the one by the depot," was the reply.

I arose to go, when it occurred to me that the brother of my old friend would be able to tell me of her movements and address, and I asked for "Mr. Smith."

The woman turned shortly around with—"What do you want of him?"

"I wish to speak with him."

The guests tittered, and Mrs. Smith's red cheek grew redder still as she said:

"If that's all you want, you can say what you've got to say to me. I'm mistress here, and, if you are what you should be, it'll answer just as well."

Had I been less weary, I should have laughed at the look of virtuous suspicion which she bestowed upon me and my baggage. As it was, I merely said:

"Of that I must be the judge, and I think not."

"Just as I s'posed! That's the door, madam!" she said, angrily, as I turned to make my way out.

"Why, Sally, you are not jealous, are you, so soon?" exclaimed one of the women. "The woman looks respectable—indeed, quite a lady, I should say."

"I dare say she is a *lady!*" I heard the bride rejoin; "for honest women don't tramp round the country after other folks' husbands. I've seen such *ladies* afore!"

Great as was my disappointment, I think this absurd termination of my interview with Mrs. Smith did me good. It turned my thoughts from myself to old Hannah and her trials; it set me to speculating upon her brother and his new wife. I felt that Hannah could never have lived with her, and, by the time I reached the hotel, I was quite reconciled to my disappointment. I obtained supper and a comfortable room, and then sat down to consider what I should do next. Uncle Steve, with whom I might have found shelter, was away beyond the Gates of Hercules; besides, Edward and Michal would be sure to seek me there. I had little Adeline's address in New York, but her husband was a stranger, and I was not willing to burden him, even had he the will and the means to aid me. I took out my money and counted it: I had seven dollars and a half; it would keep me, perhaps, a week, and, in the mean time, I must find something to do. I recalled, with what comfort I could, the theory I had so often heard advanced by Mr. Tyler and Mrs. Ellis, that "no really deserving person need suffer for food or shelter who was willing to work;" and, in order to test it, I began with the landlady, a motherly, pleasant-voiced woman, and asked her at once if she could assist me in finding employment.

She gave me a critical glance, and asked: "What sort of employment? Most young women about here go into factories."

I had visited a cotton-mill in Bubbleton with Miss Agnes once; I remembered

8

the noise, and the smell of rancid oil, and said, quickly: "Plain sewing, children's nurse, housework, any thing by which I can gain my bread honestly."

"Most people, in a place like this, do their own sewing, and take care of their own children. If you can fit dresses—"

I shook my head.

"Well, then, about housework. Are you a good cook?"

"I should not like to pledge myself as such. I know something about it, and can learn."

"That's a pity, for Squire Martin's wife wants a cook; she was here yesterday to see if I could recommend any one. But she's very particular."

Here she gave me another look, letting her eyes drop slowly from my face over my dark delaine dress, white linen collar and cuffs, to the toe of my gaiter; then they trembled back until they rested on my hands.

"Your hands don't look much like cooking," she observed. "May I ask what you are used to doing?"

"I have been teaching for some years past."

"Why don't you teach still? I dare say you could get a situation here, if you are competent, and can bring the necessary testimonials."

"Because I have not those testimonials, ma'am."

She drew back a step, and the shade of distrust which I anticipated came over her face, while she said:

"But you know such things are required. People, in these days, don't take servants without knowing something of them."

She made a movement as if to leave me, but paused when I said, rapidly but firmly:

"I do, and it is doubtless wise, but there may be exceptions, madam, and my case is one. I am willing to tell you as much of my affairs as is consistent with my own welfare. Through no fault of my own, but to secure my peace of mind

and self-respect, I felt compelled to leave the place where I have been teaching some years, and to leave it suddenly, taking with me only the baggage I have with me, and the few dollars I had in my purse. I expected to find an old friend in this place, who would aid me by her wisdom and experience. I am disappointed; she left the place months since. I know no one, and I thought I would apply to you, thinking you might possibly help me; at least, that you would believe me for the sake of our common womanhood."

She seemed puzzled, as her words implied, for she said, thoughtfully:

"I don't want to be hard or unjust, and you look and speak like an honest woman; still, we people who keep a public-house see so many—well, will you tell me the name of the friend you expected to find here?"

"Hannah Smith, the sister of Eli Smith."

Her face brightened at once. "I'm glad, for your sake, it was Hannah. I know her well, and no one who had done any thing to be ashamed of would be likely to come to her for help. My girls, who are away on a visit now, do the sewing mostly, but you are welcome to stay and help about the house until we see what can be done. Have you no relatives or friends?"

"No relatives living, ma'am, and no friends in this country; at least, none to whom I can apply."

"Poor thing! How should I feel if it were my Ellen, or Jane?" she said, as she hastened away at a call from her husband. I went into the kitchen, and wiped the dishes for the Irish cook, inwardly thanking God that, even in this noisy, dusty place, He had kept fresh and green the plant of human kindness, strengthening it, at need, by the deep experiences of maternity.

I was still in the kitchen when a train thundered into the depot, a few rods distant; presently, several people entered the house; there were much talking and some confusion; then the landlady put her head into the kitchen, and bade me "bring fresh water to No. 9—quick. The train had met with an accident, and a lady had been seriously injured." I obeyed, and found a dozen people around the bed, talking of the "narrow escape," while an elderly gentleman stood with his fingers on the wrist of the injured person, with a look that betokened anxiety and impatience. I made my way to the bedside, and began to bathe the lady's dusty and grazed face with the tepid water.

"That's sensible," said the gentleman, "she begins to revive. I think she had fainted."

"She needs more air," I said, with a glance at the crowd.

"Right!" he turned to those present, saying: "I thank all here, in the name of my friend Mrs. Lloyd, for their sympathy and kindness. She begins to revive, and I think we had better leave her with the women of the house until the doctor arrives. Before the train leaves, I hope to be able to assure you that she is not seriously injured."

He left the room, and the others followed, leaving only Mrs. Burbank, the landlady, and myself, to loosen the lady's dress and bind up, as well as we could, her mass of strong black hair, slightly streaked with gray. She seemed a woman of forty-five or more, with a magnificent bust and shoulders, and features and complexion that reminded me of my old Jewish heroines. Before we had finished, the doctor entered, and his applications soon restored her to consciousness. She was able to reply to his questions, and I inferred, from her air and manner, that she was *une grande dame*, at least, in her own opinion, for she was very haughty and supercilious, and seemed filled with horror at being obliged to stay "in such a place." But stay she must, for, although she was not seriously injured, the bruises and contusions were so severe that the physician assured her she could not travel under several days; and, as pride could not salve her wounds, she was obliged to submit.

I slept on a lounge in her room that night, to minister to her wants; and in the morning, when I went to my breakfast, Mrs. Burbank told me that the gray-haired gentleman, whom I had seen the evening before, desired to speak with me in the parlor.

"I think he wants you to take care of Mrs. Lloyd until she is able to travel, and I shall be glad if you will, for she seems to be one of those folks who don't know as there is anybody else in the world but themselves," she said, pleasantly.

She was right. When I entered the parlor, the gentleman looked at me a second, not inquisitively, but as if he were not quite certain how to address me; then he asked me to be seated, and said:

"The doctor tells me that Mrs. Lloyd's injuries will detain her here some days. My business compels me to go on, and, as she was under my care, and has no servant with her, I feel anxious to provide for her comfort as far as I can. The landlady thinks I may induce you to remain with her until she is able to travel?" He paused, and looked at me inquiringly.

"I shall be very glad, indeed, to do so, sir; for, at present, I am without employment."

"Thank you. Mrs. Lloyd is the widow of a distinguished gentleman, and has resided much abroad. She has been accustomed to a good deal of attention, and you may find her somewhat difficult and exacting, but I think you will succeed."

"I will try, sir."

"That is all I ask." He took from his pocket-book a bank-note, and offered it to me, saying, "Here is a trifle in advance."

I declined to receive it, saying, "When

my wages are due, I shall receive them from Mrs. Lloyd."

He smiled, and asked me to attend him to that lady's room, where he explained the arrangement. She looked at me as if I were an inevitable evil to be endured, like her bruises, thanked him, and gave him some messages for her daughters, who were in New York.

Thus I found myself installed as nurse, and my patient kept me very busy. But, if she was *exigeante*, I was very patient; if haughty, almost to insolence (and ladies, I found, could be insolent), I was indifferent, not caring enough about her to resent it; so the time passed quietly. Meantime, she received letters from her daughters, and, one day, on the arrival of the western train, there came sweeping into our dim room such a vision of elegance and fashion—ay, and of beauty, too, for the face was very beautiful, the youthful, unfurrowed image of the mother—as I had never seen before.

It was Miss Lloyd, and, kissing her mother, she said, gayly:

"Now, just own, mamma, that for once you are taken by surprise?"

"I am! When Miss Julia Lloyd takes to travelling alone, like a common servant-girl, it is time to be surprised," said the lady, gravely. "But I presume it was a suggestion of Cousin Anne's."

"Yes; and to tell the truth, mamma, I rather enjoyed it, for, of course, nothing could happen to *me*—nothing improper, I mean."

She drew herself up, as if, by the very motion, she set herself above the common incidents and accidents of life, and her face assumed the same haughty look that distinguished her mother's, only not so deeply ingrained in every line.

The mother smiled proudly as she surveyed the tall, superb figure.

"Certainly not, but it is not the custom of people of our position, and a disregard of the laws of society argues a lack of self-respect. But cousin never rightly understood such matters."

"No; she was much troubled about you, and insisted on my coming, and, to confess the truth, mamma, I was a little *distrait*, and, moreover, was curious to see how the Hon. Mrs. Lloyd looked in a country tavern."

She gave a glance around the room, and, with an expressive shrug of the shoulders, added: "Really, mamma, it's too bad. I don't see how you have contrived to exist."

I had approached to take her wraps, which she removed and threw over my arm, with no more apparent consciousness of my presence than if I had been a clothes-rack, and went on with the conversation. It turned upon family affairs, and, not receiving any intimation from Mrs. Lloyd to leave the room, I retired to the window, but the room was not large, and I heard every word.

But they were not so unmindful as I thought; for, when Mrs. Lloyd began urging pecuniary reasons for refusing to spend the coming season at Saratoga, Miss Lloyd, with a glance at me, replied in French, and the conversation was carried on in that language, which they both spoke admirably.

Having been accustomed to the fluent tongue of Mademoiselle Berthier, I had no difficulty in understanding them; therefore I arose, and, coming to Mrs. Lloyd's side, said:

"Excuse me, madam, but I think I ought to tell you that my knowledge of French enables me to understand all you say."

They looked at me a second with an expression which, had it been on the face of a common mortal, I should have called surprise; then Miss Lloyd said, carelessly:

"A French *bonne*, mamma! Quite a *coup de-théâtre*, though I wonder how she ever strayed here?"

"I am not French, miss, only familiar with that language."

"Your feeling is quite correct," said Mrs. Lloyd, loftily. "You can go down and tell them to send up dinner for two. I will ring when I want you."

When the bell again summoned me to her presence, the saturnine composure of the elder lady seemed undisturbed; but the daughter's cheek was flushed, and her tone irritable and impatient, as she said:

"To think of staying shut up at that horrid old country place! No society, no amusements. I shall die of *ennui* before the summer is half over! If the master were only at home, it would be a different thing."

"Yes, I wish he were. But I have stated my reasons; besides, you seem to forget Grace. She must spend her vacation somewhere."

"Let her go to Highcliff with Cousin Anne, or accept the invitation of the Pyncheons to visit Northampton. Or, if you choose to remain with Cousin Anne, I can go with the Howards. But, *à propos* of Cousin Anne, did you find a companion for her?"

"No. She must be getting into her dotage, or she never would have sent such a request to me! The person she spoke of is married. I know nothing of such people, and I certainly did not expect to look up servants for her, when I accepted her invitation. But she always lacked judgment."

The young lady smiled satirically.

"Yes; I thought when she spoke of it, that it would a new *rôle* for the Hon. Mrs. Lloyd to be exploring Yankee lodging-houses in pursuit of reduced gentlewomen; people who have seen better days, as they term it. But, mamma, we must humor her, and, though I detest that sort of people, I really hope she will find some one, for, if we are to go to Highcliff for the summer, I have no idea of playing the part of companion myself, and reading to her by the hour."

Mrs. Lloyd yawned as if tired of the subject, but my thoughts naturally reverted to it. Some lady wanted a companion: would she accept me? Would she require the usual credentials? If so, would my week's service with Mrs. Lloyd suffice? Who was Cousin Anne? Should I be brought into close and daily contact with these Lloyds, whose intolerable and intolerant pride might become unendurable?

All these queries, save the last, were solved on the following day: Mrs. Lloyd announced herself well enough to travel, and, when she came to pay me, I referred to the above conversation, and asked if she would be so kind as to recommend me to fill the place.

She lifted her eyebrows, and said, haughtily: "You might also have heard that it is a lady my cousin needs—a person of education and refinement—not an ordinary servant."

"I did, madam, but, having passed the last six years in school, either as pupil or teacher, I thought I might possess the requisite amount of culture."

"Mamma," said Miss Julia, "perhaps you had better give her a trial. It will save some explanations. If she does not suit, it's not your affair."

"Have you a character?"

"None, save such as my week's service with you may entitle me to. The only friend in this place to whom I could refer is absent, and I must trust to your kindness."

She looked at her daughter, who answered, with a curl of her rich, red lip:

"It's not essential, mamma. Your word will be sufficient. These characters are simply humbug — excuse me, *chère maman*, but it's just the word—*au reste*, she looks quiet and unpresuming— so engage her."

The matter was speedily settled. I was to receive a salary of one hundred and fifty dollars per annum, provided I gave satisfaction, Mrs. Lloyd assuming that her word would render any testimonials unnecessary.

I had sufficient money for my travelling-expenses, and an inspection of the contents of my satchel led me to think that the under-clothing and black-silk dress it contained might, with the delaine I had on, be made to cover me respectably until my first quarterly payment became due; and, with a lighter heart than I had known for many days, I bade the landlady "Good-by," and followed the ladies to the station.

CHAPTER XXI.

COUSIN ANNE.

It was almost dark when the carriage containing Mrs. and Miss Lloyd, and, by sufferance, the "humble companion," drove up to a handsome but old-fashioned house in Bleecker Street, New York. A man-servant met us and conducted us across the hall into a pleasant apartment that opened into the dining-room, where the servants were laying the table for dinner.

Mrs. Lloyd and her daughter left the room very soon, bidding me wait until I was sent for. I had waited, it seemed to me, a long time, when a smartly-dressed young woman came tripping in, and, with rather a contemptuous look at me and my little baggage, said:

"Mrs. Lloyd desires to see you in Miss Annesley's room, miss."

"Miss Annesley! Miss Anne Annesley!" I exclaimed. It was the first time I had heard my new mistress's family name, the Lloyds always having spoken of her as Cousin Anne, and I had thought it best to ask no questions. I stood, therefore, staring the girl blankly in the face.

"Yes; I'm sure I spoke it plainly enough!" she said, impatiently. "You had better hurry, miss, for Mrs. Lloyd isn't fond of waiting, and the dinner-bell will ring soon. You can leave your bundles in the hall."

I did as she directed, and followed her up a flight of stairs, like one walking in a dream, through a small anteroom into a large chamber, where Mrs. Lloyd and her daughter, in perfectly fresh costumes, sat talking with some one whose face, and almost her whole figure, was hidden from me by the high back of the capacious easy-chair in which she reclined. At a sign from Mrs. Lloyd, I advanced to her side, and, with a very perceptible abatement of her usual *hauteur*, she said:

"Anne, dear, this is the young person of whom I was speaking—Ray—Lina Ray is the name, I think. Of course, you take her only on trial, for of that class of people I absolutely know nothing."

During the week passed at the hotel, Mrs. Lloyd had persisted in calling me Ray, and, after one or two attempts to correct her, I had let it pass as a matter of no account; now, I felt inwardly grateful for an error which would leave me to conceal or disclose my real name, as circumstances might dictate. I bowed, therefore, and the small, delicate, elderly lady in the chair said, with a pleasant smile:

"Thank you, cousin; the young lady is very welcome. You look weary, my dear; sit down, and I will ring for Jane to attend to you."

There are moments when the most complete self-control is hardly proof against a simple word uttered in a loving tone, and I felt the tears spring to my eyes while the lady spoke. Nor were they frozen by the knowledge that Mrs. Lloyd elevated her eyebrows and chin with marked significance at the tone, nor by Miss Julia's emphatic shrug of her fair shoulders, as she said:

"Mamma, with Cousin Anne's permission, we will retire. I wish to give Laura some directions about unpacking, before we go to dinner."

Both ladies arose, and Miss Annesley said, hastily:

"Don't let me detain you, ladies. Cousin Lloyd, I trust you will find your rooms comfortable. If there is any thing wanting, let Mrs. Price know. Make yourself entirely at home, and don't trouble yourself about me. I didn't invite you here to keep you shut up with a cripple. For the present, you must be the hostess, and I the guest, and some evening, before long, I shall come down and take tea with you. Now, I eat here, and this young lady shall be my guest to-night."

She rang a silver bell upon the table within her reach, as the ladies swept out, and a servant entered and waited for my hat and cape. My fingers were strangely tremulous, and, seeing me pull vainly at the string of my veil, Miss Annesley bade the girl help me.

"Now," she began, but, interrupting herself with a smile, she said: "Pardon me, dear, I forgot that you had been kept waiting while my guests dressed.—Jane, show Miss Ray to her room, the one formerly occupied by Miss Lee, and see that she has every thing she needs.—When you have dressed, child, you will return to this room and dine with me. Dinner will be sent up," she turned her eye to her watch upon the table, "in just twenty-five minutes.—Jane, you see that her baggage is carried up."

My baggage! I could not but smile when I thought of it. Unwilling that it should be the subject of further comment by the servants, I said to Jane as the door closed upon us, that I would go for my satchel myself.

"No, Miss. Miss Annesley would be displeased if I permitted it. If you have nothing but a satchel, I will bring it up."

I told her where I had left it with my small bundle, and was amused at seeing her bring them to my room, and put them down as respectfully as if they had contained a queen's outfit. I was glad to be left alone a moment, that I might consider the peculiar circumstances in which I was placed; for that this was the old Annesley house, and the lady in yonder room, awaiting my return, was the relative of whom Miss Agnes had spoken as always residing there, I had not the slightest doubt.

I did not forget that her words had been: "When you are dressed," but, fortunately, my toilet did not require much thought, and all the while I was binding up my hair, and brushing out the obstinate crimps, I was querying whether, in "devising my own way," I had not walked very nearly, if not right, into the lion's mouth. Ralph Annesley was one of the executors of my uncle's will; he was the dear friend and cousin of both Rothsay and Philip Cavendish, and would he not, when a knowledge of the circumstances reached him, strain every nerve to ferret out the missing claimant, and make her either prove her claim or cover her with ignominy as an impostor? I had not thought of this before, and now I half wished that I had stayed at Oaklawn and faced him there, if necessary, for he would never understand the mood in which I left that place; and the very fact of my leaving as I did would be construed as an evidence of my guilt. Should I remain under this roof to be discovered and impaled by his keen eyes as swindler —a deliberate cheat? I let my black-silk dress, from which I was smoothing the folds, fall from my hands, body and soul shrinking before that thought. It may be that—

"To those who are sad already, it seems sweet,
  By clear foreknowledge, to make perfect pain ; "

but I had not attained that state, and, for some moments, I sat dumbly pitying myself. Then, half in shame of my cowardice, I rose up, saying to myself:

"You acted for the best, Lina, and you must not shrink from the result. He may not return before you have earned money enough to be able to procure the proof, if proof there be, of your birth, and, if he does, men don't seek the missing at their own hearth-stones; besides, he believed you once without pledge or witness, why should he not again? If he does not, the truth will remain the same, and with truth and toil you can still continue to live."

The black-silk dress went on, and I
was ready for Miss Annesley.

She received me with the same pleasant smile; a servant brought up the dinner, the girl Jane arranged the tray upon
a small table, by the side of her mistress,
placed a chair for me, and withdrew.

During dinner, my mistress questioned
me about my journey, not curiously, but
from a simple desire to put me at ease.
Then she spoke of herself, and my duties.
By a fall, last autumn, she had injured her
knee, and been confined to the house all
winter in consequence. Just before that
accident, the young lady, who had been
with her several years, sickened and
died, while on a visit to her parents, and
she had been alone, until Miss Julia Lloyd
came on with her sister Grace, who was
a member of Madame Chegary's school.
She liked to have young ladies about her;
they made a stir of life in the old house;
and, as her mother had broken up her
establishment, she had invited them to
spend the summer with her. She had
hoped to be able to go down-stairs to receive Mrs. Lloyd herself, but that, she
had found, was out of the question. She
was so glad that Cousin Lloyd had been
able to bring me with her! Was I fond
of reading aloud?

"Yes."

"Was I sure it did not tire me—in-
jure my chest?"

"Quite sure. It had been a part of
my duties for several years."

"That was fortunate. Her eyes were
poor, and she was so fond of reading.
Miss Lloyd read well—remarkably well,
as, indeed, she did every thing she under-
took, but she could not think of pressing
her guests into her service. But we
should not do much until we got settled
at Highcliff.—That was another thing.
Mrs. Lloyd had, of course, told me that
she spent her summers in the country—
perhaps I did not like the country?"

"I did, indeed; my whole life had
been passed there."

"Ay, then, I must be fond of garden-

ing. I could help her; she was so fond
of flowers, and she had so many at Highcliff—old-fashioned things like herself;
but she liked them, and she thought I
would—they might remind me of my
mother's garden."

"I had no mother!" I might have
added that my dreams of what a mother's voice might be had been more nearly realized than ever before, while she
was speaking, but I kept silent.

She looked at me pityingly. "That
was sad—she knew all about that! So
young, too! Would I have a peach?
Her peaches were raised at Highcliff.
Peter told her, when last in town, that
the trees had been full of blossoms this
spring; please Heaven, we would watch
their ripening ourselves."

"Is Highcliff far from here?" I
asked.

"No; it's among the Bedford hills in
Westchester County, a place that had
belonged to Mr. Annesley's father—Mr.
Ralph Saville Annesley I mean, to whom
this place also belongs."

"Is he often here, ma'am?"

"Not often; I always keep his rooms
ready, for no one knows when he may
come—perhaps from Egypt or Lapland,
for Cousin Ralph is a great traveller."

"Where is he now?"

"He spent the winter in Paris, I hear
from his lawyer, Mr. Spencer. He never
writes except on business, and then to
Mr. Spencer."

"He has no family?"

"No; he and I are the last of our
race." She pushed back her plate with
a sigh, and was silent for some minutes,
saddened, as it seemed, by the thought;
then, rousing herself, she added:

"It is sad to contemplate the extinction of an old family, like ours; but Mr.
Annesley has never married, and probably never will."

"Is he so very fastidious, then?"

"Not more so, perhaps, than any gentleman of his age and experience. He is
a great favorite with the ladies, but as

soon as he leaves their presence he forgets all about them, and is, in reality, more devoted to an old woman like me than to the most brilliant of them all. I don't think he cares much for domestic life, and perhaps the unfortunate experience of his youth has made him skeptical."

I wondered what that experience was. Had he been "dis'p'inted," like Polly Maria? If so, he certainly did not, as Uncle Steve said, "take to it nat'rally." But the lady did not seem inclined to speak, so I ventured to ask:

"Has he suffered, then, very much?"

"I hardly know. When quite young, he became very much attached to a young lady, but was superseded in the good graces of the parents, and, it was said, in the affections of the lady, by a half-brother, some years his senior, whose great wealth, inherited from his mother, weighed largely in his favor. Ralph went to England, but, before the marriage took place, he was recalled by his brother's sudden death. Then, the parents of the lady were very courteous to him, and it was even said that their daughter's feelings toward him had remained unchanged, her acceptance of the brother having been in obedience to filial duty; but he treated them with the most friendly but profound indifference, and the lady soon married into one of our wealthiest families. They are on friendly terms, and most of his friends doubt if he ever cared for her at all."

"I should not think her worth caring for," I said, bluntly.

She smiled. "That is the judgment of youth, and, at your age, I should have thought so too. But her chief fault was one which older eyes are inclined to view with more leniency—deference to her parents' will. She is one of the most elegant ladies in the city, and her house the centre of attraction."

"And you think this is the reason of his remaining unmarried?"

"It is the only reason I can give for

his restless, wandering life—so unlike the habits of his family; and when I see Mrs. Lincoln—that is the lady, dear—I cannot but think how different his life would have been if he had married her."

She rang for Jane to remove the table, asked me to replenish the wood-fire in the grate, a task which I had only just performed, when the Lloyds came up from dinner, and, receiving no orders to withdraw, I took a low seat, and sat trying to picture to myself Mr. Annesley, with his keen eyes and abrupt, independent speech and manners, as the husband of that elegant lady, dispensing the honors of a mansion which was the "centre of attraction" to the most aristocratic and fashionable people in the city. But, somehow, I did not succeed; the surroundings, though I painted them gorgeously enough, were too light and conventional—his dark face and lithe figure would not harmonize with them; and to satisfy myself, I had to place him alone, beneath an Eastern palm, with no background save the line of the distant horizon, where limitless expanse of sky came down to meet the limitless expanse of arid desert-sand below, with no accessories save the group of Arab attendants and their patient camels. Had I had crayon and paper, I could not have drawn the lines or worked in the shades more carefully; and so intent was my thought on this, that I scarcely noted aught of the presence of the ladies, save the intermediate ripple of their low voices, until they rose to withdraw, and Miss Lloyd said, laughing:

"Don't be too sanguine, cousin Anne. Perfection does not usually take that form!"

Miss Annesley glanced hurriedly toward me; the lady shrugged her shoulders and swept out of the room, followed by her mamma.

As soon as they were gone, Miss Annesley turned to me and said:

"Pardon me, dear. I ought to have

dismissed you before. You must be so
weary."

"Is there nothing I can do for you,
ma'am?"

"No, Jane attends to me. To-morrow, we will talk over our plans. Good-
night."

When I entered my room and saw
the (to me) elegant furniture—the bed
with its snowy drapery—and thought
how recently I had been houseless and
homeless, my heart was filled with gratitude to "Our Father" for this haven of
rest. All my doubts seemed to vanish;
I felt that I could leave my future in
His hands, only praying for grace and
strength to meet its trials and perform its
duties, whatever they might be; and
very sweet and sound was the rest I enjoyed that first night in my new home.

CHAPTER XXII.

A HUMBLE COMPANION.

It is not necessary that I should enter
into the details of the life of a "humble
companion," and mine, in the service of
Miss Annesley, must have been a pleasant exception to the general rule. She
was kind and just, very much devoted to
the usages and traditions of her family,
very fond of old friends and old books;
and the reader must fancy me reading
aloud Milton, Shakespeare, Cowper, and
Thomson, but much oftener from the volumes of the *Rambler* and *Spectator*, her
smile growing sweeter, and her eyes
brighter at the stately courtesy of good
old Sir Roger de Coverley, until I came to
take her for the living representative of
the lady whose perfections drew from
him that most graceful of all compliments:

"She is as inimitable by all women,
as she is inaccessible to all men!"

The house contained a large and valuable library, to which I had free access;
and here, among works of rare wisdom,
I found those lighter tales which, under

Mr. Tyler's rule, had tempted me into
the pit of falsehood, many of which I now
read aloud as a part of my duty. But
the apartments on the first floor presented quite a contrast to our quiet life.
Miss Annesley, with rare generosity, had
left her guests free to enjoy themselves.
They had many friends and acquaintances
in the city, and the house was often full
of company. I often amused myself by
watching from the window the elegantly-
dressed ladies and gentlemen who came
to call on the Lloyds. Sometimes I caught
the subdued murmur of their voices, or a
burst of silvery laughter, as I passed
through the hall; and I used to wonder
if they were really born to a life of doubt,
and care, and sorrow, like myself. The
Lloyds usually passed an hour or so in Miss
Annesley's room after dinner, but as they
never, after that first day, seemed to notice me any more than they did any
other piece of furniture, I gladly availed
myself of my mistress's permission to
take this time for a walk, and my first
thought was to find little Adeline Leete.
I had her address, 160 Mulberry Street,
and, not caring to take a servant with
me, I studied the great plan of the city
hanging in one of the back halls, until I
felt quite sure I could find my way there
alone. I knew nothing of the city save
a few streets in the vicinity of Bleecker,
leading to Washington Square, and Broadway, and, when I had crossed that great
thoroughfare, and turned into Mulberry,
my heart almost failed me. Broken pave-
ments; tumbling, old houses; filth of all
description; stenches of all odors; ghoul-
like swine, that ought long ago to have
perished in the water, like their devil-
infested progenitors in Galilee; lean, hun-
gry-eyed, snarling curs, hunting for bones;
reeking gutters—could any human being
live in such a place as this!—especially
Uncle Steve's Bluebird—that little tender
thing—who, as he once told me, "needed broodin' so much!"

I thought of the Cove, the fresh sea-
breeze, the broad, yellow beach, the

gleaming, glittering, blue water, the tidy cottage overshadowed by the giant pine, and grew sick and faint at the contrast. I paused before one of the houses, and said: "She is dead; you might as well expect to find here the wind-flower of the woods." But there were children there—dirty, scrofulous, pale-faced, little creatures; and, on a window-ledge, away up near the roof of one of these houses, was a pot, containing some kind of plant. Children and flowers, but, dear Heaven, what a new sense of the possibilities of life I gained during that walk! The sight of these gave me courage, and I pushed on until I stood before the house bearing the number I sought. A slatternly-looking woman opened the door, and, in answer to my inquiry, directed me to the "third floor, front." I gave a glance of dismay at the filthy stairs, which seemed but a continuation of the street, but, with Birdie so near, I was not to be turned back. I ascended rapidly, and knocked at the number which the woman had indicated. A voice said, "Come in," but the tone was so unlike the gleeful one I remembered, that I hesitated, and opened the door very carefully. But there she stood, the darling, and as I put back my veil, and walked forward to meet her, I saw a flash of surprise steal over her face; her drooping eyelids raised wide with wonder, just as was her wont when Uncle Steve told some tale more marvellous than any that had gone before, and the next instant she was in my arms, her face buried on my shoulder, crying:

"O Lina—Lina!"

I could have wept also, but I knew that would not do; so I half carried her across the room, no great distance, to a miserable old lounge, and let her weep, while I began to give an account of my endeavors to find her; I hardly knew or cared what I said, so that it calmed and diverted her mind from the direction I knew it must have taken.

At last she lifted her head, but, without the slightest effort to move otherwise, said:

"I must cry, Lina; I am so glad, you can't think how glad, to see you! It reminds me so of Uncle Steve and the dear old days!"

"Yes, they were indeed dear old days," I said, involuntarily.

Again her head was laid on my shoulder, but it was as quickly raised, and, dashing away her tears, she said, quickly:

"You must not think, because I cry, that I'm not happy, Lina. Of course, I am, and ought to be, but it's so different. One can never be a child but once, and I suppose that's what makes one feel so sad when thinking about it."

She withdrew from my arms, and sat erect with a little attempt at wisdom and dignity, which poorly hid from my eyes the little trembling heart; but now, for the first time, I got a full view of her face. It was fair, sweet, childish, lovable still, but thinner and paler, and there was a shadow about her eyes, and a tremulous curve to her lip, that convinced me that something more than regrets for a vanished childhood had been at work within. I took this in at a glance, for I could not bear that she should suspect my thoughts, while I asked:

"How do you busy yourself, Birdie? Have you made many acquaintances?"

"No; some people whom Henry knew called here, and we have been out a few times, but city people seem different from those I knew at home; besides, I haven't cared to go out much, lately. I haven't been very well."

"Well, now I am in the city, I shall look after you," I said, cheerfully, for the attempt at matronly dignity was all gone, and in its place a look of weariness that made me inexpressibly sad. "Do you like boarding?"

"No; I would rather keep house, and we mean to as soon as Henry can find suitable rooms—such as we can afford to take, for rent is so high here, Lina."

"Yes, I suppose so. But if you could keep house, you would have more to occupy you, though I suppose Mr. Heath spends all his leisure with you, now."

It was a home question, I knew, but I must know something of this husband.

"Oh, yes—that is, when he can. But he is very much confined, poor fellow, and when he has a leisure evening it seems hard to keep him cooped up here. Men can't content themselves as easily as we do; besides, I am afraid I am sometimes stupid, especially of late — you know, I never was remarkably bright, dear—but, by-and-by, I suppose—I believe, we shall have something to keep us both busy."

The blushing face was again hidden, and the blush and the action more significant than the words.

She a mother! I gave a glance around the narrow room. I thought of the vile street without, the nauseous smells and vitiated atmosphere—of her lonely life, for her simple excuses could not deceive me, if they did herself—and did not wonder that she grew sick and faint, thinking of dear Uncle Steve and the clear blue sea. For some seconds I sat with my arms folded closely about her with a yearning wish to shelter her from all sorrow and harm, before I could command my voice to say, firmly:

"Indeed, Birdie, is it so? Then I must come to you so much the oftener. I am so glad to be near you!"

Now the face was raised, and, with a still heightened color, and the light of a new hope in her eyes, it had more the look of my old pet's than before, and she went on to say:

"And I'm so glad too, Lina! I've wanted some one to talk to so much, and these women are all strangers. I s'pose it's silly, I know Henry thinks it is, but I cannot bear to talk to one of them about this. But I shall feel better now. It's almost like seeing Uncle Steve; bet-

ter for me, I s'pose, though I'd give so much to see him!"

"When will he be home?"

"Not until some time next fall. They had some bad luck going out, and were obliged to stop at some island—Madeira, I believe—for repairs. Henry read it in the newspaper. He is very careful to look about the ships, because I am so anxious."

Sitting there together, we talked over old days, and much that had happened since. I told her that I had left Oaklawn, and was residing in the city, and she was too well pleased with the news to trouble me with questions. Steps were now heard on the stairs, and she started, turning her head with a bird-like motion toward the door, her whole face flushing with pleasure while she listened.

"It's Henry's step. Now, you will see him, Lina! I am so glad he has come so early."

She went to the door, flung it open, but instantly recoiled and drew behind it when she saw that there were two men on the landing instead of one. They saw the movement, for one of them made some remark, at which the other laughed heartily as he entered the room, while the speaker passed on to the flight above. But I heard his voice, and saw his face before the door closed, and recognized them at once—it was Tom Hunt—older, more bloated, and sensual-looking, if possible, less flashily dressed, but that face and voice were too deeply impressed upon my memory for me to mistake them. Something of my old, childish dread came over me at the sight, and I sat staring at the door, half expecting him to turn back and call out, "Little devil!" with an oath, as of old, while little Adeline stood by my side, saying:

"Yes—Uncle Steve's Blackbird, he used to tell you about.—Lina, this is Henry.—He knows all about you, dear."

"Yes, indeed, and he is very glad to see you here," replied the husband, smiling, as I rose and gave him my hand. "A fine time you two have had of it, no doubt, talking over your old days. Ada, here, thinks there is nothing in New York to compare with that bit of beach, and the old shanty."

"O Henry! It was the nice, fresh air, and Uncle Steve I spoke of! You are not quite fair."

"And I agree with her, Mr. Heath," I said; "for, as yet, I have seen nothing in this great wilderness of houses that will compare with the beauty and freshness of the Cove. So, you see, you have two against you now, instead of one."

"And both ladies," he returned, with a graceful bow. "I hope, however, your judgment is not formed from this locality. Ada and I are going to get out of it as soon as we can.—Ada, dear, will you see if my cigar-case is not on the shelf? I forgot it this morning," he added, lounging indolently into a chair.

Birdie found and brought the missing case, while he went on to speak to me of the city and my residence in it.

I replied courteously but cautiously, and, in the mean time, had a good view of his face. It was what would generally be called handsome; the features were regular, the hair soft and curling, complexion smooth and fair, but the brown eye was blank and shallow, the smooth, narrow forehead wore no look of thought or power, the straight nose no energy, the small mouth and short chin no firmness or self-control—the whole impression was weak, and, the more I studied it, the more that impression was confirmed; and, while fully appreciating the attractions that had charmed little Adeline, as they would most any other young girls of like knowledge of the world, I trembled for her future. He would be the foot-ball of circumstance, and how soiled and broken might her plumage be in the race!

Promising to come again soon, and urging her to come to see me, I took my leave. Mr. Heath offered to walk with me as far as Broadway, and, to please her, I accepted the offer.

More than once, while I sat there, I had been tempted to ask about Tom Hunt, but the memory of the look on little Adeline's face, when she drew back behind the door, withheld me; but, as soon as we were in the street, I put the question.

"Yes; it was Tom. His family live in Broome Street, near Centre."

"Have you known him long?"

"Well, for some time. I was in a saloon where he was employed at one time; I believe he had formerly been the proprietor, but got into some trouble, and was obliged to sell out."

That was enough. I did not wish to excite his curiosity, so turned the conversation upon Uncle Steve, of whom he spoke in the warmest terms. As we turned into Broadway, we passed two very showily-dressed girls, who bowed to my companion, and stared boldly at my closely-veiled face. Mr. Heath seemed annoyed at their rudeness, for he walked more rapidly, saying: "That black-eyed girl was Tom Hunt's daughter, Fan. An impudent girl, as you see."

So that was the girl for whose long curls and gay dresses I had almost forgotten my Ollie! There was something ominous to me in the connection of these people with little Adeline's husband, and I was glad when he left me.

It was near the hour of dinner when I reached home, and I hurriedly changed my dress and arranged my hair, to be in time for Miss Annesley's table, for I still continued to take my meals with her.

She made some inquiries about my walk, remarked that I looked fatigued and must rest myself upon the sofa, for Miss Grace Lloyd was here to dinner, and was coming up to play for her. She wanted me to hear her; she played and sung so beautifully.

"Better than Miss Lloyd?" I asked; for I had often leaned over the balustrade, when there was company below, to listen to Miss Lloyd's brilliant playing, or to

her rich, powerful, perfectly-trained mez-
zo-soprano voice, mingling with the bass
of some gentleman guest. I noticed that
she never played save on such occasions,
but, as Miss Annesley said of her reading,
" she did every thing well."

"No, not as well," she replied, "none
but a professed artist could; but Julia
does not like to, unless she has some one
to accompany her. Grace is always
ready to oblige one, and has always
something new for me. She is a charming girl."

When the young lady came running
up-stairs after dinner, I felt the truth of
Miss Annesley's words; she was charming; quite a contrast to her mother and
sister—a blonde, with a profusion of
light, wavy hair; small, but regular features; childlike, naïve manners, and no
hint of the hauteur of mother or sister,
save in an occasional curve of the lips.
She bowed when Miss Annesley announced my name, and chatted on with
her old friend, until the latter pointed
significantly to the piano which stood in
the room.

She played well—some things which I
had heard worn out at Oaklawn—others
less hackneyed, especially some of Schu-
bert's "Songs without Words," which
were delicious as morning dreams. Presently Mrs. Lloyd and Miss Julia came up,
and the music at once became a lesson.
Miss Lloyd seated herself near the window with the air of one who expected to
be bored, but at every other bar observed, without turning her head: "You
take that altogether too fast, child," or,
"That is not the expression at all," or,
"Is that a dirge, Grace? One would
suppose so from your manner of playing
it "—until the young girl arose and pettishly declared that "Julia should play
herself."

Miss Annesley drew the pouting girl
down beside her, and, turning to Miss
Lloyd, seconded her request, but the lady
excused herself, saying that they knew
she "needed the excitement of a room

full of company to make playing any
thing but a bore."

"Then this young lady must play,"
said Miss Grace, turning to me. "I am determined that some one shall amuse me."

Mrs. Lloyd said "Grace!" in her
most imperative tone, and Miss Julia's
lip curled satirically, as she said, with a
sneer: "She doubtless would. That is
quite a bright thought, Grace."

Tranquil Miss Annesley saw nothing
but an opportunity for me to do credit to
myself, and said, eagerly:

"Yes, Miss Ray plays very well indeed." (I had sometimes practised a little when I knew the Lloyds were out.)
"Will you oblige us, dear?"

I had won self-possession, if nothing
else, since the old days when Miss Harriet
Hart's stare and rustling dress could confuse me; and, regardless of the smile that
still curved Miss Lloyd's lips, I sat down
at the piano, and began the prelude to
the old Scotch song that I had found lying open on Miss Helen Cavendish's piano
at the Pines—"The Scottish Widow's
Lament." I had studied that music thoroughly, and now, as I sung, memories of
the days when I first saw it came over
me—thoughts of all that had happened
since—and the sorrows and loneliness
of my own life—were mingled with the
touching pathos of the bereaved wife and
mother.

When I ceased, there was silence for
a second, which Miss Grace Lloyd broke
with school-girl impulsiveness.

"O mamma, isn't that lovely? So
sweet and sad! And she sings it finely! I must learn it—indeed, I must.
It is better than all the waltzes ever
written."

Miss Julia never turned her head,
but sat waving her fan (it was a warm
spring day), but the mother said, reprovingly:

"Grace, when will you learn that
repose and quiet self-possession which
mark the manners of a lady? I did hope
that, under Madame Chegary's training,

you would overcome your tendency to exaggeration."

Grace pouted and blushed, while I arose and resumed my former seat. As I passed Miss Annesley, she said:

"Thank you, my dear. That song has brought back the light of many a vanished summer.—Cousin Lloyd, you remember Helen Cavendish? You met her here about the time of your marriage. That song was her favorite, and she sung it as no one else could."

"Yes, I remember her well. What did I hear happened to her or her brother?"

"Helen was insane, or partially so, for several years before her death, which occurred about a year ago."

"And her brother—is he living? I remember him as quite a distinguished man—wealthy, too, I believe."

"Rothsay Cavendish died three months since, quite suddenly, at the Astor House. They are all gone now, not one of the name living."

Miss Annesley's eyes were full of tears, but Mrs. Lloyd went on in her *ex-cathedra* manner:

"The extinction of our families of wealth and distinction is not only very sad, but a positive wrong against society. Mr. Cavendish should have married as a matter of duty toward his class, if not for himself. What disposition did he make of his property?"

"He gave it by will to the children of a distant relative—a person of the name of Ellis, I think. The family is very respectable, I hear."

"Why, they must be the Ellises of Oaklawn!" said Grace Lloyd, opening wide her blue eyes. "It was a Mr. Cavendish who left them quite a fortune not long since. You remember, mamma, I told you Fanny Pyncheon was engaged to a Mr. Ellis? But the queerest thing has happened! Sophie Pyncheon wrote me about it last week. I should have forgotten to tell you, if Cousin Anne had not mentioned that name."

"Does Madame Chegary teach her pupils to use such words as *queer*, Grace?" asked Miss Julia, sternly.

"Well, *strange*, then!" returned the little beauty, too eager to respond to Miss Annesley's—"What is it, pet?" to be angry.

I did not need to ask. I knew what was coming, but I closed the book of engravings, which I had been ostensibly looking over, and sat with folded arms, curious to know what the world said of the affair.

"Why, Sophie says the old gentleman left them all his property, that is, to Edward, Fanny's suitor, and his sister; but there was something said in the will about a brother, who died abroad a great many years ago, when quite a boy. It was a mere matter of form, the lawyers say—a whim of the old gentleman's. But, what should one of the teachers (Mrs. Ellis the mother conducts a seminary for young ladies) do—a poor girl, a pauper, Sophie says, whom Mrs. Ellis took and educated out of charity—but step forward and claim to be the daughter of that dead brother and the heir!"

"What unparalleled impudence!" exclaimed Mrs. Lloyd. "I hope they sent her back to the almshouse where she came from, or, what is better, gave her into the hands of the officers of justice!"

"I don't see why you should be surprised at any thing from people of that sort, ma'am; after your experience with our governesses, I should think you would be prepared for any thing. I am. They are a needy, artful, unscrupulous class, and this one only acted out her true character!" said Miss Julia, whisking a fly from her fresh spring silk with her fan.

"Grace laughed. Ay, Julia never can forgive Miss Littell, my governess, for marrying Senator E——. It was a real romance, Cousin Anne!"

Miss Julia bit her lips, and shot a glance of anger at the laughing girl; the mother gave her one of her blackest frowns ; but Miss Annesley, unmindful of their displeasure, said, thoughtfully :

"It is barely possible that what this teacher asserts may be true ; for Philip Cavendish, though very young, was not a mere boy when he left the country, and there was a rumor of his marriage at the time. I have heard Ralph Saville speak of it.—But go on, dear. What came of it ? "

"The girl, I believe, had a document which gave some color to her story, and there was an old housekeeper who said Mr. Cavendish acknowledged her as his niece in her presence, before he died, and there was talk of a compromise, for the Ellises are very honorable people ; but the girl showed out what she was by running away in the night, after trying to bribe an elder half-brother of Edward Ellis to marry her."

There was James Sancroft's trail ! I might have smiled at the absurdity of his report, if I had not known that Edward Ellis himself must have told it to Fanny Pyncheon, whose grace and beauty I had often heard him describe. He must have believed it—Mrs. Ellis believed it—and these ladies believed it ! This was my guerdon for renunciation, suffering, loneliness, and toil. They had not told of the coldness, mistrust, and suspicion ; the changed looks and degrading insinuations, that made my life there, on their terms, intolerable ! I was poor, therefore dishonest ; homeless, therefore base and unwomanly ; friendless, therefore any thing in the shape of a man with friends and family, or, for aught I knew, without them, might slander me with impunity ! And this was civilization in the nineteenth century !

Is it strange that I paid little heed to the remainder of the tale—"the shock the creature's ingratitude" had given to Mrs. Ellis's nerves ; the disinterestedness of herself and son in trying to trace the fugitive—the probable postponement of Edward's marriage, or the emphatic denunciations of "such baseness" by Mrs.

Lloyd, echoed faintly by gentle Miss Annesley ; the eloquent shrug of Miss Julia's shoulders—but sat recalling some words of Mr. Ralph Annesley's uttered long ago, by the Cedar Pond, about the children of the Hindoo women, and the river Ganges?

CHAPTER XXIII.

AT HIGHCLIFF.

WE are at Highcliff once more, enjoying the fair miracles of sunrise and sunset, with still delicious noontides between. We are alone, for the Lloyds are going to Saratoga ; Miss Julia has carried her point, and they are whiling away the time, before the season commences, with some friends on the banks of the Hudson, somewhat to my mistress's disappointment. The father of these young ladies had been her favorite cousin, and she had transferred her affection to his children after his death. Her love for them completely, as it seemed, blinded her to Miss Julia's arrogant, overbearing spirit, or perhaps it did not seem out of place in one of her position, for she could not be expected to see it from the standpoint of the poor companion.

But her disappointment was soon effaced by the sunshine and fresh air, and she spent hours in the garden, sometimes leaning on my arm, for she was now able to walk with a little assistance, or seated in her garden-chair, beneath the great peach-tree at the end of the alley, planning the arrangement of flower-beds, and overlooking the labors of Peter's boy, Jim, her maid Jane, and myself. Sometimes, Peter and one of the men gave us their assistance, and, by midsummer, the old garden was a wilderness of beauty—old-fashioned beauty —for there were the flowers my mistress had loved and tended in her youth— white lilies, sweet-williams, larkspurs, columbines, marigolds, pinks in endless varieties, roses of all colors, sweet-scent-ed shrubs, lilacs, syringas, Guelder roses, flowering almonds, with beds of thyme, mignonette, summer savory, and fennel, all bordered by the ever green, ever fresh-looking box, thick hedges of which screened the lawn from the country road, and lined the walks about the grounds. This was a new feature to me; all that I had seen of this shrub before had been the small, dust-colored specimens dividing the mathematically-drawn flower-beds in some city yard, as unlike this strong, green, stalwart thing as possible; and these hedges were to me a constant source of delight, standing up so firm, and strong, and undaunted, defying summer's heat and winter's cold.

But a word about Highcliff. It was nothing more than a large, well-built, old-fashioned farm-house, standing on a plateau of some acres in extent, about half-way up a ridge of hills, that encircle the town of Bedford. It faced the south, and, from the front windows, or the long piazza, the eye ranged over ground famous in the annals of the Revolution, until it rested on a long line of hazy blue, which my heart leaped to see, for it was the distant water of Long-Island Sound. Behind the house rose the hills, not high enough to be dignified by the name of mountains, but rough and steep, and almost perpendicular in some places, seamed by deep ravines, at the bottom of which gurgled and dashed swift mountain-brooks, which united in the plain below, and rolled onward to mingle their waters with that of the sound.

Immediately back of the house was an orchard, beyond an open meadow; then a piece of woodland, where the flat ceased, and the ground began to ascend, until it terminated in a high ledge or cliff of rock, which overhung one of these swift streams. This, I presume, gave the place its name. On the top of this cliff stood a tower, now evidently going to decay, and, a few yards beyond, the remains of a rustic bridge that had once spanned the gorge. Its place was now supplied by a stout plank. The tower was locked, but the view from the cliff was much more extensive and beautiful than that from the house, for, on the northwest, far over the Croton, loomed the summits of the Highlands, Sugar-loaf, Crow's-Nest, Dunderberg, and the rest of the Titans; while to the south, like a line of silver, gleamed the waters of Tappan Bay. On the north was Bedford, nestled amid the hills, and surrounded by countless villages and farms.

I questioned old Peter about the tower and bridge one day, and he told me they had been built by old Mr. Annesley, Highcliff having been his favorite residence.

"Times are changed, miss, since the old master's day," he said, leaning on his hoe amid the hills of corn, where I had joined him. "Then, at this season, the house was full of company, and the stables full of horses. He was a master-man for horses; you should have seen a pair of bays he used to drive. An' a mighty particular man he was, too! Little went on here that he did not see, for all he was so fond o' sittin' perched up in the old tower yonder."

"Isn't the present owner a good master?"

"Mr. Ralph? Yes, miss, some would call him better'n his father, for that matter, for he's seldom here, and mighty easy when he does come. But I like to have the master here, to see what's done."

"I would like to go into that tower, Have you the key?"

"Yes, it's at the house, and if Miss Annesley don't object; but nobody has been there for years but Mr. Ralph. He fitted up the lower room, some years ago, in the trouting-season. But you must ask the mistress."

I did, and received at once the permission I craved; and I spent many an hour in the upper room of the old tower, reading or dreaming dreams as little

9

likely to be realized as those which used to float through my brain in the whortle-berry-pastures of Bradshaw; picturing a life, not devoid of trials and sorrows, but so replete with all that mine had lacked, that it set my heart to throbbing, until reason came, and, half in anger, half in grief, made me blush for my own folly.

I was happy here, even if I did build *châteaux en Espagne* altogether too costly for the child of the almshouse; happier than I had ever been, since those childish visits to the Cove, for I had books and leisure, and, better than all, was treated as an equal, a companion, by my mistress, in the truest sense of the word. Indeed, in intellectual culture, I was Miss Annesley's superior, and my mind travelled leagues while hers only beat round and round the old accustomed track. This was unfortunate for me, for I needed some one to guide if not share my life of thought; and, to tell the truth, much as I admired and appreciated the gentle goodness and benevolence of my mistress, there were times when it affected me as did the "Life of Payson" in my childhood. It was good, but I wanted something less negative, something that had doubted, and struggled, and overcome.

One thing troubled me. I heard nothing from little Adeline Heath. She never called at Bleecker Street; and, when I went to tell her of our removal to Highcliff, she was out with her husband. Since then, I had written to her twice and received no reply. I persuaded myself that she had gone to the Cove, perhaps, or to visit her husband's friends, and looked forward to a happy meeting in the autumn, glad to think that, when her hour of trial came, Uncle Steve and I should both be near her.

I often spent some hours in the kitchen, where Miss Annesley and Katty Brown, old Peter's wife, held long discussions on the best methods of pickling and preserving. One morning, when I entered, I found old Peter talking to Miss Annesley about some one whom he had heard was very ill, "nigh to her end," as he expressed it. My mistress was much concerned, for she kept fluttering her hands about nervously, and saying:

"Poor thing! What will become of her? Two children, did you say?"

"Yes; an' the girl's big enough to help some, an' there's an old woman there, some relation, they say, that takes care of her, but they be poorly off, I reckon, an' it's a long way from neighbors."

"You and Katty must drive up there, Peter. We must not let them suffer."

"Drive, miss! I doubt if a wagon can be driven there, unless you go clean round by Bedford. The road on this side was all torn to pieces by the great March storm, and has never been mended at all. If 'twas a rainy day, I could foot it up there, or maybe ride old Bony part of the way—but it's a fine hay-day, miss."

A fine hay-day was sacred from all outside interruptions with old Peter, and, as he turned doggedly away, I inquired who needed help, and if I could be of any assistance.

"A Widow Joyce, who lives on the top of the ridge yonder, where you see those tall Lombardy poplars. She was a servant in the family years ago, and Peter heard in town, to-day, that she is very ill. I am afraid they will suffer."

"I will go up there, if you please. I can easily walk there and back before night."

"You, child? Why, it's more than four miles!"

"That's nothing, ma'am. I have often walked farther than that since I came here. I like to walk."

It was decided that I should go, and, to avoid the heat of the day, I set off immediately, with the lad Jim for a guide, and the poplars for a landmark. I am not sure that the boy did not diverge from the direct path, occasionally, to show me where the crows built their nests, or some deep, still pool, famous for trout, but we reached our destination in time, and, leaving him to amuse himself outside, I entered the house.

A woman who was stirring something over the fire, heard my step, and, without turning her head, said, in a low tone:

"Be quiet, Jenny, for she's asleep."

I started, looked at her a second to be sure I was not mistaken, then crossed the floor lightly, and, laying my hand on her shoulder, said, in the same low tone:

"It's not Jenny, but don't be frightened, Alice dear."

She sprang up, stared at me in astonishment for a few moments, then clung to me, sobbing:

"O my child, Master Philip's child! Then you didn't go away to die like him, as I feared? Thank God, I see you again!"

I made her sit down, and briefly explained where I was, and why I had left Oaklawn, as I did, without seeing her. She shook her head mournfully, saying:

"It was just like your father, child. One who knew him and them, would need no other proof of your birth. But it wasn't right. I don't think Mr. Rothsay would have liked it."

"Perhaps not, Alice, but it's done, and I must depend on you to keep my secret. You must be more careful than you were with James Sancroft."

"Did he say I told him?—the false knave!" she exclaimed, flushing up as I had never seen her before.

"He certainly led me to think so, but it's no matter now, Alice."

"Yes it is, Miss Lina," she replied, "because it is not the truth. I promised you not to tell, and I didn't; but I could not tell a lie, and when he came there and asked in so many words if you were 'Master Philip's child,' I said nothing. But when he spoke slightingly of Mr. Rothsay, I told him he might find out yet that he and his wasn't as crazy as he thought."

Again I made her promise to keep my secret, and drew from her some account of herself and Oaklawn.

As soon as she heard I had left Oaklawn, she went down there and had an interview with Mrs. Ellis. She told her all that had been said at the Pines on the evening of the discovery of the certificate, and assured them that I was "Master Philip's child." But she had no proof to offer; she could not be made to see that my sudden and secret departure proved me an impostor, and she returned home with a heavier heart than when she left.

A few weeks later, Mr. Sancroft told her that the executors wished to close the house, that the annuity left herself and Mark would be paid them regularly, and she could have a home with his mother as long as she pleased. But she could not serve strangers, least of all them; and Mr. Edward Ellis, the best of them all, had himself brought her to New York—her and old Nep.

"Nep! What did you do with him?"

"Left him at Mr. Spencer's office; I think he wanted him."

"And Mark?"

"Went to live with his son in H——."

So the cottage was deserted—shut up. Well, what did it matter? They would have the wealth, I the love of an old woman and a dog; but I felt rich and glad.

I explained my errand, and learned that her niece was suffering from a low fever, brought on by overwork and exposure. She was better, and would be proud that the family at Highcliff remembered her, though, thank Heaven, through Mr. Rothsay's kindness, she herself could make them comfortable now.

I saw the girl Jenny, a rosy-cheeked lass of twelve; but the boy had gone to New York with his uncle, who had just returned from a long voyage.

I had brought a basket containing things likely to tempt the appetite of an invalid; and, when Mrs. Joyce awoke, I went in to see her, and assured her of Miss Annesley's sympathy. She seemed much pleased, and thanked me warmly for coming.

Leaving Jenny with her mother, and sending Jim (whom I found on his hands and knees, by the spring beneath the poplars, watching for frogs) ahead, Alice and I walked down the hill. She kept on until she could see the chimneys and gables of Highcliff house, when she stopped and said, with a sigh:

"Many a time have I been there with the children, in the old days, and I'm glad to know that you are there now, though it's little I ever thought that Master Philip's child would live there as a—"

"Servant!" I said, seeing her hesitate, "but, as you say, I am glad to be there—twice glad, now I know you are here. I shall come up here often; but, remember, I am Miss Lina—Lina Ray, now."

"Have you given up the name? They said you kept it."

"Only for the present. As soon as I have earned money enough, I am going West, to find, if possible, the proof of my right to bear it."

"Go now! Take my money! Indeed, we can do without it—we need so little here."

"No, Alice, at least not now; but if ever I do need help, be sure I shall come to you;" and, kissing her cheek, I said "Good-by," and ran down the hill.

I soon overtook my guide, and, gladdened by this meeting with old Alice, and invigorated by my day among the hills, I ran races with the boy across the open fields, and enjoyed them, too, with a zest which the Oaklawn teacher would hardly have thought possible six months before.

"I am going over the cliff, Jim; I want to see the sunset," I said, as we drew near home.

"Then, I'm going, too, and I know who'll get to the bridge first."

He passed me like an arrow, while I followed leisurely, in time to see him stumble when within a few feet of the bridge, and fall headlong. Thinking he might be hurt, I ran forward, but sprang back at the fierce growl of a large dog that came bounding over the rocks. I called to the boy to know if he was hurt, but he was already on his feet, and, running to my side, pointed to the bridge, saying:

"See, miss!—it's the master, Mr. Ralph."

A rapid glance showed me that he was right, but I had no time to look, for, at the sound of my voice, the dog, who had planted himself at the end of the plank, as if to prevent us from trespassing on his master's privacy, sprang forward, and came fawning around me, uttering low cries of joyful recognition. It was Neptune—old Nep, of the Pines, and with difficulty I repressed the answering cry of delight that rose to my lips. As it was, I could not afford, save by a mute caress, or some softly-uttered words, to recognize even the love of my uncle's dog, for fear it might betray me. Mistaking, as his words indicated, the cause of my delay, the gentleman came across the plank, saying:

"Down, Nep, down!—The dog will not harm you. Is the lad much hurt?"

"Not a bit, sir," spoke up, Jim. "We were running races, Miss Lina and me."

"Indeed! I was not aware that young ladies of the present day practised such classical feats. The dog's instincts are keener, for he seems to appreciate an accomplishment so much in his own line, and desires to make friends.—Down, sir, I say!"

I scarcely knew whether the smile and tone were intended to be complimentary or sarcastic, and I said bluntly, as I moved toward the bridge:

"I thank him, for neither a dog's friendship nor lightness of foot is to be despised, to my thinking."

"Very true," he replied, with a quick

glance at my face; then he moved on by my side, adding, by way of explanation: "This old plank looks hardly safe, even for one who runs races. Let me go first and try it with my heavier foot."

He stalked across the worm-eaten plank, as if it were a matter of indifference whether it held together or not, and satisfying himself, by a glance, that Jim and I had followed, ascended the rocks in the direction of the tower. Presently he paused, and stood looking over the wide landscape, apparently forgetful of our proximity, though we were obliged to pass very near him, to gain the narrow foot-path which led to the wood below, old Nep running on before, and the lad expatiating on the necessity of his father's bridging the ravine "with a first-rate, new plank," when the gentleman turned suddenly and asked:

"Who is your father, my lad?"

"Why, Peter Brown, Mr. Annesley! Didn't you know me, sir? I know'd you in a minit. I'm Jim, sir."

"Ay, I see now, and—" He paused, but his glance had caught the boy's eye, and, child-like, proud of having any thing to tell, he went on:

"This is Miss Lina, sir. She came up with Miss Annesley, and reads to her, and helps us make garden and goes with me to salt the sheep and bring the cows, and—"

"Runs races," interrupted the master, slightly lifting his hat at this introduction. "Miss Annesley is fortunate in possessing such a friend."

"You mistake, sir. I am only Miss Annesley's hired companion."

"Ay, I forgot; a pleasant walk to you," and with a grave bow he ascended the steps that led to the tower; and I hurried home, musing upon his sudden appearance, and what it might portend to me.

"He has come!" said Miss Annesley, whom I met in the hall in a flutter of excitement—"Cousin Ralph, Miss Ray. It is only for a few days, he says, but what a pity the Lloyds are not here! He will find it so lonesome."

CHAPTER XXIV.

RALPH ANNESLEY.

He did not seem to find it lonely, however, even though the days ran into weeks. At first, he was too busy over accounts and matters connected with the farm, to be dull, at least all the mornings; and after dinner, as soon as the sun began to decline, it became quite impossible to go out for a walk without meeting him on the rocks, or in the fields, or catching a glimpse of him cantering along the country roads, on a beautiful bay horse which he had had sent up from the city. He was seldom visible in-doors, save at meal-time, and I contrived to avoid meeting him at the table as often as possible, without seeming to contravene Miss Annesley's expressed wishes.

About a week after his arrival, I was in my own room, making the most of the last rays of sunlight to finish a sketch of Widow Joyce's cottage, when Miss Annesley, who had quite recovered from the injury consequent upon her fall, came in, to say she expected me to be down to tea *punctually*, Mr. Annesley having asked for me at dinner.

"You need not be afraid, child," she said, with a touch of her family pride (almost her only foible), slightly elevating her head, and stirring the delicate lace that bordered her cap; "Saville Annesley is a gentleman by birth and breeding, and appreciates intelligence and honest worth wherever he finds it. Smooth your hair, and dress as quickly as you can. That corn-colored lawn will do; the shade is almost as becoming to you as to Julia Lloyd."

The gentle lady hastened away, and I thrust aside, from some undefined feeling which I did not stay to analyze, the pretty lawn, and put on a *chambre* of neutral brown, and, thus apparelled, I went down, and found the gentleman discussing some proposed improvements about the place, with my mistress. He bowed slightly when she introduced me, and went on speaking, while I took a seat as far out of the range of his observation as possible. I might have saved myself this precaution, however, for he sat chatting with Miss Annesley, quite unconscious of my presence, leaving me ample time to study his face, which had lost nothing of its imperious character under the influence of a Parisian winter.

When the tea and candles were brought in, I was obliged to come forward and take my place at the table, where my mistress, from behind the massive silver urn, still pursued her favorite topic—the attractions of the Lloyds and her regret at their absence—until her sweet, monotonous voice, or perhaps it was the subject, grew rather tiresome. I think the gentleman's thoughts went wool-gathering as well as mine, for, at some direct question of hers, he roused himself and said:

"The Lloyds, did you say? I am glad you find them such pleasant people, cousin."

"Pleasant, Ralph!" she repeated, a little piqued at his indifference. "You should see Julia! I do not believe, in all your travels, you have ever met her superior. Such a brilliant intellect, such beauty, wit, and grace, such dignity! Indeed, she is perfect."

"Undoubtedly," he returned, with a look that reminded me of his face when talking to Miss Agnes down by the Pond. "Another proof that the world does move, cousin, since we find so common what Solomon with all his experience pronounced so rare. But you always see your friends through your heart, Cousin Anne; therefore, I will appeal to a less prejudiced observer." He turned

suddenly to me. "Miss Ray, is Miss Julia Lloyd very beautiful?"

"She is very handsome, sir."

He gave me a quick glance. "You discriminate, I see; but, her mind—what of that?"

"Very brilliant, I should say."

"Manners?"

I could not help smiling at his categorical manner, as I replied:

"Miss Annesley has described them as dignified—perfect."

"Humph! You are non-committal, I see. Now, about her moral qualities. Is she good?"

"Indeed, sir, I must decline answering. I know too little of the lady to decide."

"Yet you answered my former queries."

"Because those qualities are addressed to the eye, sir, and I am not blind."

"No, I perceive not. But you have formed some opinion upon this subject, which you do not choose to disclose."

"Upon what grounds do you base that assertion, sir?" I was getting a little curious.

"Upon my skill in reading faces. Yours is less cautious than your tongue. Am I not right?"

Here Miss Annesley came to my relief with her "Indeed, Cousin Ralph—" but he immediately interrupted, with—

"Your pardon, Anne; but let Miss Ray answer for herself. She has a tongue, as well as eyes."

"But she is not obliged to use it at your command," I thought.

He had not boasted of his skill in reading faces idly, for my eye met his as I looked up, and he answered, with a smile, as if to my spoken words:

"True, she is not obliged to answer, and I might have expressed myself in a different manner. If I sometimes am forgetful of the conventionalities and formalities of drawing-room speech, it is not from lack of respect, Miss Ray, but because a large portion of my life has been passed in lands, and under circumstances, where the scriptural 'Go, and he goeth,' is of much more practical value. Will you accept this in excuse for all such shortcomings?"

I bowed.

"And answer my question?"

"No, sir."

His forehead contracted slightly, but the next instant he smiled, as if at himself, and said:

"You are wilful, Miss Ray, and I don't like to be thwarted in the pursuit of knowledge. But let it pass. I had a reason for wishing to hear your opinion of my cousin's guest. You needn't ask why—I can be wilful too. I thought, from what I saw of you the other day, on the cliff, that you would speak the truth."

"You met Lina on the cliff, Ralph!— Why, child, you never spoke of it," said Miss Annesley, turning to me with a puzzled look.

"I met Mr. Annesley, the day he arrived here, on my way home from Widow Joyce's. He was kind enough to stand surety for his dog, which seemed inclined to dispute our passage across the ravine. I did not think it necessary to mention it," I said, gravely.

"And the dog left me for her, Cousin Anne. That fact, coupled with the knowledge that she had been running races among the hills with a lad who might have been her familiar, led me to scrutinize her closely. I fancied I had stumbled upon a witch, that had strayed across the line from Connecticut, where they used to flourish—or, at least, a fairy —for, when the lad spoke of her sheep-tending, and cow-bringing habits, I remembered their sometime freaks of usefulness, and I thought one of the race might well have a friendly feeling for you, cousin. But, when I questioned the creature, it answered in plain, prosaic English. It was Miss Annesley's companion, forsooth!"

I was greatly amused at his serious air, as well as Miss Annesley's perplexed look. She caught at his closing sentence, however; it was, probably, the only one she comprehended.

"Yes, indeed," she said; "Miss Ray is my companion, my friend, rather, and I have reason to thank Providence, every day, for giving me such a one."

"Ah, but when I suggested *friend*," returned the gentleman, somewhat to my annoyance, "the—well—I suppose I must say person, ignored the relation, and said, expressly, *hired* companion."

"That's just like Lina. She is as proud, in her way, as Julia Lloyd is in hers; but she is never presuming."

"And Miss Lloyd is?" He gave me a look that said: "I shall get my answer, after all."

"Presuming! Oh, no; Miss Julia is very independent, and that makes her, sometimes, a little forgetful of those around her. It is only natural, petted and admired as she has been, and accustomed to command from her cradle. I have sometimes feared that Lina, not knowing her well, might feel hurt, at times, by her careless way of speaking, but I see she does not, by her manner of answering you. She is right, for no one can, in a strict sense, be called *good*. It's hardly polite for you to press her so hard, Ralph."

"I have already explained to Miss Ray that I am not what would be called a polite man, cousin, and the young lady has, doubtless, faults enough of her own, to make her merciful to the shortcomings of others."

He arose and took his newspaper, leaving me to discuss, with my mistress, the best method of preparing brandied peaches.

For several succeeding days, I saw little of him. His arrival was the occasion of numerous calls from the gentlemen of the neighborhood. Then came trouting expeditions to the hills, calls to be returned, and long rides on Don, with only Nep for a companion. Sometimes, he had a word, or a pleasant smile (and his smile could be very pleasant) for me, when I chanced to meet him, but, more frequently, he passed me with a nod, or no sign of recognition at all. I was daily convinced that I had acted wisely in remaining beneath his roof. I wondered if he knew that Alice Ross was so near, and determined to go to the Ridge as soon as possible, to impress upon her the increased necessity of keeping my secret.

But Miss Annesley was deep in the mysteries of blackberry-jam that week, and my presence was indispensable; besides, a severe thunder-storm had changed to a settled rain, which made the hill-paths any thing but safe and comfortable walking.

One day, while I stood by the window, anxiously "seeking for a sign" of fair weather, I saw Mr. Annesley, who had ridden away the day before, come dashing up the road at full speed. I went up-stairs to bring down some drawings which my mistress wished to see, and, when I returned, encountered both him and Nep in the hall, dripping with water and bespattered with mud. He smiled when he saw me, and called out, gayly:

"Don't be frightened, Miss Ray. Nep and I have a fancy for racing sometimes, as well as yourself, and care as little for a soaking as his namesake of old; and we've caught it this time!"

I was not disposed to grieve, for I thought Miss Annesley would have ample time to look over the drawings before he could change his dress and join us. I was mistaken. In what seemed to me an incredibly short space of time, he entered in fresh habiliments, and, lounging into an arm-chair, began talking to my mistress of some affairs in the city, where, it seemed, he had spent the night.

Interested in his conversation, she forgot the drawings which I quietly laid aside on the table behind her, and re-sumed my netting. My movement did not escape him, for presently he said:

"Now, Miss Ray, we will look at those drawings, if you please."

I did not dare to refuse, though I remembered with dismay that the little sketch of the Cedar Pond was among them. But he laid it aside with a passing glance, as he did most of the others, until he came to some three or four in which I had attempted to embody my conceptions of some of the scenes in Shelley's "Revolt of Islam." These he examined closely for some time before he remarked:

"You have studied Shelley to some purpose, it seems. Did you understand that poem?"

"Not wholly, but I liked it very much."

"A woman's answer. I see you liked it, or you never would have executed these. The conception is good, and the execution—passable, for a school-girl. But who can hope to do justice to Shelley? You might as well attempt to seize the tremulous radiance of a star! You have left the combatants" (he had returned to the sketch illustrating the opening of the first canto) "'a speck—a cloud, a shape,' I observe, as the poet first conceived them. Why did you not represent them in their distinct forms—

'An eagle and a serpent wreathed in fight?'"

"I did try, but the effort satisfied me still less than this."

"Very likely," he returned, with one of his quick, penetrating glances, "and it's hardly to be regretted. What should you, whose life has been as quiet as a nun's, know of the fierce combats of Good and Evil? To you they are like that cloudy shape. Let them remain so."

"But, if the battle-ground be within the heart, it may rage as fiercely in the nun's cell as the king's palace—may it not, sir?" I was thinking of what Mr. Cavendish had once said about temptation.

He gave me another searching look before he replied :

"Therefore, you would say that the 'power of circumstances,' which we make the scape-goat for our false, wasted lives, is but the subterfuge by which the devil juggles us into self-complacency?"

"The inference is yours, sir—not mine."

"But you believe it. I read it in your eye. Are you as severe as you are sententious, Miss Ray?"

"I don't believe that Circumstance is a god before whom men should sink supinely, but rather an earth-born Titan from whom he may wring a blessing, as Jacob did at Penuel, if he will. As for myself, I have, as you were pleased to observe the other night, faults enough of my own to make me humble."

He smiled. "You have a good memory, it seems, and, what is more rare, can hear truth without losing your temper ; a rare thing in a woman—ay, let us be just—or, a man either."

"Show Mr. Annesley this, dear," said Miss Annesley, handing over a sketch she had been examining. "I think he will be pleased with it."

"Ah, the Ridge and the old poplars ! That reminds me, cousin, of another thing I heard to-day. Spencer says that Alice Ross, Rothsay Cavendish's old housekeeper, is living with Widow Joyce. Have you heard or seen any thing of her ?"

"No, but I wonder I have not. I remember her well.—Lina, you were at the Ridge a few days since ; did you see or hear of such a person?"

"I did."

"And I have been here a fortnight without seeing her!" exclaimed Mr. Annesley impatiently. "I wonder Spencer didn't mention it at Saratoga!"

"Saratoga! Have you been to Saratoga, Cousin Ralph?" Miss Annesley opened wide her fine blue eyes.

"Yes; on my arrival in New York, I found Spencer had gone to the Springs.

I followed, *instanter*, and, if it had not been for the illness of his wife, we should have gone West, and thus spared you the infliction of my presence here. But I have that to add," he continued, with a quizzical smile, "which will reconcile you to a much greater evil. I met Mrs. and Miss Lloyd, who are so disgusted with the pomps and vanities of Saratoga, and so full of yearnings for rural seclusion and pastoral sweets, as they contrived to make me feel, during my brief interview with them, that I could not do otherwise than second the invitation to Highcliff, which I found you had given them, and, unluckily, forgot all about it, until I saw Spencer yesterday. They will be here the beginning of the month."

"Now, that was so like you, Savillo Annesley, to come home and go to quizzing me and Lina about Julia, just as if you had never seen her! But, isn't she beautiful?"

"Superb ! I suppose ; but, really, I was too much occupied with business to think much about her."

"But you will be at leisure, now. How fortunate !"

"Not for me, Cousin Anne, for I hope to be on my way West before that time. I must see Alice Ross. Is the road to the Ridge passable—for any thing Christian, I mean?" he inquired, turning abruptly to me.

"For your horse, sir, although he may not come within that catalogue."

"Beware of the vice of slander, Miss Ray! Don has more right there than many men, judging him by the Scriptural text, the use of the gifts given him. But how did you get there? Did you walk or did you take the ancient mode of conveyance peculiar to your people ?"

"I walked, sir—as I shall again to-morrow morning," I mentally added, with a glance at the breaking clouds.

"Speaking of Alice," said Miss Annesley, "reminds me of something little Grace Lloyd told us, before we left the city, about Rothsay Cavendish's property.

She said he gave it, by will, to some relatives: and some person, a teacher, I think, in the family of these relatives, claimed it as the daughter of his brother Philip. There was a great deal of trouble about it, in consequence, and the person ran away, I think Gracie said.—Didn't she, dear?" turning to me.

"She did."

"A pretty sure proof of the justice of her claim," observed the gentleman. "I have heard this story before, for I am one of the executors of the will; and the strangest thing is, that Spencer seems inclined to credit her story. He is not the man to be humbugged by a pretty face; besides, he says the girl is plain. I don't understand it. I met the brother of the legatees, this morning, in Spencer's office."

"What sort of a person is he, sir?"

I could not resist the temptation to know his thought of James Sancroft, though I was conscious that my voice sounded harsh and unnatural.

He turned suddenly. "Come away from that window. You are taking cold."

I obeyed, and put Miss Annesley between me and his keen eyes, while he went on:

"One of the 'rising men' of whom we hear so much in these days. Do you know the species, Miss Ray?"

I shook my head.

"Well, they are usually made up of brains, *minus* heart and conscience. This fellow's manner has a velvety softness, significant of cats' claws. I distrust him, and, if his family are like him, there must be some truth in his assertion that Rothsay Cavendish was easily deceived. Another strange feature of the case is, the girl's refusal to take the property."

"What do you intend to do?" asked my mistress.

"Find her, if she be above-ground!" he replied, starting from a fit of musing, "and find out who she is. Let her deceive me, if she can! I think I should know Philip's child! Poor Phil!"

CHAPTER XXV.

THE SHIP-FEVER.

I AROSE very early next morning for my walk to the Ridge, but found that Mr. Annesley had the start of me. When I went into the garden to gather my flowers for the breakfast-table, I heard him giving some order about the horses to one of the men. I did not hear what he said, but supposed that he was, probably, going to ride to the Ridge, and I almost wished for that power of locomotion which he had ascribed to me the evening before, for, by the shortest foot-path, I could not hope to forestall Don's speed, even if I dared risk meeting him in Alice Ross's presence.

I had now seen enough of him to know what old Hannah Smith meant when she said, "if Mr. Ralph said a thing wasn't proper, she should like to know who would say it was," and I felt sure that he would draw my secret from Alice, in spite of herself.

"And why not?" I said, pausing from my work, and facing the rising sun. "Because he thinks me an impostor—because, when he gets hold of me, he will compel me to prove who I am. Before two years expire, I will do it, if possible, but not now."

I took up my basket to go in, and found him leaning over the garden-gate.

"Good-morning, Miss Ray! You are early among your flowers. Were they cropped by magic moonlight?"

"No, sir. I have just gathered them."

"They are harmless, then," he said, taking my basket. "Here are carnations, gillyflowers, phlox, marigolds—

'These are flowers
Of middle summer, and I think are given
To men of middle age.'"

He selected several, and returned the basket, but without manifesting the slightest intention to let me pass.

"What a glorious morning, Miss

Lina! See how the sunbeams light up the face of the old cliff up yonder. The whole country looks bright and fresh as a boy's dream of life—and will fade as soon."

"Not fade, but change—deepen into the rich, genial, fructifying heat of noonday. Why should not the boy's dream do the same?"

"Because of the world, the flesh, and the devil! But, I forget—you are no believer in the god Circumstance, and, on such a morning as this, I feel half inclined to defy him myself. But I'm no longer a boy. At this late day, 'Le jeu ne vaut pas la chandelle.' Is it not so, Miss Ray?"

"I think not. Few people completely exhaust their capacity for happiness or usefulness at your age, and the strength born of a struggle is, in itself, a rich reward."

"What a Quaker preacher you would have made! So you really think there is hope for one like me, who have, especially on such a morning as this, the pleasant consciousness of having wasted the best years of my life in a round of petty, selfish, idle, commonplace pleasures—call them sins if you choose, which the élite call life!"

"I do."

"But the means?"

"Faith in God and yourself."

He lifted his hat reverently, and stood for some seconds, with the wind stirring his black locks.

"True," he said, at length, "but I am human. Am I to have no human aid?"

"The warm wishes and prayers of all who love you, sir."

"The aid will be feeble enough, then, my friend, for most of those are beneath the sod."

"They may not be the less efficient helpers, for that, sir!" I said, earnestly, touched by the change in his voice. "Besides, you are still young; you have health, energy, courage, and persever-

ance, a keen intellect, and a kind heart, and we are told that our 'valors are our best gods.'"

He looked at me searchingly, until I shrunk a little at the thought that I had been speaking from my early conception of him, and not from recent, personal knowledge.

"I believe you are right," he said, thoughtfully. "Were you thinking of that apothegm when you rose from gathering flowers, and stood facing the sun, with such a firm, set mouth, and decided pose of the head?"

"Yes, I often have occasion to think of it, sir. Will you please to let me pass?"

He opened the gate, and passed up the box-edged walk by my side.

"You should like this stout evergreen, Miss Ray," he observed, breaking off a spray. "It preaches your doctrine—self-reliance."

"And trust," I added, taking the twig he offered.

"You like Highcliff?" he rejoined, pausing, and looking back over the broad valley.

"Yes. I never enjoyed the country so much before."

"Yet you have always lived in the country, I understand?"

"Yes, but for some years in a school."

"And saw it only from the pons asinorum, or through a microscope, I suppose. There comes Elliott's boy, and, instead of a gallop to the Ridge, I shall have to attend that cursed meeting of stockholders!"

I felt no sympathy with his vexation, so, leaving him with the messenger, I went in with my flowers, secured a cup of coffee and a mouthful of breakfast in the kitchen, and set off for the Ridge.

I had crossed the ravine, when I saw a young girl coming rapidly to meet me. It was Jenny Joyce, and she was crying so, that it was some time before I could get any intelligible account of her trouble:

Aunt Alice and little Billy were both sick, oh, so sick! Aunt Alice kept talking so crazy-like, calling for somebody, and her mother thought it might be me. Would I be so good as to go home with her now?

I went back to the woods, where I knew I should find Jim Brown, and bade him tell Miss Annesley that Alice Ross was sick, and I should not, probably, be at home as early as I anticipated.

I found Alice and the boy in a high fever, and delirious. Alice had been taken first, and the boy the next day. They had been ill three days, but there was no one to go for the doctor in the storm; they had sent for him the night before by the Morris boys, and expected him this morning. Alice had kept talking about her old master, Mr. Rothsay, and Master Philip's child. Sometimes she called for Miss Lina, and Mrs. Joyce thought it must be for me, and, therefore, sent off little Jenny as soon as the storm was over, to ask me to come up.

Mrs. Joyce seemed completely overcome, but little Jenny gathered courage and composure from my presence, and was a most efficient helper. The physician reached the place soon after I did, and, after a minute examination of the patients, he questioned Mrs. Joyce closely as to where they had been, and whom they had seen.

They had been nowhere, and seen no one but the Morris boys when they came up to work, for more than a week. "'Twas good eight days since Billy returned from the city."

The physician seemed perplexed.

"You say the woman was attacked first?" he inquired again.

"Yes, she had been helping me make a suit of clothes for Billy. His uncle sent him up some that were most as good as new, but she had to give up before they were finished."

"Do you know where the clothes came from?"

"No; brother George often sent such things up for Billy. He a'most clothed him."

The doctor beckoned me out of the room.

"Young lady," he said, gravely, "I feel it right to tell you that this disease is, I think, ship-fever—brought here, probably, in those clothes. I may be mistaken—I hope I am; but it is unwise for you to remain here."

"Do you think they will die?"

"I can't say. I shall do what I can, but I fear it is too late."

"The disease is very contagious, is it not?"

"It is so considered."

"Then it will be equally unsafe for me to return to Highcliff, for I have already been here some hours. I will remain, and assist Mrs. Joyce. If you will have the goodness to send a note to Highcliff for me, I shall be very grateful."

"No, miss, you must not do this. There are many chances for escape now, hardly one if you remain."

"But I have no right to expose others, sir. It is better for me to remain and meet whatever result there may be. I am not afraid."

"But your friends, young lady?"

"I have none. I am alone in the world, or none but my mistress, Miss Annesley, and she can very easily supply my place."

He took three or four strides across the patch of greensward, for we had gone out of the house, then came up to me, and placed his finger on my wrist.

"Pulse, firm and even. You are a brave girl, and there is some reason in what you say; but—"

He dropped my hand, and again commenced his walk.

"Doctor," I said, seeing him not inclined to speak, "in case your fears are realized, will you have the goodness to look after me to—the end? I have sufficient means in Miss Annesley's hands to repay you."

He came up to me again. He was a tall man, with gray hair and whiskers, reminding me of Mr. Cavendish, and said, earnestly:

"That I will, if I have to nurse you myself! But you must promise me to put yourself under my care from this moment, and implicitly obey my directions as to diet and exercise."

I promised, and we went within, where I wrote a few lines with a pencil, briefly stating my reasons for not returning, or such as I might state, for I could not speak of my desire to be near old Alice; then the doctor departed, leaving me to my task.

It was well for me that I knew nothing of the disease. To me, it was like any other fever, to be avoided if possible; if not, to be met with a brave face and trust in God; therefore, I could not share the doctor's apprehensions. Besides, I was young and strong, with a nervous system in perfect health, and, to such, death always seems an anomaly—an accident, rather than an inevitable fate. But I had little time to think of myself—my patients claimed all my time, and it was near sunset before I could go out for a breath of fresh air, as I had promised the doctor. I wandered over the hill, and sat down on a rock, to watch the sun set, but was soon roused by the measured tread of a horse's feet upon the other side of the hill. "It is Mr. Annesley," I said, and I hurried back in time to meet him just as he sprung from the saddle, beneath the poplars.

"Well met, Miss Ray!" he said. "So the lad's talk was true; you have not joined your own folk, 'the good people o' the greenwood,' but are caring for my old friend Alice Ross, like a veritable sister of mercy, as you are. I thought to meet you on the road. I hope her illness is not serious, that you stay so late?"

He spoke pleasantly, almost gayly, and I thought I had never seen his face wear such a bright, genial look before.

"She is very ill," I replied, purposely leaning upon the little gate that gave entrance to the yard, "and I sent Miss Annesley a note by Dr. Clark, to say that I should not return to-night. I hoped it would reach her before this."

"I don't think it had; she only spoke of your message brought by the boy. I am sorry to hear bad news of Alice Ross," he added, with a look of concern. "She is a very old friend, and it's kind of you to stay by her. I wanted to speak with her very much, but, if she is so ill, I'll only look in upon her, and postpone my talk to another time."

I made no reply, but was trying to devise some excuse to prevent him from entering the house, as I felt he would, if he knew of her danger.

Noting my silence, he said, with a significant smile: "Do you bear malice, Miss Ray, for my impudence this morning, that you thus keep me waiting for admittance. It is growing late, and Don and I may chance to find ourselves at the bottom of one of these gullies, unless we wait for the moon."

"You cannot see Alice to-night, Mr. Annesley; indeed, you must not enter the house at all," I said, hastily, for his hand was already on the gate.

"Must not! What is to prevent me?" he replied, impatiently. "Let me pass, Miss Ray?"

"No; Alice Ross and the little boy are dying of ship-fever, and she will not recognize you. You must not peril your life, and the lives of others, unnecessarily."

"Ship-fever!—and you here! My God! were you mad, girl, that you must come here?"

His voice was deep, almost stern, and I spoke at once to the point where his thought, as I supposed, tended.

"I was not coming back to Highcliff, sir. I would not bring danger there for the world. I explained to Miss Annesley in my note. Indeed, sir—" But, stung by the misapprehension of me which his words implied, I found it impossible to go on. He did not seem to heed my silence, but broke in eagerly:

"Worse and worse. It's not that, but that you should be here at all! Not going back to Highcliff? You will go, and with me, to-night."

He put out his hand to remove me from the gate.

"No, sir; I shall not return," I said, without heeding the movement. "I came here in ignorance, but, had I known the nature of the disease, I hope I should have had the courage to come; otherwise, these people must suffer for lack of care. I shall take every precaution against infection, for life is all I possess, and I am not ready to give it up yet; but, at the worst, there is no one to whom my death would bring more than a passing regret. With you, sir, it is different. You must not go in. You can do Alice no possible good, only expose your own valuable life to danger."

"My valuable life! Much you know of it. Who taught you to estimate lives? Am I to understand that you will not go home with me?"

"Yes, sir."

"Then, stand aside." But he gave me no time to deliberate, for, with one hand he put me gently aside, and, passing through, strode into the house.

He hung long over the bed of old Alice, who was in one of the fits of stupor that usually followed her raving delirium. He did not speak, but his face grew very sad, as he laid his hand on her forehead, and turned away. He walked to the bedside of the boy, looked at him a moment; then, with a kind word to Mrs. Joyce, asked me to walk with him to the gate.

"You are right," he said, as we went slowly down the yard. "Alice Ross is dying; I am too late. You have been with her all day, Miss Ray; has she had her reason at all?"

"No, sir. She has been delirious, or stupid, as you see her now."

"What does she talk about in her delirium? Does she mention the Cavendish family, with whom she lived so many years?"

"Yes."

"I wish, then—but you will have enough to do, and, after all, she could tell me only what I know already.—Now, what is needed for your comfort and theirs? They must want many things."

"I presume so, for Mrs. Joyce has but recently recovered from a long illness, and there are no prophets in these days to fill the widow's cruse."

"No, but money is still potent, and I will see that they want for nothing."

We were at the gate; he lingered, looked at me seriously a moment, pityingly, as I thought, before he added:

"Miss Ray, I do not often ask favors, but I beg you to return to Highcliff, and let me get one or a half-dozen nurses from the city to care for these people. I will go down for them to-night."

I shook my head. "You forget, sir. I have the safety of others to consult."

He turned abruptly away, I feared in anger, but, immediately retracing his steps, took my hand, and said, in a tone that made my heart glow:

"God bless you! You are a brave little girl."

The next moment he had sprung upon his horse, and was urging him down the hill at his usual break-neck pace.

It was a weary task that I had assumed, rendered still more so by the terror and grief of Mrs. Joyce. Little Jenny tried to keep up a brave heart, and Dr. Clark was attentive and kind, but, next to God, my chief help and support was Mr. Annesley. Not content with sending up every thing needful for our comfort, he would persist in coming himself, daily, in spite of my entreaties and commands, which I did not fail to urge, though I could not repress a feeling of pleasure at the sight of his face and the grasp of his hand. His manner was frank and cordial, a little imperious at times, when I crossed him, but that did not trouble me, and it was a rare pleasure for me to listen to his conversation. His mind was original, vigorous, and highly cultivated; and I think the conversations, at first begun to amuse and interest me, during my moments of leisure, were often continued as much for his own pleasure as mine; for he possessed the rare faculty of being able to communicate his ideas and present objects clearly and vividly, and he seemed to take pleasure in describing, to one so unsophisticated as myself, the strange countries he had visited, and opening to me glimpses of a world so different from mine. Then, he was so gentle and patient with the sick ones, so careful of their wants, that I often wondered if he was indeed the same person as the impatient, sometimes exacting, master of Highcliff.

On the morning of the sixth day, o'd Alice ceased to breathe. I think, for a half hour before she died, she was fully conscious, but unable to speak, happy in the knowledge that her master's child would close her eyes.

"True friend and faithful servant!" said Mr. Annesley, as we stood by her grave that night, after the few men who had assisted at her interment had departed. "If Philip Cavendish left a child, as she believed, this spot shall be to her sacred ground."

From that day, the symptoms of the boy seemed more favorable, and the contest between Mr. Annesley's will and my sense of right began again. He would have me go *home* immediately. Had he known the magic power of that word uttered by his lips, he might have spared me the temptation. But I was firm, and he went away annoyed, and even angry. He did not return for two days, and the time passed heavily indeed. I knew, then, how much I had relied on him; but, on the third day, he came up with Dr. Clark, and brought me a note from

Miss Annesley, saying: "Read, and disobey at your peril!"

It was a request for me to come home. If I felt that there was still any danger, I might have the east bedroom, which was quite away from the rooms usually occupied by the family, though Ralph and the doctor assured her that the critical period for me was passed. Jane had offered to take care of me, if I should be ill, and she should feel much less anxious. if I were at home, than if I remained with Joyce, where Ralph was sure that I could not be comfortable.

It was like my kind mistress, but I felt the impetus had been given by another mind, and I suppose my face expressed something of my thought, for when I looked up from my note, Mr. Annesley was watching me, and said, smiling:

"Ask Clark here, yourself, Miss Lina! Then, if you believe not Moses and the prophets, I shall use my authority as patriarch of the family, and take you by force. Those old Jewish laws worked admirably in some cases."

The doctor laughed, and reaffirmed his opinion as stated by Miss Annesley. He thought the disease would have shown itself before, had I taken it; he had faith in the precaution which I had taken. I had best keep quiet for a day or two, and get rested; he should look in and see me, etc.

Miss Annesley had had the forethought to send me a fresh suit of clothing. My toilet was soon made, and, breaking from the widow and little Jenny, whom Mr. Annesley promised should not be left long alone, I found myself suddenly lifted into the carriage and driven at a rapid pace over what was to me a new and circuitous road to Highcliff. Our drive was a silent one, for my companion seemed occupied with his own thoughts, and I was too busy recalling the ride I had taken with him ten years before, to disturb him, had I dared to do so. The day was rather chilly for the season, or seemed so to me, and once or twice he turned to ask me if I were cold, as the wind swept over the hills, or muttered a curse at his folly in not bringing another shawl.

When we drove up to the house, Miss Annesley tossed me a kiss and a bouquet of flowers from her window. We passed round to the side-door that led to my new quarters, which I was glad enough to gain, the rapid motion of the carriage having made me a little sick and dizzy. I did not like to mention it to Mr. Annesley, when he came to the door to ask if I were comfortable, thinking that the cup of tea which Jane had brought, would drive it away. One thing I missed from the room, Ollie's box, and, before I dismissed Jane, I made her bring it. My ride had stirred deeply the memories of those childish days, and I had a strange longing to look at the mementos it contained, before I slept. But the pictures in the "Whale Book" grew dim before my dizzy head and aching eyes, and Mr. Annesley's boyish face in the miniature was blurred and indistinct. I remember getting up in the night for water to quench the burning thirst that consumed me, of attempting to reach the pitcher upon the table, that it slipped from my trembling hands as I grasped it, and—no more!

CHAPTER XXVI.

THE FEVER OF LOVE.

AGAIN God is merciful; the fever with its wild fantastic visions has left me, and I lie "clothed in my right mind," but too weak to speak. I hear hushed voices in the room; one is strange to me, but the others are those of Dr. Clark and Mr. Annesley, and often I am conscious that he stands beside me, and it is his hand that raises me while some one presses to my lips the cool and refreshing drink.

Then I miss him, for I am able to sit up, and Mary Kane, the nurse, takes the whole care of me. Presently I am able to go out at the door, and every day it is his arms that bear me out to the lounge in the vine-shaded piazza, his arm that supports me along the old garden-walks, when I am strong enough for that effort, his hands that arrange the cushions and shawls in the old arbor, and bring me fruit and flowers—his voice that reads to me, or, in a few felicitous words, brings before me the solemn grandeur of Karnac and Luxor, the wild magnificence of the Indian forests, or the polished grace and factitious splendor of European life. I say little—what need?—Here is the life—the communion of which I had dreamed—a mind acute, vigorous, energetic, noble, recognizing me as its equal, appreciating my qualities, not after the utilitarian standard of Oaklawn, but for themselves, and my whole being expands under its influence, like the resurrection-flower at the touch of water. Miss Annesley is at Mr. Elliott's, where he and Dr. Clark had insisted upon her going when I was taken ill, but every day she sends messages in little notes; then, one day, he drives over and brings her home, and the old life begins again. No—not the old life—it can never be the old life to me again. I am conscious of this. I know that in thus sunning myself in his presence, a spark from the divine flame has fallen into my heart, which will live and glow through all my solitary life, because it is eternal. Pain it *must* bring, but shame, by God's help, never!

"Do not be a fool," I said, as, in the solitude of my own room, I arraigned myself at the bar of common-sense. "You are not so silly as to mistake kindness and courtesy for evidences of a more particular regard. There is no shame in loving a worthy object—it is far better than to starve the heart by feeding it upon husks as so many women do, and then challenge canonization for the act. But beware how you let this spark become a burning flame to devour you!

No dallying with vain dreams or regrets, but shut down the valves of the heart firmly upon all such, and do your duty patiently, and trust God for the rest. And the heart—the woman's quick, sensitive, yearning heart—quivered and moaned beneath the stern decision, but Reason was unyielding, and forced it to lie quiet but very sore.

"Miss Ray!—Lina!—child!—Where are you?"

I was on the back porch, shelling beans with old Mrs. Brown, when, with an open letter in her hand, and her blue eyes sparkling with pleasure, my mistress made her appearance with the above query.

"A note from the city—from Cousin Ralph, child?"

"Is Mr. Annesley in New York still? I understood he had gone West."

"No; he has changed his mind, and is coming up with the Lloyds. They will be here on the evening of the 6th—that is, the day after to-morrow. The Knights and the Lincolns are coming up to visit the Elliotts next week, and we shall have gay times. Mrs. Brown, Mr. Annesley will send up Honor and James to-morrow, and, if you need more help, he will bring up Ann." Then, turning again to me, she added: "The Lloyds are delighted with Ralph. I have a note from Julia; she says he is *magnifique*. I hope she will make him feel her power yet, just for teasing you so that evening with his questions. And he right from Saratoga! He deserves it, and stranger things *have* happened."

"I thought you considered Mr. Annesley proof against all such attractions!"

"Yes, but then he has never come under the spell of Julia Lloyd; though he must have felt something of it, even in that brief interview at Saratoga, or he never would have questioned you so closely. Indeed, I have noticed a change in him ever since he came home. I never knew him so interested in things about

the place, or so contented here, before. Peter was speaking of it yesterday.—Well, well," she went on, with a little diplomatic smile and nod, "a little prudent forethought, under Providence, sometimes, effects a good deal."

"So that is the plan?" I thought—"and why not? Why should not the high-bred, beautiful, brilliant, and accomplished Miss Lloyd become the wife of Saville Annesley, spite of the fulness in your throat at the thought?—Because, notwithstanding all this, she lacks *humanity*. He is impatient only of stupidity and conceit; she *despises* all who are, or whom she deems, beneath her; she is not earnest, sincere, or truthful; she is in no way like him!

"Hold, there! Are marriages only between those of responsive sympathies and like natures? Are these not rather the exception than the rule? Moreover, she holds a different position from you; were you of her set, you might see her with different eyes. The wisest thing you can do is, to look after the arrangement of the curtains, in the guest-chambers, as you promised, and not attempt to pronounce Star-Chamber decisions on other people's characters. *There* you will make fewer mistakes."

I did; for the next twenty-four hours, I worked busily, and had the satisfaction of knowing that I could listen to Miss Annesley's oracular hints without danger of suffocation; only my heart was a little heavy, for it was hard to sink back to my old sphere, and become a mere tool for others to use.

If I had been fool enough to cherish any hope that it might be otherwise, the arrival of the Lloyds would soon have dispelled it. It seemed a part of Miss Annesley's "wise forethought" to refer every thing to Miss Julia's taste and judgment, and the lady assumed the responsibility as by right divine. Was there a dinner-party to be given, a picnic or a drive in question, the "who and the when and the where" were all

10

referred to her, while she consulted no one but Mr. Annesley, "so happy if her arrangements were so fortunate as to meet his approval." They invariably did; I could not deny that; but the expression of his face, the shrewd gleam in his eye, the sardonic smile that sometimes lurked about his mouth as he turned from her on. such occasions, perplexed me. Had he received her homage with any of the pleasure that mature manhood so often manifests at the attentions of youth and beauty, or, even with the dignified courtesy that claimed it as a right, I should quietly have dropped the subject. But I had seen enough of him now, to know that he was very *human*, tenacious of the rights of his sex, susceptible to both admiration and reverence, and I could not reconcile his manner with this. It kept recurring to me as an unsolved problem, making me restless and uneasy.

The Lloyds, both mother and daughter, seemed to have quite forgotten my position in the household, and treated me just as they did the other servants. This did not trouble me half so much as it did Miss Annesley, whose gentle manœuvring to make Miss Julia conscious of her mistake often provoked a smile from me, and a very decided elevation of that young lady's eyebrows. I disposed of her orders quite summarily. If I was at leisure and it suited my mood, I sometimes did what she required, but if occupied, or disposed to read or walk, I simply said so, and offered to ring for one of the girls to attend her pleasure. After one or two trials of this kind, I found her look of haughty astonishment, which threatened to transfix me at first, very harmless. Mr. Annesley, if he happened to be present, appeared to neither hear nor see, but wore a face as impenetrable as marble.

It was not long before I had the pleasure of seeing Mrs. Lincoln, the ideal of his youth, according to Miss Annesley. There was a dinner-party at Highcliff,

and she came with the Elliotts. I had declined Miss Annesley's invitation to come into the parlor after dinner, but, there being several quite young people present, some one suggested dancing, and Miss Annesley sent for me to come and play for them. We were in the back-parlor, but the doors were drawn back, and I could see most of the guests very well. Mrs. Annesley, however, came herself, and pointed Mrs. Lincoln out to me. She must have been at least thirty-five, but time had touched her lightly, for she was still very beautiful—a complexion like a white rose with the blush at its heart, features delicate and regular, large dewy blue eyes, a profusion of sunny hair worn in long curls in front and gathered back by a loop of pearls, a figure *petite*, but beautifully rounded, every motion of which seemed to me the perfection of grace. I longed to hear her speak, and, after the young people were tired of their dancing, I took a secluded seat, and was soon gratified.

One of the Miss Elliotts spoke of a new poem which had come upon the public like a jet of "spring-water unawares," and the lady took up the subject with great animation. To one like me, who knew nothing of what is termed the "art of conversation," and no use of language save to express my thought in the simplest, clearest manner possible, the ease and fluency with which she spoke, the readiness and extent of her quotations, seemed marvellous. I listened attentively, but this was all; there was nothing original or individual in her remarks, nothing in her sweet, infantine face, her manner, or, best of all tests, her voice, to indicate that she had actually *lived* or felt one of the truths or experiences of that inner life upon which she expatiated so cleverly. She evidently had read much and had a good memory, but her mind was second rate and her ideas second hand, and, in her delicate azure robe, she reminded me of the beautiful blue-and-gold chrysalis which I used to find hanging under the edges of the clapboards or along the mossy rail-fences. I could well understand how she might have charmed the beauty-worshipping heart of Ralph Annesley at twenty-two—the duration of the spell was what I doubted. His manner toward her was perfectly free and unembarrassed, grave or gay as the mood happened to be, and I dismissed her for Miss Lloyd, who was in one of her most brilliant moods that day, and was decidedly the belle of the company. Elated by the admiration she excited, and the marked attention of Mr. Annesley, she exerted her powers of pleasing to the utmost. She sang and played with the taste and execution of an artist, and her satire, wit, and repartee, made her the centre of attraction.

It was a phase of life wholly new to me, and I watched it with great interest, just as I would a group of statuary or fine pictures. One group I well remember. They were talking of Highcliff, and its capabilities for improvement. Miss Lloyd and Mrs. Lincoln were the principal speakers; I could not hear all they said, but I saw that Mr. Annesley listened attentively, sometimes assenting, and at others raising objections, as I judged, until, in reply to something, Miss Lloyd rose, and said, gayly:

"Difficulties! I, for one, ignore the word! If you will step to the piazza, I will give you ocular demonstration of the feasibility of my plan."

Mr. Annesley gallantly offered his arm, and they passed out of the French windows, opening on the piazza, followed by the others. She was dressed in pure white, with the exception of a corn-colored sash, and a Solfataire-rose in her hair. The light, airy texture of her dress, and the amplitude of the skirt and train, seemed to add to her stately proportions, as she stood, with one finely-rounded arm raised, pointing with her jewelled hand to a certain portion of the grounds, while, with the animation of conscious belleship, she indicated the line of a new carriage-way, which would greatly enhance the beauty of the place; he listening the while, with a quiet, happy smile, that gave his dark face an indescribable charm.

"Now, what say you, sir?" flashing upon him a brilliant smile. "Have I not made it clear?"

"Yes, indeed; and I owe you a thousand thanks. Your suggestions shall be carried out to the letter."

I saw the smile of triumph wreath her lips, Miss Annesley's look of delight, heard Mr. Elliott's "Bravo, Annesley! under the supervision of Miss Lloyd's fine taste, Highcliff will soon be perfect. I never, in fact, appreciated half its beauties before!" and Mr. Annesley's quiet, "Certainly, it has never seemed half so pleasant to me," and felt it was time for me to withdraw.

CHAPTER XXVII.

THE RETURN TO THE CITY.

It was the middle of September, and we were still at Highcliff. The Elliotts, and several other families, remained in the country also, for the weather was still warm, and there were rumors of cholera in the city. I regretted this only because I heard nothing from little Adeline Heath. I feared some evil had overtaken her, and should have gone down to the city myself, had I not been afraid of meeting Mr. Annesley there (he was down two or three times a week), and, by some inadvertence, giving him a clew to my history. Miss Annesley said we should all go by the first of October, so I withdrew as much as possible from the gay life about me, and sought to make my old shell of reserve cover my sore and foolish heart. But some words of Mr. Annesley's, one morning, came near crushing in that covering, and laying my secrets bare. He was sitting with the ladies, when the mail was brought in; I, who never received any letters, was arranging flowers in the vases, at a little distance from them, smiling at the desultory, disconnected remarks elicited by their letters, when he laid down the one he had been reading, and said to Miss Lloyd:

"You spoke of Mr. Sancroft the other day. Did you know his brother or sister?"

"No. We met Mr. Sancroft at Saratoga with Mr. Spencer.—You remember him, mamma, the gentleman you and Amy Clayton thought so handsome? His brother is engaged to one of Grace's friends. He gave us such an amusing account of that beggarly *protégée* of his mother's, who claimed to be Mr. Cavendish's heir; and the trouble and anxiety she had caused them. It was very foolish for them to notice her, or try to find her. The brother is to be married as soon as his sister reaches home, and Grace is to be one of the bridesmaids."

"They wait in vain, then, for Miss Michal Ellis is dead."

"Dead!" The exclamation was Miss Annesley's, for my lips refused to utter a sound, but the crash of the vase, as it fell from my trembling hands, drew all eyes upon me.

"One of that exquisite pair of antiques! Such carelessness is intolerable!" exclaimed Miss Lloyd; "I wonder, Cousin Anne, that you can endure it."

"Don't be so frightened, child," said my good mistress, seeing my blanched face.—"Of course, it was an accident, Miss Julia.—Why, you look ready to faint, Lina! Run out in the fresh air, and I will ring for Honor to clear up this litter."

As I turned to leave the room, I met Mr. Annesley's eye, and, for a second, its singular expression held me fast; then, I hurried away across the lawn and orchard, into the woods—I seldom ventured to the cliff now, unless the master was absent—and gave way to my tears.

Not for her, for, selfish as I was, I knew that "she had outlived the shadow of our night," and stood face to face with the eternal truth she had so worshipped here, but that she had died before I could see her—died, probably, doubting me! I had been looking forward to the time when I should see her and tell her all; and, knowing as she did her mother's peculiar character, I felt sure she would understand my position, and appreciate, if she could not approve, the feeling that led me to leave so suddenly.

Then, I recalled my intercourse with her—her patience, her wisdom, her goodness—clear insight, and deep religious faith, and slowly but clearly I began to apprehend that what I so selfishly deplored was a blessing even to me; for there was no need of stammering explanation and cloudy speech, now that she could discern truth with the clear eyes of an angel of God; and I rose up comforted, seeming to hear again, mingling with the murmur of the leaves above, her own words: "God is eternal, blessing us even in our memories—remember that, child!"

I walked slowly homeward, and, just as I entered the orchard, I saw Mr. Annesley leaning over the fence and watching the gambols of a couple of colts in a small paddock adjoining. These colts were the special pets of Peter and his boy, and usually very gentle, but to-day they seemed bent on a frolic, and had showed Jim their heels, while the master stood laughing at the lad's discomfiture. I hoped to pass him unobserved, but he saw me, and called out:

"Come here, Miss Ray, and see these beauties. What grace, what freedom, what conscious but honest pride! What a comment on the conventionalities and proprieties which have ruled at Highcliff for the past six weeks! Ugh! if it were not for an occasional hour spent with these fellows, or Don, I should be a fit subject for a strait-jacket."

"Yet that life seems very beautiful

and attractive to me," I said, drawing my sun-bonnet more closely over my eyes.

"That's because you have never been behind the curtain; it's the glamour of the foot-lights, child. It's none the less slavery because the chain is gilded or wreathed in flowers. Not one, I dare be sworn, of the hearts beating under those silken bodices, at Highcliff, yesterday, but went to its rest more weary and discontented than ever yours was, even after a scolding from some crabbed old teacher. So you really think all these people happy, myself included?" he added, after a pause.

"No, not exactly; but it seems to me that people who hold in their hands so many facilities for making themselves and others happy—who are so richly endowed with all that can win the eye and heart, can hardly be—unhappy. The certainty of being able to give pleasure to others—the knowledge that one's life is necessary to the happiness of others —must, in itself, be happiness, I think."

He turned suddenly, and his whole face glowed brightly, as he said:

"Then you—" He paused, took out his cigar-case, deliberately lit one, and, without so much as saying, "By your leave," drew two or three long puffs, before he added, in his driest tone, "you must think Miss Lloyd supremely blest. Rumor has doubtless informed you, before this, that she is necessary to the happiness of the master of Highcliff, though this was not needed, for every movement of her frank and independent nature discloses her assurance of it."

His tone was certainly not that of a happy lover, but I did not feel called upon to answer, and he went on:

"Such evidence of pure and disinterested attachment is very gratifying to a man of my experience, for, until very recently, I have been quite skeptical of the existence of such a thing in your sex. You look surprised, but at your age I was as green as you, and had faith enough

to have removed Dunderberg yonder. I put women among the beatitudes, the possession of which made heaven. Well, I found mine in Louise Ashmead—you know her as Mrs. Lincoln—and, boy-like, thought my life or death lay in her hands. She was gracious, she granted me life, and assured me that I possessed a like power over her, which I religiously believed until—

"When, sir?" I ventured to ask, seeing him pause.

"The jingle of the gold in my brother's breeches-pocket made her deaf to my voice—oblivious to my presence."

"Did you suffer much?"

"Suffer? No—yes, that is, when I got over my jealous rage, I was conscious of that regret one always feels for a vanished dream."

"What did you do then?" I was curious to know if his version would tally with that of my mistress, though I expected a rebuff.

"Tried a dose of sea-sickness (let me assure you, Miss Ray, it's an excellent remedy), crossed the Atlantic, returned in a few weeks to bury my brother, and find the lady and her family disposed to follow the old Hebrew custom, of brother succeeding brother in marital rights. I declined, returned to Europe, ran the treadmill round of folly common to the rich and the idle, offered lip-service at many shrines, and found them, as I deserved, fair and false, until, disgusted with every thing, myself included, I became a wanderer, sometimes returning to find myself more of a stranger in my father's house than in the midst of the Great Desert or a Siberian steppe, and glad to return to my Ishmaelitish life again, until this summer. Summoned home by business, I returned to find light, and hope, and life, faith in my early dream, harried by doubt at times, but still faith in one word—*regeneration!*"

"May you accept it as God's blessing, sir, and be very—very happy!" I could hardly steady my voice, for the tone in which he pronounced the last words, so different from the scornful sarcasm that marked it in the beginning, moved me almost to tears—it was so heart-felt, so earnest.

"As such I do accept it!" he replied, reverently. "But I want you to help me. You see, I have a great respect for your judgment; it's like the sunbeams yonder, clear and direct. What shall be done for the one whom the king delighteth to honor?"

"If it be a woman, as I infer" (I could not bring myself, just then, to pronounce Miss Lloyd's name), "do not clothe her in royal apparel, or proclaim her abroad in the streets, but crown her with your love, give her a home in your heart of hearts, and, trust me, if she be a true woman, she will be content."

His eye sparkled, his face again glowed with that bright, joyous light, as he said, fervently:

"I will! and may God so deal by me as I by her!"

Some further word seemed trembling upon his lips, but he repressed it, and said, in his usual tone: "Will you walk to the house with me, Miss Ray, or does your path lie another way?"

I had already been absent a long time, and I walked back with him in silence.

When we reached the lawn, he said, suddenly:

"You had been crying when you joined me. Will you tell me why?"

"No, sir. It was about nothing that concerned any one but myself."

"Not for the broken crockery, certainly," he said, with a smile. "I did not suppose it. But it is something unusual to see you thus moved—ah, I forgot —Miss Lloyd's anger! Well, I am sorry to say that she is not quite perfect; *entre nous*, I have observed in her a disposition to snub you occasionally, as to-day, all owing to an excess of that quality by which, according to Milton, the angels fell. But I am a man of leisure, and it

will be a delightful occupation to mould her plastic mind to my standard. I did intend, when I married, to keep a corner of my heart for one or two friends, yourself among them, Miss Lina; but, if she is to be enthroned there, you'll find it rather a tight squeeze, I am afraid, a taste of the old punishment by pressure, with which some of your forbears were probably acquainted in the old days of witchcraft."

Ridiculous as was his way of stating it, I knew it was the truth, and it struck my heart like ice.

Miss Lloyd was on the veranda when we crossed the lawn and ascended the steps, and the look she gave me proved the truth of his words. I think he noticed it, for there was a curious expression about his mouth when he addressed her with some common phrase of gallantry; but I did not stay to analyze it, being glad to escape to my room.

The next morning Mr. Annesley left for the city, to be absent for some weeks, as I understood from my mistress. In his absence the country lost all its charms, for the Lloyds and Miss Annesley were easily persuaded that the mornings were getting too cool for them; so, two weeks earlier than we had anticipated, we were settled in our city home.

Miss Annesley, having quite recovered from her lameness, went into society much more than she had during the first months I was with her, and my office of companion became almost a sinecure, or would have become such, if Mrs. and Miss Lloyd had not seemed bent upon reducing it to that of seamstress and lady's-maid. Sometimes I found it quite difficult to baffle their plans without coming to an open rupture which might end in my dismissal—a result which I fancied would not be unpleasing to Miss Julia, for my indifference to her authority at Highcliff, as well as here, was a crime not to be overlooked by one of her disposition.

But I was not quite ready for this—I

knew I must go, for nothing would tempt me to remain there if she became the wife of Mr. Annesley; but it required more strength to break, at one strain, the ties that bound me to the place where I had first truly tasted life, because no longer repressed by narrowness or formality. I tried to ascertain from Miss Annesley when the marriage would take place; but, notwithstanding her oracular "perhapses" and diplomatic nods, I was convinced she was really as ignorant on the subject as myself, and I was weak enough to cherish a feeling of relief at the indefiniteness that still left me the shelter of his roof.

As soon as possible after my return, I went to Mulberry Street to find little Adeline Leete, and was told by the woman of the house that the "Heaths left the first of July, and took rooms in Sheriff Street near the corner of Delancey, she believed—the number she did not know."

It was useless to ask if she had received my letters; so I turned slowly homeward, pondering upon the best course to find her, for I dared not attempt to explore that portion of the city alone. I might, doubtless, hear of her through Tom Hunt, but I shrunk with horror from the thought of renewing my acquaintance with him or his mother. There was one of the old servants, Honor, who had been born, and always had lived in the city; I was quite a favorite with her—might I not take her into my confidence and ask her advice or aid? I was thinking this over one afternoon, about two weeks after our return to the city, while unpacking and arranging some books in the library according to my mistress's wish, she having gone out to dinner somewhere with the Lloyds. My work progressed slowly, for my heart and my fingers were both heavy. Finally, I opened one of the volumes, and sat listlessly looking it over, when I heard a voice in the hall, which sent the blood tingling through my whole frame, saying:

"This way, sir. We will go into the library, if you please."

There was no time nor way to escape, for the only other door communicating with that room was locked; and the next instant, Mr. Annesley opened the door, and ushered in—James Sancroft.

"Ah, Miss Linn," he said, carelessly, as if he had come home after a three-hours' instead of a three-weeks' absence, "you are busy as ever, I see. Don't let us disturb you.—Mr. Sancroft, Miss Ray. Please be seated, sir, while I let in a little more light. This 'dim, religious' medium may do for women, but not for lawyers."

I have a memory of standing bolt upright, stiff and unbending as the statue of the commander at the famous supper in "Don Giovanni," while James Sancroft saluted me with as perfect *sang froid* as if he had never met me before in his life.

But while Mr. Annesley swept back the heavy curtains and attempted to raise a sash to fling back the blind, muttering anathemas at its obstinacy, Mr. Sancroft uttered a few low words that put life into that statue. They were these:

"So you thought to hide from *me!* What folly! I traced you long ago, and have sought you, now, to say that, being a patient man, as I once told you, the conditions for peace are still open. Do you accept?"

"No."

"As you please—you know the consequences. Betray your identity even by so much as a hint to that man, and you will soon learn what the word *enemy* means!"

The words were hissed in my ear, and, before I could recover from my surprise, he had advanced to meet Mr. Annesley, and was complimenting him on his library with the utmost grace and suavity of manner.

I immediately left the room, and sat for a long time, thinking over his words, and what new evil to me his presence in the house betokened. Finally, Honor appeared with Mr. Annesley's compliments, and a request that I would come down to the library.

James Sancroft was gone. I made sure of that before I ventured down, and Mr. Annesley sat in a large easy-chair, with Nep at his knee, vividly recalling, by his position, the night I had seen him at the Pines. He greeted me with a bright smile, saying, as he pointed to the sofa:

"Please be seated, Miss Ray. I believe my life at Highcliff has spoiled me, for Nep and I are lonely. What have you been doing these three weeks?"

"Sewing, chiefly, sir; helping to make the ladies' dresses."

"Humph! What possessed you to turn seamstress? You look as if you had been making your own shroud. Are you sure you are not going to have fever again?"

"Yes, sir."

"Don't attempt to cheat me. I am somewhat skilled in the pathology of disease, and I say you are either ill or in trouble. But, sit down there—you will have the more sympathy for me, for I am troubled too, not merely because, upon coming home after an absence of three weeks, I find that bird of paradise, the queenly Julia, on the wing, but by another matter in which I have a fancy your common-sense can help me."

I obeyed, sitting as far back in the shadow as possible. But he seemed to forget all about me and his trouble, and sat for some time silent, occasionally passing his hand slowly over old Nep's head. Finally he roused himself, and said:

"Miss Ray, you have heard some talk about the estate of my old friend Rothsay Cavendish, and the young girl who, after his death, suddenly laid claim to it, as the child of his brother, and then quite as suddenly disappeared?"

"Yes, sir." The reply was hardly above my breath, but he did not seem to notice it, and went on:

"That brother was the dear friend of my boyhood, and, as soon as I learned these facts, I gave Spencer, Mr. Cavendish's lawyer and mine, orders to spare no effort or expense in trying to find this strange claimant. He set his agents to work, and more than once thought he had succeeded, but the scent proved false, or the game turned out something quite different from that he sought, and he has been disappointed. The fact that a mere girl, not older than yourself, I judge, ignorant of the world, who never went twenty miles, it seems, from the place where she was brought up, could, for so many months, baffle and elude the search of one of the shrewdest lawyers in the city, added to the interest I already felt in the case, and I have actually caught myself, this summer, staring divers ugly girls out of countenance (Spencer says she is plain), or chasing down some algebraic-looking figure, with a zeal deserving of better success. For the past three weeks, I have been searching the State of Michigan, to find, if above-ground, the witnesses to Philip Cavendish's marriage, Spencer having made a copy of the certificate upon which the girl founded her claim."

He paused, and I drew still farther back into the corner of the deep sofa, almost breathless in my eagerness to hear the next words.

"I was successful: the Catholic mission, where they were married, has long been abandoned for a more eligible locality, still farther West; but, after much fruitless inquiry, I unearthed an old Frenchman, who proved to be the very man I wanted. He witnessed the marriage, and grew garrulous in his recollections of the handsome young couple. But, I forgot—to understand this, you should know something of the circumstances of this marriage."

He briefly related the story I had heard from Mr. Cavendish, and again took up the account of his search:

"From this man I gained a clew to the poor girl's fate. It seems, when up in the region of Mackinaw, some years afterward, he learned, from the wife of an old comrade, that the old man and his daughter had found shelter in their cabin, and that she had died there in giving birth to a child. The good woman kept the baby, and the old man, whom the Frenchman described as a little unsound in mind, wandered about the country, returning at intervals to see the child. When it was about three years old he stole it, and left poor Margot Lefranc *désolé*.

"I went to the place and heard the story from the lips of Margot herself. That poor young thing, who hid her shame, as she thought, on the extreme verge of civilization, was the idolized wife for whom Philip Cavendish was searching. You weep, Miss Ray, and, indeed, it is a sad story; the only fault of the young people seems to have been in concealing their marriage from their friends. The knowledge of his daughter's condition seems to have driven the father wild, and, believing herself deceived and deserted, she was but too ready to follow him into the wilderness and die."

He paused, and seemed lost in some sad reminiscence, while I, by a strong effort, repressed my tears.

"I could not hope to trace the old man's wanderings after so many years," he added, "neither was it necessary. I was satisfied that the child, born under the roof of that French cabin, was the daughter of my friend, for the mother bore the name of Harriet Day; and the name which Margot's husband, who had once belonged to the chorus of an opera-troupe, insisted upon giving her child, was identical with that of this Oaklawn teacher—Zerlina. And one of the most singular circumstances in the whole story is, that upon comparing notes and collating evidence with Spencer, I find that this same child was thrown into my hands some years ago. I was just ready to sail for Europe, and transferred her to the care of a cousin, who took it into her head to marry some little time after, and the girl proving stiff-necked and rebel-lious, it is said, and, quite likely, a stumbling-block in the way of the husband's children (he was a widower, I hear), she was sent as a sort of charity-scholar to this Oaklawn school. My cousin left the country after her marriage, but I have written to her, to make confirmation sure."

"I think I heard you once say that you should recognize your friend's child," I said, as steadily as I could.

"Well, I certainly did not, though for some time I recalled the spirited, elf-ish, tawny imp (you need not wince, Miss Ray, she was twice as dark as you, without your transparency), with a strange interest, and felt glad that she had a home with gentle Agnes Lathrop. One thing is certain—she must have developed a character of some strength and originality, for she was, it is admitted, a favorite with Rothsay Cavendish; moreover, was early promoted to a position of trust and responsibility in the school, which she continued to hold up to the hour of her leaving. Found she *must* be, and I have a kind of faith that your woman's wit may suggest some way in which it may be done."

Should I do it? Should I yield to the almost uncontrollable impulse that moved me to kneel at the feet of my father's friend—my own friend—and say, "It is done! I am Philip Cavendish's child!"—Had there been, in his face or manner, the slightest indication that he suspected this, I should have yielded, but there was not, and that reflection saved me. I thought of Edward's approaching marriage, of the change soon to take place in his own household, and I said: "When I make this confession, I will hold the lines of my destiny in my own hands; I will be my own mistress, and make it deliberately, and not from impulses; I have plenty of time yet." These thoughts occupied but a moment, but he was getting impatient, and said:

"Have you nothing to suggest, Miss Lina?"

"I hardly feel competent, sir. Of course, she changed her name."

"Yes, and, if we ever hear of her, it will be as Hannah, or Deborah, or Eunice, I dare swear!"

"She might have gone West on the same errand as yourself."

"I thought of that, and we have made every possible inquiry. Besides, Spencer says she had no means, for she left the pittance owing to her in the hands of Mrs. Ellis. That seems like Philip! Poor girl! there was doubtless some sharp filing under their apparent kindness, or she would never have left as she did. I distrust that Sancroft, I was tempted to kick him, just now, when he ventured to insinuate that the girl wanted to marry him—Philip Cavendish's daughter!"

"I wish, from my soul, you had, sir!" The words broke from me unconsciously, but I recollected myself, and added: "I think any man who says such a thing, or even assumes it, ought to be kicked!"

"Bravo! Miss Lina! I like to see you fire up on that will-o'-the-wisp way when any thing touches you! Then I get a glimpse of you as you really are; I look right into your heart and see—"

"See what?"

"A brave, true, womanly spirit; the same that spoke to me one bright morning at Highcliff, of faith in God and man, as if the words had a meaning—were a reality."

"So they are, sir, and I trust you feel it."

"It's growing clearer, my friend. But the power to discern such things is not quite as clear at forty as at nineteen. The fogs that arise from the *débris* of a misspent life would be respectable even in Egypt. But with such a spirit as—" He paused, bit his lip, and added in a totally different tone—"Miss Ray, I believe you were about to suggest something with reference to the business of which I have been speaking."

Curious as I was to know what the words so suddenly and forcibly repressed might be, I was obliged to answer:

"I think the wisest plan would be to give over the search, for the present. The fugitive is probably aware of it, and has taken her measures accordingly. Drop your search, and she will be likely to drop her caution."

"Exactly! It shall be done. How is it you always contrive to say just the right word, Miss Lina?"

"I don't know, but I am very glad if I am able to assist you in any way," I said, as I arose to go.

"Yes; I believe that, and I somehow find my intractable self quite disposed to accept your help. But you needn't be in such a hurry, when, very likely, I shall not have another opportunity to speak to you before I leave for England."

"Are you going to England, sir?"

"Yes, immediately."

"Alone?"

"Yes; I should be glad to take my wife with me, but it is necessary for me to go immediately, and I shall have to postpone that pleasure, possibly, until next spring. It is a great trial to me, my friend, and I would not go if it were not for some information brought me by the last foreign mail. But, I shall return all the sooner for leaving my treasure behind—probably, in about six or eight weeks."

So the time was fixed—in the spring, at the latest. I must go, and go before he returned. My limbs began to fail me, and I had hard work to keep back the tears, while I said hurriedly, and not very steadily, I fear:

"Then, good-by, sir; and, as I may not have another opportunity to say it—God bless you for all your kindness to me!"

Now the tears would no longer be repressed, but it was too dark for him to see them; he rose hastily, and confronted me, saying:

"Not see me? What nonsense is

this? Are you going to run into ship-fever again?"

"No, sir; but the changes of which you have been speaking will make it necessary for me to find a new home."

"You'll find the Northwest passage! Have not I just said that I shall return in two months, when I intend to be married, *Deo volente*, and take my bride to Europe? You can surely stay until then."

"I would rather not, sir."

He went on without heeding me: "The woman whom you bade me crown with my love, and treasure in my heart of hearts."

"Yes, sir—Miss Lloyd."

"Miss Lloyd be hanged!" was the impetuous, uncivil answer. "Miss Ray—Lina!" He came toward me, his whole face kindling with intense, passionate emotion, "you must know—your heart has surely divined the truth! Who should that woman be, but yourself—the dearest—"

There was a bustle, the sound of foot-steps in the hall, and Miss Annesley's voice was heard saying, in glad surprise: "Ralph! Mr. Annesley in the library!" and his sentence was not finished in words, but I was suddenly gathered close to his breast, and his lips pressed to mine. The next instant, I had struggled from his arms, and had barely time to escape, before I heard the ladies enter and welcome him home.

CHAPTER XXVIII.

AN UNEXPECTED VISITOR.

"Miss Ray, a person below desires to see you."

It was well Jane came with that mes-sage—well that something occurred to break the spell that had held me for the past twenty-four hours, lest I should grow selfish in my unspeakable happi-ness.

I knew he was gone—my master—I might never see him again—I might be a stranger and a hireling all my days, but I did not think of this; only that the dream, that I had set myself to overcome as something hopeless, was realized. I was beloved—beloved by the noblest, truest man I knew; and, henceforth, nei-ther the sorrows of life nor the agonies of death could take me from that blessed consciousness. Fear and doubt were, as yet, outside the gates of my paradise; but I found them both in the honest old face waiting for me in the hall.

There was no mistaking that blue roundabout and tarpaulin, and, in an instant, I had the two horny hands in mine, crying:

"Uncle Steve! dear Uncle Steve, how glad I am to see you!"

"Yes, Blackbird, I knew you'd be! An' I'm glad," with a loving glance at my face, "ter see you're all right, an' how you've grow'd a good bit. But do you know where Birdie is? I can't find her, nor I can't make nothin' out o' the folks where she lived."

I drew him into a small anteroom which I knew would be vacant at that hour, but he would not be seated, evi-dently seeming to think he should lose time by so doing. So he stood restlessly moving his feet, while I told him of my one interview with little Adeline, and my subsequent efforts to find her.

"The woman there said somebody had come to look for her, and she give this ticket, else I shouldn't a' known your bearin'," he said, holding out the card on which I had written only the word, "Blackbird," with Miss Annesley's ad-dress, and left it with the woman in Mul-berry Street, in case little Adeline should come back. "She was well, and havin' a good time, Lina, when you saw her; flyin' about, just as she used to be, of course?"

Dear old soul, how the anxious face and restless foot contradicted that "of course!" I could not impart to him my misgivings; I had no right to contradict her own assertion that she was happy; so I spoke only of her health, and her longing for the pure air and blue sea of the Cove.

"No wonder, for it does seem to me, Blackbird, that 'ere place where she lived ain't right wholesome for anybody. I hain't nothin' ag'in cities; they are well enough for 'em that likes 'em, but I never can see how folks can bear to live jammed together thicker 'n black muscles, when there's a plenty of room on the airth and sea."

I agreed with him, and went on to tell him about Mr. Heath's acquaintance with the Hunts, and my thought of applying to them for information.

"I guess I'll try Sheriff Street first," he said, thoughtfully. "Not that there's any reason why I shouldn't put an honest question to an old neighbor, but Birdie never sot much by 'em, nor I don't think the lad would, arter he came back here, for you see, Polly, she kinder bore down on him about the Hunts, but he didn't seem to think much more on 'em than she did, arter all."

"Very well, and, if you will wait a minute, I will go with you to Sheriff Street."

"Sartinly, child; that's just what I wanted ter ask, 'cause she'd be so glad to see us together. But, if it don't matter, I'll wait outside; it won't seem so long out there."

When I joined him, he was walking up and down the pavement energetically, as if every step brought him nearer the goal. During our walk, I tried to learn from him something of little Adeline's husband, but he seemed to be almost as ignorant on that subject as myself.

He had made one of a party of young men who had come up from the city to shoot ducks, and encamped for some weeks on the islands in the vicinity of the Cove. On one of his visits to shore, he had met Birdie, and "they took to each other 'mazin'ly."

Without any definite address, we were forced to make many inquiries, and my forebodings were by no means lightened by the appearance of the dwellings or the manners of their inmates. At last, we stumbled upon the right house; a woman met us at the door, a coarse, bedizened creature, who, in reply to our inquiries, burst into a tirade of abuse and imprecation worthy of a fiend. I clung to Uncle Steve in affright, while, for a few seconds, he stood as if stunned and bewildered; then, hearing his darling's name again coupled with epithets, vile as the breath that uttered them, his face grew almost bloodless, and, shaking my arm from his, he confronted the virago with a look of simple, manly anger, that had power, for an instant, to check even her tongue.

"Woman!" he said, "that child is as innocent of the things you talk about as her little unborn baby. She's his *wife*, I tell you! I saw 'em married, with my own eyes; an' if he had another wife— O Lina! I can't believe it!—'twill kill her!"

Oh, the sorrow and anguish of that look and tone. It reached even that woman's heart through the crust of sin and vice, for, in language still coarse, but free from foul indecency, she said:

"Believe it or not, the woman who came here claimed him as her husband, and she had her papers in black and white, and, what's more, he hadn't the face to deny it, but sneaked off, owing me ten dollars for a week's board."

Uncle Steve took out his pocket-book and placed the money in her hand, saying:

"Where is she? Where did she go, then?"

"Back to where she come from, I s'pose—'twas some place in New Hampshire, where they lived afore he quit her."

The old man groaned, and turned an appealing look to me.

"The wife we know," I said, in reply to that look. "The young girl he brought here, from Mulberry Street, whom he married in Connecticut. Where did she go?"

"I don't know. I didn't turn her out; she didn't wait for that. She'd spunk enough, for all she seemed so soft. At first, she flared up in that woman's face like a tiger, but when the woman faced Hen. down, and made him own the truth, she walked right out of the house without a word, and I've never seen nor heard of her since."

We turned away, and had reached the corner of Broadway, before I ventured to break in upon the anguish that was rending that old man's heart, by again suggesting the possibility of tracing her through the Hunts.

"No, no, Lina, she'd never go to the likes o' them in her trouble. They were *his* sort, and I—'twouldn't be well for me to see him or them just now. I'm going home, for where should the homeless little thing go to but the old place—to them as loved her better 'n their hearts' blood, an' she knew Polly an' the children did that, and Nat, too? O Lina! to think of it's bein' our Birdie!"

He completely broke down, and, catching at the possibility his words suggested, I tried to encourage him to hope.

"No, Blackbird, I know she couldn't stand it. She'd set her heart on him, an' ter have such a thing come on her now when she's jist as you say, 'twill kill her sure, an' there's nothin' to hope about."

I felt that words were, indeed, useless, and so we parted, he promising to have Polly Maria write if the child were there; if not, he would come back and we would search the city together.

There was no letter, and on the third day he returned, but looking so changed—so worn and haggard, that it seemed as if those brief days had done the work of years.

I had explained to Miss Annesley that some friends of my early childhood were in trouble, and, with her usual kindness, she had given me permission to go out,

so that Uncle Steve and I soon found ourselves at Tom Hunt's door. It was a tippling house of the lowest class, a very gate-way to hell, judging from the appearance of its patrons and their conversation, but we did not shrink back. Behind the counter, or bar, a couple of tawdrily-dressed girls were gossiping in the corner, and a man making change. We applied to the latter, and asked for Mr. Hunt. Our inquiry brought all eyes upon us, and one of the girls, coming forward— the one whom I had met when with Adeline's husband—said:

"He's out, but, if you owe him any thing, you can pay me."

"No, no, Fan, you don't come that game," said the man by her side, with an oath. "I am chief clerk here, and if you've any thing to pay," turning to us, "you must deal with me!"

"Thank ye, sir; we only want to see Mr. Hunt," said Uncle Steve.

"Well, he's out, and will be for some time," returned his daughter, turning to pour out a dram for a customer.

"Yes, he's gone on a tour," said the other girl, with a laugh.

Uncle Steve turned hopelessly to me, and made a movement to go, but I had determined to appeal to the girl, so, raising my veil, I said:

"Miss Hunt, since we cannot see your father, perhaps you will be so kind as to give us a few minutes' conversation in a more private place."

She stared at first, but my respectful tone was not without effect, for, passing out from behind the counter, she opened a door into a private room, saying:

"Yes, indeed, if it will be any satisfaction to you. Walk in."

The room was small, and the furniture reminded me of Sally Hunt's favorite adjective—"hogged out." Uncle Steve remained standing, but I took the seat she offered, saying:

"You are acquainted with a Mr. Heath, I believe, who lived, not long

since, in Mulberry Street, and more recently in Sheriff?"

"Yes; but I tell you beforehand, if
you are going to arrest him, I'll have
nothing to do with it!" she exclaimed
bluntly.

"Our business does not relate to him,
but to the young girl he married in Bradshaw, and brought here as his wife. You
probably know, some two weeks ago a
woman appeared here who claimed to
be his wife by a former marriage, and
the young girl left the house in Sheriff
Street alone. Have you heard any thing
about her? Where she went?—or where
she may be found?"

"Didn't she go back to the Cove?"

"No."

"Then Hen. was mistaken. He
thought—" She paused, and, eying us
suspiciously, said, "You aren't trying to
bamboozle me?"

"No, no, we don't want any thing of
him!" exclaimed Uncle Steve, impatiently. "We never desire to set eyes on him
ag'in."

"Not that I care a red for Hen.
Heath," she returned, "but I despise to
'peach. There's a warrant out for his
arrest, but I'll not get him into trouble.
I've seen him once, since the fray in
Sheriff, and he was taking on terribly
about that girl, little Adeline as he called
her. We all thought she'd go straight
home, and finally got him off, but, Lord,
he's too sappy to keep out of the way
long. He didn't even deny that he married t'other woman, but said she made
him do it, when he was nothing but a
boy, and she old enough to be his mother."

"Then you can give us no clew to her
at all?" I said, rising.

"No; though, if she didn't quit the
city, most likely she's been picked up
by the police, and sent to the almshouse or hospital."

I thanked her, and we were turning
away when I heard some one in an adjoining room cry out:

"Fan, you idle slut, bring me some
water!"

I recognized the voice at once, though
it was weak and somewhat tremulous,
and I did not need the girl's angry—
"Hold your tongue, granny!" to tell
me that it was my old mistress—and I
said to the girl:

"Your grandmother is living, then?
Can we see her? We knew her once—
this man is, or was, her neighbor."

Her bold, rude manner had returned
at the sound of that voice, and she retorted, angrily, "See her! You wouldn't
want to if you had her to live with!
She's the crossest old torment that ever
breathed!"

She flung open the door of a small
room or closet, and there, upon her bed,
lay my old mistress. She was emaciated
to a skeleton, and it was fortunate that
she was "blinder than a bat," as her
granddaughter said, for the room, the
bed, and her person, were filthy beyond
description. I confess, my first impulse
was to turn away, but the look of pity
on Uncle Steve's face withheld me.

"Granny!" yelled the girl, "here's
somebody from your old place come to
see you!"

The bleared eyes stared straight at
us, but evidently without recognition,
and I drew as near to her as I could bear
to, and said:

"It is Steve Leete from the Cove, and
another friend. You remember Steve
and Polly Maria, Mrs. Hunt?"

She made an effort to raise herself
upon her elbow, but fell back, muttering
querulously:

"Steve Leete!"

"Yes. I'm right sorry to see you so
poorly," said the old man.

"No, you ain't! It's a lie!" she
screamed. "You all want me to die.
But I won't, I tell you! I'm only sixty-
eight, and sixty-eight's young. I'll not
die yet!"

"No; no such good news as that,"
said the girl, mockingly.

"Hold your tongue, you blasted—"
a fit of coughing interrupted the anathe-
ma, and threatened to shake the life from
her. Catching breath again, she rolled
her eyes toward Uncle Steve, saying:

"Where did you come from? What
do you want?"

"I come here to find my little gal,
Adeline. You remember her, *Miss*
Hunt?" said the old man, kindly.

"More fool you! Children are nothing but a cuss. When Tom was a baby,
an' had the scarlet fever, I carried him
night arter night in my arms; if I'd
known he'd a' lived to sarve me as he
has, I'd a helped him to die!"

The old, white head shook with im-
potent rage; and, feeling how truly the
sins of youth become the fate of age,
I turned away sick at heart. She observed the movement, and asked:

"Who's that? You've got somebody
with you, Steve Leete!"

"Why, I s'posed you knew. It's
Lina, *Miss* Hunt—Lina Day, that used to
live with you."

"Lina Day! Who said she was rich?
—some great man's child?—Are you
rich, girl?"

"No; I am almost as poor as when
I left your house, Mrs. Hunt."

"I'm glad on't. I told the man that
come here to pump me 'twas all a lie.
What right had Harri't Day's come-by-
chance to be rich, an' I poor, cheated
out o' my just rights?"

"So you are the girl that used to
live with granny," said the granddaughter, eying me curiously. "And you didn't
get a fortune, after all?"

"No. Who came here to inquire for
me?"

"A lawyer from up-town. He wanted
to find out something about your folks,
but granny was a match for him, as she
is for the devil himself! I'm sorry you
didn't get the money, for I believe it
would have killed her right off," she returned, with an unfeeling laugh, as we
left the room.

When we reached the pavement, we
looked silently and hopelessly in each
other's face. The almshouse, or hospital, the girl had said, but we were both
strangers, and to whom should we apply
for aid. I thought of Mr. Spencer; to
seek him would be to betray myself, but
what was that to the sorrow of that poor
old man; and I was about to suggest this
to him, when a cheery voice, that I recognized at once, said:

"Shure an' it's Miss Lina! an' aren't
I glad to see your face once more!"

It was Mary Kane, the nurse Mr.
Annesley had brought from the city, to
care for me in my illness, and I immediately told her our trouble.

"It's to Bellevue they'd be after taking the poor thing," she said, her honest face aglow with sympathy. "I was
nurse there for more than a twelvemonth
myself, and I'll go with you. Many's
the poor young thing that finds shelter
there, in her anguish and trouble."

She led the way, with rapid steps, to
that quarter of the city where the hospital, so inaptly named, overlooks the
East River. The officials recognized her,
and our inquiries met with a courteous
answer:

"Adeline Leete Heath," said the
clerk, running a finger down the pages
of the record. "No such person—ay,
Adeline Leete, entered November 5th,
child born on the 8th—dead—woman
delirious, escaped November 20th, eluding vigilance of the nurse. Subsequent
fate unknown."

"She's dead, poor little Birdie!"
groaned Uncle Steve, turning away with
a look I shall never forget.

"No, not so bad as that sir," replied
hopeful Mary Kane. "If she's crazy,
she'd be the more likely to hold out. It's
the 25th now, most likely she's gone
home. Wait till I speak to one of the
nurses."

Permission was given, and, while de-
taining my impatient companion by the
hand, my eye fell upon the following

news item, in the daily paper lying on the desk before me:

" An old fisherman of Southport, upon going down to the beach very early, a few mornings since, was surprised to find a young, delicate-looking girl cowering beneath the sail of his boat, where she had evidently passed the night. She was supposed to be a lunatic who had escaped from her friends. She was kindly cared for by the family, but contrived to escape the next night."

I seized the paper, and read the item to Uncle Steve. His face brightened, and, without waiting for me to finish, he started for the street, saying:

" 'Twas her, Lina! She thought 'twas the Dart, poor thing! I know'd she'd steer for the old place.'"

I followed, and we were soon overtaken by Mary, who had learned nothing further from her friend, save that the patient " had been very quiet-like, and moaned constantly to go home."

" To be sure," said the old man hurrying on at a pace that left us breathless in the attempt to follow ; " an' she'll be so taken aback to find the old house shut up. We must hurry, Blackbird."

His *we* expressed just my own feeling. I must go too. I could not leave him to face what I feared alone. When we reached the vicinity of the New Haven Depot, I seized his arm and spoke to him of the necessity of my notifying Miss Annesley of my intended absence. He simply turned his haggard, anxious face toward me, without slackening his pace, and said, with such an imploring look :

" But she may be waitin', child! "

" It will not delay us a moment. I shall have ample time to go home and back before the next train leaves. If you do not choose to go with me, you can wait at the station. I will be back in half an hour."

" If you mind leavin' him alone, miss," whispered my Irish friend, with a look of commiseration at his haggard face, " I'll just step into the depot with him

myself. He's a good bit distraught, I fancy."

She had laid her hand on my arm as she spoke, and, turning to reply, I looked right into the faces of Miss Lloyd and James Sancroft. Although our eyes met, the gentleman betrayed no evidence of recognition, save a rapid, sneering glance at my companions ; but the look with which the lady surveyed us was one of unspeakable disdain. I hardly noted it, however, for, just a little in advance, assisting a fair young girl into a carriage, was Edward Ellis. He was too much occupied to observe me ; Miss Lloyd and his brother entered the carriage, and, parting from my humble friends, I walked rapidly toward Bleecker Street, and reached the house just as the empty carriage drove from the door.

" Miss Annesley had gone to the parlor to see some friends of the Lloyds," Jane said, in answer to my inquiries, and I waited in the upper hall, what seemed to me an age, but there was no cessation to the murmur of voices in the parlor below. At length, I ventured to send Jane down to beg permission for me to speak with my mistress a moment. My heart beat fast when I heard some one step into the hall, and I was about to run down when I heard Miss Lloyd give Jane some order, and when the girl explained that I had sent her, she replied, sharply :

" Let Miss Ray deliver her own messages henceforth."

I hurried down, and said, respectfully :

" I do not like to disturb Miss Annesley, ma'am, but it is of the utmost importance to me that I should see her at once. I will detain her but one moment."

She drew herself up haughtily, gathering back the ample folds of her heavy *gros grain*, as if there was contamination in my touch, for, in my eagerness, I had advanced quite near her, and said :

" The company in which I saw you, not an hour since, accounts, I suppose, for your neglect of your duties for the past week, miss. It is perfectly congenial, I learn, however, from one who knows something of your past life, and Miss Annesley will be duly informed. At present, she is engaged."

She turned into the parlor, and closed the door behind her. So James Sancroft had spoken! But how much — and what? Should I go into the parlor and confront him, trusting to the candor and honor of Edward Ellis to support me? I glanced at the clock on the landing. I had but half an hour left, and it would take twice that time to set this matter right, and the thought of that sorrowful old face, watching for me at the depot, silenced all feeling of self, and, returning to my room, I wrote a brief note explaining my absence, left it on Miss Annesley's table, descended to the street, and hurried to the station.

CHAPTER XXIX.

THE SEARCH FOR BIRDIE.

It was quite dark when we got off at the lonely little station put up to accommodate visitors at the "Beach" and "Cove;" a gloomy November night, with a sky threatening rain; a raw, east wind which, sweeping right off from the water, seemed to penetrate to the bones. We were two miles from the Cove, and, as soon as we touched the ground, the old man started with those long strides, upon the well-remembered path, while I followed, doing my best to keep up. Presently, he seemed to remember, for pausing, he said, in a tone of humble apology:

"I'm tiring you to death, Lina. I didn't mean ter, but I don't mind anything when I think mebbe she's waitin' for Uncle Steve. You'll kinder think how it is, child."

I did, and there was a strange excitement for me in that rapid night-walk.

The old man's expectation of finding her grew more reasonable to me, and more than once, when the moon struggled through the driving clouds, I found myself starting at some fancied resemblance to a human figure or the flow of female drapery among the rocks and white birches that lined our path. The excitement was too deep for words, and we pressed on in silence until the light from Nat Frisbie's kitchen-window gleamed athwart the darkness. Then we paused to take breath, and I could see by the dim moonlight that the old man's eyes were fixed—not on that, but on a point beyond, where the pyramidal form of the old pine was dimly outlined against the sky—with an intentness that seemed to pierce the darkness and the distance, while the hand that I took in mine trembled like an aspen-leaf. Seeing he did not move, I suggested that we should call on Polly Maria.

"Yes, " he murmured, and we started on. In a few minutes, we stood in Nat's long, narrow kitchen. Polly Maria was alone; she dropped her knitting upon her open Bible and came toward us, every line of her dark, melancholy face alive with grief and foreboding. Uncle Steve glanced at it and sank into a chair. She pressed my hand in silence, and turning to him, while natural grief, struggling with her unquestioning faith, gave a deep, solemn pathos to her voice, said:

"It's the hand of God, Stephen, and though He slay me, yet will I put my trust in Him! Last night the warnin' came ag'in. I see her as plain as I see you, standin' by my bed, the water a streamin' from her hair and dress just as it did when she fell over the Dart. It was the third time, and I know now that she is drownded as well as if I see it."

Uncle Steve moaned like a child, while I briefly told her of our search, and our hope to find her here.

She shook her head hopelessly. "Some folks may slight such things, miss, but I've never known 'em fail.

Nobody dies without a warning, if they or their friends would have the grace to heed it."

"Polly," said Uncle Steve, impatiently, "I allers know'd you was great on dreams, but this one can't be true, because, you see, Birdie ain't on the water. But your head allers run on her bein' drownded."

"Wait and see, brother. But you must stay here to-night. You can't be comfortable down there."

He glanced at me anxiously.—"She's tired out, poor girl, mebbe she'd better stay."

"I shall go with you, Uncle Steve; but if Aunt Polly will give us a bit of food, I'll be glad—*she* may be hungry, you know," I added, seeing how impatient he looked.

A small basket was filled, Polly promised to come down early in the morning, and we turned away. We had not gone above two rods when, as if to second Mrs. Frisbie's warnings, there came from the back yard the long, startling howl of a dog, wailing through the air, and died mournfully away. We did not speak, but I felt the old man's fingers tighten on my wrist, and we hurried as if drawn by some invisible power. The old cabin was dark and silent, and the unbroken stillness without and within soon convinced him that she did not *wait*. I was thankful for the darkness, for I felt that, at that moment, it would be almost sacrilege to look upon that old man's face.

I do not think he attempted to sleep or even rest that night, for, long after I had flung myself upon the bed in her room, I heard him moving about, sometimes in the house and sometimes on the beach. He said little to his sister or myself the next day; the excitement that had buoyed him up for the past few days had left him, and he seemed weak and trembling. When I saw him bring out all her old treasures and playthings, the box of shells, the "History of Beasts," "John R. Jewett's Narrative,"

and the volume of "Shipwrecks," and arrange and rearrange them with his trembling hands, I began to fear for his reason. Yet a moment's reflection taught me that the intuitions of that loving heart were better than my highest wisdom, for if our poor wronged Birdie had, as the nurse said, "moaned so constantly for home" at the hospital, what home would her poor, crazed brain be so likely to recognize as the one of her happy childhood? All deep emotion is electric, and the tremor in the old man's hands was communicated to mine when I brought from the beach the little "silver shells" and the smooth, variegated pebbles in my apron as of old, and began to lay them down upon the sand by the door in the quaint patterns we were wont to fashion years before. The old man smiled faintly when he saw them, saying:

"That's right, Blackbird; we must make it seem as nat'ral as we can. If we could only coax her to forget!"

Forget! No need of that! The cruel, pitiless east wind, laden with sea-spray, and driving before it long racks of clouds, that seemed to almost touch the green, yeasty wave, was preparing a Lethe for all her troubles—even Death!

The night set in dark and gusty, with showers of rain which the wind caught and beat into a blinding, driving mist, which soon shut out from sight the fish-houses and the great reels, and left the black stakes of the nearest fish-pound visible only at intervals. I shuddered at the thought of our darling exposed to such a storm, and bitterly regretted that I had not searched every town and hamlet on the coast between there and Southport, instead of yielding to what now seemed a mere monomania in Uncle Steve—the expectation of finding her at home. But I could not speak of this to that bowed and broken man, who sat gazing out into the darkness with such a look of unutterable anguish; I could not so much as let a hint of a mistake touch that sore and quivering heart! I could only pace the room and shudder at the mournful wailing of the old pine, and the long wash of the rising tide, which had now come to add new strength to the turbulent water. As my eye rested again and again on the motionless figure of the old man, it struck me that his whole appearance was that of one who waits and listens intently. Once or twice he went out into the storm, to return in a brief space, with dripping hair and garments, and resume his watch. At last, he roused himself, and begged me to go to bed. Knowing a refusal would only add to his trouble, I consented and went into the small room, and, seating myself by the window, with my head resting on a small pine table, I waited for the morning light. I suppose I must have fallen into a drowse, for I was again with little Adeline in the boat off the island—again I saw her go over the side, clutching at the fronds of the waving sea-weed, and, just as I sprang forward to catch her, a cry of—"O Lina! Lina!" uttered in fear and deathly anguish, rang in my ears with startling distinctness, and I sprang to my feet, shivering, trembling, and expectant.

All was still, save the surging of the waves and the moaning of the old pine-tree; the violence of the storm had abated, the clouds were broken, and the scene without was made dimly visible by the moonbeams that struggled from behind the fast-flying scuds. Not being able to realize then, nor even now, that the cry, so awfully distinct, was a mere delusion of the imagination, I flung open the door into the next room. It was unoccupied, and the outside door was wide open. Without staying for hood or shawl, I ran out and joined Uncle Steve on the beach.

"Did you hear any thing?" I cried, breathlessly.

"Nothin' but the fallin' of the big dead limb of the old bass-wood on the p'int, yonder; an' I kept watch ever sin' you went ter sleep."

He had not heard it; I must have been dreaming. What ear so likely as his, to catch the agonized cry of his darling! It was thus I reasoned, but reason did not bring conviction, and, feeling it impossible to stay in the house, I ran back for some covering, and then drew the old man on, along the curving beach, peering into the moaning waves, with the expectation of seeing—I dared not whisper to myself *what*.

The tide was now on the ebb; and, keeping close to the water, with the wet sea-weed clogging my feet, and clinging to my ankles, I went on, across the slippery old timber that spanned the narrow creek, between our beach and the fish-houses—beyond these, to the extreme verge of the rocky point, on the west. I dared not hint my thought to the old man who followed my lead in patient, unquestioning silence; so, with a mental "Thank God!" I retraced my steps. We had reached the creek, and were again crossing the timber, when my eye fell upon a portion of an old, long-disused weir, which was still standing near the mouth of the creek. Many a time had little Adeline and myself waded off to it at low tide, in our childhood; but now, the sight filled me with horror, for, lodged against it, rising and falling with the motion of the waves, was a dark object, something like a human figure. Speechless from terror, I caught Uncle Steve's arm, and pointed to it. In an instant, he was in the water, and I knew our long watch was over. In a few moments, our darling lay stretched upon the beach, not a dozen rods from her old home, but deaf to our anguish, cold, and white, and still. So changed, too—so worn and thin with the shipwreck of all her earthly hopes!

Oh, was it not in mercy rather than wrath, that God had called her to follow her little baby thus, rocking her poor crazed brain to its long rest in the waters which had cradled, as it were, her childhood!

We bore her home just as the dawn was breaking. Friendly hands wrung the water from her long, fair hair, and straightened her shrunken limbs for the grave. A dark, discolored wound on her temple proved that her death had not been premeditated—that in crossing the timber she must have lost her footing and struck against some sharp, shell-incrusted rock.

I hardly know how the weary day wore away. The house was full of people, but I thought but for two; that bowed old man who seemed to see nothing, to be conscious of nothing but the white figure stretched upon the old pine table, and Polly Maria, whom this great sorrow had suddenly taken out of the atmosphere of commonplace quotations, and set face to face with simple, natural grief.

She remained and occupied part of my bed that night, for no entreaties could induce Uncle Steve to let us take his place by the dead. Worn out by excitement and lack of rest, I slept soundly, until suddenly awakened by the touch of Polly Maria and her startled "Hark!"

There were voices in the out-room; some one was speaking earnestly in tones of entreaty, and I hurriedly dressed myself, and opened the door.

I shall never forget that scene. At the head of that still form, whose outlines were distinctly visible beneath the white sheet, stood Uncle Steve; his face was ghastly, but there was a fire in his eyes that I never saw there before, and his whole face and figure, even to the outstretched arm, were rigid with anger, scorn, and immitigable resolve, while cowering before him, by the side of the corpse, was a man, who pleaded in a voice hoarse from anguish and remorse.

"Curse me! you can't do it worse than I curse myself! Kick me—trample on me! but, for the love of God, let me see her once more! only this once!"

It was Henry Heath, the miserable, conscience-stricken husband of the poor girl, that cowered there; but there was no relenting of that look of awful sternness in the old man's face, only a spasmodic movement of the fingers, as he replied:

"I never cuss'd livin' cre'tur yet, God be thanked; so don't tempt me now! Go away, out of my sight. You had her livin'." Now the voice began to tremble, the iron nerves to relax. "I giv' her to you 'cause you said you loved her, an' I thought you'd be tenderer of her—make her happier than I could. She went away from here innocent, happy, and loving—she has come back—*that*—"

With a motion toward the dead body of his child, he covered his face with his hands, and groaned aloud.

By this time I had gained his side, followed closely by Polly Maria. Recognizing me, the young man clutched at my dress, pleading:

"O Miss Lina, let me see her this once! I was false, and mean, and wicked—false in all but my love for her, for I call Heaven to witness that I never would have taken her away if I hadn't believed myself a free man. They told me that curse of my boyhood was dead!"

I glanced at my companions. Uncle Steve's face was still buried in his hands, but the anger and abhorrence that had gleamed from Polly Maria's black eyes, when she first recognized the man, were fast giving place to a look of sorrowful commiseration. Suddenly she sunk on her knees, in doubt of all save the wisdom and love of the Highest, and exclaimed:

"Our Father which art in heaven, we are poor, and weak, and sinful; teach us, we pray Thee, to forgive!"

I interpreted the expression of the old man's face, as the hands were slowly removed, and raised the covering from the face of the dead.

The young man arose, looked for a moment with widely-distended eyes at the calm, cold face; then, with a groan of agony, turned and went out into the night.

We buried her on the following day.

For a brief space the coffin rested on the bank above the house, while friends and neighbors took the last look of her face; and the voice of the minister, as it rose in prayer, mingled with the murmur of the pines and the swell of the sea. Then we bore her to the small district burial-ground and laid her in the grave.

CHAPTER XXX.

A MEMORABLE INTERVIEW.

In the note left on my mistress's table I had spoken of a necessary absence for a few days. Nearly six weeks elapsed before I could think of leaving that desolate old man to go back to my duties; but I had written her briefly meantime, and thought that I could trust to her kindness. The parting with Uncle Steve and his sister was very sad; but, as the train bore me along, thoughts, and queries, and anticipations, which had lain quiet under this sudden weight of grief, began to stir again. I wondered if Mr. Annesley had arrived; I recalled our last interview—his look, his words, the passionate tenderness of his embrace—and a new feeling, strange as delightful, sent a warm thrill of joy through my frame, the feeling that I was going *home—home*, for the first time in my life. It may seem selfish —I know it did to me at the time, in the shadow of the terrible scene through which I had just passed—but *that* could only temper it. The human heart is a curious thing, and Joy treads too close on the heels of Sorrow, in most experiences,

"To keep a dream or grave apart."

Fast as was the speed of the cars, my longings travelled faster. Yet, when I sprang from the coach at Miss Annesley's door, and heard the clock upon the neighboring church-tower strike three, I was conscious of a sudden feeling of relief at the thought that I should not, probably, meet any of the family until after dinner. I hurried to my room and flung off my dusty travelling-suit, and dressed myself in a perfectly fresh merino. The house was unusually quiet, so much so that the silence seemed to oppress me. For the first time a doubt as to the wisdom of the anticipations in which I had permitted myself to indulge crossed my mind, but I shut it out as unworthy of the atmosphere of that house, and went down to Miss Annesley's room to wait her coming, as was usual, after dinner. In crossing the hall I met Jane, and the warmth of my greeting seemed to surprise and gratify her; I was so glad to be at home!

"Won't the mistress be glad to see you back?" she said; "she's been rather poorly of late."

"Has she been ill, Jane?"

"No, not exactly, but a little low-spirited. But I'll tell her you have come, miss."

"Stop, Jane! Is there company to dinner?"

"No; only the family, miss."

"The Lloyds and Mr. Annesley?" I said, as carelessly as I could.

"Not Mr. Annesley. I think he went away before you did, miss, and has not returned. The mistress has been quite lonely, after having him here so long."

He had not returned. "Well, what then? Six weeks is surely a short space of time in which to cross the Atlantic Ocean twice; *that* is not a woman's heart to be swayed by Saville Annesley's eyes or voice. Beware of the sin of idolatry, Lina!"

Still waiting for my mistress's step on the stairs, I sat musing thus, striving to collect my wandering thoughts and feelings and hold them under the strong leash of common-sense. I was too much occupied to note the time, but I think a half hour or more must have passed, when Miss Lloyd's maid appeared to say that the ladies desired to see me in the library.

The girl's manner was always pert

and self-sufficient, therefore a rather un-usual display of these characteristics did not surprise me; and, with a feeling of annoyance at being forced to explain my absence in the presence of the Lloyds, I obeyed.

But one glance at the group in the library, especially at the faces of Mrs. Lloyd and her daughter (Miss Annesley's was turned away) convinced me that this feeling was unnecessary. I should not be permitted to explain, for there was unalterable decision in every line of Mrs. Lloyd's face, every knot and fold of her head-dress and heavy black-satin dress. For a moment, I paused—not in fear of that Semiramis figure in the arm-chair in the foreground, but in memory of the last time I had stood in that room; and, as I did so, I saw Miss Julia smile and glance at her mother. The smile and movement were the perfection of im-measurable disdain, slightly modified by impatience and sarcasm. It acted like a tonic on me, and, collecting myself, I gave a hasty glance around the room before advancing to my mistress's side. The *mise en scène* was perfect. Miss Lloyd, looking, as I could not but confess, magnificent in a heavy purple silk, was lounging on a sofa, a little to her mother's right, just below a bracket, upon which stood an exquisite copy in marble of the head of Juno, looking scarcely more stately in its lofty self-poise than the lady below. To the left sat my mistress, a little more bowed, I thought, than was necessary to overlook the illustrated volume that lay on the table before her.

One glance took in the scene as well as a conception of its meaning. I made a movement to reach Miss Annesley's side, but Mrs. Lloyd motioned me back with a sweep of her jewelled right arm, saying:

"Keep your place, Miss Ray. I will detain you but a few minutes."

It was evident there was to be a scene of some sort, but it did not suit my present mood, and I determined to avoid it if possible; so, waiting until she had settled back against the damask cushions of her chair, I said, quietly:

"I merely wish to speak with Miss Annesley and explain the reasons of my long absence."

Before Mrs. Lloyd, who was ever de-liberate in her movements, could reply, Miss Annesley turned quickly toward me, saying:

"Yes, yes, let her speak, cousin. Per-haps she can explain."

"As you please, Cousin Anne," re-turned the lady, haughtily; "doubtless she will, but I must beg you, in that case, to dispense with the presence of my daughter and myself. I have never been accustomed to permit, much less *accept*, explanations for remissness or neglect of duty from my servants; and, had I not felt personally implicated by introducing her into your service without any defi-nite knowledge of her character, I should not consent to be present here at all. No explanations can change the facts with which we are already acquainted."

She half rose from her seat, and Miss Annesley said, hastily:

"Don't mistake me, Cousin Lloyd. I am truly grateful for your interest and advice in this matter, and beg you not to reproach yourself for any remissness in bringing Lina into my service. She has been a good, faithful girl, an intelligent companion, and,—these charges—I do not know what to make of them!"

Miss Annesley looked really dis-tressed; but, before I could ask what the "charges" were, Mrs. Lloyd said, with a slight smile of contempt:

"If so good and faithful, she should also be *truthful;* and she may be able to make you see that it is right and fit-ting that a person introduced by *me* into this house, as a companion for Miss Anne Annesley, should frequent some of the lowest and most infamous houses in this city — that she should associate with sailors and Irish vagabonds, even leave her place without permission, to go travelling about with the same disreputable set!"

The tone, so ironical at first, was replete with concentrated scorn and anger as she went on. My conduct had cast an imputation on *her* judgment—a sin beyond redemption with Mrs. Lloyd; but, nothing daunted by this knowledge, I said, calmly:

"If she cannot make it right and fitting, she can and will tell the truth. To *one* such place, perhaps, two, she has been!"

There was a grim smile of triumph on Mrs. Lloyd's face, and a look of surprise, disappointment, not unmixed with displeasure from my mistress, but I was too much in earnest to heed them.

"Not from any improper motives, but to help those whom she was bound, from gratitude, to assist. So much of the charge is true. That which touches the character of my companions—one, the nurse, which Mr. Annesley selected for me in my illness—the other the friend of my childhood, an old man and an honest one, is falsehood itself!"

"Will you tell me why you went to such places, Miss Ray?" said Miss Annesley, with a look of wounded dignity.

"To seek some tidings of that old man's niece, the playmate and friend of my childhood, madam."

"Who had been living for months in a disreputable and criminal connection with a married man," interposed Mrs. Lloyd.

"That is not true!" I said, indignantly. "She was married to him in the presence of her family, and believed herself his lawful wife. The knowledge that she had been deceived crazed her brain, and broke her heart. The week I went from here, we laid her in her grave as pure, and innocent, and stainless, as are your own daughters, Mrs. Lloyd. It was pity for the sorrow of that poor old man, who had been a father to her from her birth, that kept me so long from my duty here, as I told Miss Annesley in my let-

ter," I said, trying to keep back the tears.

"Did you write, Miss Ray?" asked my mistress.

"I did, explaining the cause of my absence."

"I never received the letter. Had it reached me, it would have explained the motives of your conduct, not *excused* its impropriety in a young, unmarried girl, and one, as Mrs. Lloyd justly observes, holding such an intimate relationship to this family. That is, I regret to say, inexcusable."

It was not my mistress that spoke thus, but the family pride of whole generations of Annesleys. It was her one foible, and I forgave it.

"I was not aware," she continued, "until a few days since, of the circumstances under which Mrs. Lloyd engaged you. She was so kind as to take you, after a week's trial, and your recent conduct has grieved me deeply. I trusted you so fully—" here the woman began to break through the ancestral shell—"O Lina, if you must needs have any thing to do with such people, why did you not consult me?"

Her emotion touched me, and I said hurriedly: "Because I could not; there were reasons, circumstances, which I was not free to explain. Indeed, Miss Annesley, I could not."

"Then that must be true which we have heard hinted," she said, sadly. "That you are not what you seem—that you have imposed upon us all. I say *hinted*, for the person who spoke of this was too delicate and generous to betray you, or do more than express a very natural surprise at seeing you here under a name which he felt sure you yourself would not deny was false. Is this true, Miss Ray?"

"It is."

Even Miss Lloyd started and looked up from the copy of *Blackwood*, with which she affected to be busy, at this direct avowal.

"But," I added, "the name of Ray is

a mistake of Mrs. Lloyd's. She persisted in calling me by that name, and, as it suited me as well as any other, I have continued to answer to it."

"What unparalleled impudence! Dear cousin, will you ever forgive me for bringing you in contact with such a person? I shall never forgive myself.—Julia, my love—"

"Excuse me, mamma," interrupted that young lady. "I protest against being mixed up with this absurd farce. This person, Ray, or whatever her name may be, has the tastes and vices of her class, as is natural, and she has showed them out. I'm not surprised in the least. The only thing to be done is for Cousin Anne to show her the door at once; though, if you get a dozen in her place, cousin, it will only be a choice of evils. They are all alike—*canaille!*"

"It may be so, Julia," said Miss Annesley, sadly; "but you must admit that Lina has great natural refinement, and a well-cultured mind. I thought—" she interrupted herself, arose, and came toward me, saying earnestly—"if I could only understand this! Girl, will you tell me your real name?"

My limbs trembled, and the words rose to my lips, so much did her sad, anxious, troubled face move me; but I thought of the Lloyds, and the storm of incredulity which would follow such an avowal, and I answered, faintly—

"No."

She came to my side, placed a roll of bills in my hand, saying:

"Such persistence in concealment argues something wrong, especially in one so young. I feel that I ought not to countenance it, and the relation between us must cease. You will find your salary there, and something more. I could not rest in peace, if I thought you were exposed to want."

She did not withdraw the hand I took, and I pressed it to my lips, before I replied:

"I can take gifts only from those who love or trust me, madam, therefore I can retain of this only my salary. Have no fear for me. The same honest old sailor of whom Mrs. Lloyd thinks so meanly will give me food and shelter until I can find employment."

Miss Lloyd arose, saying: "Really, Cousin Anne—mamma you must excuse me. The farce grows tiresome as they always do, unless you have some one to laugh with you! If Mr. Annesley were only here—"

"I wish he were!" eagerly interrupted Miss Annesley.

"Thank you, ladies!" said a voice that thrilled through every nerve in my body. "The man who meets such good wishes on his threshold may count himself fortunate."

The door which had been left ajar had been flung open, and Mr. Annesley stood on the threshold. Miss Julia, with a flushed cheek and proud smile, came forward to greet him. He returned their congratulations briefly and gravely, I thought, walked to the fire, and, leaning on the mantel, looked round the room with a quick, curious glance. For a second, it rested on me, but was instantly withdrawn, and he remarked, carelessly:

"In spite of the old adage, it is well to be a listener sometimes, ladies; for, if I had not overheard your wish for my presence, I should suppose I had intruded on some solemn and secret conclave, met to discuss some vexed point in feminine ethics, and expect the just indignation of the gods to follow my presumption. But in what can my masculine wisdom aid you?"

Miss Lloyd made a grimace expressive of weariness and disgust, but my mistress burst into tears, saying:

"O Ralph, it's about that girl there! She has deliberately deceived us all— and you know how I trusted her!"

"Deceived! What has the girl done? Broken another Etruscan vase, and denied it?" he asked, gravely.

Before Miss Annesley could reply,

Mrs. Lloyd began in her most magisterial manner:

"It is no matter for jesting, let me assure you, sir. I speak, because I feel responsible for having introduced her into this house. She has disgraced herself and us all, by not only associating with the lowest and most vulgar people, but has actually frequented, in their company, some of the worst places in the city. Our dear cousin is altogether too kind-hearted and sensitive to deal with such characters, and your arrival is opportune. It is no very agreeable task to any one of refined mind, but duty is duty, and must be done."

It was hard to keep back the burning words that struggled for utterance, but I *did* it, waiting impatiently for his next words.

They came after a brief silence, during which his face, or what I could see of it, was as unreadable as that of the Sphinx.

"Very true, Mrs. Lloyd, but what reasons does the young girl give in excuse for such conduct?"

"Oh, as usual, disinterested friendship! Some worthless associate in trouble. These people never look for reasons; but you and I know the world, Mr. Annesley!"

"Cousin Lloyd, you forget. She says these people were kind to her in her childhood," interposed Miss Annesley.

"No, indeed, Anne! I would have no one ungrateful, but, when *we* condescended to employ her, we took her out—away from that low set, and duty to us should have taught her to ignore them. The injury that the mere recognition of them would bring her, in her present position, would more than counterbalance any favors they could ever have bestowed. She should have quietly dropped them!"

Mr. Annesley bowed gravely. "A very lucid statement, madam; but I was thinking, as you spoke, of a certain historical personage whose teachings upon this subject have, somehow, contrived to get a pretty strong footing in the world. He not only associated with the poor and the outcast, the leper and the Magdalen, but actually sat down to eat with publicans and sinners. To be sure, he was only a mechanic, the son of a carpenter, a despised Nazarene, but as he is historical, as I said, you may have heard of him, Mrs. Lloyd — at Grace Church and elsewhere."

She could not but feel the mocking irony of the tone, through all its seeming gravity, and her dark cheek flushed with anger, and in a manner more measured than usual she replied:

"We will not speak lightly of sacred things, Mr. Annesley, and I confess I should be surprised at your, to say the least, bad taste, did I not know how much of your life has been spent abroad, where the general laxity on such subjects is notorious. The girl has acknowledged herself to be an impostor, besides; we have it from unquestionable authority that—Julia, my dear, will you tell—"

"Mamma, pray have some mercy on Mr. Annesley, if not on me!" cried Miss Julia, laughing. "Here, he has just arrived after such a weary absence"—he might have been the Man in the Iron Mask for all the impression that look of languishing softness had upon him—"and you bore him to death with such nonsense. The truth is," she continued, crossing over and taking a position at the opposite corner of the grate, "the girl is an impostor, and Miss Annesley has very properly dismissed her.—Better join with me, mamma, and beg Mr. Annesley to forgive us for bringing such a person beneath his roof."

"There is no necessity. *That* was done long ago." The words were for her, but the look was mine, and I stood erect and unshrinking.

He was silent a moment, and Mrs. Lloyd gave me a look that said very plainly that my presence there was unnecessary. I did not heed it; and Miss Annesley, observing this, said:

"Cousin Ralph, Miss Ray refuses to accept any thing from me but the small sum due her for the past quarter. I wish you would talk with her. I fear she may be driven to continue these low associations from lack of means. She always seemed grateful for your kindness when she was so ill; perhaps she will listen to you."

"I trust she will, cousin; be at rest," he returned, with a curious smile; "but, first, I wish to say a few words to you ladies on my own affairs. You are all such kind friends that I find it a pleasure as well as duty to speak to you on a subject which so nearly concerns my happiness."

Turning round until he faced his auditors, he continued:

"You, Cousin Anne, as well as Mrs. Lloyd, have often told me that it was my duty to marry; and even Miss Julia, though so careful to keep clear of the fetters herself, thinks it not amiss for a person of my age to *settle*—I believe that is the phrase."

He paused, and that queer, mischievous smile changed to an expression of deep and serious feeling. I doubt whether he even noted Miss Lloyd's blush and self-conscious manner — for, looking straight in Miss Annesley's surprised face, he continued:

"There was little hope of my acting upon your advice at first, for I felt myself a world-wearied, pleasure-surfeited man; what had I to offer in exchange for the love of a good and pure woman, and such I must have, if any; and, to tell the truth, I had never lost faith in the possibility of such a thing, in spite of my general and avowed atheism in matters of the heart. But I mistook myself. I met a woman, whose simple independence, frank truthfulness, *naive*, sagacious mind, and unaffected manner, had for me a strange fascination. I studied her, and found no trace of the selfishness, hardness, or littleness, that had so often disgusted me in others of her sex. Have patience, ladies; it is not often, you know, that I confess. All was bright, serene, and clear, and her presence became to me like dew to the desert. New hopes, thoughts, and feelings awoke—or, rather, old ones became conscious of a miraculous resurrection. I was a man again, with all a man's best hopes and joys before me. I know that I love her with my whole heart; and I think, I believe, my love is returned."

He paused, came to my side, and whispered a word in my ear that made my veins to throb with tumultuous joy. I replied by placing my hand in his, and he led me up to Miss Annesley, saying, while his voice trembled from intense emotion:

"Cousin Anne, permit me to present to you my bride!"

"Ralph, Ralph Saville!" stammered the lady in amazement.

"Bride!" exclaimed Mrs. Lloyd, angrily; "you are carrying this jest too far, sir! Such things are beneath you and your guests, Mr. Annesley!"

A dark frown knotted his forehead, and I felt the quickened throbbing of his heart, when, drawing me still closer to him, he said, sternly:

"I do not jest, Mrs. Lloyd! It should be enough for you that I take this young girl to my heart without a question of those absurd charges. She is poor and friendless; I care not: I can shelter her in my heart, and I will stake my life on her purity and truth!"

Hastily, almost frantically, I broke from his clasp, and knelt at his feet, crying:

"Forgive me, sir! It is true—I am not what I seem! I am Zerlina Day, the Oaklawn teacher, Agnes Lathrop's ward, whom you have sought so long!"

"Philip Cavendish's child!" he exclaimed, as he raised me again, his face radiant with joy. "My Philip's child! Oh, but this is wonderful!"

"Mamma," said Julia Lloyd, with a discordant laugh, "this is really getting absurd as well as tiresome. Let us withdraw."

They swept out of the room, but I doubt if he heard the words or noted their departure; for he had put me from him a little, and was eagerly scanning my face, and saying:

"Yes,—I see it now, in the forehead, and mouth, and the deep-set eye;" then turning to Miss Anne, who had been watching him with a look of hopeless bewilderment, he said, solemnly:

"Anne, it was God Himself who sent this girl, Philip Cavendish's friendless child, to you! To be with us when he returns, for he is not dead, but on his way home even now, after an absence of so many years. It was to satisfy myself of the truth of this, that I went to England so suddenly. Will you not bless her as my wife?"

"Not only as your wife, Ralph, but as my own faithful friend with whom I have been hasty and unjust.—Will you forgive me, dear?"

I kissed her hand, I could not speak; then laying her hands on my head, she stood a moment, while her lips moved inaudibly; while Mr. Annesley withdrew his arm from my waist, and stood with bowed head and clasped hands.

Then she glided from the room, and we were alone.

CHAPTER XXXI.

CONCLUSION.

SAVILLE ANNESLEY made good his promise. He took his wife to Europe with him in less than two months, but our wedding-trip was to the Cove, for he could not rest until he had clasped hands with Uncle Steve. In Paris we met my father, whose solitary heart seemed to revel in an atmosphere of silent joy at the sight of his friend and child thus united.

After an absence of six months, we began to yearn for home. It was strange, as pleasant to me, to hear those two wanderers talking so earnestly of *home*, and laying plans for the future.

After a brief winter in New York, we came out to Highcliff, which, with the exception of a few weeks in midwinter, and midsummer, has been our permanent home. My father's return, of course, settled the succession of the Cavendish estate, but, at my request, the Pines, with the exception of the pictures, and some other mementos, was settled upon Edward Ellis, whose joy in my happiness was unmistakable. Mrs. Ellis is helpless from paralysis; and James Sancroft, I see by the papers, has just been elected to a seat in Congress by one of our latest-born Western States. This is fortunate, for I hear, through Cousin Anne, who spends most of her time with us, that the Lloyds are in Washington, Miss Julia still unmarried, and it is always pleasant to meet friends.

Every summer we visit the Cove. My father, between whom and Uncle Steve there exists a bond of sympathy as deep as it is silent, has amused himself by building a summer-residence on the bank beneath the great pine. It is a curious affair, half Oriental in its construction and arrangements, but very comfortable as we find, when the heat at Highcliff becomes unendurable, and we join him at midsummer. He usually precedes us by several weeks, for he is as fond of the fisherman's quiet craft as Uncle Steve, and in the evening they sit together on the bench by the old cabin-door, smoking silently, until enveloped in clouds of their own making.

But when the children come, then there is a stir. There are lines to rig for Master Philip Rothsay, who boasts the mature age of four years; stories to be told him of mamma's childhood; the wonderful picture of the Dart, which still hangs in its old place to be exhibited; shells to be gathered for baby Ralph; albeit Uncle Steve's eyes grow so dim and misty in the effort that many a dingy pebble is brought in among them. He never plays at porpoises or kangaroos now—that part of the programme falls upon Saville Annesley, who is ready to transform himself into any thing, no matter how absurd, to please his boys; and to be honest, reader, his wife only loves him the better for his folly.

But within the past year we have had a little girl added to our family; a small, quiet, blue-eyed girl of six; the child of Agnes Lathrop, and her dying legacy to my husband and myself. So Mr. Tyler wrote, and as such we thankfully received her. She is very dear to us all, but Uncle Steve manifests, if possible, a tenderer love for her than for my bold boys. My husband and I often speak of this, with grateful hearts, as we watch him leading her about the beach, or carefully lifting her over the rocks. Recent information of her father's marriage to the widow of a missionary has relieved us of the fear of losing her, and now we hold her entirely as our own.

Of my married life I need not speak. Where there is perfect love, there must be perfect accord. Reader, may a like blessing be thine!

THE END.

MORTON HOUSE,

A Novel.

By the Author of "VALERIE AYLMER."

One volume, paper covers, with four Illustrations, price, $1.00; cloth, $1.50.

"'Morton House' proves to us that at last we have a writer who understands her public. The story is located in the South; yet there is not a word of glorification of lost institutions or lost causes. This species of rubbish is simply brushed aside, and we have society as it is—not a brawling debating club, but an assemblage of individuals concerned in the ordinary ways of life. The plot serves; is thoroughly sensational, and yet tolerably reasonable. The characterizations are good—the conversation is excellent. Above all, the tone is healthy and unostentatiously American. For the sake of our literature, we trust that the author will not pause in her new career, which certainly opens with the bravest promise."—*Henry Ward Beecher's Christian Union.*

"The plot is interesting, the characters good, the dialogue amusing, and the whole book well done."—*N. Y. Albion.*

"One of the most brilliant writers whom the South has produced. * * * There is intense power in many of the scenes."—*N. Y. Evening Mail.*

"A very readable story. The interest is sustained from the first suggestion of mystery to the final *dénoûment.*"—*Boston Christian Register.*

"There is so much freshness in the tone, so much nature in the personages, and so much interest in the story, that 'Morton House,' so neatly printed and well illustrated, is one of the most attractive of Appleton & Co.'s standard novels. It has the topping merit of being very readable."—*Boston Transcript.*

"The plot and characterization of this story are more than good. They are marked by great force and originality. Few finer specimens of manhood have ever been conceived than the two suitors of the heroine. The author has shown an elevation of sentiment and good taste, combined with an effective style."—*Philadelphia Age.*

"A charming picture of life in the South."—*Wilmington (N. C.) Star.*

"The author's style is flowing, easy, and vivid. Her delineations of character graphic and true to nature. There is a fascination in all she writes, that betokens an original genius."—*Baltimore American.*

"The author of 'Morton House' has the genuine dramatic perceptions which are indispensable to whoever would depict human character; and she is possessed of a literary style which is rarely found except in conjunction with other and higher mental qualities. In natural, easy, and graceful dialogue, we do not know a single living writer who surpasses her. Her books are interesting from beginning to end, and there are few pages which the most inveterate novel-reader will feel disposed to skip."—*The Eclectic Magazine for January,* 1872.

D. APPLETON & CO., Publishers,

549 & 551 Broadway, New York.

POPULAR WORKS OF FICTION

PUBLISHED BY

D. APPLETON & CO.,

549 & 551 BROADWAY, NEW YORK.

APPLETONS' ILLUSTRATED LIBRARY OF ROMANCE.

In uniform octavo volumes,

Handsomely Illustrated, and bound either in paper covers, or in muslin.

Price, in Paper, $1.00; in Cloth, $1.50.

₌ In this series of Romances are included the famous novels of LOUISA MUHLBACH. Since the time when Sir Walter Scott produced so profound a sensation in the reading world, no historical novels have achieved a success so great as those from the pen of Miss MUHLBACH.

1. TOO STRANGE NOT TO BE TRUE. A Novel. By Lady Georgiana Fullerton.
2. THE CLEVER WOMAN OF THE FAMILY. By Miss Yonge, author of "The Heir of Redclyffe," "Heartsease," etc.
3. JOSEPH II. AND HIS COURT. By Louisa Muhlbach.
4. FREDERICK THE GREAT AND HIS COURT. By Louisa Muhlbach.
5. BERLIN AND SANS-SOUCI; or, FREDERICK THE GREAT AND HIS FRIENDS. By Louisa Muhlbach.
6. THE MERCHANT OF BERLIN. By Louisa Muhlbach.
7. FREDERICK THE GREAT AND HIS FAMILY. By Louisa Muhlbach.
8. HENRY VIII. AND CATHARINE PARR. By Louisa Muhlbach.
9. LOUISA OF PRUSSIA AND HER TIMES. By Louisa Muhlbach.
10. MARIE ANTOINETTE AND HER SON. By Louisa Muhlbach.
11. THE DAUGHTER OF AN EMPRESS. By Louisa Muhlbach.
12. NAPOLEON AND THE QUEEN OF PRUSSIA. By Louisa Muhlbach.
13. THE EMPRESS JOSEPHINE. By Louisa Muhlbach.
14. NAPOLEON AND BLUCHER. An Historical Romance. By Louisa Muhlbach.
15. COUNT MIRABEAU. An Historical Novel. By Theodor Mundt.
16. A STORMY LIFE. A Novel. By Lady Georgiana Fullerton, author of "Too Strange not to be True."
17. OLD FRITZ AND THE NEW ERA. By Louisa Muhlbach.
18. ANDREAS HOFER. By Louisa Muhlbach.
19. DORA. By Julia Kavanagh.
20. JOHN MILTON AND HIS TIMES. By Max Ring.
21. BEAUMARCHAIS. An Historical Tale. By A. E. Brachvogel.
22. GOETHE AND SCHILLER. By Louisa Muhlbach.
23. A CHAPLET OF PEARLS. By Miss Yonge.

Grace Aguilar.

HOME INFLUENCE. 12mo. Cloth. $1.00.

MOTHER'S RECOMPENSE. 12mo. Cloth. $1.00.

DAYS OF BRUCE. 2 vols., 12mo. Cloth. $2.00.

HOME SCENES AND HEART STUDIES. 12mo. Cloth. $1.00.

WOMAN'S FRIENDSHIP. 12mo. Cloth. $1.00.

WOMEN OF ISRAEL. 2 vols., 12mo. Cloth. $2.00.

VALE OF CEDARS. 12mo. Cloth. $1.00.

"Grace Aguilar's works possess attractions which will always place them among the standard writings which no library can be without. 'Mother's Recompense' and 'Woman's Friendship' should be read by both young and old."

W. Arthur.

THE SUCCESSFUL MERCHANT. 1 vol., 12mo. Cloth. $1.

J. B. Bouton.

ROUND THE BLOCK. A new American Novel. Illustrated. 1 vol., 12mo. Cloth. $1.25.

"Unlike most novels that now appear, it has no 'mission,' the author being neither a politician nor a reformer, but a story-teller, according to the old pattern; and a capital story he has produced, written in the happiest style."

F. Caballero.

ELIA; or, Spain Fifty Years Ago. A Novel. 1 vol., 12mo. Cloth. $1.

Mary Cowden Clarke.

THE IRON COUSIN. A Tale. 1 vol., 12mo. Cloth. $1.50.

"The story is too deeply interesting to allow the reader to lay it down till he has read it to the end."

Charles Dickens.

The Cheap Popular Edition of the Works of Charles Dickens.

Clear type, handsomely printed, and of convenient size. 18 vols., 8vo. Paper.

	Pages.	Cts.		Pages.	Cts.
OLIVER TWIST	172	25	BLEAK HOUSE	340	35
AMERICAN NOTES	104	15	LITTLE DORRIT	330	35
DOMBEY & SON	356	35	PICKWICK PAPERS	326	35
MARTIN CHUZZLEWIT	342	35	DAVID COPPERFIELD	351	35
OUR MUTUAL FRIEND	330	35	BARNABY RUDGE	257	30
CHRISTMAS STORIES	162	25	OLD CURIOSITY SHOP	221	30
TALE OF TWO CITIES	144	20	SKETCHES	196	25
HARD TIMES, and ADDITIONAL CHRISTMAS STORIES	200	25	GREAT EXPECTATIONS	184	25
			UNCOMMERCIAL TRAVELLER, PICTURES		
NICHOLAS NICKLEBY	340	35	FROM ITALY, Etc.	200	35

THE COMPLETE POPULAR LIBRARY EDITION. Handsomely printed in good, clear type. Illustrated with 32 Engravings, and a Steel-plate Portrait of the Author. 6 vols., small 8vo. Cloth, extra. $10.50.

OUR MUTUAL FRIEND. With Illustrations by Marcus Stone. London edition. vols., 12mo. Scarlet Cloth, $5.00; Half Calf, $9.00.

Mrs. Ellis.

HEARTS AND HOMES; or, Social Distinctions. A Story. 1 vol, 8vo. Cloth. $2.

"There is a charm about this lady's productions that is extremely fascinating. For grace and ease of narrative, she is unsurpassed; her fictions always breathe a healthy moral."

Margaret Field.

BERTHA PERCY; or, L'Esperance. 1 vol. 12mo. Cloth. $1.

"A book of great power and fascination. . . . . . In its pictures of home life, it reminds one of Fredrika Bremer's earlier and better novels, but it possesses much more than Fredrika Bremer's descriptive power."

Julia Kavanagh.

ADELE. A Tale. 1 thick vol. 12mo. Cloth. $1.50.

BEATRICE. 12mo. Cloth. $1.50.

DAISY BURNS. 12mo. Cloth. $1.50.

GRACE LEE. 12mo. Cloth. $1.50.

MADELINE. 12mo. Cloth. $1.

NATHALIE. A Tale. 12mo. Cloth. $1.50.

RACHEL GRAY. 12mo. Cloth. $1.

QUEEN MAB. 12mo. Cloth. $1.50.

SEVEN YEARS, and Other Tales. 12mo. Cloth. $1.

SYBIL'S SECOND LOVE. 12mo. Cloth. $1.50.

WOMEN OF CHRISTIANITY, Exemplary for Piety and Charity. 12mo. Cloth. $1.

DORA. Illustrated by Gaston Fay. 1 vol. 8vo. Paper, $1.00. Cloth, $1.50.

"There is a quiet power in the writings of this gifted author, which is as far removed from the sensational school as any of the modern novels can be."

Margaret Lee.

DR. WILMER'S LOVE; or, A Question of Conscience. A Novel. 1 vol. 12mo. Cloth. $1.25.

Olive Logan.

CHATEAU FRISSAC; or, Home Scenes in France. Authoress of "Photographs of Paris Life." 1 vol., 12mo. Cloth. $1.25.

Maria J. Macintosh.

AUNT KITTY'S TALES. 12mo. Cloth. $1.

CHARMS AND COUNTER CHARMS. 12mo. Cloth. $1.25.

EVENINGS AT DONALDSON MANOR. 1 vol., 12mo. Cloth. $1.

THE LOFTY AND LOWLY. 2 vols., 12mo. Cloth. $1.50.

TWO LIVES; or, To Seem and To Be. 12mo. Cloth. $1.

TWO PICTURES; or, How We See Ourselves, and How the World Sees Us. 1 vol., 12mo. Cloth. $1.50.

"Miss Macintosh is one of the best of the female writers of the day. Her stories are always full of lessons of truth, and purity, and goodness, of that serene and gentle wisdom which comes from no source so fitly as from a refined and Christian woman."

www.ingramcontent.com/pod-product-compliance
Lightning Source LLC
Chambersburg PA
CBHW022356020726
47500CB00002B/309